The Klindrel Invasion

The Klindrel Invasion

JASON A. HOLT

Published by the author.
JasonAHolt.com

print ISBN: 978-0-9860717-5-1
epub ISBN: 978-0-9860717-4-4

For those who decide to fight even when it looks like they can't win.

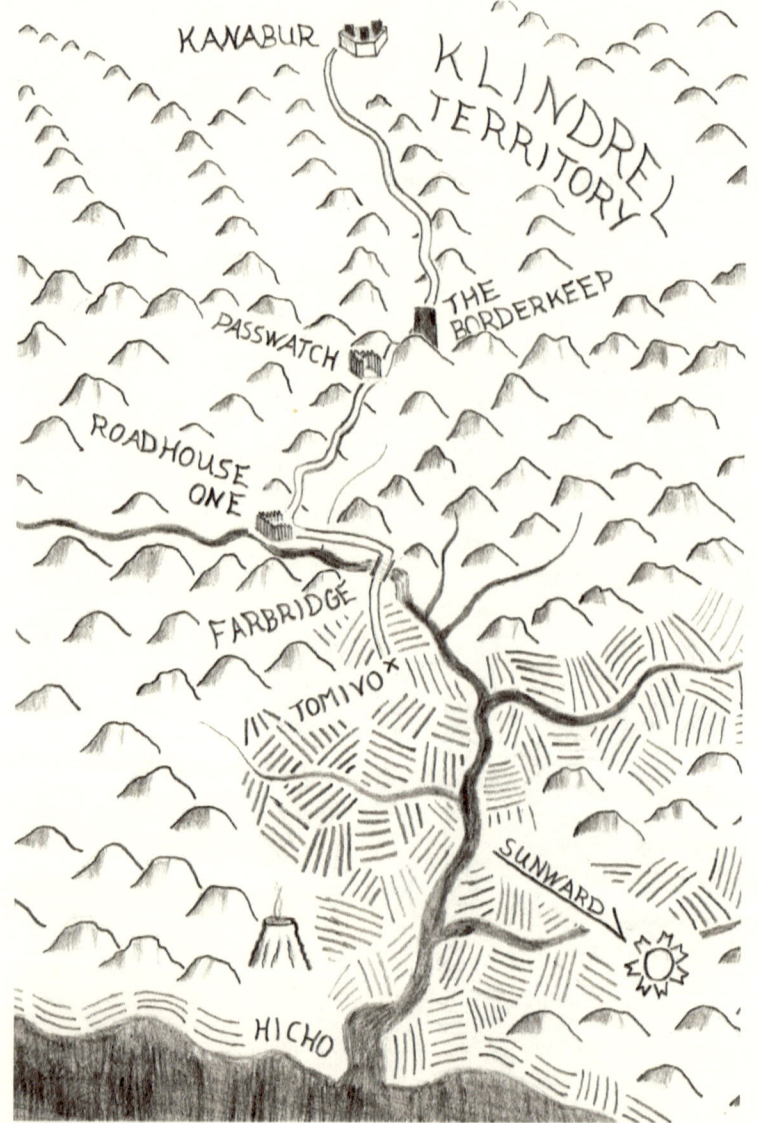

CHAPTER 1
Before the Invasion

THE CHILDREN OF LITH ARE NOT LIKE US. They do not read. They do not go to school. They study nothing except combat. Lith created them to be warriors, just as Knowledge created us to be scholars.

The Children of Lith are like the heavenly body that gives their creator his name. The lith moves swiftly, circling the sky nine times a day in an orbit as predictable as that of the sun or the moon. But this predictability contains chaos. Irregular metallic facets sparkle, flash, and fade as the lith spins through the sky. Whenever we look, we see a face we have never seen before.

So, too, are the Children of Lith always in motion, always in chaos, always changing. Even when we know where they are going, we do not know what side they will show us next.

Of all Children of Lith, the Klindrel are the most civilized. We had traded peacefully with the Klindrel Empire for years and years and years. We were trading with them before they built their empire, before there was even a road. When they invaded, we were caught off guard.

Perhaps we should have paid more attention to the calendar. Like us, the Klindrel begin the new year on the first day of Yellowmonth, the winter solstice. But unlike us, the Klindrel count by tens. The year of the Klindrel Invasion, the Year of Blood and Famine, was written in the Klindrel counting system as *1 5 0 0*.

You and I understand that this is merely an interesting numerical artifact created by an arbitrary choice of counting system. But the Klindrel do not think like us. To the Klindrel Emperor, the zeroes seemed filled with cosmological significance. This numerical artifact prompted him to order the invasion of the Redwood Valley, causing death and destruction that rivaled the greatest drought, flood, or wildfire.

On the first day of that year, no one in the Redwood Valley guessed at the calamity that lay ahead. Neighbors visited each others' houses, sharing pouches of dried grapes and apricots, wishing each other the blessings of wisdom in the new year. If anyone remarked that the year was a multiple of ten times ten, no one suspected that the numerical fact would have political implications.

High in the snow-covered mountains, within the stout wooden palisade of the Passwatch Roadhouse, the members of the Passwatch Road Patrol were not worrying about the new year's arithmetical properties. Their anxiety was directed at one of the crates of apples that had begun to rot in the cellar. Every patroller was helping the quartermaster categorize the contents as "rotten", "rotting", or "still good", and every patroller was trying to calculate what rationing would be necessary to stretch out the remaining supply until the snow melted and the road was passable again. Even those who had claimed they were sick of eating apples now discovered that they cared deeply for the sweet, colorful fruit which broke the monotony of daily potatoes and flatcakes.

Was the Road Patrol aware that an invasion was possible? Yes. But the dangers of avalanche, equine misstep, and cougar attack were much more real to them. The Road Patrol understood that they were the Redwood Valley's only defense against the Klindrel Empire, but that concern was secondary and theoretical. When the road was passable, their main concern was traveler safety. In the winter, their main concern was apples.

In a snow-bound cabin on the other side of the pass, near the top of a mountain claimed by the Klindrel Empire, a black-bearded giant was eating bear meat. He would be the first Child of Lith to arrive at the Passwatch Roadhouse that year, although he had no such plans. He had no plans at all.

On the Cataract River, in Kanabur, the capital of the Klindrel Empire, the emperor had plans. On the first of Yellowmonth, he and his advisors were plotting to invade the Redwood Valley. The emperor won a crucial argument that day: His advisors accepted that he would lead the invasion himself.

The citizens of Kanabur had noted that certain military units had been recalled from Mazibo and the Saltland Provinces. They knew the recently ascended emperor had promised to reestablish the glorious tradition of conquest. But they did not know their emperor was planning to attack our people. They believed the target was Penwargo. You see, the Klindrel had always warred with other Children of Lith and never with peoples created by the other deities. And most of the citizens of Kanabur did not know the year was a multiple of ten times ten. They did not keep track.

Although the *citizens* of Kanabur may not have given much thought to the number of the year, some *residents* of Kanabur kept careful track of dates and figures. Among these residents was Tim Hill, a Child of Wealth.

Children of Wealth do not think of themselves by that name. They think of themselves as "Clanfolk" because they are organized into forty clans. Clan Hill had held land near Kanabur for a dozen generations. Tim's ancestors had been among the first to use the Klindrel Road. In fact they had built the road and used it to build wealth for their clan by trading Klindrel iron for our glass and our glass for Klindrel iron.

Tim had grown comfortably wealthy on such trade. He owned a well-furnished townhouse from which he could do business in the cold, snowy months. He owned a well-maintained wagon with which he could transport goods in the warm, dry months. And he shared with his brother a large herd of cattle. His brother profited from meat, leather, and cheese, while Tim profited from the oxen which pulled his wagon.

Tim was a merchant, and he felt great satisfaction on the first day of Yellowmonth as he wrote *1500* into his ledger. The round zeroes on the clean page promised beginnings, changes, and new business opportunities. In this assessment, as in so many others, Tim would be proven correct.

His first new business opportunity came on a chilly spring morning exactly three months later, on the first day of Purplemonth. The puddles in the muddy street had been refilled by the previous night's rain. The sunlight soaking through the low, wispy clouds had not yet dried the thatch on the townhouses in Tim's neighborhood.

Despite being damp and chill, the air held the kiss of spring, not the bite of winter. The mountains above the Klindrel Valley were topped with new snow, but the sunlight gleaming on the puddles made Tim think of melting snow, drying roads, and wagon wheels rolling across the pass.

The wagon was at his brother's farm. Tim decided to go see how it had fared over winter. After all, his annual departure date was only thirty days away.

Tim left the hood of his woolen cloak down. He adjusted his woolen hat so that it covered his ears without shading his eyes from the beautiful morning. He splashed up the street, pleased to see that he was not the only one out and about.

A boy was poking a stick into the mud, engineering a canal between two puddles. His tightly closed fist betrayed that he held coins for a neglected shopping errand—the allure of the mud had exceeded even the thrill of commerce. Two sisters, each carrying a basket of freshly baked rolls, discussed their husbands' relative merits as they walked past wooden doors and white-washed townhouses. Three of the old, bearded neighbor men were engaged in a serious conversation concerning the weather—or so Tim gathered from the way they squinted at the sun and glowered at the dispersing clouds. Tim waved, and two of the old men waved back. The third poked at a puddle with his cane.

An ox wagon turned onto Tim's street, moving through the mud with slow grace, as though it were a river barge. The weather was poor for wagons. Tim reckoned the wagon was not heavily loaded.

He recognized the driver as Van Fairweather—also of the Clanfolk, but from a different clan. Fairweathers had enclaves elsewhere in the Klindrel Valley, but they made occasional visits to Clan Hill's enclave, especially in the spring, when Tim and his cousins were preparing for a season of travel.

It was a bit unusual for a Fairweather to enter the Hill Enclave with wagon guards, but Van had two. They were Children of Lith, black-bearded men twice as tall as anyone else on the street, with long, straight, black hair and skin as red as rosehips in late autumn. They walked on either side of the oxen, scanning the street warily, keeping their hands near the hilts of their swords. Their swords were nearly as long as Tim. Even though the guards were on foot, they could still see over the backs of the oxen. They were giants.

The word "giant" is perhaps a misnomer. It implies that taller peoples are unusual. When one considers that, of all the nine peoples, only Tim's people are as short as we are, it might be more objective to admit that it is we who are unusual. Regardless, we refer to all other peoples (except Children of Wealth) as "giants". Children of Wealth do the same.

The Klindrel have an analogous perception of our two peoples. They call us both "Drelfin". If they make a distinction, they might call our people "brown Drelfin" and Tim's people "red Drelfin". This is amusing because it is actually the Klindrel who are red. Tim's people have the ability to mimic their neighbors' skin color. The God of Wealth—whom they call Yolim—wanted them to match whomever they were trading with. Because of this, Clanfolk tend to see other peoples in terms of their skin. They call us "Brownfolk".

Tim wasn't planning on trading with the wagon guards, so he kept his skin the yellow-brown color of lightly tanned leather—which was considered a neutral color suitable for any kind of business among Clanfolk. Van drew rein as Tim approached, but he remained on his wagon, looking about the street nervously.

"Good morning, Van," Tim called.

"Good morning, Tim." Van's voice was not pitched to carry far.

One of the guards turned his back to Tim, so that he could watch for anything coming from behind. The other continued looking down the street, over Tim's head.

Tim walked to the wagon. The nearer ox looked down at him and snuffled at his hat. Tim reached up to pat the ox on the shoulder.

"Why are you out on streets like this?" Tim asked Van. "What are you hauling?"

"Come back and see," Van said. "I might have something you could sell to the Brownfolk."

Tim found a ladder built into the side of the wagon and climbed up. The bed was empty except for …

"A basket and a stick?" Tim could not believe Van Fairweather had bothered to hitch up his oxen so that he could haul a basket and a stick around the Hill Enclave.

"It's not a stick," said Van, rising from his seat. "It's a bow."

He climbed into the wagon bed and lifted up the item in question. The stick had been bowed and a string had been tied between the ends so that the stick pulled the string taut and the string prevented the stick from straightening.

"Oh," said Tim. "I've heard about these, but I've never seen one before. How does it work?"

"You need a special stick called an 'arrow'," Van explained. "It has a knife on one end and feathers on the other, to help it fly. You put it on the string, pull, and when you let go—" the string twanged, "—the arrow pushes its knife into your target."

Tim nodded in approval at the explanation, but he made no move to reach for the smooth stick of wood. "Have you sold many?" he asked.

"I only have the one," said Van. "And I can't convince any Redman to buy it."

Van's eyes darted nervously up the street. No one was there.

"What about the Stripedfolk?" Tim asked. His cousins had told him of Stripedfolk on the plains, and he knew Van had cousins who traded with them.

"The Stripedfolk *make* bows," Van said. "They don't buy them. I was hoping you could sell this to the Brownfolk."

"Hm," said Tim. "What is in your basket?"

"It's not a basket," said Van. "It's a wicker cage. Take a peek inside."

Tim knelt down and did so. He hoped it would be a possum. Tim did not know what a possum was, but possums were occasionally mentioned in the lore of Clan Hill. They lived in the trees of the Heartland.

This animal, however, was not a possum. It appeared to be a small cougar or lynx, with a long twitchy tail, fine whiskers, pointed ears, and inquisitive yellow eyes.

"It is a 'cat'," said Van. "My cousin bought it in the Heartland, but it came from the lands of the Silverfolk."

"Oho!" Tim said, much impressed.

The Heartland, the center of Clanfolk civilization, was surely far away. Anything wonderful could be purchased there, even animals from the other side of the world.

"Is it a cub or is it full grown?" Tim asked.

"Full grown," Van replied.

"Magically shaped?"

Van shook his head. "Natural born."

Tim peered at the creature.

"Mer?" the cat asked.

Van glanced up the street.

"Is it vicious?" Tim asked.

"No. It's tame," Van said.

"Tame? What would you tame it for? Meat?"

Van shook his head. "Too stringy," he said. "It catches mice."

"Well, I don't have any mice," Tim said.

"Everyone has mice," Van said.

"I don't," Tim said. "I plug every hole."

"But the Brownfolk have mice, don't they?"

"Oh, aye," Tim said. "But I wouldn't know what price to ask for it."

"No one will," said Van. "Find the richest person you can, and name the highest price you can think of. No one over there has ever seen a cat before … or a bow."

"I have a good stock of iron I can move," Tim said. "I don't reckon I need to risk money on exotic goods." *Besides,* he thought, *I'd probably lose my temper if I knew how much you wanted to charge for that stick-and-string.*

"Well perhaps your cousin Shom had a better year than you," said Van.

Tim nodded. "Perhaps," he said. And then, not because he was boastful but rather because he was honest, he added, "But I doubt it. Shom made only one trip over the pass last year; I kept my wheels moving and made it twice."

Van Fairweather stared at him, unimpressed—which probably meant he was envious.

"Nonetheless, you should try him," Tim advised. "Cousin Shom always likes a chance to trade rare goods."

Tim was about to bid Van Fairweather a good day when he saw his brother, Lon Hill, trudging down the street. The wagon guards did not react—Lon was not the threat the guards were watching for—but Tim was worried by the sight of his brother slopping into town. Mud globs clung to Lon's woolen leggings and spots splattered his woolen tunic.

"Isn't that your brother?" Van asked.

"Aye," said Tim. "I hope one of the animals isn't hurt."

"I reckon it's worse than that," Van said. "Look, I have to leave Kanabur. Now. Tell you what: I'll *give* you a stake in the cat and the bow. If you can sell them, you can keep fifty percent."

"I don't even know what to charge," Tim said. His brother's shoulders were slumped. He wasn't looking beyond his own feet.

"All right, sixty percent."

"I reckon you had better talk to Shom," Tim said. He climbed down the ladder and went to meet his brother.

Van followed him, wringing his hands with anxiety. The wagon guards remained at the wagon, standing by the oxen, watching in all directions.

"Lon, are you all right?" Tim asked.

Lon looked up with dazed eyes, as though he had just slammed his head into the barn door.

"What happened?" Tim asked.

Lon swallowed. "Soldiers took the cattle."

"I was afraid of that," Van said.

"Which cattle?" Tim asked.

"Our cattle," Lon said.

Tim was confused. Only a few of the oxen were for sale. The rest of the herd had been magically marked in the womb. All livestock with white stockings on both front feet belonged to Clan Hill. Under clan law, marked cattle could never leave the clan.

Lon held out a small bundle—a piece of linen tied around a handful of imperial coins. Tim took the bundle and shook it. Even through the linen, he could estimate their number and denominations. It was enough to buy one trained ox or two yearlings.

"How many did they take?" Tim asked.

"All of them," Lon said.

Tim's fingers deftly untied the bundle. No, his estimation of the coins had not been wrong.

"All the unmarked oxen?" Tim asked.

Lon shook his head. "All the cattle, Tim. The oxen, marked and unmarked. The bull. The cows. The yearlings. Everything."

"But—" Tim looked at the coins in his hand. "They can't buy them. They're not for sale." Selling marked livestock was not illegal; it was impossible.

"Tim, the soldiers had spears and swords," Lon said. "There was nothing I could do."

Tim looked at Van's hired guards. He realized they were standing guard over the oxen, not over the exotic pet in the wagon bed. He looked at Van. "You knew," Tim said.

"The innkeeper warned me to get my oxen out of town," Van said. "The emperor wants them."

"But he can't have them," Tim said. "Your oxen are clan-marked."

"He has *our* clan-marked beasts," Lon said.

"No he doesn't!" Tim said. He flung the coins down into the mud. "He can't buy them. He can't keep them. They don't belong to him. I'm going to take them back."

Van Fairweather put a hand on Tim's chest. "You aren't going anywhere," he said.

"Yes I am," Tim said. "I'm going to legion headquarters and demand my cattle back."

"No, you're not," Van said. "If you go in there looking for a fight, they'll take you up on it and stick a sword in your belly."

"I don't fear them," Tim said.

"I can see you don't," Van said. "And that's why your brother and I will stop you." Van looked to Lon.

"He's right, Tim." Lon put a hand on Tim's arm. "Let's go inside and talk this out."

"Nothing needs to be said," Tim replied. "They can't do this. They just can't do this. They have no jurisdiction. They can't violate clan law."

"But they did," Lon said. "Let's go inside and talk about it." He took Tim by the arm and gently led him to the door of the mouse-proof townhouse.

CHAPTER 2

Tim Reconnoiters

TIM LIVED IN A THREE-STORY HOUSE typical of those in the Hill Enclave. The walls were made of a type of mud brick that would not last three winters on our side of the mountains. But it rains much less in the Klindrel Valley. Tim and a few of his cousins had rebuilt the walls only a few years before, so the house was new, even though it was also centuries old.

Inside, the freshly whitewashed walls reflected the daylight from an open window near the hearth. A flight of stairs led up to bedrooms and Tim's office. The ground-floor room was dominated by a waist-high table made of finished pine covered with a Hicho tablecloth. Arrayed around this table were pieces of furniture called "chairs". A chair is essentially a tall, four-legged stool, but two of the stool's legs extend up through the seat to provide a framework for a wicker backrest. Clanfolk do not sit on the floor.

Tim's floor was packed earth. If you have lived on the cobbles of Hicho all your life, perhaps you cannot imagine it, but go to the village of Goshivo during their Harvest Fair. By the end of the week, the fairgoers' sandals have packed the earth into a hard, brown plaza that gleams like glazed earthenware. Tim's wife accomplished this same effect by pounding the floor with a pole.

Tim's wife did most of the work inside the house. She prepared the meals, washed the clothes, and looked after the children. (Tim and his wife had four, ages five to fifteen.) If she regretted being married to a man who was home only half the year, she never mentioned these regrets to Tim. Her name was Besi, and Tim loved her very much.

Tim didn't notice how Besi reacted to the news that their cattle had been confiscated. He was too busy raging and shouting. Besi swiftly sent the children outside.

Lon suggested he calm down, and Tim slammed his fist into the table, knocking over the tea cups. Then Tim did quiet down. Besi fetched a clean tablecloth. Tim apologized and hung his head. After that, he became quite morose. Tim never actually told me that he sobbed, but who could blame him if he did? Imagine that someone had come to your home and taken all the books in your library—all those you had received as graduation gifts and all those you had labored to transcribe. That is how Tim felt when the Klindrel Empire confiscated his cattle.

By the time Tim had calmed down enough to be talked to, Van Fairweather was long gone from Kanabur and Shom Hill had come over to show off his new cat.

(Shom, too, had rejected the bow. And wisely so. At that time, none of his customers would have recognized the weapon's effectiveness. Of course, bows would prove essential to the Klindrel conquest of the desert provinces, but that began a few decades later. The invasion of our lands would have gone differently had either side used such weapons.)

Tim had no interest in the cat, but the striped-furred, lynx-like beast did seem interested in him. It sat on the floor near Besi's hearth and watched him placidly, as though it were enjoying the conversation. Every so often, its long tail would twitch.

Besi leaned across the table and touched Tim's brother's hand. "How is your savings, Lon?"

Lon shrugged. "We'll get by."

"At least you still have the geese," Besi said.

"Should be good money in eggs this year," Shom Hill said, helping himself to another roll from the basket on the table.

"We've got a bit stashed away," Besi said. "So let us know if you need help with Varthi's wedding celebration."

"Oh," said Lon. He'd obviously forgotten that his daughter was getting married that summer. "Thank you."

Lon, Shom, and Besi were sitting on the chairs. Tim normally found chairs quite comfortable, but now he was in no mood to sit. He paced. All his livestock had been stolen and the thief commanded legions of soldiers. In all of Klindrel history, no one had ever brought an emperor to justice. But Tim would. He had to find a way.

"What about the horse?" Tim asked. "Did they take Ludo?"

Lon shook his head.

"Did you hide him?" Tim asked.

"No," Lon said. "They didn't ask for him."

Tim nodded. "So they have all the horses they need, but they're short on oxen."

"Not so short anymore," said Lon.

"Where are they keeping the oxen?" Tim asked. "The Broomfield Meadows?"

"I doubt it," said Cousin Shom. "I reckon they're out at the mustering grounds. That's where they're keeping the oxen that came in with the Saltlands troops."

"There's not enough pasture out at the mustering grounds," Lon said.

"They supplement with hay," Shom said.

"Have you been there?" Tim asked.

"Aye," said Shom. "I went to see if they wanted a wagon driver for the season. They turned me away. Said the emperor didn't want any Drelfin in his army."

"Well, that's surely odd," Tim said.

"Not if you think like Redfolk," Shom said.

"What do you mean?" Tim asked.

"Well, who else do they call 'Drelfin'?" Shom asked.

Tim was puzzled. Having been called a "Drelfin" all his life, it took him a moment to remember that there was another people whom the Klindrel called "Drelfin":

"You think the emperor is planning to attack the Brownfolk?"

"Where else could the army be going?" Shom asked.

"I reckoned they were going downriver," Tim said, "to take the kingdom of Poldwen."

"Not Poldwen," Shom said. "I know a wagon maker who says the army has been building horse wagons for three months. You wouldn't want to take horse wagons on the Poldwen Trail."

"Well, that's so," Tim said.

"What about Penwargo?" Lon asked. "All the Redfolk think it's time for the emperor to conquer Penwargo."

Shom shook his head derisively. "He wouldn't muster troops here to attack Penwargo. And he wouldn't pull companies out of Mazibo. No, he's planning to march into the Redwood Valley. Mark my words."

Tim scratched his chin. Could be he had an opportunity here. He knew a lot of Brownfolk.

Besi asked, "What is it?"

"Well," said Tim, "I can't fight the emperor's army, but if he's attacking the Brownfolk, could be I can aid his enemies."

"The Brownfolk will get slaughtered," Shom said.

"The Brownfolk were made by Thafarsi, the goddess of knowledge," Tim said. "They're smart."

"That doesn't mean they can win," Shom said.

"Do they even have weapons?" Lon asked.

"They do," Tim said.

"Are you sure?" Lon asked.

"I'm an iron trader," Tim said. "I know their weapon crafters."

"Do you know any Brownfolk who would be interested in a cat?" Shom asked.

"Tim has no oxen," Lon reminded him. "He won't be visiting the Brownfolk this year."

Shom waved his hand dismissively. "Oh, the Enclave Council will get our oxen back."

Besi turned her worried face to Shom. "You think so?"

"I surely do," Shom said. "That's their job—making sure the Empire respects clan law."

"I don't know," Lon said. "I reckon the emperor thinks he bought those cattle. And anyway, he needs them for his war."

Shom shrugged. "Well, then, the Council will make him pay a fair price. Either to you or to the Clan. Don't worry. It will all get settled."

That was easy for Shom to say. He hadn't lost any cattle. He hired a new team every spring.

"But he took clan-marked beasts," Besi said. "Those can't be sold to the emperor for any price."

"Well, technically I suppose you're right," Shom said. "But if the Council can't get the oxen back, I reckon they'll have to bend the law a bit."

"Bend the law?" Tim exclaimed. "That law comes from Yolim."

"Well," said Shom, "I reckon Yolim understands that the party with the army has a superior bargaining position."

"Aye," said Lon. "I'm sorry, Tim. They all had swords. I couldn't stand up to them, but Yolim knows I'm sorry."

Besi reached out and touched Lon's hand. "We aren't blaming you, Lon. Are we, Tim?"

"No," said Tim, unequivocally. "No, I blame the emperor. He's the one responsible. He's the one who must be punished."

He could see that Besi didn't like him talking that way, but she held her tongue.

"Might be tricky to punish the man with the army," Shom observed.

"The Brownfolk have an army, too," Tim said. "I'm going to help them win this war."

"How will you get weapons to them without oxen?" Shom asked.

"They don't need weapons," Tim said. "They need information. And I can get it for them without leaving sight of Kanabur."

Tim enacted the first step of his plan two days later. One of his cousins had negotiated a hay contract with the Klindrel Army's supply master. (Tim and Lon were not the only ones who suddenly found themselves with more hay reserves than they needed.) Tim convinced his cousin to bring him along when he made the first delivery.

They rode past neat rows of tents set up on the mustering grounds. Fire pits were scattered haphazardly among them, each pit serving two, three, or sometimes four tents. Women and their daughters tended cook pots. Small boys, barely taller than Tim, danced through the camp waving sticks at each other. Tim reckoned that each tent represented at least four mouths the army had to feed. He would have to think of a way to hide Lon's barley in case the soldiers came for that next.

Tim's cousin drove the wagon up to an immense haystack and the boys in the back began unloading, with assistance from several Klindrel soldiers. While his cousin chatted with the supply master, Tim picked up a stick and calculated the number of tents, soldiers, and camp followers, scratching his figures in the mud. He did not notice the approaching sentry until the giant was nearly upon him.

"What are you doodling, Drelfin?"

Tim looked up: leather boots, wool trousers, long tunic, leather apron, sword-and-dagger, segmented armor, and finally, way up there underneath the soldier's iron helmet, an apple-red face.

"Good day!" said Tim. He was too startled to control his skin color, but it reddened autonomically to match the Redman. "I was just, uh, writing. Numbers."

The giant squinted down at him. "Why are you writing them in the mud?" he asked.

"Well, I left my pocket ledger at home," Tim explained. This was true. He had not brought it because he had feared it would make him look like a spy. Which he was.

Please, Yolim, Tim prayed. *Please don't let him arrest me.*

The giant snorted and shook his head like a grumpy old bull. "Drelfin," he muttered.

Tim kept silent, resisting the urge to wipe out his figures with his boot.

Still shaking his head, the giant stalked away.

Thank you, Tim prayed.

Tim checked his figures to be sure they hadn't been scared out of his head. Good. He had a count. He stepped on his calculations and walked over to the supply tent.

Sacks and sacks of grain were piled up to giant height under a gray canvas ceiling supported by dozens of poles and cross-poles. The ground underneath the canvas was not much drier than the ground outside.

Poor drainage, Tim thought. *That will waste grain.*

He could see how many sacks were in a pile, but how many piles were in here? He reckoned five or six deep. How wide was the supply tent? Did the piles go all the way to the end?

Tim glanced at the supply master, who was still conversing with Tim's cousin. He had affected not to notice Tim entering the tent. Would he notice if Tim started wandering through the tent counting sacks?

Oh but the Redmen have you spooked, Tim told himself. *Don't be daft. Just do this the easy way.*

Tim didn't need to count sacks. The supply master had done it for him. Tallies had been scored into the tent pole behind the supply master. Tim sidled around his cousin and pretended to be interested in the giant's pontifications. From this angle, he had a good view of the tallies. Now he knew how many wagon loads of grain were in the tent.

But how many wagons were there?

"I'll go see how the boys are coming along," he murmured.

His cousin nodded and then launched into a counterargument. Good. That would keep them occupied.

Tim went to help his cousin's sons stack the hay. Only a bit of finish work was left, which suited Tim just fine. From the top of the haystack, he could see the ox herd grazing on the meadow. He reckoned about half of the cattle were marked with two white stockings. The sight made him sick, but he kept looking until he had a count. The number of oxen told him the number of wagons.

That evening, in the after-supper candlelight, Tim Hill took out his ledger and started putting the pieces together. From the amount of grain in the tent, he reckoned the army was planning on a four-month campaign.

Moving this grain through the mountains would be tricky. The army would use some horse wagons for speed, but the bulk of the supply chain would be supported by slow-moving oxen. The animals had to haul their own hay—at least in the mountains—so not every wagon could be loaded with grain for the soldiers. The army would need to establish supply bases, and the wagons would need to make multiple trips.

Tim penciled out a plausible supply chain—what he would do if he were running the army. He now had an estimate of how long it would take to haul the grain across the mountains.

That was valuable information, and Tim knew just the man who would value it.

The next day, Tim called at a boarding house near the Kanabur ferry docks. A Brownman (that is, a Child of Knowledge) lived there under the name of "Blueglass". As the moniker implies, Blueglass specialized in delivering glassware and other expensive goods from Hicho to Kanabur. Blueglass had managed two-and-a-half trips the previous year, and the snow had forced him to rent a room for the winter. Blueglass could afford it.

Tim's knock at the door was answered by a Klindrel with bloodstained trousers. Tim, being on eye level with the blood-stains, was startled. But a feather sticking to the trousers told him he was being silly. The giant had just killed a duck for the noonday meal.

Tim put on his negotiation smile and tilted his head back to meet the giant's eyes. He wished he hadn't. The giant was enraged.

"What are you doing here?"

"I— I came to see Blueglass. Is he—?"

"Get out!" the houseman shouted, although Tim had not even come in. "Get out! I want nothing to do with either of you!"

The door slammed.

Tim stepped back, stared at the door, and scratched his head in puzzlement. Tim surmised that Blueglass was no longer at the boarding house, but where could he have gone?

Where would Tim have gone, if he were homeless in a foreign city? Well, Tim would have gone to one of his clients. Fortunately, Tim knew all of Blueglass's clients, because Tim traded in glass, too.

Tim found Chenalko minding his luxury goods store on the edge of Kanabur's only cobbled plaza. After an exchange of pleasantries—and before the topic of conversation could turn to the emperor's military intentions—Tim asked about the Brownman:

"I went down to Blueglass's boarding house this morning," Tim said. "The houseman seemed a bit upset. Do you know? Has he thrown Blueglass out?"

Chenalko looked around his empty shop nervously. Then he leaned down and murmured quietly into Tim's ear, "No."

Chenalko straightened up and nodded gravely.

"So Blueglass is still staying there?"

Chenalko shook his head. Deliberately. Once left, once right.

"He went back to Hicho?"

Shake. Shake.

"He died?"

Chenalko shrugged. "Only the Imperial Guard knows. They put him in prison."

"In— in prison?"

Chenalko nodded. "For spying."

"Oh," said Tim. He rubbed his chin thoughtfully. "Well, do *you* have any gilded wine glasses, then? My niece is getting married."

That night, as Tim lay in bed next to his beloved, snoring Besi, he wondered two things: He wondered why he hadn't been quickwitted enough to think of silvered wine glasses (they would have been good enough for his niece) and he wondered how he could travel over the pass during the snow melt without alerting the suspicions of the Klindrel Army.

The first question was moot. But before Tim fell asleep, he answered the second: He would take the horse and carry some small luxury item. If he were stopped, he could claim he was trying to get his treasure to Hicho before his rival crossed the pass. For that story to work, he would need something rare and valuable enough to warrant making such a trip. The gilded wine glasses were almost expensive enough, but no one would believe a merchant was carrying glass *toward* Hicho. Tim needed something small that the Brownfolk didn't have.

He needed the cat.

CHAPTER 3
The End of Tim's Quest

TIM ACQUIRED THE CAT THE NEXT DAY. Shom offered to let him sell it on commission, but Tim bought the whole cat outright. His true goal was to deliver information that would thwart the emperor's invasion, so he didn't want to be obliged to extract the best price for the cat.

He paid too much for it. Oh well. Cousin Shom would need the money.

Tim's house had no mice, but his brother's stable did. Tim took the cat there.

As soon as he opened the cage, the cat bolted out and scampered up a pole to the hayloft. Ludo, the long-maned bay gelding, shied and snorted.

So the cat was afraid of the horse, and the horse was afraid of the cat. Tim needed everyone to get along. He couldn't pretend to be crossing the pass to sell the cat if the cat ran away.

Over the next few days, as the purple moon deepened, Tim spent much time in the stable trying to convince the cat that the horse would not eat it and convince the horse that the cat would not eat him. Ludo was the more even-tempered of the two, and he soon learned to ignore the cat. The cat was willing to tolerate Tim—it even let Tim stroke its fur—but it remained in the hayloft from where it often peered down at the giant gelding below. (I should clarify, perhaps, that Ludo was a full-sized, grass-eating horse. If you have only seen the deer-sized, fern-eating horses ridden by our Road Patrol, then you may not know that horses can grow to be as big as elk.)

Coaxing the cat down was not easy, but Tim was fortunate to have such a problem. He needed something to do. He had many days to wait through. Although the ground was bare and the air was warming in the valley of the Cataract River, the pass would be choked with snow until the end of the month.

He faced each morning with a sickening dread. What if the houseman told the soldiers that Tim had been looking for Blueglass? What if the army found out about the ledger in which he had written all he knew about their supplies? If Tim were imprisoned, could Lon protect Tim's wife and children from being imprisoned, too? Who would protect Lon?

Tim hated to risk his family's security, but the alternative was worse. The alternative was to stand with helpless clenched fists as the emperor pillaged the wealth of Clan Hill. That's what the Enclave Council had decided to do. Tim couldn't stomach that.

Tim planned to leave on the twenty-fifth, but once he had taught the cat to sit a trot, he had nothing left to do but worry. And besides, the army had already started work on road repairs. Tim saddled up his horse on the twentieth.

"When is Daddy coming back?" his littlest son asked.

"Soon," Besi said. "This year, he'll come home early." Besi's beautiful forehead was wrinkled with worry.

"I'll come back as soon as I can," Tim said.

"Ludo is a fast horse," his eldest son said.

"Aye," said Tim. He put a hand on the boy's shoulder. "You remember those prices? In case anyone wants to buy our iron?"

"I wrote them down, Dad."

"Good. Well … I reckon I should be going."

He hugged each of them in turn. Besi saved herself for last.

"I wish …" she said. But then she pressed her lips together and shook her head.

Tim looked into her eyes. "It has to be done, Besi. You know it has to be done."

"I know *you* think it has to be done," she said.

"We can't let him get away with it," Tim said. His cattle could not be bought, but he *would* make the emperor pay.

She put her forehead on his chest. "Do what you must," she said. She looked up. "But be as safe as you can."

"Don't worry, Besi."

"I will, though."

Tim sighed. "I know."

Lon shook Tim's hand. "Don't push him too hard on the downhill."

"I won't," Tim said. Except for the pass itself, the downhills were pretty gentle, but Tim knew what his brother really meant.

"Well," said Tim. "I reckon I'd best get going."

He reached up and slipped the knot that held the saddle ladder. The wooden rungs clicked together as the ladder unrolled.

The cat—whom Tim had named Mister Whiskers—was already in his cage behind the saddle. Thanks to Tim's training, Mister Whiskers could now be trusted to ride uncaged, but Tim feared something might spook the cat as they passed through Kanabur.

Tim climbed up and sat astride his saddle with his feet on the horse's withers. He rolled the ladder up carefully and retied its slip knot.

"Well," he said, looking down on his brother, his wife, and his four children. They looked somber. Besi was biting her lip. He should leave before she started to cry.

His eldest son smiled up at him. "May Yolim bless your journey, Dad."

Tim smiled and took up Ludo's ear-reins. "May Yolim watch over you while I am gone. Ho-hey, Ludo."

Tim rode out of the Hill Enclave vowing to come back.

In addition to the cat, Tim had brought enough food to get himself over the pass and down as far as the Passwatch Roadhouse. He planned to eat none of it, for he could purchase food at the inns along the way, but he brought it in case the road proved more hostile than he expected. Tim had one pouch of imperial coins to pay for food, lodging, and tolls on the Klindrel side of the pass and another pouch of Academy coins to pay for whatever he might need on our side. He also had his cloak, his woolen cap, his pocket-sized ledger, and five changes of socks. Tim was prepared.

The first day of his journey was uneventful. On the second, he met soldiers.

Tim and Ludo were stopped at a stream. Mister Whiskers was lapping water from Tim's cupped hands when Tim heard the rumble of wagon wheels—not one wagon, but many, coming down the road from the mountains.

Tim let the water fall from his hands. He picked up the cat.

"Mer?" asked Mister Whiskers as Tim carried him up the saddle ladder.

Ludo stood still as they mounted. The rumbling did not frighten him, but he was interested. His ears were pointed toward the sound.

The wagons rolled into view, two abreast, taking up the entire road. Every ox had two white stockings. Stolen.

Tim's hand clenched the saddle leather. He was seized by the urge to confront the wagon drivers and demand the return of his clan's oxen.

The cat squirming in his arm brought him back to his senses. Tim stuffed Mister Whiskers into the cage behind the saddle and hastily rolled up the ladder.

Tim Hill, don't be a fool, Tim thought. *You can't balance this account by getting beaten by soldiers and thrown in jail.*

His hands were shaking so much that he couldn't tie the knot to hold the rolled-up ladder in place.

He could tie it later. He dumped the bundle of rope and wood in his lap and gestured with his ear-rein.

"Ho-hey, Ludo."

The horse allowed himself to be directed off the road.

Tim wanted to hide, but it was too late for that. He would just keep Ludo out of the way and hope for the best.

Please, Yolim, make them ignore me.

But the soldiers were not ignoring him. Those in the front wagons eyed him with suspicion.

As the first pair of wagons passed, a soldier leapt off and strode toward Tim, scabbard slapping against his thigh. From his raised saddle, Tim could look down on the Redman, but even so, the soldier's muscular arms and armored torso were intimidating.

"Ho, Drelfin. Whither do you ride?"

Gesturing toward the caged cat, Tim said, "I have a rare beast to sell."

"In the mountains?"

"No," said Tim. "In the lands of the brown Drelfin."

The soldier folded his red arms across his broad chest, considering. Behind him, the wagons continued to roll by.

The wagons were mostly empty. Each had just enough hay to get its team back to Kanabur. So: They were already building the supply chain.

"The pass is still blocked by snow," the soldier said.

"For wagons, it is," Tim agreed. "But if my horse can get through, I shall be able to make a great profit by arriving before my competition."

The soldier frowned, still considering.

Tim looked at the wagons then back at the soldier. He asked,

"Is there some reason I shouldn't be trading with the brown Drelfin this year?"

The frown deepened to a scowl. "No," said the soldier. "We are only hauling supplies to the forts. As we do every spring."

"Oh," said Tim. "Of course."

The soldier glanced over his shoulder at the rolling wagons. "I must get back," he said. "Good day, Drelfin."

"Good day," said Tim.

After that, Tim didn't worry about meeting soldiers. If they couldn't admit they were preparing an invasion, then they wouldn't be able to send him home. Each day, the road took Tim higher and higher into the mountains.

Ludo complained about being saddled each morning, but Tim could tell the gelding was pleased to be traveling. Mister Whiskers enjoyed it as well. Frequently, he would climb up Tim's back and ride with his paws on Tim's shoulder so he could get a better view of the pine-covered slopes, the blue ridges in the distance, and the mottled gray sky above. When Mister Whiskers was particularly pleased, he would make a throaty throbbing noise in Tim's ear. Tim tolerated this because it amused him.

Every day, they rode through wagon tracks and dung. Tim was no tracker, but he knew animals. He noted the point where fresh horse dung began to appear, indicating that he was now following horse wagons. He reckoned the fort they had just passed must be the midway supply base between Kanabur and the Borderkeep. Tim did not push Ludo, and the horse dung aged over the next two days.

The road still had ox dung, too, from a supply train sent out several days ahead of the horses. Tim could tell they had been timed to reach the Borderkeep on the same afternoon. The Klindrel were clever.

Tim met both the horse wagons and the ox wagons on the morning they came rumbling back from the Borderkeep. He got a good count. Once they were gone, he took out his pocket ledger and did some arithmetic. It would be at least twelve days until the army would have all their grain at the Borderkeep. That meant the legion had probably not yet left Kanabur. Tim figured to cross the pass into Brownfolk territory after noon. He would be able to give the Brownfolk a good head start.

The Borderkeep is the last Klindrel outpost before the pass, and the village below it is called Zweebin. Tim was tempted to ride around Zweebin, around the toll booth, and especially around the Borderkeep, but toll takers have sharp eyes. If anyone caught him trying to circumvent the toll, he could be imprisoned in the keep. That would never do. Not when he was so close.

After locking up his furry alibi in the wicker cage, Tim rode into Zweebin. Keeping his reins in his lap to hide the shaking of his hands, Tim tried to appear bold and confident.

The giants stared as he rode through their village. Tim began to realize what a daft thing he was doing. The villagers had all seen the loads of supplies taken up to the Borderkeep. They knew war was coming. And here was this Drelfin riding jauntily through their village as though nothing were happening.

By the time Tim reached the toll booth, he was feeling queasy. When he saw the guards, his stomach clenched like a fist.

These weren't familiar faces from the Borderkeep garrison. They looked like scouts. Their helmets were covered with leather so that the gleam of iron would not give them away. Leather-hilted swords were tucked into black scabbards on their belts. Their boots were soft leather and they wore no armor, so that they could move soundlessly if they needed to go afoot. Under gray woolen cloaks, their linen tunics were quartered gray and brown. From innkeepers' and villagers' descriptions, Tim recognized the uniform of the Chumwarl Scouts, a company from the Saltlands that had been sent to escort the supply trains.

Tim reined Ludo to a halt. The horse shuffled his feet nervously. From inside the wicker cage, Mister Whiskers asked, "Mer?"

There were three scouts, but one of them had a leather patch sewn on the breast of his tunic. From this and from the scar on his eyebrow that innkeepers had mentioned, Tim realized he had chanced upon the toll booth just as the guards were receiving a visit from their captain.

Oh, Yolim, Tim thought, *this is unfortunate.*

The captain called, "Good day, Drelfin!"

"Good day," said Tim. He allowed his skin to redden as the Redman drew near. He hoped there was a way he could turn the captain's presence to his advantage.

The white scar through the captain's eyebrow gave a sinister aspect to his placid, round face. His eyes were the color of Kanabur steel. "I hope you weren't planning on heading over the pass," the captain said.

"I am, actually," Tim said.

The captain shook his head. "Conditions are not so good right now."

"Oh, I reckon my horse can handle a bit of snow," Tim said, in what he hoped was a casual voice. "I want to get across the pass before Clan Fairweather can."

"Such a hurry? Would you not prefer to wait a month?"

"Oh, no," said Tim. He swallowed and prepared to put his story to the final test. "You see, I am carrying a rare beast from the other side of the world." He placed a hand on the wicker cage. "The brown Drelfin have never seen anything like it. I must be the first to sell them one."

"Why?"

"Why? Oh ... well, because the first shall be able to demand the highest price, of course," Tim said. "But I admit it is also a matter of pride."

"If the animal is as rare as you say, Drelfin, I doubt anyone else will be able to deliver one before you, even if you must wait a month or two."

"Well, I reckon the pass is clear enough now," said Tim. "For horses, at least. Um, hasn't the weather been warm here?"

"It has, it has," agreed the captain. "But still I must ask you to wait. Fravvin, check his cage."

The scout named Fravvin said, "Yes, sir." He approached Tim's horse with his right hand on his sword hilt.

Fravvin glanced up at Tim. "Untie it," he ordered.

Tim untied the straps that held Mister Whiskers's cage to the saddle.

Watching Tim and the horse warily, Fravvin reached for the cage. Perhaps because he was paying more attention to Tim than to what he was doing, he knocked the cage off Ludo's back. The cat cried out. The cage struck the ground. The gelding danced nervously, giving the cage an inadvertent kick that sent it sliding along the road. Amid all this tumult, the door popped open.

"Rrrrrrrowr!" screamed Mister Whiskers as he bounded off into the forest.

"What was that?" asked Fravvin.

"Was it a lynx?" asked the scar-browed captain.

"That was my cat!" cried Tim.

He untied his saddle ladder and dismounted. "I've got to get him!"

"I think he's gone now," said the captain. "Perhaps you should turn around and ride home, now that you have no reason to cross the pass."

"But I *do* have a reason to cross the pass!" Tim said. "I'm going to sell that cat. I just need to get him back. Please let me pay my toll so I can be on my way."

"I am disturbed by your reluctance to return home," the captain said.

"Beg pardon?"

"You seem to be a right stubborn Drelfin."

"Oh, I am," said Tim.

"Wait a moment," said the captain. He frowned in thought. "No," he decided. "I can't take the risk."

"What risk?"

"I fear that if I let you go, you will attempt to sneak around this position and cross the pass anyway," the captain explained.

"But I will pay the toll," Tim said. "That is why I stopped here at the toll booth."

"Haven't you wondered what the Chumwarl Scouts are doing in Zweebin?" asked the captain.

"No," said Tim.

"No?" repeated the captain. "You have no curiosity whatsoever?"

"If I did I wouldn't admit it," Tim mumbled.

"I would like to let you go," said the captain. "But if you were to sneak around me and warn the brown Drelfin, then the emperor could order me to report for my execution, do you understand?"

"Execution?"

The captain nodded. "My men could be executed, too."

His subordinates shifted uncomfortably.

"I have orders to prevent anyone from crossing the pass," the captain said. "So please forgive me, Mister Drelfin, but we'll be taking you to the Borderkeep now. You have my word that you will be free to go as soon as this war is over."

And so Tim Hill was imprisoned at the Borderkeep on the edge of the Klindrel Empire, less than a day's ride from our Passwatch Roadhouse. Had the Passwatch patrollers known of Tim's valuable information, they could have organized a rescue mission, but of course, they knew nothing.

CHAPTER 4
Sabu Meets Dusi

ON OUR SIDE OF THE PASS, the patrollers at the Passwatch Roadhouse waited hopefully for the third sign of spring.

The first sign of spring was that the apples ran out. Garrison Captain Zhaku urged her patrollers to be strong, to accept their fate, and to stoically endure the days until the road up from the Redwood Valley would be passable once more.

The second sign of spring was that the heaps of snow that had built up against the palisade began to diminish. By the middle of Purplemonth, the courtyard was deep in water and mud. Patrollers sent to rampart duty would cross the ground between the barracks and the palisade wearing nothing below mid-thigh except heavy clogs, preferring to don their moccasins, riding pants, and woolen leggings only after they had passed through the muck.

Bare patches began to appear on the road. At the end of Purplemonth, a messenger was sent to inform Roadhouse One that the pass would soon be open.

Roadhouse One, the headquarters of the Road Patrol, lies in the heart of the Redwood Forest, where the Klindrel Road meets the Redwood River. The region rarely receives snow. In many years, the meadows stay green all winter long. For this reason, Roadhouse One has the task of caring for all the Road Patrol's horses over the winter.

The Passwatch messenger notified Roadhouse One that it was time to send the horses up the road. The arrival of these horses was the third sign of spring for which the patrollers at Passwatch were waiting so eagerly.

Lieutenant Sabu, second-in-command at the Passwatch Road-house, was just as eager as his subordinates, but he did not show it. He was a veteran. The arrival of the new recruits would mark the beginning of his seventh year with the Road Patrol.

Sabu was young for a lieutenant, but most of the Passwatch Garrison was younger. Headquarters kept patrollers with children at the lower roadhouses, closer to civilization. At Passwatch, the patrollers were either so young they had not yet married, or so old—like Captain Zhaku—that Headquarters believed they never would marry. At thirty-three years old, Sabu was beginning to suspect he belonged in the second category.

On the day the horses were due to arrive, the mud at Passwatch was dry enough that Lieutenant Sabu could use the courtyard as a training ground. He had paired off the patrollers according to what they needed to learn and what they could teach. Sabu himself was standing on "the giant", sparring with Jamidu.

The giant is like a high wooden stool, except that two of its legs are carved to resemble giant flesh-and-blood legs. The stool is about as tall as an average person, so the effect of standing on it is to make one twice as tall. Sabu wielded a wooden sword as long as he was, simulating a flesh-and-blood giant's height and reach. He was teaching Jamidu how to fight bandits.

Jamidu needed training. He would be a second-year as soon as the horses came, but the Passwatch Garrison had seen no combat in Jamidu's rookie year. Sabu didn't mind a year with no combat. In fact, he preferred it when bandits surrendered peacefully. But his subordinates needed to know what to do when the blades started flashing. So Sabu taught them to fight, while hoping they would not have to.

Jamidu hopped around in front of Sabu just out of reach, waving his wooden practice blade. Like a real battleblade, it had serrated teeth for ripping tendons, but the point was blunt and the slicing edge, being wood, was harmless. The patrollers' battle-blades were much shorter than the swords the giants used, and the purpose of this exercise was to teach Jamidu to attack without getting killed.

"You shouldn't dance about," Sabu told him. "Just wait for your opening; then dart in."

"But Thaki said I should go in and out, in and out."

Curly-haired Thaki was indeed employing this technique against her training partner, Perga. Without interrupting her sparring, Thaki said, "But I didn't say, 'Bounce around like a love-crazed bunny.'"

"The problem," Sabu explained, "is that you keep putting yourself within my reach. You need to wait for the moment when I can't hit you."

"You haven't hit me yet," Jamidu said.

Sabu considered setting Perga against Jamidu. Perga was good with the giant sword. In truth, he was good with every technique. Perga would be able to drive the lesson home. But, no. This was something Lieutenant Sabu had to handle himself.

"Again," Sabu said.

Jamidu nodded and began dancing again. By unspoken agreement, Perga and Thaki stopped sparring so they could watch. Sabu cleared his mind and allowed his focus to expand. He held his wooden sword ready to strike.

Jamidu bounced in, out, in, out, i— "Ow!" he cried as his forehead met the swing of Sabu's wooden blade.

Hikafa, the quiet third-year, looked over at his friend's cry. He turned his worried gaze to Sabu, as though expecting Sabu to explain what had happened.

Sabu returned Hikafa's gaze and shrugged. He hadn't wanted to hurt Jamidu, but he wouldn't apologize. Jamidu was a second-year, now. He needed to learn to keep his head out of reach.

"And that's why you shouldn't bounce so much," Thaki said.

"How goes *your* training?" Sabu asked.

Thaki shook her curly head. "Poorly," she admitted. "I don't think the Goddess meant for me to use two blades."

Perga scoffed. "You have two arms, woman. You can use two blades."

"But I only need one to stab a giant," Thaki said.

Perga held up his wooden practice blades. "One is for offense; the other for defense."

"No one can block a blow from a giant," Jamidu said. "That's why they don't issue us shields."

"They don't issue you a shield because they know you would use it wrong," Perga said. "I said 'defense', not 'blocking'."

"What's the difference?" Thaki asked.

Now the other patrollers were gathering around. When Perga had something to say about combat techniques, they were wise to listen.

"Block this," Perga said. He raised his practice blade and swung it down in a slow arc at Thaki's head. She raised her blade to meet his and stopped its motion.

"Could you have blocked it if I'd been swinging an axe?" Perga asked.

"No," Thaki said.

Perga nodded. "And that's because you are meeting force with force. Your arm has to be strong enough to withstand the blow. Now block this."

He thrust, quick as a fox. Thaki parried, quick as a rattlesnake.

"Look at what you did," Perga said. "Did you put your force against my force? No. You pushed my force off to the side. It doesn't matter how hard I thrust as long as you can use your blade to change my aim."

"Very well," said Thaki. "If a giant thrusts at me, I know what to do. But how do I defend against a slash?"

"I'll show you," said Perga.

He went to stand in front of Sabu's wooden giant. Jamidu gladly made way for him.

Perga looked up at Sabu. "Backhand diagonal, please. Top to bottom. And don't pull your blow."

Sabu nodded. He knew Perga would not let himself get hit.

Sabu poised for a backhand slash. Perga shifted into reach of the long wooden sword. Sabu pulled the sword through the air, slicing at Perga's head.

Perga ducked, sidestepped, and caught the sword with his practice blade, adjusting Sabu's blow so that it would miss him. He spun inside Sabu's guard, slipped behind the tall stool, and stabbed at the wooden leg. With a jerk of his practice blade, he snapped the strip of rawhide that simulated the giant's tendon.

"Hamstrung," Perga declared.

"That's cheating," Jamidu said. "You didn't block Lieutenant Sabu's blow. You sidestepped it."

"I moved one way and pushed the blow the other. If that's cheating—" Perga shrugged, "—well, we *are* fighting bandits."

Sabu climbed down and tied a new leather tendon on the giant. It had been a good demonstration ... for Thaki. Sabu didn't think many of the other patrollers were ready to learn Perga's two-weapon technique.

Sabu was about to ask Hikafa to change places with Jamidu when the call came from the ramparts: "Horses! The horses are here!"

Grins broke out on the patrollers' faces.

"Put your practice blades away," Sabu said. "Then you can come back to greet the horsemasters. Just don't forget to be kind to the rookies."

"Are we getting any good ones?" Perga asked.

"They're all good at something," Sabu said. "We just have to learn what."

"We'll find out soon enough," Thaki said. "Want help carrying the giant?"

"Please," said Sabu.

By the time they had the wooden giant put away in the storage room, the gate in the palisade was open. Sabu went to stand in the middle of the courtyard to welcome the arriving horsemasters.

They rode mountain steppers, the deer-sized horses that were magically bred to carry the Road Patrol through the rugged terrain where bandits think they can hide. Each horsemaster held the lead ropes of four more mountain steppers bearing sacks of grain to supplement the forage available on the roadhouse's meadow. Ox wagons carrying food for horses and patrollers were expected to arrive a few days later.

The courtyard was filled with greetings, some for the horse-masters, some for the horses. Many patrollers were fond of the animals, but even those who felt no emotional attachment were glad to know that spring had arrived and that they would soon be getting back to patrolling the road and providing a safe haven for travelers.

If you have never seen a roadhouse, let me describe the layout: A wooden palisade encloses three long buildings sitting on three sides of a rectangular courtyard. On the left is the barracks. On the right is the stable. On the side opposite the gate is the road-house proper, the building in which travelers stay.

The roadhouse is also where the patrollers eat. The arrivals were welcomed with a celebratory meal (potatoes, flatcakes, and cheese). Someone showed the rookies to the barracks. Someone else showed the horsemasters to their rooms. And Sabu was summoned to the garrison captain's office-and-quarters.

Sabu entered and reached to close the sliding door separating the office from the rest of the barracks. Captain Zhaku shook her head. Sabu shrugged and left the door open.

Zhaku's first question was, "What do you think of the new recruits?"

"Fermigo seems bright enough," Sabu replied. "Although it looks like they fed him too well at the College of Forestry."

"And what did you think of Dusi?"

"Dusi?"

"The little one."

"I didn't see him."

Captain Zhaku chuckled. "Obviously not. She's female."

"Oh."

Captain Zhaku gave his shoulder a friendly slap. "We need a few more women around, don't we?"

"If you say so."

"What do you mean by that?" she asked.

"Everyone's approach to the job is unique," Sabu said. "I don't think gender has much relevance."

Zhaku shook her head. "If you were one of only seven women stationed here, you would think it has relevance."

"Oh," said Sabu. "I see. Thank you."

"For …?"

"For showing me something I haven't been taking into consideration." He wondered if the other women at the roadhouse felt outnumbered.

"Ah, here she is now," Zhaku said.

Sabu turned to see a short, slightly-built woman standing in the doorway. Her eyes were brown, and so deep that they seemed to drink in the light from the captain's oil lamp. The woman gave Sabu a lopsided smile that made him wonder how long she had been standing there and how much she had overheard.

"Sabu, this is Dusi. Dusi, this is Lieutenant Sabu."

They nodded to each other.

Dusi closed the door. Captain Zhaku offered them cushions and invited them to sit down around her knee-high dining table, which also functioned as a reading desk.

Sabu sat down cross legged and noticed a spot he had missed when washing his feet that evening—a smudge of light gray mud on his dark brown skin, just below the ankle. Embarrassed, he tucked that foot under his knee.

His embarrassment surprised him. He wasn't worried about being unhygienic in front of his captain; he was worried about the impression he was making on the stranger—who was really just a soft-footed rookie.

He glanced at Dusi's pink feet. She had washed them.

"Dusi is our new tracker," Zhaku said.

Sabu nodded. All patrollers were trained to track, but some rookies were better than others.

Zhaku put a finger to her lips, considering. "No, perhaps I should say she is our new *stalker*."

Sabu looked at Dusi.

"I like the term 'mind finder'," Dusi said. "But call me what you will."

Zhaku gestured to a rolled-up piece of paper on her dining table. "Headquarters says that Dusi tracks using elemental Thought."

"In truth?" asked Sabu. "The College of Forestry now teaches Thought magic?"

Dusi shook her head. "No, I just learned tracking. From Elder Manido."

Sabu nodded. All patrollers had learned tracking from Elder Manido. "And where did you learn to use elemental Thought?" he asked.

"Also from Elder Manido," Dusi said. "But only for tracking."

"This is the part that intrigues me," said Zhaku. "How can someone without an affinity for Thought train you to use it?"

"My affinity allows me to sense people even when they are out of sight," Dusi said. "Elder Manido showed me how to apply that to finding people in the forest—people like lost travelers, or bandits who think they can hide."

Sabu grinned.

Dusi gave him her lopsided smile. Good. He'd wanted to see it again.

"How far is your range?" Sabu asked.

Zhaku chuckled. "You'll have a chance to test her tomorrow, Lieutenant." She turned to Dusi. "What I want to know is: Why were you trained by Elder Manido? Why didn't you study under someone who knows Thought magic?"

"No one at the College of Forestry knows Thought magic," Dusi said.

"So why didn't you study elsewhere?" Zhaku asked.

"Because I wanted to join the Road Patrol," Dusi said.

"Good for you," Sabu said.

Dusi smiled at him. "Thank you."

The garrison captain did not smile. She studied the rookie. "Dusi, I am glad to have you at my roadhouse, but what will happen when a secret society finds out about your illicit training?"

Dusi shook her head. "It wasn't illicit." She slipped her hand inside the bosom of her tunic and withdrew a small rolled-up paper. She untied the red linen string and smoothed the paper out on Captain Zhaku's table.

Zhaku read it.

"I see," she said. She gestured toward Sabu and asked, "May I?"

Dusi shrugged, then nodded.

Zhaku handed the paper to Sabu. He read it:

The Order of Joined Minds wishes to inform the reader that the bearer of this message, Dusi, born in the Coldwallow District of Hicho, daughter of Perzofi, is authorized to use her affinity for elemental Thought for the purpose of detecting other minds, unless such use violates the law or the directives of local authorities. She is, however, forbidden to examine another's thoughts for any reason. Furthermore, she is forbidden from undertaking any course of study that could improve her ability to examine or manipulate another's mind.

The message was signed with verification symbols which Sabu, not being a member of the Order of Joined Minds, could not verify.

Sabu handed the paper back to Dusi. She rolled it up, retied it, and returned it to the pocket hidden inside her tunic. Sabu did not know why this pocket intrigued him.

"That is an unusual document," Zhaku said.

Dusi shrugged. "It's what I have. Does it make you feel better?"

"It does," Zhaku said. "But it leaves me with a new question."

"Ask it," Dusi said. "I have nothing to hide."

"Why wouldn't the Order of Joined Minds accept you as a member?"

"I would never join them," Dusi said.

"Why not?" Zhaku asked. "At the very least, you could have asked them for ethical training."

The rookie looked Zhaku right in the eye. "Captain, I can handle my own ethical training. And if I wanted to learn more ethics, I wouldn't turn to a secret society. My mother was murdered by a secret society."

"Ah," said Zhaku.

"I— I'm sorry," Sabu said.

Dusi sighed. "No, I'm sorry. I shouldn't be so ... intense. She was killed nineteen years ago. I've dealt with it. It's behind me, now." She shrugged. "And I've learned my own ethics."

"Thank you for clarifying," Zhaku said gently. "And forgive us for prying into your past."

"No matter," Dusi said.

Sabu looked into Dusi's deep, brown eyes. Nineteen years. She would have been a little girl, not even in local school yet. What crime had her mother committed? Had Dusi known about it? Sabu did not believe a secret society would kill without cause, but what had Dusi's mother known that had made her too dangerous to leave alive?

Sabu wanted to know the answers, but he had no right to ask the questions. Dusi was not responsible for her mother's transgressions. She had already divulged more than was necessary.

"Thank you for telling us," Sabu said. "Sometimes people's lives depend on our decisions. To make the right decisions, we must know the people we work with. So, thank you."

"You're welcome," Dusi said. And again she gave him that smile.

CHAPTER 5

Ganadarm Comes Down the Mountain

IN A REMOTE SECTION OF WILDERNESS claimed by the Klindrel Empire, the mining village of Shardook had been thawed out since early Purplemonth. As the days advanced toward Redmonth, spring crept higher and higher up the slopes of Shardook Peak. When the snow finally melted, it uncovered a tiny cabin secluded among the pines. The cabin was large enough for a giant to lie down in, but no larger. Its only occupant was Ganadarm, a black-bearded Child of Lith.

Ganadarm was a Child of Lith, but he was no Klindrel. He was from the Saltlands, a desert province that had been conquered by the Klindrel Empire some three dozen years earlier.

Children of Lith do not like to stay conquered. Ganadarm's father had united several landholders in a rebellion against the Empire. After a few years of skirmishing, the Klindrel Army cornered them all inside a hill fort and burned it to the ground. Only one rebel survived.

Ganadarm was not that survivor.

Ganadarm's father had foreseen defeat and sent his mother away before the battle. Ganadarm, being an infant at the time, had gone with her. No, the lone survivor of the Klindrel assault was a fire-scarred youth known forever after as "Ugly Lem". Ugly Lem recovered from his injuries, gathered together a gang of bandits, and eventually married Ganadarm's mother. By the time Ganadarm was fourteen, he was a bandit, too, and that was the life he had known until Ugly Lem's band earned the attention of the Chumwarl Scouts.

The Chumwarl Scouts were led by Captain Bannom, a Klindrel who pursued the bandits all across their native Saltlands. Captain Bannom was not as clever as Ugly Lem, but the bandits had to outsmart the scouts every time, and the scouts only had to win once. Inevitably, Bannom's men found the bandits and surrounded them. Ugly Lem fought and died. The others were captured and executed. Only one bandit escaped and survived.

Ganadarm was that survivor.

And Ganadarm had kept surviving. That was why, three years later, he was in the mountains far lithward of the Saltlands. He was in hiding. He was surviving.

On the eighth day of Redmonth in the year of the Klindrel Invasion, Ganadarm was surviving on roasted squirrel. Earlier in the winter, he had killed a bear, but the bear meat was gone. He had not rationed it; he preferred to eat it. Now all that was left of the bear was a furry black hide. Ganadarm hoped to trade this hide for food in the village of Shardook.

Ganadarm hadn't been to Shardook for several months, and he wanted to make a good impression. He went to the stream and washed away the winter's dirt and smoke until his skin was once again a ruddy terra-cotta. He washed his long, black hair and gathered it into a neat queue on the back of his head, securing it with a strip of braided leather. He washed and combed his bushy beard and in the process discovered two pine needles, a morsel of squirrel meat, and a tick which he flicked into the coals of his hearth. He had grown the beard as a disguise, but after three winters, it felt like a part of him.

Ganadarm did not take time to wash his trousers and tunic. Laundry was women's work. He did not need to sharpen his sword. During the five months of winter, he had sharpened it enough. He threw the bearskin over his shoulders like a cloak and set off down the mountain. Along the way, he practiced talking.

The outpost of Shardook lay at the base of the mountain, squeezed between the steep hillside and the whitewater creek. Like mushrooms on a tree stump, shacks and houses grew almost on top of one another. Ganadarm passed through freshly tilled terrace gardens and then he was splashing though the puddles that served as streets, weaving his way between the houses toward his destination.

His destination was Halaman's Public House of Wares, which was more commonly known as "Hal's House" or simply "the store". Ganadarm knocked at the door to be certain Hal was in. This was bandit country, and it wouldn't be good to be caught in the store when Hal was out. One of Hal's daughters opened the door for him, and Ganadarm stepped into the most cluttered place of business one can imagine.

Flour sacks sat in a pile near the door. Pots, snowshoes, and even furniture hung from the ceiling. A barrel standing next to a bolt of cloth held shriveled balls of wrinkles that had once been apples. The rear wall was dominated by shelves of pottery under which lurked lumpy sacks of potatoes. Another wall was pegged from floor to ceiling to display hammers, rakes, axes, hatchets, hoes, picks, awls, drills, shovels, fishing poles, and every kind of saw. Knives and swords had a special display stand in the center of the store. The silver mine was Shardook's only industry, but the industry was strong enough to support one merchant, provided he was willing to dabble in everything.

A long-armed Klindrel with silver streaks in his black hair, Hal greeted Ganadarm before he was three steps in. "Mister Musky! I feared you had died on the mountain."

"It takes more than a winter to kill me," Ganadarm said. "You should know that by now." It was the third winter he had survived on Shardook Peak. If he wasn't careful, he might turn into a mountain man.

"Tell me about it, tell me about it," Hal said. "I see you found a bear ... or did he find you?"

" 'Twas a little of both," Ganadarm said. He removed the bearskin from his shoulders and spread it on top of the sacks of flour. "What do you think? Is it worth a little credit?"

"It is, it is," laughed Hal. "Now let the wench take it up to my attic before the flour turns the fur white and the fur turns the flour ... musky."

"Oh," said Ganadarm.

Hal chuckled. "No harm done. (Git, girl.) Now what can I interest you in? I know you didn't walk all this way for the pleasure of my conversation."

"Bread and ale to begin with," Ganadarm said. He looked around the room. "And then I'll see what else I need."

"Take your time, take your time." Hal went into an adjacent room and shouted orders at his women. Moments later, his older wife appeared with a loaf of bread and a lump of cheese.

"Cheese?" asked Ganadarm. "Are the cows producing already?"

" 'Tis Redmonth," Hal observed.

"Oh, aye."

"You should winter in the village. You forget what spring looks like."

Ganadarm shook his head. The village was full of Klindrel. What he said was, "I like my cabin."

A daughter came and set two wooden cups on the table. Once she had poured ale into each, Ganadarm asked, "So what news?"

Hal took his knife from his belt and hacked off the end of the loaf of bread. "Much news," he said, keeping the end and offering the loaf to Ganadarm. "It has been a while since you last came down the mountain. Tulabo and Lame Willim tried to do a little extra mining of their own this winter. The foreman caught them and hung them both."

Ganadarm winced. He hated the Klindrel practice of hanging.

"Then Granite Dalk wanted to marry Willim's widow, but she got Penadral to duel for her. Penadral won, ripped Dalk's belly wide open. Penadral left in early Bluemonth, hoped his father would give him some land to support his new wife. I expect he'll be back before the year is out."

Ganadarm was not particularly interested in the feuds and squabbles of the locals. "Is anyone looking for a sword arm?" he asked.

Hal shook his head. "Not yet," he said. "I heard the Sunny Creek Band was planning to work the road this summer, but the baron sent some men to drive them out of hiding. Killed Sunny Creek Sam, and the rest of the band dispersed. At least for now."

Ganadarm did not mourn for the Sunny Creek Band. He knew them. He had joined them for the duration of one wagon robbery. The battle had been disgusting: only four wagon guards against ten bandits, and Sunny Creek Sam had not bothered to offer a chance to surrender. His men had killed the Drelfin wagon drivers, too. Ganadarm did not mind killing men and taking their money, but he thought it was dishonorable to slay the small, weak Drelfin.

Ganadarm hadn't argued with Sunny Creek Sam. The only acceptable way to dispute a leader's decisions was a contest of knives, and Ganadarm knew the Sunny Creek Band would not follow him if he won. So he simply left. They were all Klindrel anyway.

That was the story with every band Ganadarm had tried to join since coming to Shardook. He hadn't liked them, and they hadn't liked him. Ganadarm had come to these mountains with the hope of meeting new people and forming his own band, but the territory held too many Klindrel for his tastes. He wondered if perhaps he should go back to the Saltlands and try to recruit a band there.

"You know, you could get a job at the mine," Hal said.

"No," said Ganadarm. "I don't think I'll be a miner."

Hal laughed. "Didn't think so," he said. "Mountain man suits you much better, Mister Musky. Trapping wolves, killing bears."

Eating squirrels, thought Ganadarm.

Hal said, "Hell, you look like you're half bear yourself." He gestured to indicate Ganadarm's beard.

Ganadarm grunted.

"You might try mining for a summer, though," Hal said. "The baron raised everyone's pay by half to keep them from running off to join the war."

"War? What war?"

"Oh, that's the biggest news yet!" Hal said. "The emperor has made himself a new legion in Kanabur. Word is, he had to pull cohorts out of Mazibo and the Saltlands to do it."

"How many cohorts were pulled from the Saltlands?" Ganadarm asked.

"Oh, who knows? Not enough to make a full legion yet. Last I heard, they were still recruiting in Kanabur."

"So where is this war?" Ganadarm asked.

Hal grinned. "The emperor hasn't said, but they're moving supplies on the Drelfin Road."

"Where does that go?"

"To the lands of the Drelfin, of course."

"The Drelfin? Has the emperor run out of *men* to fight?"

"He's only been emperor a year," Hal said. "Perhaps he thought he should start small."

Hal laughed. Ganadarm did not find the joke funny.

Hal shrugged. "Anyway, all the bandits I know are lying low, Mister Musky. I don't think you'll find much work while the army's supply trains are moving."

"I see," said Ganadarm. "They are heavily guarded?"

"Not from what I hear," Hal said. "But the scout unit billeted at the Borderkeep has a reputation for being relentless bandit hunters."

The ale turned to ice in Ganadarm's stomach.

"What scout unit?"

Hal shrugged. "Just some band of horsemen the emperor recalled from the Saltlands."

And they were at the Borderkeep, only one day away.

Ganadarm asked, "Is their leader a man called Bannom?"

"I don't know his real name," Hal said. "Folks along the road are calling him 'Scarbrow'."

Ganadarm raised a hand to his face.

"That's right," Hal said. "Because it looks like somebody tried to slice his eyebrow in half. You know him?"

"Perhaps," Ganadarm said. He knew the man and he knew how he had gotten that scar. "When did they arrive at the Borderkeep?"

"Oh, sometime last month."

A month. That was plenty of time for Bannom to hear stories about a mountain man on Shardook Peak. It was time to run.

"What's wrong, Mister Musky?" Hal was looking at him with concern in his eyes.

"Nothing," said Ganadarm. "Nothing is wrong. Perhaps I've just been on the mountain too long."

If he traveled high and avoided roads, he could be far gone before Bannom came looking. Bannom was a man, not a wolf or an eagle. Ganadarm could outrun him.

For that matter, Ganadarm could outfight him. When Bannom's scouts had surrounded Ugly Lem's Band, the others had surrendered, but Ganadarm and Ugly Lem had charged. Bannom was competent with a blade, but Ganadarm had proven he was better. In the first exchange of blows, Ganadarm had nicked Bannom's eyebrow and dashed to freedom.

But Ugly Lem had not escaped. The Chumwarl Scouts had cut him down.

Those who surrendered had met an even worse fate. They were hung by their necks and left to desiccate in the desert wind. That was no way to get into Kashram's Heaven.

Ganadarm thought about this. Truth be told, hiding in the

forest eating roasted squirrels was no way to get into Kashram's Heaven, either.

Ugly Lem had died fighting the Chumwarl Scouts. Ganadarm's father had died fighting the entire Klindrel Empire. His grandfather had died defending the king of the Saltlands. They were heroes.

But Ganadarm—how would *he* die? Hiding in the forest like some wild beast?

No. For three years he had lived this way, but it was no way to die.

Ganadarm gestured at the empty ale cup and the half-eaten loaf of bread. "Do I still have credit?"

Hal smiled, almost affectionately. "Yes, Mister Musky, you still have credit. What do you need from me?"

"A razor," he said. "And my real name is Ganadarm."

CHAPTER 6
A Fateful Animal

ONE'S FATE AFTER DEATH is influenced by how one lived. Everyone knows that. However, theologians tell us that an equally important factor is how one dies. Ganadarm never studied theology, but he understood this in his bones.

You see, the God of the Lith—or "Kashram", to use Ganadarm's language—wants his people to be warriors. So he notices battles. He is more likely to be aware of a warrior who falls in battle than of, say, a thatcher who falls from a rooftop. So Ganadarm's decision to confront the scar-browed Captain Bannom was based on sound theological principles. It may seem foolish to us, but in truth, it was pious.

Ganadarm felt joyful when he awoke the next morning under a pine tree not far from the road. He was a free man with control over his own fate. He was clean shaven. He was ready to die with glory in a hopeless cause. He grinned a broad grin and continued up the road to Zweebin, which he estimated to be less than a lithic away.

His plan was to walk up to the first soldier he saw and demand to be taken to Captain Bannom. After some walking, it occurred to him that the soldiers might not let an armed criminal get within sword's reach of an officer. He needed a *good* plan, which was problematic because he had never been a military tactician. He had always done what Ugly Lem said to do.

So what would Ugly do? Well, Ugly would stay hidden until he had a good plan.

With that thought in mind, Ganadarm left the road and climbed up into the forest. Walking among the trees, he would be able to watch the road and see any Klindrel before they saw him. Also, he did not have to worry about the rocky road wearing out his elk hide moccasins so fast.

Considering he planned to die in a lost cause before noon, he probably did not have to worry about his moccasins in any event, but Ganadarm was still thinking like a mountain man. Finding food required covering ground. Covering ground required healthy feet. Healthy feet required good moccasins. Although Ganadarm's conscious mind was determined to die in a heroic duel, his habitual mind was still thinking like a survivor. The habitual mind is not changed easily.

So while Ganadarm was thinking about how to infiltrate an enemy fortress, he was still alert for signs of animals that could be his next meal. When he crossed a trickling stream, he looked for tracks. And the tracks he saw were so unusual that his planning was entirely driven from his head.

They looked like lynx tracks, but smaller. Perhaps a cub? Ganadarm thought it was too early in the year for a lynx cub to be on his own.

The animal was not long gone. Getting close to the ground, Ganadarm could find its trail. A pine needle was out of place. There was a dab of mud that had shaken loose from the creature's paw. There was a tiny piece of bark fluttering down from the branch of a tree.

"Mer?"

Ganadarm looked up to see a skinny, striped, long-tailed lynx with yellow eyes. In other words, it wasn't a lynx at all. It looked to be part lynx, part weasel, and part squirrel. He wondered what its pelt would be worth.

The creature regarded him warily, but made no move to run away. Perhaps it was just a cub. Ganadarm did not know how big the mother would be. Perhaps it was best to leave the cub alone. He took a step back.

"Mer?" the creature asked.

What if it had no mother, though? What if something had happened to the mother?

The little creature looked down at him. It almost seemed tame.

Ganadarm reached up to it. The branch was a handslength beyond his fingertips. The tiny beast had chosen its perch well.

"What say you, little cublet? Will you come down to me?"

The creature reached out a paw, as though in effort to bridge the gap. "Mer?"

Ganadarm waited. The little beast bobbed its head a few times. Then, with a gentle leap, it landed on Ganadarm's bicep.

"Your claws prick," Ganadarm commented.

With mincing steps, the squirrel-lynx arranged itself on Ganadarm's shoulder. Its tail flicked among the strands of Ganadarm's long, black queue.

"So you will ride on my shoulder? Can you stay on?" Holding up a hand to catch the beast if it should fall, Ganadarm took a step. Tiny claws poked through his tunic. Ganadarm took another step. Another.

"I see you are an accomplished rider," said Ganadarm. "I ride horses, myself ... or I did whenever Ugly could steal one for me."

Something in the middle of the animal began emitting a low, buzzing rumble. Ganadarm guessed it was the creature's stomach.

"You sound right hungry," he said. "Well, let me see if I can find some food for you before I go off on my errand. The day is yet early."

And so Ganadarm persuaded himself to return to the road and visit the outpost of Zweebin in the guise of a traveler. Of course, now he risked being recognized by one of the Chumwarl Scouts. Ganadarm reasoned that if he were recognized, he could start a fight and perhaps draw Captain Bannom out. This sort of "reasoning" is not atypical for Children of Lith. Whereas we apply logic before we make our decisions, they apply logic afterward, to justify the decisions they have made. If this sometimes puts them in dangerous situations, well, perhaps that is what Lith—or "Kashram"—intended.

As Ganadarm approached the village of Zweebin, the first thing he noticed was the Borderkeep. The square tower squatted on a round summit a short distance above the village. It was built entirely of stone, except for a flight of wooden stairs leading up to the entrance on the second story.

He could see one guard posted at the foot of the stairs and another in front of the door. More guards looked down from the top of the tower. In the village ahead of him, he saw soldiers patrolling the road and two soldiers standing guard in front of a barricade made of freshly felled pine poles. They wore shiny cuirasses made from interlocking steel segments and shiny steel helmets. They were too shiny to be Chumwarl Scouts. Ganadarm guessed they were members of the Borderkeep Garrison.

"Good day," he said, raising his hands to show that he was not reaching for his sword. The beast on his shoulder shifted at his sudden movement. Ganadarm stroked its warm, soft fur and it relaxed ... and rumbled.

"What is that?" asked a guard.

"Oh, I don't suppose you've ever seen a squirrel-lynx," Ganadarm said. "They live deep in the forest."

"What is your business here today?" the other asked.

Ganadarm shrugged his free shoulder. "I wanted a bite to eat. Does this village have an inn?" All villages on the Drelfin Road had an inn. He was certain of it.

"You may go to the inn," said the guard, indicating a wooden house with a steep shingled roof. "But do not think to go farther. No one is to cross the pass."

"No one?" said Ganadarm. "How then shall the Empire trade with the Drelfin?"

"We're preparing to negotiate a trade agreement," said the guard, patting the hilt of his sword. "The pass could be open before the end of the month. It is up to the emperor."

"Oh, well I wouldn't want to do anything that might anger the emperor," said Ganadarm. "That is the inn, did you say?"

And so Ganadarm passed into Zweebin. For a moment, he felt a desire to keep on walking and see how far he could get before the soldiers stopped him. He had never thought of crossing the pass, but now that he knew the emperor had forbidden it, it seemed like a fun thing to do. But he was in Zweebin on business: first find someone to look after the squirrel-lynx; next go die in a glorious battle against Bannom and his scouts. He entered the inn.

For someone accustomed to the dining establishments of Hicho, with their finely woven reed mats, soft linen cushions, and cozy dining nooks, the inn at Zweebin would seem filthy and cluttered (not to mention huge, being made for people Ganadarm's size). Ganadarm, however, judged the inn by the standards of his people, and he found it to be clean and spacious. The rectangular tables were arranged in an orderly (if unaesthetic) pattern. The abundance of chairs did not disturb him, for he knew no other civilized way to sit. The wooden floor, though sticky from spilled drinks, dropped food, and perhaps a bloody duel or two, was being swept even as he entered. Glad that he had bathed recently enough to meet the inn's high standards of hygiene, Ganadarm walked confidently to a table and sat down.

A pleasant-faced girl in a gray woolen dress asked, "What will you be having today?"

"Nothing just yet," said Ganadarm, "until I have spoken to the innkeeper."

"As you like it," she said. "Father, this traveler wants to speak to you."

A skinny, clean-shaven man sat down in the chair opposite Ganadarm. Wooden beads clicked among his fine, shoulder-length braids. "Red-Eyed Drago," he said, fixing Ganadarm with a gaze revealing that his irises were truly that color—a rare color, to be sure, but not unknown among the Children of Lith.

"I am Ganadarm," Ganadarm said. And to raise the stakes, he added, "From the Saltlands."

"Oh are you with, ah, Captain Bannom?"

Ganadarm spat on the floor. (He wasn't the first to do so.)

Drago raised his hands in placation. "I meant no offense," he said.

The animal hopped off Ganadarm's shoulder and walked along the table, its long tail twitching.

"So, ah, where did you find the gray weasel?" Drago asked.

" 'Tis no weasel!" said Ganadarm. " 'Tis a squirrel-lynx!"

"As you like it," said the innkeeper. "We've been calling it a weasel around here, but I don't think anyone saw it clearly. You are right, of course. It looks much more like a long-tailed lynx."

"You know this beast?" Ganadarm asked.

"Just the story," said Drago.

"Tell it to me," said Ganadarm.

"Oh. Well, a Drelfin merchant came to town last month, just a couple days after Scarbrow—I mean, Captain Bannom—had given the order that no one was allowed to cross the pass. The Drelfin said he meant to cross the pass anyway, and so Captain Bannom ordered him to get off his horse. As the Drelfin was doing so, he opened up a cage he was carrying and let loose a snarling gray weasel that ran off. It's been leaving little signs around the village."

"What sort of signs?"

"You know: turds. And chipmunk tails. It will crunch up the bones and puke them out later, but it doesn't eat the tails at all. How did you catch it?"

"The beast is tame," Ganadarm said.

The beast sat on the corner of the table and began licking its paws.

"Can you spare anything to feed it?" Ganadarm asked.

"Perhaps," said the innkeeper. "Do you have any coin?"

"No," said Ganadarm. "I was hoping to trade the squirrel-lynx to you for a bite of bread and a cup of ale."

The innkeeper shook his head. "I don't want it. Besides, the Drelfin will want it back once he gets out."

"Is that likely?"

Drago shrugged. "Perhaps. Once Scarbrow leaves. I don't think our garrison captain wants to waste food on a prisoner, but he can't let the Drelfin go while Scarbrow is here."

"The garrison captain takes orders from Bannom?"

"Captain Bannom has orders from the emperor," Drago said. "He seems to be in charge for the moment."

Ganadarm studied the spit-bathing animal and wondered about its owner. Ganadarm didn't know much about Drelfin—in fact, he didn't even distinguish between red Drelfin and brown Drelfin—but he knew they were too small to be worth fighting. Poor little merchant, sitting there locked up in the dark, wondering what happened to his squirrel-lynx, while the Klindrel made preparations to invade his country. That wasn't right. Ganadarm was ashamed that Kashram-created men could treat a Drelfin so.

But what else could he expect from a Klindrel like Bannom? Ganadarm had planned to die fighting Bannom's scouts, but now he was angry enough to fight all the way to Bannom. He wanted to teach that Klindrel a lesson.

On the other hand …

Wouldn't it be more heroic to die trying to free the Drelfin merchant? And wouldn't it be funny if no one died at all and Bannom's prisoner escaped?

Yes. Yes, that would be best. But could Ganadarm do it? Was he actually clever enough to outwit Bannom and his soldiers?

Ganadarm wanted to find out.

CHAPTER 7

Ganadarm Meets Tim

GANADARM HIKED UP TO THE KEEP with the squirrel-lynx on his shoulder. The beast still rumbled, despite the kindly innkeeper's donation of a raw grouse heart. The innkeeper had also given Ganadarm enough information about the layout of the Border-keep to enable Ganadarm to begin a plan. It was Ganadarm's tactical opinion that beginning a plan was good enough, because the end usually didn't work out anyway.

As Ganadarm approached, the guards atop the tower leaned over the parapet to look down on him. The guard by the door at the top of the stairs stood up straighter. The guard at the bottom of the stairs watched him warily.

Ganadarm smiled. Evading so many guards would be right heroic!

He was within five strides of the keep before the guard at the bottom asked, "What business do you have here today?"

"I am here to visit the Drelfin," said Ganadarm. "I heard he was offering a reward for the return of his unusual pet."

"Has anyone approved your visit?"

"Can *you* approve my visit?"

"I'll need orders from Captain Tavin … or from Captain Bannom. The Drelfin is *his* prisoner."

Ganadarm lowered his voice. "Suppose I offer you and your comrade atop the stairs a share of the reward?"

The guard shook his head. "I need orders," he said. "Besides, the Drelfin has no money. At least, not in his cell."

Ganadarm shrugged. "Perhaps he will give me credit."

"Perhaps," said the guard.

"I don't want to bother your captains," Ganadarm said. "Could I talk with the prisoner through a window?"

"The prison doesn't have windows," the guard said.

"Isn't that heartless?"

" 'Tis normally used for storing wine."

"Oh."

Ganadarm stood a moment, listening to the squirrel-lynx rumble in his ear. "I'll just have a look around, then."

"Ho! Where are you going?"

Ganadarm ignored the guard and walked around to the side of the keep. As the innkeeper had said, there was the entrance to the cellar. It was guarded, too. This guard wore a leather-bound helmet and a tunic quartered brown-and-gray. Ganadarm recognized the uniform of the Chumwarl Scouts, but he did not recognize the man wearing it. He hoped the scout did not recognize him, either.

"Good day," said Ganadarm. "I was hoping to—"

"Ho, there!" cried the brightly armored garrison guard behind him. "I have to ask you to leave."

"Who gave you permission to leave your post?" Ganadarm asked.

"What?"

"You said you don't have the authority to let me see the prisoner. Do you have the authority to leave your post?"

"You want to see the prisoner?" asked the scout.

"If I may," said Ganadarm. "*He* doesn't have the authority to let me in, but I thought *you* might."

The scout looked at the guard.

The guard said, "No civilian is allowed into the keep without orders from an officer."

Ganadarm looked at the scout. "I just want to return the Drelfin's pet. Do we really need to bother the officers with this?"

The scout thought a moment. "I don't think Captain Bannom would mind letting the prisoner have a visitor."

Ganadarm smiled.

"Go ahead and ask him," the scout told Ganadarm. To the guard he said, "Could you let this man in to see Captain Bannom?"

The guard frowned. "You'll have to give me your sword," he said.

"Very well," said Ganadarm, drawing his sword. "Here it is."

He planted his feet and drove the point through the guard's armor with a powerful thrust. With a howl, the squirrel-lynx leapt from Ganadarm's shoulder and bounded away.

Behind Ganadarm, the scout reached for his own sword, but Ganadarm smashed his elbow into the scout's nose. The scout's leather-covered helmet hit the stone wall of the keep with a clunk.

"Hello?" called a voice from the other side of the wooden door.

Ganadarm put a foot on the dying guard's chest and pulled his sword out of the man's stomach.

"Come out here, quick!" Ganadarm said. "I need your help!"

Behind the door, a wooden bar scraped against brackets, then ...

"Hey, wait. Who—?"

Ganadarm lunged and slammed his shoulder into the door. The half-lifted beam popped free of its brackets and Ganadarm was inside.

The prison guard lay at Ganadarm's feet, still holding the beam. In the torchlit cellar, all Ganadarm could see was that the soldier wore the quartered tunic of a Chumwarl Scout. Ganadarm thrust at the fallen man's neck.

The prison guard deflected the thrust with the beam and rolled to a crouch. Ganadarm kicked him in the chin before he could draw his sword.

"Where is the key?" Ganadarm demanded.

The prison guard lay outstretched on the floor, not moving.

Ganadarm was alert for tricks. He still could not see well in the torchlight. He pointed his sword at the fallen man's throat and demanded, "Give me the key."

"There is no key," said a muffled voice that came from a shadowy corner. "The door is latched."

Ganadarm pulled the torch from the wall sconce and went to investigate the source of the voice. He found a musty wooden door latched with an iron bolt. Ganadarm slid back the bolt and pulled open the door. A fuzzy-headed man half Ganadarm's height stood in the middle of a damp-smelling room. The room was lit by an oil lamp on the corner of the table against the wall.

"To whom do I have the honor of speaking?" asked the Drelfin.

"Bring that lamp," said Ganadarm.

He turned his back on the Drelfin and bent over the prison guard. Eyes closed. Breathing. Unconscious. Not a threat right now. Good.

The Drelfin, holding the lamp, came to stand beside him.

Ganadarm put a hand on the little man's shoulder. "Follow me. Stay close. Do what I say, and we might both live."

Sword in one hand, torch in the other, Ganadarm dashed out the door.

"Hyah!" said the scout whose head had been slammed into the wall. He staggered toward Ganadarm swinging his sword in a wild arc.

Ganadarm's sword caught the scout's swing at the wrist.

"Aaah!" cried the scout, dropping his sword.

Ganadarm kicked the man in the stomach and he went down.

Ganadarm stood over the vomiting man. "I wish I'd killed you instead of him," he said, pointing with his torch at the guard with the fatal stomach wound. "But since you live, deliver this message: Tell Bannom that Ganadarm was here. I'll be seeing him soon."

Cradling his maimed hand, the scout gave Ganadarm a baffled look.

Ganadarm sheathed his sword and took the lamp from the Drelfin. "Run for those trees."

The worried Drelfin hesitated only an instant before complying.

Ganadarm dashed around to the front of the tower. The guard at the door above stood with sword drawn.

"A good soldier you are," Ganadarm called up to him, "sticking to your post."

The door opened to reveal more armored men.

"I think you should stay inside," Ganadarm called to them.

He slammed the oil lamp into the middle of the wooden steps and threw his torch after it, kindling a cheery blaze.

"Good luck with your war!" he called and set off after the fleeing Drelfin.

If Ganadarm had not been running so hard, he would have laughed. It felt so *good* to be in battle again. He was glad he had come down the mountain, glad to have abandoned his hideout, glad he had decided to rescue the Drelfin. Fights like that made life worth living.

He heard an eerie buzzing in the sky. A rock struck the ground and bounced in front of him.

"Run faster, Drelfin! They have slings!"

Zzzzp! A stone brushed Ganadarm's bicep, leaving a hole in the sleeve of his tunic and a red stripe on his arm.

"Mrowr!"

The squirrel-lynx!

Ganadarm turned to see the small gray creature bounding

across the meadow after him. A stone buzzed overhead.

Ganadarm charged back toward the keep. Smoke was coming from the fire at the front. A handful of slingers were on top. Slings weren't accurate, Ganadarm knew, but if the slingers sent out enough rocks, they were likely to hit *something*.

Ganadarm bent low and scooped up the squirrel-lynx. He reversed direction. Cradling the animal in his arm, he sprinted after the Drelfin as slingstones danced along the grass.

The Drelfin's tiny legs were stumbling by the time he made it to the edge of the pines. The little man slumped against a tree and collapsed to the ground.

"No more," he said, shaking his head. "I can't run anymore."

They were out of sling range, but not out of sight. Ganadarm picked up the Drelfin with his free hand and tossed him over his shoulder. He couldn't run fast with his burdens, but he could run farther. Ganadarm settled his pace into a gentle lope that allowed him to recover his breath as he ran.

He didn't know this terrain, but he knew how a fleeing man would think. And so, once he had caught his breath, he began to take paths a normal fleeing man would not see. When faced with a choice between an easy descent and a steep incline, he chose the incline. When faced with a stream crossing, he ran downhill and doubled back away from the crossing. In this haphazard manner, Ganadarm, carrying the Drelfin and the squirrel-lynx, finally came to a shallow draw choked with trees and deadfall. It looked impenetrable, so Ganadarm set the Drelfin down and began penetrating it. He invited the Drelfin to follow.

"Haven't we gone far enough?" asked the Drelfin.

"Perhaps," said Ganadarm. "But they will let us know if we haven't."

Ganadarm released the squirrel-lynx and slithered under a fallen log. The animal and the Drelfin followed him.

Ganadarm tucked himself underneath a young pine. "Here might be a good place to rest for a moment, though." He pushed aside a sharp-toothed cone so he could sit more comfortably. "I guess I don't have to tell you to stay low."

"I am Tim Hill of the Hill Enclave in Kanabur," said the Drelfin.

"Oh. Call me Ganadarm."

"Thank you for getting me out of prison," said the Drelfin.

" 'Twas fun," said Ganadarm.

Tim looked at him. The squirrel-lynx settled itself down into Tim's lap and started growling. Tim began to pet it.

"Is that thing always hungry?" Ganadarm asked.

"Oh, the growling? That just means he's content."

"Oh," said Ganadarm. Now that he thought about it, that fit the facts better.

"You shouldn't have gone back for him, you know. He wasn't worth the risk." To the squirrel-lynx Tim added, "No offense, Mister Whiskers."

"Some might say *you* weren't worth the risk," said Ganadarm.

"Could be I wasn't," admitted Tim. "Why did you come for me?"

"I like risk."

"Well, thank you."

"You're welcome." Ganadarm gestured to indicate the growling squirrel-lynx. "It seems glad to have you back."

"I'm glad to have him back, too," Tim said. "Even though I don't need a pretext anymore."

"Oh, is that what it is? I was calling it a squirrel-lynx."

Tim smiled. "That's as good a name as any," he said. "The previous owner called him a 'cat'."

"What is it?" Ganadarm asked.

Tim shrugged. "He is just what he is, I reckon. Cats are common in the forests of the Silverfolk."

"Who are the Silverfolk?"

"They live on the moonward side of the world," Tim said. "I don't know what your people call them. I don't think they've ever met the Klindrel."

"They are indeed fortunate," said Ganadarm.

Tim's eyes asked for explanation.

"To have not met any Klindrel," Ganadarm said. "The Klindrel befoul every place they step."

The Drelfin looked at him appraisingly. "You don't like the Klindrel much, do you?"

"I do not," Ganadarm said.

"I get along with most Klindrel most of the time," said Tim. "But I'm fighting against their emperor."

Ganadarm looked at the tiny man. "The emperor has an army. Do *you* have an army?"

Tim shook his head. "I have information."

"You can't stop an army with information."

"Could be I can't," admitted Tim. "Then again, could be I can. I won't know until I try."

"Try what?"

"Try to get my information to the Brownfolk—the brown Drelfin, as you call them."

"Aren't you Drelfin?" asked Ganadarm.

"I'm red Drelfin," said Tim. "One of Yolim's folk. The brown Drelfin are Thafarsi's folk."

"Oh," said Ganadarm. "I see." He was vaguely aware of other deities besides Kashram, but he didn't think about them much. Ganadarm believed that if he minded his own business, the deities would mind theirs.

"But you want to help them anyway?" Ganadarm asked.

"Aye," said Tim. "The emperor stole my clan's cattle."

"The Klindrel stole my family's land," said Ganadarm. "My grandfather was a baron in the Saltlands."

"But you don't have any barons in your family anymore?"

Ganadarm shook his head. "I'm a bandit," he said.

"Oh," said Tim.

"What?"

"Nothing, it's just that, well, I'm a merchant."

Ganadarm waved his hand dismissively. "I don't steal from Drelfin," he said. "Much. I'm a bandit so I can attack the Klindrel and steal from them as they stole from me and my family."

Tim nodded. "Well, then, would you like to travel with me?"

"Where are you traveling?"

"Over the pass," said Tim patiently. "To the lands of ... of the other Drelfin."

"To fight on their side?"

"Well maybe not fight," said Tim, with a wobble in his voice. "But I'll do what I can."

"Then I shall come with you," said Ganadarm. He grinned. "Because I can fight!"

CHAPTER 8
Our Friends Meet

THE ROAD from the Passwatch Roadhouse to the Klindrel Pass was not so much "built" as it was "hewn". Rocks and earth were carved out of the mountain's side to make a flat road wide enough for a Klindrel ox cart—or two ox carts if they pass each other very carefully.

Originally, the road was built on a "half-and-half" principle: Remove enough earth from the mountain to carve out half the road, and deposit that earth on the downhill side to make the other half. Over time, however, this loose fill crumbles away, so whenever the road is improved, more rock is hewn from the uphill side. The result is a low, sheer cliff.

Given that one side of the road is a cliff and the other side is a steep drop into a thickly forested gorge, all legitimate travelers stay on the road. Bandits, however, prefer to lurk in the forest. You see, thieves are willing to put in extraordinary effort, as long as they believe they are avoiding honest work.

But on the tenth day of Redmonth in the spring of the Klindrel Invasion, the people hiding in the forest were only playing bandits. They were Lieutenant Sabu and his old friend Thaki, waiting in ambush for their trainees who were due to pass on the road below.

Or perhaps the trainees were overdue. Time is difficult to measure in the mountains because the lith is frequently hidden behind peaks and trees.

"They're riding slowly," Thaki observed. "I think we've been waiting an entire lithic."

Sabu checked the shadow of the stick Thaki had poked into the ground to measure the progress of the sun.

"I hope they're just being cautious," Sabu said.

"They're being slow," Thaki said. "Or maybe they gave up on trying to find us and rode back to the roadhouse."

Sabu shook his head. "Jamidu might give up. He's impatient. But Hikafa and Dusi wouldn't quit."

"Hikafa wouldn't have any say in the matter," Thaki said. "It's the rookie who's in charge. You know that as well as I do."

Thaki was right. "She's a remarkable young woman," Sabu said.

Thaki snorted so hard her brown curls bounced. "Sabu, she's also a show-off and a braggart."

"What? No she's not."

"She is," insisted Thaki. "You just can't see it because she's showing off for *you*."

"She's not showing off. She's demonstrating her talents."

Thaki rolled her eyes.

"Because I asked her to," Sabu said.

"You've been getting demonstrations every day," Thaki said.

"I have to find out what she can do. I don't know her that well yet."

"But you hope to know her better," said Thaki.

"Of course," said Sabu.

Thaki snorted again—like a horse.

"What?" Sabu asked.

"Nothing."

"Tell me, Thaki."

"I almost think you're silly for her."

"What?" That was absurd. Sabu was getting too old to think of a woman in that way.

Thaki said, "She's silly for you."

"Is she?" Had she said something to Thaki? Or was Thaki just guessing?

"She is," said Thaki. "The way she smiles at you, the tone of her voice, the way—"

"She's just friendly."

"The way she stretches in front of you."

"She's probably just sore from riding," Sabu said. "She's a rookie."

"She's been riding all winter," Thaki said. "They made her ride every day at Roadhouse One."

"Oh," said Sabu. "True. I'd forgotten."

"And it seems you've forgotten what it's like to be twenty-seven," Thaki said. "Newly graduated. Childhood behind you. Adulthood before you like paths into the forest of possibilities."

"Poetic," said Sabu. "But I don't remember it like that."

"I remember," Thaki said. "So many options. Which to choose? Seize the chance to make new discoveries? Pursue a career that will benefit society? Find a man who will give you perfect babies? Why not all three?"

"You make it sound so dramatic," Sabu said. *Perfect babies?*

"Life *is* dramatic when you're twenty-seven," Thaki said.

"It wasn't for me."

"No?"

"No. I wanted to be in the Road Patrol, so that's what I did."

Thaki gave him a look.

"Well, I was excited," he admitted. "And I suppose it was a dramatic year." They had confronted a band of thirteen Children of Lith who refused to give up without a fight. Three bandits had been killed before they surrendered, and a patroller named Hibo—from the same year as Perga—had died of his wounds before they could get him back to the healer at the roadhouse.

Sabu shook his head. "Quite a time. I believed every year would be like that."

"I'm glad they weren't," said Thaki.

Sabu nodded. "So am I. And yet, I was lucky."

"Lucky?"

"Lucky I had a stressful rookie year. I saw real fighting. I learned why we need to avoid it. And I learned why we need to be prepared for it."

Sabu waved down at the empty road to indicate the three trainees who had not yet arrived. "Hikafa's never seen a fight. We cornered the Green Falcon Gang in his rookie year, but he was on rampart duty that day. And poor Jamidu. Frankly, Thaki, last year was no test at all for the rookies. I don't want Dusi to have the same rookie year I did, but I do want her able to handle it."

"That's why Zhaku made you lieutenant," Thaki said. "Because you're always looking out for us."

Sabu bowed his head to acknowledge the compliment. "Thank you, friend."

That was all it was. He was just looking out for Dusi. Training her. Discovering what she could do.

Oh, he liked being around her. She was intelligent, like Captain Zhaku. And she had a good sense of humor, like Thaki. And sometimes when she flashed her lopsided smile, her eyes would twinkle with secrets hidden in their depths. Dusi intrigued him. But it was just friendly interest.

Or what if it was more than that? What if he really was silly over Dusi? Well, there was no rule against patrollers marrying each other, of course. But people in love could be so … well, silly. It was like a head injury, really. If he fell in love with Dusi, would that put his subordinates in danger? Should he bring the problem to Captain Zhaku?

Focus, Sabu, he told himself. *This is a personal problem, not a Road Patrol problem. You have to deal with it yourself.*

He resolved to—

Afterward, Sabu could never say what he had almost resolved to do. The silence of the forest was broken by a chittering squirrel. The sound came from beyond the bend in the road. Sabu suspected their tardy trainees were approaching.

"Finally," Thaki said.

Thaki snugged herself into her hiding spot behind a pine. She would not be visible from the road below.

Now Sabu could hear hoofsteps on the rocky road. He crouched behind a juniper on the edge of the cliff. He could see the road, so they had a fair chance to see him—perhaps his eye, or a tuft of his hair. Not that they needed to see him. Sabu had tested Dusi's range, and he judged that she would be able to sense his mind shortly before the horses came around the bend.

Jamidu rode in front, his feet jittering, his hands twitching on the reins. Hikafa followed, looking about warily. Hikafa was leading Dusi's horse.

Where was Dusi? Had something happened to her?

Be logical, Sabu told himself. *Or Thaki will think you really are silly for the rookie.*

If Dusi had been hurt, the other two would not still be on the training exercise. They would be calling Sabu's name, asking him to come out of hiding.

"Caught you," said Thaki.

Sabu looked over his shoulder.

"Behind the pine with the downward-pointing bough," Thaki said. "Come out."

Dusi, on the slope above them, stepped out from behind the pine Thaki indicated. She lifted her arms and stretched her back.

"What gave me away?" she asked.

"You startled a nuthatch," Thaki said. "But you got closer than I would have liked."

Dusi smiled her lopsided smile. "I could have gotten even closer, but I had to hurry. You were about to ambush my partners."

"We *will* ambush them," Thaki said.

"I'll warn them," Dusi said.

"We are two and you are one," said Thaki. "First we kill you, then we ambush Hikafa and Jamidu."

Dusi rolled her eyes. "If I'd thought you would kill me, I wouldn't have come out from behind the tree."

Sabu didn't want Hikafa and Jamidu to think they had won just because they could hear voices. He stood up and called, "Caught you!"

This startled Jamidu more than Sabu would have liked.

Sabu turned to Dusi. "Interesting tactic. Did you follow our tracks, or were you just guessing you would find us up here?"

"I guessed," Dusi admitted. "But if you had been on the downhill side, I would have ambushed you when you confronted Hikafa and Jamidu."

"Clever," said Sabu.

Dusi smiled. Sabu did like that smile.

"But foolish," said Thaki. "You put yourself in a two-on-one disadvantage."

"When you don't have numbers, you have to use other advantages," said Dusi. "Such as surprise."

"But you *do* have numbers," Sabu said. "You shouldn't weaken your defense by sending one person off alone. That's how people get hurt."

Dusi nodded. "I see. So if I had brought Hikafa and Jamidu with me ...?"

"That would have been impressive," Thaki said, "considering how difficult it is to make Jamidu move slowly and quietly."

Dusi cocked her head. Her eyes lost focus, as though she were paying attention to something else.

"What is it?" Thaki asked.

"Someone on the road," Dusi said. She pointed in the direction of the pass.

Sabu frowned. He hadn't sent anyone up there yet.

"Could it be merchants?" Thaki asked. "The pass should be clear by now."

"I sense only one," Dusi said.

"On foot, or with a wagon?" Thaki asked.

"I can't tell," Dusi said. "Animals have quiet minds."

"Let's get down to the road," Sabu said. He scrambled down the face of the low cliff. The women followed him.

"What is it?" Hikafa asked.

"Dusi senses someone on the road ahead," Sabu explained.

"People don't usually travel the road alone," said Thaki. "Especially not across the pass."

"Could it be a nature spirit?" Sabu asked.

"I've never seen one on the road before," Dusi said. (Nature spirits are invisible, of course, but Dusi's talent allowed her to "see" them anyway.) "And this mind isn't thinking like a nature spirit."

"There he is," said Jamidu.

"No," said Thaki. "There they are."

Indeed, two figures came around the bend ahead. Both wore cloaks, tunics, and trousers, but one was Sabu's size and the other was twice as tall. The taller one, a Child of Lith, wore a sword and no armor, which was not unusual for a wagon guard. However, what was unusual, aside from the fact that they had no wagon, was that the Child of Lith wore a live animal on his shoulder.

Sabu judged the shorter one to be a Child of Wealth because he wore tunic and trousers instead of a chiton. Of course, Sabu himself was wearing tunic and trousers, but he knew this traveler was not in the Road Patrol. As the two men drew nearer, Sabu could see that the shorter one's complexion matched the giant's terra-cotta color and his head was covered with that lamb's-wool fuzz that distinguishes male Children of Wealth.

They were an unusual pair. Sabu judged they were not dangerous. And if his judgment were proven wrong, he had a five-on-two advantage that should discourage aggression.

The strangers advanced vigorously, as though traveling the lonely road had left them eager for contact.

Dusi was scowling at the Child of Lith. Sabu suspected she was upset that she had detected only one traveler.

"Well," said Sabu. "Here is your chance to show us how well you learned Klindrel."

That startled the scowl off the rookie's face. "You want me to speak to them?"

Sabu nodded.

"What should I say?"

"The usual," Sabu said.

Dusi pressed her lips together and nodded. She stepped forward and took a deep breath. "Good day," she said. "Welcome to our fort. Ah, I mean, road to our fort."

Sabu was impressed. The rookie was nervous, but she could still speak the Klindrel language better than he could. And she had remembered that the Klindrel think of roadhouses as "forts".

The Child of Wealth turned pale as he approached, matching Dusi's complexion.

"Good day," he said. "I am Tim Hill of the Hill Enclave in Kanabur. But you may call me Tim."

Sabu nodded. He recognized Tim now. The merchant stayed at the roadhouse four times a year.

Tim stopped in front of Sabu. The giant took up a stance behind Tim, weight evenly balanced on the balls of his feet.

Tim said, "This is ... my associate, Ganadarm."

A broad grin split the giant's terra cotta face. "Good day," he said.

The creature on his shoulder looked down at them with quizzical yellow eyes.

Sabu's patrollers echoed the "good day", and he added, "I am Sabu."

Tim smiled. "Yes, Sabu, I remember you."

"You are early," Sabu observed. "And you have no wagon. Did accident happen?"

"What happened to me was surely no accident," Tim said. "But I did not come here to tell my story. I came to warn you and your people."

"Warn me and my people what?"

"Warn you that the Klindrel Army is preparing to seize your lands."

CHAPTER 9
Our First Council of War

OUR PEOPLE'S FIRST-EVER COUNCIL OF WAR convened in the garrison captain's quarters at the Passwatch Roadhouse. Captain Zhaku presided. She requested that Lieutenant Sabu act as her advisor and secretary. Ganadarm, the former bandit and former fugitive, served as strategic and tactical consultant. Tim Hill of the Hill Enclave took the role of intelligence officer and foreign diplomat.

Tim was glad to finally be delivering his information to Zhaku. He sat on a floor cushion, with Mister Whiskers on his lap. Tim stroked the cat's soft, striped fur as he explained the situation to the Brownfolk:

The Klindrel were massing supplies at the Borderkeep. One shipment had arrived just ahead of Tim. A second shipment had arrived while Tim was in prison, probably on horse wagons. A second pulse of ox wagons should arrive soon. Assuming the Klindrel soldiers could also carry provisions on their backs, Tim reckoned the army would be ready to invade as soon as they reached the Borderkeep. And the Borderkeep was only a day from Passwatch.

He showed these estimates to Sabu, who copied them into the message that Captain Zhaku was preparing to send. Tim thanked Yolim that he still had his pocket ledger. The illiterate Klindrel had not realized that his compact book was as dangerous a hundred swords.

Once the last figure was scribbled into Zhaku's message, Tim's shoulders sagged with relief. He had done it. The Chumwarl Scouts had confiscated his gelding and his traveling money. He had spent ten days shut up in a windowless wine cellar reckoning time according to the arrival of soft apples and cold boiled potatoes. He had dodged deadly slingstones and sprinted until his lungs ached. But he had done it. He had delivered his information to the Brownfolk. Now it was up to them.

Tim spoke in the Brownfolk language to be sure he was understood. He felt bad about leaving Ganadarm out of the conversation, but the giant didn't seem to mind. Ganadarm lounged against the wall with easy, affable grace. One leg stretched lazily across the reed floor mats, terra-cotta toes almost touching Zhaku's table. Even sitting, Ganadarm was tall enough that his head crowded the ceiling. His physical presence and his broad grin seemed to take up half the room.

"You should put some work into improving your fort," Ganadarm suggested. "Wooden walls won't stop the Klindrel."

"We can build no stone walls," said Lieutenant Sabu in his clipped accent. "Tim says we have few days."

"You can dig trenches," said Ganadarm. "And put in another line of stakes. You can put in road blocks to slow the Klindrel down. When they stop, you can ambush them. You can set their supply wagons on fire. Or push them off a cliff! You can sneak into their camp in the dark of night and steal their horses! You can slit their throats! You can—"

"Ganadarm dislikes Klindrel," Tim explained to the wide-eyed Brownfolk.

"You are not Klindrel?" Sabu asked.

Ganadarm spat. On Zhaku's pretty reed mats.

"Ganadarm is from the Saltlands Province," Tim said. "His father was killed in the Saltlands Uprising."

"Ah," said Captain Zhaku, trying not to notice the spittle. She turned to Sabu, but spoke in Tim and Ganadarm's language: "Lieutenant, how much time will it be taking to prepare our fort for defense?"

"I can't say I see any percentage in that," Tim interjected. "The Klindrel have a legion. Five thousand men. Once they get close, you need to retreat."

"He will not retreat!" said Ganadarm. "Look at him! He is a warrior. He will fight to defend his people, even if he must die with his fortress burning around him."

Tim was momentarily confused by the misplaced pronoun, but Ganadarm's gestures indicated that he was speaking of Zhaku. The garrison captain seemed pleased with the giant's assessment of her ferocity.

"Perhaps not so drastic," she said with a smile, "but yes, we must fight if it helps."

"But will it helps?" asked Sabu. "Will it helps?"

"I think we must try," said Zhaku.

"Aye!" said Ganadarm.

"What do you think?" Sabu asked Tim.

"Me? Well, I reckon—"

"Mister Tim is not a fighter," Ganadarm said. "He does not understand that some battles must be fought even if you cannot win."

"I have many people here," Lieutenant Sabu said, nodding in the direction of the barracks. "If they can win no battle, I will not send them fighting."

"But I intend to win," said Captain Zhaku gently. "Please, Mister Hill, you brought us information to help us win this war. What should I do with it, do you think?"

"Well," said Tim. "I reckoned you would send it to your commanders."

"Yes, I do that," Zhaku said, waving at the message Sabu had drafted for her. "But what should *I* do? I. Captain Zhaku. Leader of this thirty-six patrollers."

"Well, if you aren't going to run away ..." Tim tried to recall Ganadarm's helpful heap of suggestions. "I reckon attacking a wagon is the smartest risk. One wagon can feed a company of soldiers for five days."

"And making fort stronger?" Zhaku asked. "Should we do that?"

Tim shrugged. "I don't know anything about fortifications."

"I think maybe Klindrel can go around fort," Sabu said.

"The road is within sling range," Ganadarm observed.

"Few of my people know sling," Captain Zhaku said.

"No hunters?" Ganadarm asked.

"We have some hunters," Zhaku said. "But mostly we hunt bandits." Her eyes twinkled, and Tim had no doubt that she had guessed Ganadarm's profession.

The giant grinned.

"But we hunt no armies," Sabu said.

The captain laid a gentle hand on his arm and slipped back into the Brownfolk tongue. "This is part of guarding the road, my friend."

Tim wondered if he should pretend to not be listening. But Zhaku and Sabu knew he was fluent.

Sabu swallowed. "I can't order them to get killed. If they have to die, it has to mean something."

"Sabu, old friend, you know I don't want them to die. They are my children, too."

"Then what, Zhaku? Our garrison against five thousand Klindrel? That is nonsense."

"We do what we can, Sabu. Perhaps we must let them pass, but we can be the pebble in the moccasin that worries them all the way down to the river. We can make them pay for every step."

Yes! thought Tim. *Make them pay.*

Sabu sat quietly for a moment, his ink-stained fingers pressed to his lips.

"Their wagons will have to travel on the road," Sabu said, mostly to himself. "And we can ride our mountain steppers through the forest."

"We can hide where the bandits hide," Zhaku said. "We know all the good places."

Sabu looked at the numbers Tim had given him. "The road is narrow. They will have to be spread out over a long distance. We can attack any part of their column and fight only a small number of them."

"Now you're thinking like a lieutenant," Zhaku said.

Sabu scowled as though he had swallowed a bug. "I'm thinking like a bandit."

Zhaku chuckled. "I suppose so. But you will support me?"

"Of course."

Zhaku smiled at Ganadarm and said, "We fight."

The Redman's amiable face had registered no understanding during the entire exchange, but at the sound of these words in his own language, Ganadarm widened his grin and said, "Aye! We fight."

"You fight with us?" Zhaku asked.

"Right willingly." Ganadarm slapped the hilt of his sword for emphasis.

Zhaku inclined her head. "Thank you, Ganadarm. Then you will be under Lieutenant Sabu. Is that clear?"

"Aye!" said Ganadarm. "My blade is yours to command, Saboon."

Sabu acknowledged this pledge with a grave nod.

Zhaku turned to Tim. "And what of you, Mister Hill?"

"Me? Well, I reckon I need to find a way to get back home. Somehow."

"Tim is red Drelfin," Ganadarm explained, as though he had not just learned the difference from Tim the day before. "His people are not fighters."

"Our people are not fighters, too," Lieutenant Sabu said. "We are ... perhaps say librarians."

Ganadarm looked puzzled. Tim reckoned he didn't know what a librarian was. Could be he didn't even know what a book was.

"And Tim is merchant," said Captain Zhaku. "I can pay you, Mister Hill, but not enough. Not enough for what you have done."

Tim shook his head. "Money cannot return what has been taken from me. Make the emperor pay. That is what I ask."

Zhaku nodded. "My people will do the best we can," she said. "If you will not name price, I will give you credit here. Credit at all forts. Your next visit will be much cheaper."

If there are any forts left, Tim thought. *Or any Tim Hill left to visit them.* "Thank you," he said. "You are most generous."

"Lieutenant," said Zhaku, "Tim wants to go home. I think he should leave tomorrow. Can you find two or three people to take him through forest? Hide him from Klindrel until he is home?"

Sabu frowned.

"It's a long way," Tim said. "I reckon if you can just get me past the Borderkeep, I'll be able to make it home myself."

"Evading the Chumwarl Scouts may not be so easy," said Ganadarm. "Do you want me to go with you, Tim?"

In the Brownfolk tongue, Sabu murmured, "If we send the Child of Lith instead of our patrollers, then we don't have to weaken our force."

"True," Zhaku admitted. "I like the Child of Lith. I think he has expertise we can use. But I agree, he is the logical choice."

Sabu turned to Tim. "What do you say, Tim? Would it be all right if we sent you home with the giant?"

"Yes. It would be all right with me. But—"

Well, the truth was, Tim was a bit proud of having recruited Ganadarm to the Brownfolk cause. He knew Ganadarm was good in a fight, and he reckoned Ganadarm could be a big help in their planning, too. Ganadarm was a Redman. He knew how the

Klindrel thought. He'd fought against their scouts. The qualities that made him such a good choice to take Tim home were precisely the qualities that made him valuable to the Brownfolk. Tim wanted them to keep that asset. They needed all the help they could get.

All they could get.

"Oh no," said Tim in his own tongue. "Oh Yolim."

"What is it?" asked Ganadarm.

Even the smallest thing could make a difference. A little grease on a wagon wheel could be the difference between a wagonload of profit arriving safely home or two lame oxen stranding a man in the middle of the wilderness. Tim reckoned the Brownfolk would need Ganadarm. And he realized they might need him, too.

He shook his head. "Never mind about an escort, Captain. I reckon I have to stay."

CHAPTER 10
The Lieutenant's Office

AS I HAVE SAID, the Passwatch barracks was built along one side of the courtyard. A distance of only three steps separated the wall of the barracks from the palisade. By tradition, this narrow, shadowy space between the two structures was known as "the lieutenant's office". And this is where Sabu went to think after the council of war.

He tucked his arms inside his brown woolen cloak and leaned against the barracks. The moss had crept up again during the snowmelt. Sabu needed to assign a squad to scrape the walls.

No. No he didn't. The Klindrel would take Passwatch before the moss did.

Sabu had to fight a war. He knew little of war. Oh, he had studied Terkisho's *Theory of War* at the College of Forestry—it was required reading for all patrollers—but Terkisho's ideas about arraying cohorts on the battlefield had little to do with leading a garrison company against a legion. Sabu knew what Terkisho would have said about that: Don't do it.

But Sabu had to. Captain Zhaku was right. Nothing separated the Klindrel Army from the Redwood Valley except the pass, the road, and the Road Patrol.

Zhaku had sent a messenger to Headquarters at Roadhouse One. Until a reply came back, the Passwatch garrison was responsible for slowing the Klindrel Army. Zhaku wanted defenses strengthened in case the order came to hold the roadhouse. And she wanted a lookout post established at the pass to watch for the enemy.

Sabu thought Perga would be a good person to oversee the defenses. Perga was three years Sabu's senior and the best fighter in the garrison. Perga wasn't good at leading people, but Sabu could present the task as a tactical puzzle for him to solve. Perga would figure out how to get the job done, and Captain Zhaku would be here at the roadhouse to watch over his shoulder and help him organize his squad effectively.

Sabu would take a squad to scout for the best lookout post. Sharp-eyed Thaki would be a good lookout. Sabu wanted her advice. And Ganadarm claimed to know how to evade the Klindrel scouts. Perhaps he would have some ideas for watching the opposite side of the pass without being seen. Furthermore, Sabu needed a chance to work with Ganadarm so he could discover the giant's strengths and weaknesses.

Maybe he should take Dusi, too. Thaki would tease him, of course, but Sabu had good reasons for wanting her along. It wasn't just because he liked the way she looked in riding pants ...

No. Of course not. Sabu wasn't certain why Dusi's round bottom drew his attention at all. He wanted Dusi in his squad so that she and Thaki would start to get along. Despite being eight years apart, the two women had a lot in common. Sabu was certain Thaki would see that once she knew the rookie better.

And Sabu wanted Dusi to be near Ganadarm, too. Sabu was troubled by—

"Lieutenant?"

Sabu blinked. Dusi was behind the barracks with him, standing not ten paces away.

"Dusi," he said.

"I'm sorry. Am I disturbing you?"

"No," said Sabu. "I'm just disturbed that I let you sneak up on me."

Dusi looked down at her clogs and the mossy ground. "The ground is soft," she said.

Sabu nodded. "What can I do for you?"

"I just wanted to know where you were," Dusi said.

"Well, I am here: in my office."

"Your office?"

Sabu gestured to the mossy ground, the shadow-darkened walls, the cloudy sky above. "The lieutenant's office," Sabu said. "This is where I come to think. They didn't tell you?"

"Who?"

"Whoever told you where to find me."

"But I didn't ask," Dusi said, giving Sabu her lopsided smile. "I—"

"Oh."

Dusi nodded and tapped her head. "Mind finder."

"Well, you found me," said Sabu.

"Do you object to company?" Dusi asked. "In your 'office'? I need to think, too."

"In truth, Dusi, no one ever comes back here with me unless I ask them to."

"Ah." Her voice wavered. "I've invaded your privacy. I'm sorry."

"No, don't be sorry," Sabu said. "I enjoy your company. Come talk with me."

Dusi wrapped herself up in her cloak and leaned against the poles of the palisade opposite him.

She asked, "Are we going to fight in the war, Lieutenant?"

Sabu nodded. "Yes, Dusi. Yes we are."

"I trained," she said. "I trained hard. But—"

"Combat frightens everyone," Sabu said. "But you will do well."

"How can you be certain of me?"

"You have had the best combat training in the Redwood Valley," he said. "You are a patroller of the Passwatch Roadhouse. As long as you remember that, you will do well."

Dusi nodded and bit her lip. Something else was troubling her. Something beyond the fear that strikes all patrollers who know they may soon face combat.

"It's natural to be afraid of dying," Sabu said.

Dusi nodded.

Sabu said, "It's natural to be afraid of letting your fellow patrollers down."

Her dark eyes glistened. That was it.

Sabu studied her. "You feel a need to prove yourself."

She nodded.

"And you fear you have already failed."

Her lips grew tight and she nodded again.

"Dusi," he said, "just tell me."

She took a deep, shuddering breath. "All right," she said. "Lieutenant, I think I might have trouble sensing Children of Lith."

"I noticed you miscounted our guests today," Sabu said. "That was because you sensed only Tim?"

Dusi nodded. "Ganadarm's mind is ... fuzzy. It's like seeing through a fog."

"Do you think it's because he wears too much iron?" Sabu asked. He hadn't studied any metaphysics in college, but he remembered from local school that iron interferes with elemental resonance.

"His sword and his knife aren't the problem," Dusi said. "I can detect you just fine even though you are wearing your battleblade. The problem is that Ganadarm has iron in his blood."

"In truth?"

"Well, elementally, we all have iron in our blood," Dusi said. "But Children of Lith have more. It makes them difficult to resonate with."

"So you knew Children of Lith might give you trouble."

Dusi nodded. She looked miserable.

"Why didn't you tell me?"

"I wasn't certain," Dusi said. "I hoped my range would be good enough."

"If you had doubts, you should have told me."

"I know. Please don't tell Captain Zhaku."

Sabu looked at her.

Dusi put her hands to her face. "Oh, I'm so sorry. Of course you have to tell her. Or … I suppose I have to tell her myself." She shook her head. "I just didn't want to let her down. I truly did not want to let her down."

"Captain Zhaku will understand," Sabu said. "She may seem intimidating, but she loves us like a mother."

Dusi looked up sharply.

"Oh, I'm sorry," Sabu said. "I'd forgotten about what happened to your mother."

"No," said Dusi. "It's— Well, a daughter wants to live up to her mother's expectations."

Sabu nodded. "And you will," he said.

"I've already failed," Dusi said.

Sabu chuckled. "You haven't failed, rookie. You've just discovered a limitation."

"I don't *want* a limitation."

Sabu shrugged. What the rookie wanted was irrelevant.

"I want another chance," Dusi said. "I want to work on Ganadarm and improve my range."

"Can you do that?" Sabu asked.

Dusi's shoulders sagged. "I don't know. Maybe I can't. But I will anyway."

Sabu laughed.

Dusi looked him in the eye. "I worked hard in school, Lieutenant. I wasn't big or strong like the other girls and boys. So I had to work harder. I'm not going to quit working just because I graduated. I'll find a way to do this."

"Well," said Sabu, "perhaps now that you know what to look for—"

"Exactly," said Dusi. "Elder Manido said anybody can see the signs, but most people don't know how to look. I can learn how to look."

"All right, Dusi."

"You'll give me a chance to get better?"

"Of course," Sabu said. "Did you think we would send you down the road?"

"Maybe."

Sabu put a hand on her shoulder. "You have a useful gift, Dusi. It has limitations, but we all have limitations. Now that I have a better idea of what you can't do, I can make better use of what you *can* do."

"I'll get better, too," she said.

"I know you will."

"Captain Zhaku was so proud of me," Dusi said. "She told me how glad she was that the Road Patrol's only mind finder had been assigned to Passwatch."

"She'll still be proud of you."

"And you?" Dusi asked.

"Dusi, I don't expect my patrollers to be able to find bandits with their minds. I *do* expect them to be honest with me—"

Dusi nodded.

"—and I do expect them to tell me things I need to know. But as long as they do their jobs to the best of their abilities, I am proud of them. Understood?"

"Understood, Lieutenant."

"Good." Sabu smiled at her.

She smiled back.

Sabu liked that smile.

CHAPTER 11

Lookouts

CAPTAIN ZHAKU ordered the Passwatch Roadhouse to prepare for war, and each patroller reacted in his or her own way. Jamidu kept asking whether the garrison would fight or run. Hikafa went to the healer, complaining of stomach cramps. Thaki warned everyone to be skeptical until Tim's news was confirmed. Perga just sharpened the teeth of his battleblades.

Sabu thought like Perga: He had a job to do. But Sabu's job was more complicated. Yes, he would have to fight—or run, if Zhaku so ordered—but he also had to ensure that the others were ready to fight. He had to protect them as best he could, and he had to show them their duty so they could do it. Sabu prayed to the Goddess for wisdom.

Sabu selected Thaki, Dusi, and Ganadarm for the lookout mission. The foursome set out early in the morning, the patrollers mounted, Ganadarm on foot. With his long stride, the giant could keep pace with the mountain steppers, if they were held to a medium walk. Sabu sent Dusi into the forest above the road so that she could practice riding along deer trails while focusing her senses on the people below. She was ordered to report back each time she got too far to detect Ganadarm. Sabu warned her that if she did not report back promptly, he and Thaki and Ganadarm would come looking for her. He believed this threat to her pride would be sufficient to make her report frequently and honestly. And he was correct.

Sabu told Ganadarm only that Dusi was in training, leaving the impression that the riding was the primary object of the exercise. And in truth, riding a mountain stepper is every bit as challenging as one would assume. The nimble animals are capable of bounding up and down slopes normally traversed only by mountain goats and bighorn sheep. To help the rider stay astride, the saddle has a knob called a "saddle horn" on each of the four corners. In steep terrain, the rider will drop the rein and grab two horns, allowing the horse to pick its own path.

The sixth time Dusi dashed down the mountainside, astride a horse that bounded over fallen logs and wove its way between trees, Ganadarm commented, "Your recruit is a very good rider."

"Yes, she is," said Sabu.

"How long has he been training?" asked Ganadarm.

"Nine years," said Sabu.

" 'She,' " said Thaki. "Recruit is woman."

Sabu would not have quibbled about the pronoun, but then, his was not the gender misidentified.

Ganadarm had trouble understanding. He looked at Thaki, then at Dusi, who was descending with a rapid clatter of hooves.

"Do you mean to say he rides like a woman?" Ganadarm asked.

"No 'he'," said Thaki. "She is 'she'. Like me."

Ganadarm looked bewildered.

Then he laughed. "Ah, 'tis a fine jest! I almost believed you."

Dusi reined the mountain stepper to a halt beside Sabu and asked, "What's so funny?" in the language of Knowledge.

"Ganadarm thinks you and I are male," Thaki explained.

Dusi thought about that for a moment, then grinned. "Should we show him?"

"That won't be necessary," Sabu said.

Thaki giggled.

"We have at fort seven women," Sabu told Ganadarm.

"And well you should," said Ganadarm.

Sabu had dealt with this misunderstanding before, so he tried to explain. "They are not cooks," he said. "They are soldiers like me."

Ganadarm frowned in confusion. "Drelfin women can be soldiers?"

"Hello," said Dusi.

Thaki waved.

Ganadarm tilted his head to one side, as though trying in vain to see any signs of gender. "And what about you, Saboon? Are you a woman, too?"

"Lieutenant is man," Thaki said.

"But our captain," Dusi said with a grin, "is a woman."

"What captain?"

"Captain Zhaku," Sabu said. "We discussed with her last night."

"Captain Zhakoon is a woman?"

In our language, Dusi said, "If they are all this stupid, this will be a very short war."

Thaki laughed.

Sabu tried to explain the concept of logical gender differences versus cultural gender differences—not an easy task in his second language. A pointless task, too, for Ganadarm just kept asking, "Your women wear trousers?" and "You let your women fight men?"

Thaki and Dusi rode behind, engaged in some private conversation involving more giggling than was typical for patrollers. Whenever Thaki laughed, her curls bounced. Dusi's dark eyes sparkled. Sabu decided that anything which made Thaki more friendly with Dusi must be a good thing, so he did not send Dusi out to resume her training exercises. Anyway, he already had a good idea of how close she had to stay to detect Ganadarm. The group remained together as they approached the tree line.

The tree line at the Klindrel Pass is a result of geology, not elevation. The ridge above the forest is mostly exposed granite. Occasionally, enough dirt will collect in a crack to allow a juniper bush to grow, and if the bush captures enough soil, a pine might set root. The result looks more like a rock garden than a forest.

"Welcome to the Klindrel Pass," Thaki said to Dusi.

"Thank you," said Dusi with a grin. "That's nicer than what the nature spirit said."

"What did the nature spirit say?" Sabu asked.

" 'Intruder! Intruder!' " said Dusi. "Or thoughts to that effect."

"You told me you couldn't read minds," Thaki said.

"I don't look at thoughts that are inside a mind," Dusi said. "But when nature spirits want to talk, they send thoughts out."

"How often do they want to talk?" asked Sabu.

"To me? Never. They don't like me much. But sometimes they talk *about* me."

"Perhaps we should speak in the Klindrel tongue," suggested Sabu. "So our friend won't think we are talking about *him*."

"But *is* he our friend?" Thaki asked.

"He's not our enemy," Sabu said.

"Is our enemy's enemy our friend?" asked Dusi.

"Are the Klindrel our enemies?" Thaki asked. "This Child of Lith says he is the enemy of the Klindrel, so he would have reason to lie to us about them."

"He isn't smart enough to lie," Dusi said.

"I don't know if Ganadarm is smart or not," Sabu said. "But I doubt he and Tim are lying."

"We'll find out in a few days," said Thaki.

"We will," Sabu agreed. "Speaking of which—" he gestured at the rocky pass, "—where would be a good place to watch from?"

Thaki studied the ridgeline and pointed to one of the peaks flanking the pass. "Let's go up there," she suggested. "That should give us a good view of the other side."

"Isn't that somewhat exposed?" Dusi asked.

"I'm not suggesting it as a lookout spot," Thaki said. "We'll need to build some sort of blind among the trees. But we can't pick a good spot for the blind until we know something of what the other side looks like."

"Oh," said Dusi. "Of course."

"You still have a few things to learn," Thaki said. "They didn't teach you everything in college."

Dusi opened her mouth to say one thing, then changed her mind and said, "You're right, Thaki. I'm sorry if I seemed ..."

"Arrogant?" suggested Thaki. "Impertinent? A show-off?"

"Yes, that."

Thaki sighed. "Ah, no matter. Frankly, I admire your confidence. It took me years to become arrogant."

Dusi smiled.

Sabu explained Thaki's plan to Ganadarm, tactfully omitting the detail that it was Thaki's plan. Ganadarm agreed that a high altitude preliminary survey was a wise course of action, and so the four of them set off up the slope.

Mountain steppers bound from rock to rock like mountain goats. In such terrain, only a foolish rider would try to dictate the horse's pace. It is not possible to "bound slowly". Even so, Ganadarm kept up. His powerful legs drove him up the slope. His amiable smile became a determined grimace. His panting turned to gasps. But he kept up.

Sabu signaled a halt so the giant could catch his breath.

"That is ... well thought ... Saboon," the giant said between gasps. "From here ... on foot."

"On foot?" Dusi echoed.

"Aye," said Ganadarm. "The Klindrel might have a patrol. You don't want to be seen spying on their side of the pass."

Sabu had not called the halt because he wanted to climb the rest of the way on foot, but Ganadarm was right.

"Thaki, you and Ganadarm go see what you can observe from the peak. Dusi and I will hold your horse."

Thaki raised an eyebrow. "It takes two of you to hold my horse?"

Sabu must have let his irritation show on his face, for Thaki raised her hands defensively and said, "All right, all right."

They all dismounted. Thaki handed Dusi the lead rope. Then she explained the plan to Ganadarm, and the two of them set off on the short hike to the peak.

Dusi looked at Sabu quizzically.

"Two are less likely to be seen than three," Sabu said. "I don't know why Thaki is acting so silly." *And why am I defending myself to a rookie?*

Dusi nodded.

They stood in the wind and watched the other two clamber up the slope.

"I am glad you and Thaki are getting along," Sabu said.

Dusi grinned. "Yes, she's very kind to me even though I am just an ignorant rookie."

Sabu shook his head. "Thaki knows you're not ignorant."

"No she doesn't," Dusi said. "But I'll prove myself to her in time."

"I admire your confidence."

"Thaki thinks it's arrogance." Dusi gave him a vixen's grin. "What do you think?"

"I think—" *I think my judgment is clouded by your pretty face. May the Goddess help me, Thaki is right.* "I think if it were truly arrogance then you would not be so worried about proving yourself."

"Oh." The rookie seemed to deflate slightly. "It shows?"

"It shows to me," Sabu said. "But it's my job to understand you. All of you. All my subordinates, I mean." *Clouded judgment and slippery tongue. Oh, Knowledge, what am I to do with myself?*

Dusi just nodded solemnly.

Thaki clambered down the slope, almost as rapidly as if she were riding her mountain stepper, her brown curls bouncing with every jump. Her eyes were wide with fear.

"Sabu," she said, "the Klindrel are invading today."

CHAPTER 12
Dusi Meets Bannom

BY THE TIME OF THE KLINDREL INVASION, our people had developed many theories to explain why the Klindrel had never invaded our lands. We had a theological explanation: Lith allows his people to practice warfare only on each other. We had an economic explanation: The Klindrel benefit more from our trade than they would from extortion. We had a sociological explanation: Klindrel fight for prestige, which they cannot gain by defeating physically weaker people. And we even had a military explanation: Our population advantage is too great to be overcome by military tactics.

Most people believed the Klindrel would never invade. People always believe the future will be similar to the past.

When Dusi peered over the Klindrel Pass, she realized that her future would not be the one she had trained for. She would not be hunting bandits. She would be fighting an army.

The Klindrel were too distant for Dusi's elemental resonance, but she could see mounted scouts in brown and gray tunics riding up the switchbacks of the Klindrel side of the pass. The first company of regular soldiers was some distance behind. Dusi could see their weapons and armor gleaming through gaps in the forest below.

Her eyes followed the contour of the road to a place laid bare by a recent year's avalanche. More soldiers. And more in that exposed place where the road went around a bend. Was there no end to this army? Dusi realized that our population advantage would not protect us: We teach our children writing, not fighting.

But I was trained to fight, Dusi thought as she climbed quietly down from the summit. *And now my people need me to use that training. I am a patroller of the Passwatch Roadhouse. As long as I remember that, I will fight well.*

That was what Lieutenant Sabu had told her the day before. And if wise, pious, handsome Sabu believed in her, how could she doubt? She had wanted a chance to prove herself. Now she would get the biggest test any rookie ever had.

As Dusi drew near the others, she could hear that Sabu and

Thaki were in the midst of an argument:

"Sabu, if you stay here, then who will warn the roadhouse?"

"I'll send Ganadarm."

"Our horses can go faster than Ganadarm. Do you want me to do it?"

"No, Thaki. I need your sharp eyes on the enemy. I want an accurate count."

"And you want the rookie to shadow their scouts," Thaki said. "So you're the one who has to ride back. Can you see reason?"

"Someone experienced should go with Dusi," Sabu said.

"Ganadarm seems to know what he is doing."

"Yes, he is quiet and competent," Sabu said. "But there are other factors to consider."

"Such as?"

"Such as relationships."

Thaki snorted. "Don't let your heart fool your head."

Dusi almost stumbled over a rock. Relationships? His heart? Dusi had assumed that Sabu's interest in her was simply professional ... or friendly. She hadn't dared hope—

"That's not what I meant," Sabu protested. "I mean that Dusi and Ganadarm might not get along."

"They barely know each other," Thaki said.

"Precisely," said Sabu. "That's why I'm worried about sending them off alone."

The giant in question sat on a wind-smoothed outcropping of granite watching the debate. His face held an affable expression of interest, as though the approaching army were irrelevant and he could find nothing more entertaining than listening to people speak a language he couldn't understand.

The horses shifted restlessly. They were intelligent enough to tell that a crisis was at hand. Plainly, Ganadarm was not.

But Dusi could tolerate the giant's stupidity as long as he did as he was told. "I can work with Ganadarm," she said.

Sabu turned, surprised to find her back.

"I'm not certain we can trust him," Sabu said.

"I'm certain we shouldn't," Thaki said. "But you have to trust *us*, Sabu."

"I trust you," said Sabu. "But it's my duty to make certain everyone returns safely."

"We will," said Thaki. "You need to worry about those at the roadhouse."

Sabu opened his mouth to say something else, but then he shook his head. "Ah, you have the truth of it, friend. I am glad I brought you along."

Thaki smiled.

"Very well," said Sabu. "I will take the road back to the roadhouse. You hide your horse on the back side of the ridge, then go up to the peak so you can get us a count. I want everything. Soldiers, wagons, camp followers, everything."

Thaki nodded.

"And make certain you live long enough to bring us that information," he said. "That's an order."

Thaki smiled. "Yes, Lieutenant."

"Dusi, I want you and Ganadarm to follow those scouts when they come over the ridge. If it looks like the scouts are riding for the roadhouse, you must get there first and warn us. But I'm hoping they are just scouting a place to camp. I want to know where they stop."

"What should I do if Ganadarm can't keep up?" Dusi asked.

"Use your judgment. But remember that we cannot afford any losses. You will both be safer if you stay together."

Dusi could take care of herself, but she saw no need to argue with Sabu. "Understood," she said.

"Good."

Sabu changed languages. "Ganadarm, you go with Dusi," he said. "You guard her. Keep her safe. Yes?"

Ganadarm rose from his rock until he was towering above them. He looked down on Sabu and said, "I will keep Dusi safe, Lieutenant."

Wonderful. Couldn't the lieutenant have just told Ganadarm to follow her orders?

"I hope I see you all soon," Sabu said. He climbed astride his mountain stepper and rode off down the mountain.

Dusi looked at Thaki.

"Be careful," Thaki said.

"You too," said Dusi.

"I have done this sort of thing before," Thaki said, implying that Dusi hadn't.

"I've been well trained," Dusi assured her.

"Yes," said Thaki. "But if you get hurt, Sabu will blame me. So be careful."

Dusi grinned. "All right."

Dusi wrapped her tongue around her second language: "Follow me, Ganadarm."

One of the things we had yet to learn was chain of command. Oh, we studied the concept in our military theory classes, but we did not believe in it. The Goddess taught us to think, to question, and to push toward logical solutions. She never said, "Do this just because I say so." She always gave reasons. And so our people can be very bad at following orders.

If the Road Patrol had been a more disciplined, more hierarchical, more military organization, then Thaki would never have questioned Sabu's judgment and Dusi would not have been paired with Ganadarm. That would have been a shame, for Dusi had much to learn from the Child of Lith. At the time, however, she wished she were working alone.

"We will hide there among the trees," Ganadarm said.

"No," said Dusi. "We will go down to the road."

Ganadarm shook his head sadly. "No, I fear they will see us if we wait for them on the road."

"Not on the road," said Dusi. "To the road. We will be near. Above." She pantomimed "above" with her hands. "You will see."

"And they will see us," said Ganadarm.

"No they will not."

"Yes, they will. We will hide in those trees."

"Those trees are too far," said Dusi.

"Those trees are close."

"We need to be closer, so we can follow them."

"I say we are hiding in the trees. Are you a woman or not?"

"What?"

"I said, are you a woman or not?"

Dusi shrugged. "I am a woman."

"Very well, then." Ganadarm seized the lead rope of Dusi's mountain stepper and began marching toward the trees. The horse dutifully followed. Dusi was too surprised to protest. She hurried to keep up.

The place Ganadarm chose for them to hide was not blatantly stupid. Rough terrain and thick clumps of juniper would discourage anyone on the road from coming up to have a look. And if the scouts did find their trail, Ganadarm and Dusi could easily withdraw deeper into the forest. In truth, the hiding place was tactically advantageous. The only problem was that it was too far from the road for Dusi's elemental affinity to work. To sense Children of Lith, she needed to be very close.

But she didn't want to explain that to Ganadarm. She didn't know the Klindrel word for "elemental affinity" and she didn't want to admit that she had spent the morning testing the range at which she could detect his feeble mind. So she gave in and accepted Ganadarm's hiding place.

Dusi led her mountain stepper deeper into the forest, where it could browse without being seen. Then she rejoined Ganadarm to observe the road. Except that Ganadarm was not observing the road. He was observing Dusi.

"The Klindrel will be over there," she said, pointing. "They will not be on my chest."

"Of course," said Ganadarm.

They sat in silence for a while.

A chickadee came to inspect the pine above their heads.

"You know," said Ganadarm, "among my people, women nurse babies."

"Good for them," Dusi said.

"They have, ah, teats," he said, gesturing to indicate where his teats might be if he had them.

"That is how it is done," Dusi agreed.

"So ..."

Dusi looked at him.

"... how do your people nurse babies?" he asked.

"Same way," she said. An army was coming, and he wanted to discuss infant nutrition?

"But, Dusi, if you are a woman ..."

"Yes?"

"... never mind."

After that, Ganadarm stayed silent and kept his eyes on the road. Mostly.

They had a long wait.

Finally, the scouts came into view. They wore leather helmets and their tunics were quartered gray and brown.

" 'Tis the Chumwarl Scouts," Ganadarm said, "the Klindrel who captured my comrades three years ago."

"Let us go into the forest more deeply," Dusi suggested. "So they do not capture us, too."

"Yes, you should go," Ganadarm agreed.

"And you will come with me," Dusi said.

"No, I will confront them," Ganadarm said.

"Our job is not the confronting," Dusi reminded him. "Our job is the hiding and watching and following."

Ganadarm shook his head. "I've hidden from them long enough. Now is the time to make my stand."

He moved as if to rise from their hiding spot. Dusi grabbed his belt.

"Do not stand," she said. "They will see us."

"They will see me," said Ganadarm. "But the diversion will give you a chance to make your escape. Every man has the right to choose how he will die, and this is what I choose."

The fool! Anyone that stupid deserved to die, but Dusi had promised Sabu she could work with Ganadarm. If he died, Dusi would look bad.

Well, she was the intelligent one. She would just have to talk him out of it.

"Why do you want to die this way?" she asked.

"Because it is my will. Now let go of my belt, woman."

"They captured your friends—is that not so?"

"They killed my friends," Ganadarm said. "And I should have died with them."

"No," said Dusi. "Then would your friends be sad. You do not want the death; you want the revenge."

"Revenge would be sweet," admitted Ganadarm. "But the scouts are many, and I am—"

"You will have more soldiers beside you," said Dusi. "When we go to the fort, we get all the fort's soldiers."

"Hm," said Ganadarm. "Then we would outnumber them."

"That is good," said Dusi.

Ganadarm looked at her skeptically. Clearly the imbecile could take no pride in defeating his adversaries easily.

"But the fighting will not be easy," Dusi said. "Because Captain Zhaku will want to fight the army."

"The whole army?"

Of course not. What an idiot. "Yes," said Dusi. "The whole army."

Ganadarm was wavering.

"And remember that you promised you will guard me," said Dusi. "Lieutenant Sabu will be—" angry? sad? "—disappointed if you do not guard me as you said you will do."

Ganadarm's shoulders sagged. "All right, little woman," he said. "We shall do this your way."

"Yes," said Dusi, smiling to herself. "Good. Follow me and be quiet."

They scuttled into the forest to where Dusi had left her horse. She coiled the lead rope and tied it snugly to her saddle, so that it would not catch on anything as she rode.

In the distance, one of the scouts' horses snorted. Dusi's mountain stepper shuffled its feet, but Dusi calmed it with a hand on its shoulder. She vaulted into the saddle.

"Easy, now," she murmured. "Keep quiet."

They could hear the percussive steps of hooves on stone. Dusi closed her eyes and invited her mind to enter a state of deep concentration.

So close to Ganadarm, she could feel his mind listening. The other Children of Lith would have minds like his, Dusi thought. They would be fuzzy, muffled, as though masked by iron. Could she make use of the similarity?

Dusi's skill with elemental Thought was limited to what she had learned from her mother. The secret societies of Hicho had forbidden her to practice deeper techniques. She had a graduate's knowledge of metaphysical theory, but only an eight-year-old's understanding of practical application.

The key was resonance—her mind resonating with theirs. Their minds were so unlike hers, but she had spent all morning aware of Ganadarm's elemental Thought. If she could attune herself to Ganadarm, then perhaps she could sense a resonance between Ganadarm and other nearby minds.

She reached for the fuzzy mind that was Ganadarm's. Her thoughts buzzed with the contact. She relaxed her mind to let her Thought flow into his.

Have you ever swung an axe at a chunk of wood and hit a knot so hard that the vibrations stung your hands? That was how Dusi's mind felt when she tried to attune herself to Ganadarm's mind. It couldn't be done.

Ganadarm stood alert, his head cocked to listen to the hoof-steps on the road below, but his stance was not tense. He looked springy, as though he could, at the slightest whim, leap down the slope and fly into the middle of the scouts.

The enemy riders were passing into the forest. Dusi's own horse shuffled its feet, but it made no more noise than would a browsing deer.

Dusi shifted her weight and the mountain stepper began creeping through the forest. She could not hear Ganadarm following, but when she turned to check on him, he was right behind her.

Good. At least he was quiet.

Dusi guided her horse on a descending path, trying to get close enough to resonate with the Klindrel.

She caught a glimpse of the road below. Her seat tightened and her mountain stepper froze.

She had not realized she was so close. They passed below her, twenty riders, backs covered with gray cloaks, heads covered with leather helmets.

Of course. The helmets.

Dusi kept her horse still, as the sound of the scouts' passing faded around the bend.

"Ganadarm," she murmured, "are their helmets made from iron?"

"Yes," he said. "But covered with leather so that the light will not reflect off them."

"Ah. Thank you."

The iron was completely blocking her resonance. Of what use could she be in this war? Her unique talent was the ability to find people she could not see, but the Klindrel defenses—iron in the blood, helmet on the head—completely thwarted her.

Gold blocks creation. Iron blocks resonance. Silver blocks destruction. Dusi had learned that lesson in local school. She hadn't forgotten, exactly. She had just ignored the fact that iron could be a problem. In general, bandits did not wear helmets. So Dusi had decided to not worry about it.

What would Sabu and Zhaku think? How long could she hide it from them?

"Why are we following them?" Ganadarm asked. "We know where they are going."

"We want to find out where they stop and go back. Lieutenant Sabu thinks they are scouting for a camp."

"Very well."

Ganadarm set off through the forest, quick and graceful as a deer. Dusi urged her mount to catch up. They would shadow the scouts by sound. *Anyone* could do that.

How could she train for nine years and have it be for nothing? Oh, she was a competent patroller, but she could have been a *brilliant* tracker. She *was* a brilliant tracker. But her quarry was immune to her techniques.

Why did they wear helmets anyway? It was not like a Child of Knowledge could reach high enough to club them over the head. Stupid iron. Stupid iron-blooded Klindrel.

Dusi took the lead from Ganadarm when they crossed a flowing stream. Ganadarm was quick, but not quite as quick as Dusi's mountain stepper. She pushed the pace, letting the noise of the stream mask her horse's hoofbeats.

It was odd how a tiny stream could make so much more noise than a great river. Dusi realized that it wasn't the amount of water that mattered, but rather how fast it went downward.

Downward.

The elements of the universe are like a stream flowing downward from Creation to Destruction. That, too, Dusi had learned in local school. Gold and silver had the power to block this flow, but iron would only interfere with resonances on the same level—in the same elemental pool.

Thoughts are like water, Dusi realized. *They flow through the mind, they shape it, they are shaped by it, and then they flow away. The iron blocks me from the mind, but can I reach the flow?*

Dusi dropped the reins and let her horse choose the path. She reached out with her mind, searching for the flow of Thought through the Elemental Realms. As she concentrated, she could feel her other thoughts drain away.

That was it! That was the phenomenon she was seeking. Let her thoughts drain away, and resonate with other thoughts flowing into the negative Elemental Realm.

She caught one.

She was so excited by the sensation that she lost it immediately, as though she had seized the tail of a slippery fish.

That thought had been close behind her: Ganadarm.

Dusi needed to resonate with the soldiers on the road. She took a deep breath and let the thoughts slip from her mind again.

There it was—a resonance between her mind and the falling thoughts on the road below. They flashed through her awareness like minnows in a pool. She could sense them! She knew exactly where the riders were!

The riders were a little too close. Dusi opened her eyes and took the reins again, guiding her horse away from the road.

"I cannot hear them," Ganadarm said.

"No problem," Dusi said. "I know where they are."

She smiled to herself. How pleased Lieutenant Sabu would be to learn that she was useful after all!

Ganadarm had broken her concentration. She reached again for the destructive half of the Elemental Realms. Negative resonance felt slippery, but surprisingly strong.

Dusi shadowed the scouts, creeping ahead of them as they neared the massive crag at Broken Handle Bend. There was no place to hide on the steep granite face, but Dusi hoped to pass behind the crag and thus keep herself and Ganadarm hidden while shortcutting the road.

Flashes of falling thoughts told her the scouts were still behind, out of sight. Dusi emerged from the trees and rode toward the gap behind the crag.

A thought hit her mind like a slap across the forehead. She reined to a halt. The thought had come from the crag.

Take your conflict elsewhere, it said, with wordless Thought.

A nature spirit. Dusi had suspected one was hiding there.

"I'm not the one bringing war," Dusi said, speaking softly so that Ganadarm could not overhear. "They are." She gestured in the direction of the scouts.

"To whom do you speak?" Ganadarm asked.

The horses below hit a stony section of road. Their hoofsteps echoed faintly in the breeze.

No. The war is inside your soul, said the crag.

"I don't understand," she murmured. "What are you talking about?"

Be gone, evil woman!

A squirrel climbed up on a rock and flicked its tail to emphasize the spirit's point. "Ch-ch-ch-ch-ch-ch-ch-ch!"

"Don't talk to squirrels," Ganadarm said with a sigh. "Never talk to squirrels." He held up a hand to forestall her protest. "Listen: The horses have stopped."

Ganadarm headed toward the granite wall of the crag.

"Wait," said Dusi. "They'll see you."

"You have already revealed us," Ganadarm said with disgust. "When Bannom hears a squirrel scolding from a perfect lookout point, he knows exactly what that means."

He began climbing the face of the rock.

Hooves scraped on the stone below. Dusi reined away from the crag so the nature spirit's squirrel would stop scolding her. But it was too late. In her mind, she could see that the scouts were indeed turning back to report to the army.

Ganadarm, now on the exposed side of the crag, called after them, "Why do you run, Bannom? Do you fear Ganadarm? Come back and fight!"

The retreating scouts ignored him, and his words fell out of their minds like splashes of moonlit raindrops.

CHAPTER 13
Zhaku's Decisions

ANYONE who has studied Terkisho's *Theory of War* can confirm that Terkisho is mostly concerned with battles between opposing armies. He explains how a well-trained army can defeat a smaller, less disciplined force. He explains the value of an organized retreat. Nowhere does he explain how to defeat a legion of thousands with three dozen bandit catchers. This was unfortunate for the Passwatch Road Patrol, because Terkisho's was the only theory of war they knew.

When Sabu returned with the news that the Klindrel Army was approaching, Captain Zhaku convened an ad hoc committee to devise a new theory of war, with the stipulation that they do so in less than a quarter-lithic. The other people in Zhaku's office were the merchant Tim Hill and the patroller Perga, with whom Zhaku had been planning fortifications before Sabu's arrival.

Sabu described what he had seen of the invasion force. Zhaku frowned thoughtfully. Stalwart Perga looked relaxed standing by the door, but Sabu noted that Perga's folded arms were in position to draw both his battleblades at once. Perga was ready to fight.

As Sabu concluded his report, Tim Hill displaced his cat from his lap, opened his ledger, and scratched a few figures. "If they are at the pass," he said in our language, "then they left Kanabur on the first. Or the second. No later."

"They *are* at the pass," Sabu insisted. The scouts were most likely already across. He hoped that Dusi, Ganadarm, and Thaki were staying out of sight.

"How fast can they get to the roadhouse?" Zhaku asked.

"Ox wagons cannot go fast," Tim said. "Oxen will be tired from the hill. But foot soldiers and horse soldiers—" he shrugged, "—they could be here by midday."

"It seems we don't have time to dig that trench I was thinking of," Perga said. "Do we make our stand here anyway?"

Tim said, "Excuse me, but you cannot stand here. They have many, many men. Many more than you."

"But we must engage their forces somehow," Zhaku said. "I sent word that Passwatch would slow the Klindrel down. The other roadhouses are counting on us to give them time to prepare."

Tim turned pale.

"Don't worry," Zhaku said. "Defending the road is not your concern. I will be sending noncombat personnel down to High-cliff Roadhouse. Lieutenant, what is the minimum number of patrollers we can send to escort the evacuees?"

Sabu was uncertain. "It depends on what the Klindrel scouts do," he said. "I counted twenty of them. If the riders choose to wait at the pass for the rest of their army, then we need send no escort at all. If they keep coming, we would want our entire company to guard the withdrawal."

"Would we?" Perga asked. "Suppose we remained in the roadhouse while the noncombatants withdrew. The Klindrel would most likely fight us and leave the noncombatants alone."

"Why is that?" asked Tim.

" 'Never leave an enemy fortification behind your line,' " Perga quoted.

Zhaku frowned. "I'm not certain the Klindrel have read Terkisho."

"Hm," said Perga. "Then perhaps we should ride out and confront the horsemen. We would have a two-to-one advantage."

"But some of our people would be killed," said Sabu.

"This is war," said Perga. "There will be losses."

"We have to take care," said Sabu. "We are few. Even a victory could be a devastating loss for us."

Zhaku nodded. "They are stronger and more numerous. We need to be smarter."

"Smarter would be to flee," Tim said.

"If the horsemen overtake us, we will have to fight anyway," said Perga.

"We must fight," Zhaku said. "But we don't have to fight their scouts. Lieutenant, did you see any wagons?"

"I saw a few horse-drawn wagons interspersed among the vanguard," Sabu said. "It was difficult to count them. The road is somewhat obscured by trees."

"We only need to disable one," Zhaku said.

Perga nodded. "I see. If we disable a wagon, then they must stop to repair it."

Sabu thought the plan had merit. "We can retreat as soon as the job is done," he said. "If we are quick, we might not need to fight at all."

"But what about the escort for our noncombatants?" Perga asked, indicating Tim. "Do we split into two squads?"

"We will leave only a minimal garrison," Zhaku said. "As soon as we have disabled the wagon, we come back here and guard the withdrawal to Highcliff."

"But the scouts might get here before we can come back," Sabu said.

"I am hoping they will hear the fighting and ride to defend their vanguard," Zhaku said. "But if they choose to attack the roadhouse, well, that is why we have a palisade."

Sabu nodded.

Zhaku looked to Tim. "What do you think?"

The Child of Wealth shrugged, pale-faced. "You know best, Captain. I am just a merchant."

"Lieutenant?"

Sabu was not certain what to think. "If it works, we will have most of our force at the point of attack and then our entire force covering the withdrawal. But if it doesn't work—"

"Every option has risks," Zhaku said.

That was true. Sabu hated risking lives, but Zhaku was right: Stopping the Klindrel was their duty, regardless of the cost.

"I will organize the company to leave at once," Sabu said.

"Thank you, Lieutenant. Please leave only a minimal garrison."

In the end, Sabu left only seven people: Tim Hill, the stablemaster, the quartermaster, a cook to help the quartermaster get ready to leave, the healer, the ritesmaster, and Jamidu, whom Sabu put on rampart duty. He simply couldn't trust the fidgety second-year to wait silently in ambush.

The remainder of the Road Patrol mustered in the courtyard and mounted their light-footed mountain steppers. Sabu explained their mission with a confident smile. He could not let his fear show. They had to see that he believed in their ability to fight. Then they would believe in themselves. And that belief might be enough to keep them alive to see the sun set on this terrible day.

They rode out of Passwatch and up the steep, forested slope above the Klindrel Road. Initially, Zhaku led them on a high trail to avoid meeting the enemy scouts. As a result, they almost missed Ganadarm and Dusi, who had decided to return along the road. But Ganadarm hailed them, so they came down from the trees.

"You make as much noise as a herd of elk," Ganadarm told Zhaku.

Zhaku began explaining the plan, and Sabu took the opportunity to speak with Dusi.

"Hello, Lieutenant." Dusi smiled her lopsided smile.

Sabu grinned back. He wanted to hug her. He didn't, of course.

"I'm glad to see you," he said. "Did you have any trouble?"

"Not with the scouts," Dusi said. "We followed them as far as the crag at Broken Handle Bend. Then a squirrel began chattering at us, and Ganadarm took that as an excuse to reveal himself and taunt the enemy."

The fool! Sabu thought. "What happened then?" he asked.

"The scouts turned and trotted back up the road."

"So they'll be watching for us now."

Dusi nodded. "But I can watch for them, too." Her deep brown eyes gleamed. "I found a way to detect Children of Lith almost as well as I can detect you."

"That is good news," said Sabu. "You will have to tell me about it later."

For he saw that Zhaku had explained the plan to Ganadarm and now wanted to speak with him.

"Dusi informs me that she and Ganadarm were discovered," Sabu reported.

"Yes," said Zhaku. "But that changes nothing. It just means we must hide ourselves carefully."

Sabu nodded.

"I wanted to set up by Yellow Spring," Zhaku said, "but if the scouts' report makes the vanguard hurry, we may not have time. I don't want to be caught exposed on the scree slope."

That made sense. "So we set up here, then?"

"Yes," said Zhaku. "Choose six patrollers to take our horses up to the avalanche meadow. Then organize the remainder into an ambush force."

Sabu wanted to choose Dusi to stay with the horses. He was so glad to see her out of danger that he wanted to keep her that way.

But that was unreasonable. He needed her help with the ambush. Instead he chose six quiet people whom he trusted to be calm around horses. He put Hikafa in command.

"Once you hear the fighting," he said, "start walking the horses down to us. The lives of those in the roadhouse may depend on how quickly we can remount."

The clatter of hoofbeats made him look upslope.

"It's Thaki," Dusi murmured, a moment before the curly-haired patroller rode into view.

Thaki dismounted. Hikafa took her horse.

"They're still coming," Thaki reported. "The vanguard isn't camping at the pass."

Captain Zhaku smiled. "They may regret that decision. Let us prepare for them."

CHAPTER 14
The First Battle

IN *ANALYSIS OF INVASION*, Boshi implies that Captain Zhaku could have ended the war right there on the Klindrel Road by killing the emperor. I suppose I should be grateful to Boshi for mentioning the Road Patrol at all. All other accounts of the war (except for Maburbi's *Defense of the Redwoods*) leave us out entirely. Still, gratitude has its limits.

In the first place, Zhaku had no way to know that the emperor had chosen to lead the invasion. In the second place, a clever cohort commander could have used the emperor's death as an excuse to seize the army for himself and lead it on a conquest of vengeance. But I am ahead of myself. I shall make this argument later. Suffice it to say that Captain Zhaku did the best she could with the information she had. I shall leave it to others to comment on whether Boshi has done the same.

The patrollers hid themselves on the upslope side of a turn where the road was crossed by a running stream. Ganadarm and Dusi had left tracks when they crossed the water, and those tracks would tell the story of two lookouts heading back to the roadhouse with news. Ganadarm portrayed the Chumwarl Scouts as competent, and Zhaku's plan relied on them finding signs of Ganadarm and Dusi. If the scouts focused on the tracks leading away, they would be less likely to find signs that an ambush party lurked among the shrubs.

Sabu crouched beside Dusi, so close he could smell the sweat in her hair. The first time he had crept up on a den of bandits, his sweat had stunk with fear, but Dusi smelled good. She was alert, listening with her supernatural sense, yet her posture did not seem anxious. She simply looked ready for action.

Dusi held out four fingers, the sign for the four-legged horses riding in front. In a short while, Sabu heard them himself. The hoofsteps blended into the noise of the stream flowing across the road.

Dusi showed two fingers, indicating that a company of foot soldiers would come next. Thaki had reported that the soldiers marched in ten ranks of ten, led by one or two men on horseback.

Dusi could identify them by this formation.

Sabu could not hear the infantry yet, but the scouts were already splashing across the stream. One of them made a comment—Sabu hoped it was about the tracks—but they did not stop. Two of the horses whickered to each other.

As the hoofsteps diminished, Sabu heard a sound he did not recognize. The rhythm reminded him of a moose crunching determinedly through the snow, but this sound was louder than a moose.

It was the booted feet of the enemy soldiers. Their steps were synchronized, as though it were only one person walking. Sabu's stomach tightened, and he remembered what Terkisho says about the fighting power of a disciplined army.

Dusi's two fingers remained resting in her palm. Sabu's fingers pressed against his spear. The roadhouse had six hunting spears, and Sabu had given himself one of them because Zhaku had assigned him the task of initiating the ambush.

But not yet. Zhaku wanted to attack a wagon, and as long as Dusi showed two fingers, Sabu had to stay hidden.

With a muted *clip clop*, two riders led a company of two hundred boots past Sabu's hiding place. Before the marchers had faded away, Sabu could hear the approach of the next company. The sound of so many giants marching on his road was unsettling. But at least he could take pride in the discipline of his subordinates. Not a foot shifted. Not a leaf stirred.

As the second company marched past, Dusi held up her hand: Five fingers was the sign for a five-horse wagon. Dusi could recognize it because it had a guard and a driver—two minds close together, isolated from the rest of the army.

Sabu took a deep breath, and suddenly he was calm. He felt the Goddess giving his mind mastery of his emotions. He was trained for this. He was prepared. He was ready to do his duty.

Sabu could hear the wagon wheels rumble along the stones as the enemy company marched through the stream. The foot soldiers began passing Sabu's hiding place as the wagon sloshed through the water. The wagon driver shouted something, and one of the horses snorted. Another wagon was following behind.

Dusi's hand remained in the air and Sabu waited as the marching soldiers passed. He was trusting the lives of everyone in his command to Dusi's judgment. But not without reason. The rookie was sharp. He could rely on her.

Dusi made a fist.

With a cry of "Now!" Sabu burst from his hiding place and threw his spear at the rear rank of giants. It pierced a Klindrel soldier's armor and stuck in his side. The soldier reached to draw his sword, even as he collapsed to his knees.

The soldiers turned at Sabu's cry. Five more spears flew toward them. Ganadarm drew his sword, Perga drew both his battleblades, and together they led the charge.

Trusting Perga's squad to do their duty, Sabu turned his back to them and ran toward the wagon. The horses were frozen in panic. Zhaku led Sabu's squad out of the bushes to attack the wheels with hatchets. Zhaku herself slid under the wagon to chop on the axle.

The wagon guard drew his sword and leapt down to the road. As he drew back to strike, Dusi slipped behind him and thrust her battleblade into the back of his knee. With a yank, she snapped his hamstring. He collapsed on the road.

Sabu reached the wagon and climbed up to confront the driver. The Klindrel was unarmored and terrified. He had a sword on his belt, but he did not reach for it. Sabu waved his battleblade under the driver's chin.

The driver backed away.

"Get off," Sabu suggested.

The driver did so.

From his high perch, Sabu had a good view of the battle. The Klindrel ahead were in confusion as they tried to turn around and reorganize their formation. Ganadarm was wielding his blood-streaked blade in a frenzy. Perga's patrollers were darting through the Klindrel ranks, dealing crippling blows to the soldiers' unarmored legs.

Dusi climbed up to join Sabu on the driver's seat. Spokes popped as his squad assaulted the wheels. A hatchet thudded into the axle below his feet. He believed that to be Captain Zhaku.

Sabu checked on Thaki's squad. Thaki had taken the driver's seat of the wagon behind, and her patrollers were attacking the wheels madly.

Behind Thaki's wagon, a mounted Klindrel captain shouted

something at the next company of foot soldiers. He waved his sword in the air, kicked his horse forward, and the ranks of soldiers behind him charged toward Thaki's wagon.

The moment of surprise had passed. Now it was time for Sabu to get his people out of here.

"Fall back!" Sabu yelled. "Retreat!"

The sword-waving captain galloped along the narrow gap between Thaki's wagon and the steep slope below the road. He leaned toward the driver's seat, but Thaki ducked away from his slash. The enemy captain rode on past.

"Retreat!" Thaki called to her squad.

Thaki's horses started as the rider passed them. Her wagon began rolling. She tried to rein the horses in, but the wagon just rolled faster.

The horses in front of Sabu rolled their eyes and turned their ears back toward the sound of hooves. Sabu's wagon started with a jerk.

Sabu couldn't see Zhaku. He thought she might still be under his wagon.

Dusi exclaimed, "Captain!" and jumped from the driver's seat onto the tent canvas in the wagon bed. As the wagon rumbled forward, Captain Zhaku appeared behind it. She was unharmed.

Thaki's horses were gaining, threatening to overrun the captain. Zhaku leapt for the wagon bed, caught it, and tried to swing herself up.

"Behind you!" Dusi screamed.

The Klindrel captain rode past Thaki's lead horse. As Zhaku put her foot on the wagon bed, the Klindrel thrust his sword into Zhaku's back. Her eyes went wide and she fell to the road below.

"No!" Dusi shouted.

The rookie ran along the tent canvas and leapt from the back of the wagon.

"Dusi!" Sabu yelled, but she was gone.

The enemy captain drew abreast of Sabu's seat. The point of his sword whirred past Sabu's nose. Sabu raised his battleblade and backed away. The rider had a long reach, and Sabu saw no way to get inside his guard.

The rider checked the road ahead. Sabu did likewise. The soldiers were scattering to make way for the accelerating wagon.

Perga's squad was retreating upslope, except for Ganadarm, who stood in the middle of the road, grinning.

The terra-cotta giant held a spear he had taken from one of the fallen soldiers. As Sabu's runaway wagon closed the distance, Ganadarm drew back his arm and let the spear fly.

It pierced the Klindrel captain through his armored chest. With a grunt, he fell from his saddle.

A clacking sound announced the disintegration of one of the wagon's wheels. Splintered spokes flew into the air. One end of Sabu's seat dropped an armslength, but the wagon continued ahead on three wheels, still accelerating toward Ganadarm.

The lead horse veered. Ganadarm grabbed its mane and vaulted astride. Taking the reins in hand, Ganadarm tried to tug the lead horse away from the brink, but the wagon was already askew.

One wheel slipped over the edge, kicking up a spray of dust. Then the horses were plunging off the side of the road. The wagon slammed into a tree, but Sabu kept going, flying through the air. He hit the back of a horse, bounced off, rolled, and crashed into a juniper, finally coming to rest on his back, looking at the world from a crazy angle.

Sabu looked beyond the wreckage of the wagon and the bodies of the screaming horses. His gaze focused on a man hanging by one hand from a tree branch.

The man was Ganadarm. He was laughing.

CHAPTER 15
Zhaku's Death

IN *DEFENSE OF THE REDWOODS*, Maburbi says Zhaku was our first soldier to die in the Klindrel Invasion, but this may not be true. Thaki said one of the men in her squad was impaled by a spear as he turned to retreat.

Two of Perga's squad were surrounded by Klindrel and never seen again. Some of the patrollers held out hope that they had been captured, but the Klindrel took no prisoners that day.

It seems most probable that Fermigo died in that battle, too, but only the Goddess knows. No one saw Fermigo fall, and afterward, no one could remember seeing him fight. Sabu always felt guilty about Fermigo—guilty that he had lost a rookie, and guilty that the only thing he knew about him was that he was fat.

Dusi felt guilty, too, because she had not known Fermigo well, even though they were in the same classes in college. She had only one clear memory of him: When the students were making their first moccasins, Fermigo had shown her how to sew.

Every person at the Passwatch Roadhouse had his or her own story. Some of those stories ended that day, the eleventh of Redmonth, the first day of the Klindrel Invasion. Every story deserves to be told, but I can tell you only the stories of those people I knew best.

I will tell you of Zhaku's ending. I hope the families of the others will forgive my lack of knowledge.

Zhaku was stabbed in the kidney. The Klindrel rider ran her through from behind. The point of his blade emerged from Zhaku's abdomen in exactly the place that Dusi had seen the assassin's blade exit her mother's body nineteen years before. Dusi knew the wound was fatal.

Zhaku's eyes went wide. The Klindrel rider withdrew his blade and Zhaku fell to the road below.

"No!" Dusi cried.

She ran to the back end of the wagon, ignoring the Klindrel murderer riding past. Zhaku was lying in the road, looking up at Dusi with confused eyes.

Dusi leapt from the wagon and landed with a roll. She scrambled to Zhaku's side and asked, "Captain? Captain, can you hear me?"

Zhaku shuddered and her eyelids slid shut. Life was leaking from her body, and her soul was slipping loose.

The road shook from the thunder of hooves and the rumble of iron-bound wheels. Dusi looked up to see horses bearing down on her and Zhaku.

From the seat of the onrushing wagon, Thaki shouted something. The lead horse veered, but the wagon was rolling too fast to change course.

Dusi grabbed Zhaku under the shoulders and dragged her toward the downslope edge of the road. As the smell of hot horses rushed past, one of the beasts caught Zhaku's legs with a kick that sent her toward the wheels. Dusi hung on and was spun to the ground.

The wagon wheel hit Zhaku's legs with a crack. Sabotaged spokes splintered, and the metal rim rolled free. For a moment, Dusi thought the wagon would continue on three wheels, but then it hit another bump and tipped onto its side, spilling tent canvas out of the bed. Thaki jumped clear. The horses dragged the wreckage away down the road.

Coming in the wake of the wagon was an entire company of infantry, boots scuffing against the rocky road as they hastened toward Dusi. She stood up, still holding Zhaku under the shoulders. Thaki grabbed Zhaku's mangled legs.

A wise woman would have had more fear of the oncoming line of spearpoints, but Dusi felt mostly cold hatred. The murderers had killed Captain Zhaku and she would find a way to make them pay.

But not right now. She had a soul to save. Dusi and Thaki carried Zhaku over the edge of the road.

The Klindrel did not pursue them down the steep slope. Dusi, Thaki, and Zhaku were soon hidden among the trees.

Dusi and Thaki laid their captain's body on the ground. Dusi opened her supernatural senses and focused her concentration. She found Zhaku immediately. The captain's thoughts were bright. Zhaku was no longer unconscious. She was dead.

Zhaku was dead and her soul was waiting to go to Heaven.

Or to Hell. Dusi knew well that either was a possibility. But she would make certain that Zhaku went to Heaven.

"We need a funeral," she said. "And we need it now."

Thaki looked at her as though she were crazy. And in a way, Dusi was. She had risked her life to save a dying body. But she needed that body. She would not let Zhaku be claimed by the Deceiver. She was determined to fight the demon for possession of Zhaku's soul.

Later, when Dusi calmed down enough to reason things out, she would realize that the Deceiver had no claim to Zhaku, that none of the demons could take the garrison captain's soul. But at the time, Dusi could only think of what had happened to her mother.

I hope that explains why Dusi reacted so emotionally.

CHAPTER 16
Ganadarm the Messenger

THE MORALITY OF KILLING IS RELATIVE. We say the teachings of the deities define good and evil, but we forget that different deities have different teachings.

To our people, life is sacred. Knowledge has allotted us twenty-seven years for studying, twenty-seven years for putting our knowledge to use, and twenty-seven years for passing on what we have learned. Murder stops life short, leaving the victim unable to pass knowledge on as the Goddess intended. That is why, among our people, murder is a sin.

Children of Lith also spend time learning skills, using them, and passing them on, but they do not see this as their purpose in the world. Their purpose is to fight the demons. Until that battle comes, the only thing they can do is prepare.

So when one Child of Lith kills another, the killer learns something and becomes more prepared to fight the demons. The victim would not have lived long enough to fight the demons anyway, so it does not matter whether the victim is sent to Lith's Heaven early or late. And that is why Children of Lith see combat as a pious act.

So when I tell you that Ganadarm felt giddy from the battle on the road, do not judge him harshly. Perhaps he enjoyed killing Klindrel, but more than that, he enjoyed surviving. His survival proved that he had bested them, and that was why Ganadarm felt so ebullient as he raced to the aid of Lieutenant Sabu—whom he thought was named Saboon.

"Saboon!" he cried. "You still live!"

The dark-skinned Drelfin was getting to his feet. Strewn on the slope above him were dying horses and chunks of wagon. The Klindrel occupied the road above, but none yet dared to come down into the forest.

"Ganadarm!" the Drelfin cried. "Quick. Follow me."

Saboon crawled under a log and disappeared into a patch of shrubby oak. Ganadarm was too big to do likewise, but he followed downhill, pursuing glimpses of the little man, until Saboon sat down to rest under a stout yellow pine.

Massaging his knee, Saboon asked, "Who else is here? On our side of the road?"

Ganadarm thought about it. Pergan had led most of his squad upslope. But Ganadarm had seen, while hanging from a tree branch, two Drelfin dragging a body away as an entire enemy company charged at them.

The two Drelfin had been astoundingly brave, and Ganadarm suspected they were female because only women could be so brave about something so pointless.

"I think perhaps I saw Dusi and Thaki dragging a body off the road," Ganadarm said. "Should I go find them? Should I bring them to you?"

Saboon shook his head. "I will find them," he said in his clipped accent. "Perhaps they find me. You must warn fort."

"Right willingly," said Ganadarm. "What message should I carry?"

"Say captain is dead. Say I am at distance from patrollers—wrong side of road. Say army comes tonight."

"Very well," said Ganadarm. "That sounds simple enough." Zhakoon was dead? Ah, the poor Drelfin! They would miss their captain.

"Do you have any orders for them?" Ganadarm asked.

Saboon shook his head. "They must think," he said. "Do what is wise."

Ganadarm put a hand on the little man's shoulder. "How is your knee? If you cannot walk, I can carry you back to the fort."

Saboon shook his head and stood up. "I will be well," he said. "Please go warn."

"Very well," Ganadarm murmured.

Saboon limped away.

Ganadarm checked upslope. No one was coming down to look for him. The Klindrel were unlikely to descend this far from their easy-march road. Evading them would not be difficult. Beating them to the fort, however, could be a challenge. The vanguard had a head start, and Bannom's scouts were horseback. Ganadarm would have to run fast to overtake them.

Ganadarm smiled at the thought of outrunning Bannom, warning the Drelfin at the fort, guarding the road as Tim Hill and the other Drelfin retreated behind him, and then humiliating the

Chumwarl Scouts by defeating them in twos and threes as they tried to get past. He set off at a lope.

Running on the sidehill was difficult, so Ganadarm allowed himself to lose elevation until he found a trail. Deer trails were only wide enough for one foot, but when running, he only needed room for one foot at a time. Last summer's growth brushed against his legs. He leapt over rocks and tree roots. His lungs filled with the joy of running.

Ganadarm decided not to worry about how much noise he made. Let the Klindrel come down after him! He would lose them among the trees. He was a mountain man and a bandit. The Klindrel would never catch him.

Bannom was riding somewhere on the road above, but Ganadarm would confront him *after* he had done his job. He would warn the fort. Not just because he had promised Saboon, but also because he wanted to keep Tim safe.

Little Tim knew nothing of combat. He had allowed Bannom to capture him without a fight. Ganadarm was glad they had left him in the safety of the fort, but if the Klindrel vanguard had a cauldron of hot coals, that wooden fort would not be safe for long.

Ganadarm thought of his father's burning stronghold, how the heat had melted Ugly Lem's skin. He ran faster.

If he had known the terrain better, perhaps he would not have lost so much elevation during his run. If he had not lost so much elevation, perhaps he would not have chosen the wrong line of ascent the first time. And if he had not been forced to backtrack and try again, perhaps he would have arrived at the fort before the Klindrel vanguard.

But Ganadarm did not know the most efficient route back, and the vanguard had been sent ahead at double time.

CHAPTER 17
Captain Sabu

UNLIKE OUR DEAR FRIEND GANADARM, Lieutenant Sabu had spent several years patrolling that forest. He knew exactly where he was. He was on the wrong side of the road.

High above him, in an avalanche-cleared meadow, Hikafa and his squad were waiting with the mountain steppers. Or with luck, they had heard the shouts of the soldiers and the screams of the injured horses and were already descending toward these hideous cries.

Perga and his squad were somewhere above the road, climbing up toward Hikafa. Sabu hoped his own leaderless squad would find Perga.

Thaki's squad might be leaderless as well. Ganadarm had suggested that Thaki might have helped Dusi carry someone off the road. If anyone was on Sabu's side of the road, it was his duty to find them and keep them out of the hands of the invading army.

Sore from his wagon crash, Sabu limped through the trees. On the road above, horses were crying in pain and a Klindrel was shouting orders. With so much noise, Sabu had no fear that someone would hear him sneaking through the forest. But the noise also prevented him from hearing anyone else sneaking through the forest.

Dusi could find him. But Sabu could not be certain the rookie would calm down and act rationally. Her leap from the wagon had not seemed like a well-reasoned decision. Where had she jumped off? Had Sabu walked far enough? Perhaps he could find her tracks.

Snap! Someone broke a stout branch nearby.

Sabu heard Thaki's voice: "Have you lost all reason? They'll hear you!"

"I need to make a litter," Dusi said.

They were alive! Sabu forgot his sore knee and hobbled up the slope toward their voices.

Another branch snapped.

"We have to leave her," Thaki said.

"I can save her!"

"Dusi, she's dead."

"I know. We don't have much time."

So Dusi was still irrational. She would need his help. They both would.

Thaki saw him first. "Lieutenant Sabu! Make this rookie see reason."

Thaki was standing, hands on her hips, glaring at Dusi. Between them lay the body of Captain Zhaku, her legs bent in unnatural places, her dead eyes staring at the sky. The women had chosen to hold their argument close to the road. Sabu could see glints of armor upslope, although no Klindrel were yet descending.

Dusi knelt among the pine needles, trying to use Zhaku's belt to bind two poles to the body. "I need to make a litter," Dusi said. "The soul is still attached to the body. It needs a proper funeral."

I need my mind finder sane enough to help me gather the rest of the company, Sabu thought.

"Dusi," he said, "the captain is dead. We must leave her. If she were alive, that is what she would order us to do."

Dusi paused a moment, staring, then glaring at nothing Sabu could see. "You keep quiet," Dusi said, addressing the air. "You're dead. I don't want to hear a word from you."

Thaki made a worried face and shifted her feet uncomfortably.

"Help me tie her to the poles," Dusi insisted. She looked at Sabu. "Please, Lieutenant? I can't let her go to— I just can't let her go."

Sabu contemplated the body of his dead friend. He would abandon the dead body because he had to, but could he also abandon Dusi?

Sabu looked at Thaki. "Let's do it," he said.

Thaki's eyebrows rose, but she nodded.

"We're near a scree field," Sabu said. "We'll bury her there. Good enough?"

Dusi nodded.

Thaki gave him a look, but she nodded, too. She was too smart to ask about a ritesmaster.

One *can* perform a funeral without a ritesmaster, of course, just as one *can* perform surgery without a healer. Neither of these

actions is recommended. But in war, soldiers learn to make do
with what they have.

They took turns carrying the makeshift litter. Sabu wondered
why Knowledge had not taken Zhaku up to Heaven. Was the
Goddess punishing Zhaku for foolish decisions?

That seemed too harsh. Zhaku had done the best she could.
No one in the Road Patrol could have done better.

Zhaku *was* consecrated to Knowledge, wasn't she? Sabu had
never thought to ask. He knew it was possible to give one's soul
to another deity, but—

No. Zhaku occasionally sought a blessing from the ritesmaster,
just as Sabu did. And when she prayed, she prayed to Knowledge.
Her soul belonged in Knowledge's Heaven. But for some reason,
her connection to her body was stronger than her connection to
Heaven right now.

Sabu saw no shame in that. He understood that even the most
pious people occasionally need extra help to get to Heaven. That
is why the Goddess taught us funeral rites.

The Klindrel Army had already resumed its march by the time
Sabu and the women reached the scree field. That was bad for
those who were still at the roadhouse, but good for Sabu's plan to
cross the road and reunite with the rest of the company. The road
above the scree field was empty.

Sabu, Thaki, and Dusi displaced the loose stones until they had
cleared a shallow hollow for Zhaku's body. It was shallow for two
reasons: First, they needed to be quick. Second, Sabu wanted to
keep the body close to the surface where the rocks were baking in
the sun.

Sabu didn't have an easy way to start a funeral fire, but as the
reader doubtless understands, the fire is not as important as the
Heat. For the Earth element, rocks are even better than the loam
that our people are buried under in the cemeteries of the Redwood Valley. And the Thought element is never lacking at a
funeral, for people cannot help but recall their memories of the
dead. So you see, Sabu had assembled all three of Knowledge's
primary elements, just as the ritesmasters do.

"Zhaku was our friend," Sabu told the Goddess. "And she was
our captain. She died defending her people. You alone can judge
whether her actions today were wise or foolish, but I ask you to

remember that this is your people's first war. We are lost right now, doing the best we can. Those of us who have survived have learned something today. Please take the soul of the woman who taught us this lesson."

They waited, heads bowed.

Sabu looked to Dusi.

She shook her head.

Please, Sabu prayed. *I can't take the body to a ritesmaster.*

That was an excuse, not a logical argument.

Your people need this, Sabu prayed. *We try to be logical, but you made us emotional creatures. Everyone in my company reveres their captain. Please let me tell them that you took her into Heaven. They need to believe you will catch them if they fall in battle. Without this hope, they will have no courage to fight and no chance to win.*

Dusi's eyes widened. Her mouth opened as she looked up into the blue sky.

The Goddess loves a good argument.

Thaki gave Sabu a nervous glance. Sabu gave Thaki a reassuring nod. The idea that Dusi could see a dead person's soul disturbed him, too, but Thaki did not need to know that right now.

Tears ran down Dusi's cheeks. "Captain Zhaku said, 'Thank you.' Just before she left, she told us, 'Thank you.'"

Sabu thanked the Goddess for allowing him to serve his captain one last time.

Sabu took Dusi's hand and gently pressed his fingers against hers. He looked into her deep, brown eyes.

"Dusi, we need to find the others," he said. "Can you do it?"

Dusi snuffled. "I can find the close ones," she said. Her voice was shaky—not at all the brash, confident rookie who had come to the roadhouse the week before.

"Do so," Sabu said.

After a moment, Dusi reported, "No one is close."

Sabu nodded.

"Follow me and keep looking," he said. "Thaki, you look for tracks."

Sabu led them up the scree field and across the road as swiftly as possible. Once they reached the cover of the pines on the other side, they breathed more easily, although Sabu continued to push the pace.

The first patrollers they found were three men from Thaki's squad. They had hidden themselves under a log uphill from the battle site. Sabu and Thaki convinced them to come out, and now Sabu had a squad of six.

Shortly thereafter, they found riders.

"Lieutenant Sabu!"

"Vomijomi! Did Perga send you out to look for us?"

"He did," Vomijomi replied. "He's established a line of defense upslope."

So Perga had the horses and was organizing the patrollers. That much was good. But why did he need a line of defense?

"Is he under attack?" Sabu asked.

"No," said Vomijomi. "But he wanted a defensible position for us to return to."

"Has he sent anyone to warn the roadhouse?" Sabu asked.

"Ah … I don't think so," said Vomijomi.

Sabu hoped he could rely on Ganadarm.

Vomijomi asked, "Would you like my horse, Lieutenant?"

"No … or rather …" He turned to Mishu, a second-year riding a stout mare. "Do you know how to get back to Perga from here?"

Mishu stared at Sabu with glazed eyes. It had not been a good afternoon for Mishu. Sabu waited patiently.

Mishu blinked, and the dazed look on his face was replaced with confusion. "Lieutenant?"

"Mishu," Sabu said. "Do you know where you are? Can you take me to Perga?"

Mishu looked around, as though he had just awoken. But apparently he recognized the place, for he nodded.

"Good. Please dismount."

Mishu did so. Sabu handed the horse off to Dusi.

"Ride with them," he said. "Help them gather the others."

Dusi nodded.

"And be safe," he added.

She gave him the faintest of smiles, but for now, that was enough.

Vomijomi, Dusi, and the others rode off. Mishu led Sabu, Thaki, and the three from Thaki's squad along a trail and then up a steep climb to Perga's position. Branches had been piled to restrict their path of approach. Trees and shrubs provided ample cover for ambushes. Sabu admired how quickly Perga's squad had made their position defensible, but he wished they had raced to the roadhouse instead. They had plenty of horses.

"Sabu!" Perga called. "You survived!"

"Yes," Sabu agreed. "But Captain Zhaku did not."

"Ah," said Perga. "I had hoped … Never mind. I hope she is with the Goddess now."

"She is," Thaki said. "Sabu gave her a funeral."

Perga looked to Sabu for an explanation.

You don't question my decision to take time for a funeral, Sabu thought, *and I won't ask why you decided to regroup here instead of taking your squad to evacuate the roadhouse.*

But in truth, he understood why Perga had decided to regroup here. Perga had not known that Zhaku was dead and that Sabu and Thaki were on the wrong side of the road. He had not realized he was in charge of the entire company.

"I'm glad you're back," Perga said. "What are your orders, Captain?"

Captain? Sabu now realized that *he* was in charge of the entire company.

"How many search parties do you have out?" Sabu asked.

"Three."

"We'll wait for them to return," Sabu decided.

Perga nodded.

"And we'll pray that the Klindrel make camp tonight before they get to the roadhouse."

Perga nodded again.

I hope Ganadarm convinced them to leave for Highcliff, he thought.

They waited. In time, all three search parties reported back, but only Dusi and Vomijomi had found any more people—a few stragglers from Sabu's squad. The other missing patrollers were either dead or hiding too far away for Dusi to detect.

Now what to do? Sabu was still missing people. They could be dead, lost, wounded, or simply hiding. Sabu hated to leave anyone behind, but he had a duty to check on the roadhouse.

Captain Sabu led the line of riders—and riderless horses—at a rapid walk, covering the distance swiftly. He kept them high above the road, to minimize the threat from the Klindrel Army. Their first goal was to discover the fate of Passwatch Roadhouse—and then, if possible, reunite with the people who had been left there.

As they descended toward the roadhouse, Dusi reported sensing Klindrel minds. When Sabu asked if they were making camp, she replied, "They could be."

Ah, the Klindrel Army *was* making camp on the road that evening. It was so. But the smoke Sabu smelled was more than just campfires.

He led his patrollers to the edge of the forest above the roadhouse and then crept forward on foot so that he could look down on the situation himself. The army's tents were arrayed below. The charred poles of the palisade had been knocked down. And the buildings of the roadhouse were smoking ruins.

I HOPE the reader will forgive me for implying that Tim's life was consumed by the flames that destroyed the Passwatch Roadhouse. I admit that my presentation of the facts is misleading, but this is because I want the reader to understand not only the facts but also the people. I want the reader to understand how Sabu felt when he saw his beloved roadhouse reduced to charred timbers. I want the reader to understand why the patrollers suspected that the people at the roadhouse had perished.

But they had not perished. This is what happened at the roadhouse after the majority of the garrison had left:

Tim spent some time in calculation. He considered a number of logistical options, devoting a separate page of his pocket ledger to each. The scratching of his pencil intrigued the cat, Mister Whiskers, who came over to watch.

Tim reckoned that the horse wagons could travel three times as fast as the ox wagons, but he knew the Klindrel had fewer of them. That meant most of the supplies had to be moved by oxen.

The smart thing to do was to use the horse wagons to resupply the legion and use the ox wagons to shuttle food between supply bases. The supply bases couldn't be too far apart. If the oxen had to haul their own feed all the way from the Borderkeep to Roadhouse One, then there wouldn't be much room in the wagons for anything else—each team would eat up the load of its own wagon.

The trick was to put a supply base in the middle—somewhere between Deermeadow and Tuma's Bend. Then the oxen could haul supplies (and their own fodder) in two or three trips.

Tim went to see the quartermaster. The Brownman was in the cellar, holding a roll of twine.

"Good day," said Tim in the quartermaster's language.

"Good day," the quartermaster replied in Tim's.

"What are you doing?" Tim asked.

"I am making together potatoes," he said.

"Oh, you're tying them into panniers."

The quartermaster nodded. He had a long face with skin like worn leather. Tim liked the color. His own color changed to match it.

"You plan to haul the potatoes on the horses?" Tim asked.

The quartermaster nodded. "Captain Zhaku said, 'Prepare to leave.' I do not want to leave much behind."

"What about the spare wagon?" Tim asked. He knew that every roadhouse stable had a wagon that the Brownfolk were willing to rent out to broken-down merchants for an exorbitant fee. Tim always kept his own wagon in good repair.

"We have no oxen to pull it," said the quartermaster. "Besides, we may need to ride through the forest."

"Off the road you mean?"

The quartermaster nodded.

That wasn't good. Tim could ride the Brownfolk's tiny horses—he had discovered that the day before—but he didn't like the idea of ducking tree branches, jumping logs, and bounding through boulder fields. He wondered if the road behind the Klindrel Army was clear. If he hid and waited for them to pass, could he just walk home?

He reckoned not. Anyway, it didn't matter. He had told Zhaku he would stay to help with the figures.

"I reckon the Klindrel Army will want to establish a supply base somewhere between Deermeadow and Tuma's Bend," Tim said.

The quartermaster nodded. "I think they will want all the roadhouses."

"Well, I don't mean to scare you," Tim said, "but Ganadarm says the Klindrel don't have much use for wooden forts. He thinks that if we stay here, they'll try to burn us out."

"Zhaku did not say we would stay here," the quartermaster said. "So they get this fort for free." His gaze took in the pile of empty crates, the heap of empty sacks, and the remaining sacks of potatoes. "At least it is the spring. They will not get so much of the food from the Passwatch."

"Can your horses carry it all?"

The quartermaster shook his head. "Too many potatoes. And I want to take all the flour we have upstairs."

"Could you make potato flour?" Tim asked.

"No. No time to dry it."

That was a problem.

In fact, it was more than a problem. It was a moral dilemma. Tim didn't want the Klindrel to get any of the Brownfolk's food, but destroying potatoes was a sin.

You see, Tim believed that all wealth is a gift from Yolim. Perhaps you do not see potatoes as wealth, but according to the Clanfolk, wealth is "health, land, and stock". Now "stock" includes livestock and seedstock—anything that can reproduce. Potatoes are not technically seeds, and so the first Clanfolk to encounter potatoes were not certain whether they were wealth or not, but by this time, the question was long settled. Because potatoes can be used to grow new plants, they are wealth—at least according to the law of Clan Hill, which for Tim was as good as the word of Yolim.

Of course, it would be absurd to think that no one in the Hill Enclave ever lets a potato go to waste. Like us, they have a surplus nearly every year. Those surplus potatoes grow sprouty and wrinkly and inedible, and by springtime they have more sprouty potatoes than they need for planting. Their solution to this problem is something a nature worshipper might think up: They grind up the potatoes and till the mash into their gardens and fields, thus storing the wealth in the land.

"Could you mash them up and spread them on the horse pasture?" Tim asked.

"I think I could burn them in a fire," the quartermaster said.

That would just be wasting good seed. "No don't burn them," Tim said.

The quartermaster nodded. "They do not burn well," he said. "When the captain returns, I will ask her what I do."

They had orders to be ready to evacuate as soon as Captain Zhaku returned. Once they were ready, they had nothing to do but wait.

Each waited in his or her own way. Once the quartermaster had selected sacks of flour and potatoes, he sat on top of them reading a book. The guard on the ramparts above the gate paced back and forth nervously. The healer and the stablemaster sat inside the roadhouse playing pegboard. The priest sat in seclusion somewhere. The cook, not knowing what else to do, made a potato soup.

Tim sat on the steps of the roadhouse, petting Mister Whiskers. He wanted to keep his pet close.

Afternoon shaded toward evening. The cook announced he was serving supper. Tim put Mister Whiskers back in their room and went to join the others.

The roadhouse dining chamber was a large, high-ceilinged hall with tables built for Redfolk caravan guards. Tim shook his head. There would be no caravans this year.

He climbed the short flight of steps up to the Brownfolk dining alcove. Here, the tables were six-sided and shin-high. These made him feel foreign. And sitting with his legs folded underneath him gave him cramps, no matter where he put the cushion. He should be home, with Besi and the kids. Yolim curse the emperor!

The personnel left at the roadhouse could fit around one table. The healer with her long, pretty, brown hair sat opposite Tim. She folded her legs underneath her with a feminine grace that made him miss Besi more. The stablemaster, smelling pleasantly of horse, was on Tim's right. Beside him sat the gaunt quartermaster with skin like worn leather.

The cook put six bowls of soup on the table, then sat down beside Tim. In two decades of visiting Brownfolk roadhouses, Tim had only seen the cook eat with the guests a handful of times. Then again, could be Tim was not a guest. Could be he was in the Brownfolk army now.

A man wearing a blade climbed up the steps. Tim recognized him as the guard who had been pacing the ramparts. He looked nervously from one face to another and said, "The ritesmaster said I could come to supper."

The quartermaster sighed. "Sit down, Jamidu."

Jamidu sat. Then he stood up, fetched a seating cushion, and sat down again.

The quartermaster looked at the stablemaster. "I don't think the ritesmaster should be playing soldier on a day like today."

The stablemaster nodded and stood. He picked up his bowl and spoon from the table.

"Get a blade from the armory," the quartermaster suggested.

The stablemaster nodded again and went down the dining platform steps, still carrying his soup.

The exchange took place in the Brownfolk language, indicating it was Brownfolk business. Tim knew that a ritesmaster was something like a priest. Apparently the quartermaster was upset that the priest had volunteered for guard duty.

"He just wants to do his part," the healer said.

The quartermaster shook his head. "His part is blessings and funerals."

"He has already blessed everyone as best he can," the healer said. "And I hope he doesn't have to perform any funerals."

"There will be funerals," the quartermaster said. He switched to Tim's language. "When do you think the Klindrel Army will arrive?"

"Well, if they were climbing the pass around mid-morning, and if they don't have ox carts to slow them down …"

"They could be here now," the quartermaster said.

But the Klindrel did not arrive then. They arrived a short while later, just as the errant ritesmaster came into the roadhouse to get his soup.

The diners heard a loud clanging outside. Tim had never heard the sound, but he knew it meant trouble. Everyone ran out the door. The stablemaster was standing on the ramparts banging a hammer against an iron pipe.

They ran across the courtyard and scrambled up the ladders. Tim didn't know what he could do, but he followed the others. If the Klindrel were approaching, he wanted to know how many. He wanted to know what supplies they carried.

When he reached the top, the first words out of his mouth were, "We have to get out of here."

The Chumwarl Scouts were trotting toward the Passwatch Roadhouse, led by scar-browed Captain Bannom. A hundred Klindrel soldiers led by another captain came marching behind them. The soldiers in the fifth and sixth ranks were acting as porters, with wooden poles resting on their shoulders. Suspended from the poles were iron pots swaying on iron chains.

Tim appealed to the Brownfolk: "Open the gate! We must run!"

"We won't be able to get everyone on horses in time," said the stablemaster.

"We can run on foot," said Tim. "Open the gate!"

"The palisade is solid," said the quartermaster. "And not even giants can breech our gate. We'll hold these walls until the captain returns to relieve us."

"She can't relieve us," Tim said. "She would be outnumbered nearly three to one."

"We'll hold the walls," the quartermaster repeated. He looked at the others. The Brownfolk nodded.

"Get us seven axes," he told the ritesmaster.

"Not blades?" the ritesmaster asked.

"Who here knows how to use a battleblade?" the quartermaster asked. "I said axes. One blow, straight down on top of the head ... Oh."

"What?" asked the ritesmaster.

"The captain took all the axes with her. I forgot."

"I'll get my frying pans," said the cook. "And my cleavers."

The quartermaster nodded.

"We have two more blades in the armory," the stablemaster said.

"I'll fetch them," said the ritesmaster.

"Yes," said the quartermaster. "But you won't wear one. I get one and—" he looked over their faces, "—Tim gets the other."

Tim said nothing, because he did not want to undermine the quartermaster's authority. But he didn't want a sword. He wasn't a soldier. He was a merchant. He wanted to get away.

"We have pitchforks in the stables," said the stablemaster.

"Get them," said the quartermaster. Then: "No. Stay on the ramparts." He turned to the healer. "You get them."

She nodded and followed the ritesmaster and the cook down the ladder.

Of course, while the quartermaster organized his paltry force, the Klindrel were not idle. Bannom led half his mounted scouts past the roadhouse. They took up a position to prevent any escape down the road. The first two ranks of foot soldiers spread themselves along the road facing the gate and readied slings.

Tim reckoned a battleblade would do him precious little good.

"Here's the situation—" the quartermaster said. He glanced over the wall at the company of giants below.

"Ah," he said, "why don't they have ladders?"

"They plan to burn us out," said the stablemaster. "Those cauldrons hold live coals."

Beside the two ranks of slingers arrayed in front of the gate stood an infantry captain. He raised an arm and looked to Captain Bannom, who nodded. The infantry captain lowered his arm and pointed at the other ranks of his soldiers.

Ranks three, four, seven, and eight raised their shields. This was some special company Tim was not familiar with. Their shields were small and round. Each was painted yellow and decorated with a black, scowling eye. The forty fearsome eyes formed a roof over the shield bearers and the porters of the cauldrons in between. Ranks nine and ten stood in reserve.

"We should have gotten something to throw down on them," the quartermaster said.

We should have run, Tim thought. "Is there a back way out?" he asked.

"The pipe for the spring might be big enough to crawl through," said the soldier called Jamidu.

"No it isn't," said the quartermaster.

"Besides," said the stablemaster, "can't get the horses out that way."

"Just stay calm and hold the wall," the quartermaster said. "Here comes the ritesmaster with our blades."

"One blade to each wall?" the stablemaster asked.

"That is what it adds up to," agreed the quartermaster.

This is crazy, thought Tim.

At a shout from the Klindrel captain below, slingstones began pelting the walls. The four men dropped to their bellies behind the cover of the pointed-tipped palisade.

The quartermaster squinted through a gap between the palisade poles. "The cauldrons are advancing."

The healer called from the courtyard: "Should we come up?"

The stablemaster clambered down a ladder. "To me!" he said. "Come to me."

Stray slingstones bounced across the courtyard.

On the ramparts, Jamidu asked, "Now what should we do?"

"I'm thinking," the quartermaster replied. "It looks like they are dumping hot coals at the base of the gate. Oh look: That one has a bellows. These Klindrel think of everything."

He glanced down into the courtyard. "Hey!" he yelled. "Where are you going?"

The cook and the stablemaster were racing back toward the roadhouse. The cook had left a small pile of pots, pans, and cutlery at the base of one ladder.

The healer, standing atop that ladder, cautiously poked her head over the edge of the rampart. She set a pitchfork on the rampart and went back down for another.

Tim decided to help her. He slithered over to her ladder and looked down. She looked up with eyes that said she could not believe she had found herself in the middle of a war. Tim agreed with her. He thought of Besi. He prayed to Yolim.

Tim and the healer transferred the makeshift arsenal from the base of the ladder to the ramparts, with Tim on the top rungs, low enough that the slingstones flew over his head. The ritesmaster climbed a different ladder and ran along the ramparts. Could be he thought his goddess would protect him from the slingstones. Anyway, he didn't get hit. He handed scabbarded battleblades to the quartermaster and Tim. Tim buckled his on while he was waiting for the healer to fetch a heavy iron frying pan.

I wonder if the cook has a pot I could use for a helmet, he thought. But then he realized that the barrage of slingstones had stopped.

"They're just watching us," the quartermaster said.

Jamidu poked his head up over the wall. "No they're not," he said. "They're moving to surround us. So we can't escape over the back wall now. Wish I'd thought of that before they did."

The cook and the stablemaster were crossing the courtyard now. Between them they carried the soup cauldron, hanging on a spit.

"You're too late," the quartermaster called. "They fell back after dumping coals at the gate."

The two men ignored him and began muscling the soup up a ladder. The stablemaster pulled it up one rung at a time. The cook, with his hand protected by a cooking mitten, pushed up from below. The healer wrapped a bandage around her hand and added her strength to the endeavor.

Jamidu grabbed the handle when it got close, and with a final grunt, he and the stablemaster heaved the soup up to the ramparts.

"They already fell back," the quartermaster said again.

"Soup's not for them," panted the stablemaster. "For the fire."

"Aha! Good thinking."

The quartermaster and the stablemaster wrestled the heavy pot along the ramparts until it was directly over the flames that were consuming the gate. With help from Tim and Jamidu using the pitchforks as levers, they tipped the cauldron up and over, pouring the liquid onto the fire.

Burning wood hissed. The flames fell. Steam billowed up into their faces, carrying the odor of burning potatoes.

They set the cauldron down. It was nearly empty.

The steam turned to choking smoke, and the flames began creeping up again.

"We could fetch water from the cistern," Jamidu suggested.

The quartermaster looked dubious. "Can we fetch enough in time?"

"Why aren't they doing anything?" asked the stablemaster, surveying the ranks of soldiers outside the roadhouse. The Klindrel now had twenty soldiers watching each wall, plus the slingers and horsemen on the road.

"They've done enough," said the quartermaster. "They've set us on fire, and they can slaughter us if we try to escape."

Tim took the scabbarded blade off his belt and held it out for the quartermaster.

The leather-skinned Brownman looked at him questioningly.

"We've tried it your way," Tim said. "Now we do this my way."

"And what is your way?"

"We negotiate."

The quartermaster considered. He nodded and took the blade from Tim.

Tim called down to the infantry captain on the road: "What are your terms?"

The captain looked at him impassively.

"We surrender!" Tim called. "What are your terms?"

He waited.

No reply.

"I think they mean to burn the wall down and slaughter us all," Jamidu said. "I think they mean to burn down the whole Redwood Valley."

Tim shook his head. "The Klindrel can reason. I trade with them every year."

"Yes," said the quartermaster. "But do you trade with *these* Klindrel?"

Tim decided to try the scout captain. "Captain Bannom!" he called. "Will *you* accept our surrender?"

The captain of the Chumwarl Scouts looked over to the infantry captain. Or perhaps he was just looking away from Tim.

The healer called up from the courtyard: "The flames are creeping inside the wall now. You should come down."

"I should let the spare horses out of the stables," the stablemaster said.

Tim looked at the impassive Klindrel soldiers. The walls of the roadhouse were likely to burn entirely, but the seven people trapped inside could stay in the middle of the courtyard away from the flames. If the wind was good, they could survive the smoke, too. Then what would the Klindrel do? Take them prisoner, or slaughter them all?

The quartermaster put a hand on Tim's shoulder. "He's not going to answer, Tim. Please come down."

"Aye."

"We could hide in the potato cellar," Jamidu was saying as Tim descended the ladder. "They'll think we all burned up in the fire, and in a few days ..."

"I think it will not work," Tim said in Jamidu's language. "They will find us there when the flame is cool."

"They want to destroy the palisade," Jamidu said. "If we aren't fighting them and we have no palisade, they will have no reason to hunt for us. Believe me. We studied this in college."

"They find us in the cellar," Tim insisted. "Not because they seek us, but because they seek potatoes. The army must eat."

The quartermaster nodded.

The stablemaster was emptying the stable. Horses pranced nervously about the courtyard. The stable doors were wide open— except for one. The stablemaster had not bothered to open the door to the stall that held the spare wagon.

Tim looked at that closed door. He looked at the burning gate.

Tim had an idea. He shared his idea with the Brownfolk.

A short while later, the wagon was sitting in the middle of the courtyard. The hitch and driver's seat had been sawed off, so that it was just a box on four wheels. Two sacks of flour were tied to the front. Potatoes filled the bed, and among them, tied up in a sack, was Tim's cat.

CHAPTER 19
What Ganadarm Saw

GANADARM WAS LATE. He had not gotten lost, exactly, but he had chosen a wrong path and been forced to backtrack. Now the sound of shouting told him he was near the Drelfin fort, but that was not a comfort. The sky, which he could see only through gaps in the treetops, held wisps of rising smoke. Ganadarm was too late.

Too late to rescue Tim Hill, perhaps, but not too late to kill Captain Bannom. Ganadarm was certain the Chumwarl Scouts had a hand in this. He crept up the slope toward the road.

A familiar voice shouted, "Captain Bannom! Will *you* accept our surrender?"

So good Mister Hill was not dead after all. At least not yet. Ganadarm wanted to warn Tim against surrendering. Ugly Lem's band had surrendered to Bannom, and they had been hung.

Could you hang a Drelfin? Were they heavy enough? Ganadarm didn't want to find out.

He crept from tree to tree. Judging from the smoke in the air, he was getting closer, but he heard no more sounds from above. How many Klindrel were up there? Just the Chumwarl Scouts? Or did they have other companies with them?

Ganadarm wasn't afraid to take on a company or two, but he didn't want to die until he had gotten Tim to safety. That meant he needed to find a fight that would offer him some chance of winning. He needed to challenge Bannom.

Near the road, the slope leveled out. Ganadarm found a place from which he could survey the situation while crouching in the cover of the shrubs growing at the edge of the pines.

He saw a smoking black gate underneath an arch of flame. The fire had started at the base of the gate and climbed upward. It was spreading, conquering the palisade one pole at a time.

The timber of the gate was ashy black and brittle. The Klindrel would have no trouble battering it down now. But they were immobile, waiting for the flames to cool. Ganadarm would have time to sneak into position.

Ranks of Klindrel soldiers stood everywhere the Drelfin were likely to try an escape, but no one was looking in Ganadarm's direction.

Ganadarm's target, Captain Bannom, stood off to the side with nine other mounted scouts, blocking any escape down the road. The Klindrel planned to do more than burn down the fort. They wanted to ride down and kill any Drelfin who survived the fire.

Yes, Bannom, Ganadarm thought. *You like to be thorough. How it must gall you to know that one of Ugly Lem's band escaped! Every time you overhear one of your men referring to you as "Scarbrow", I suspect you think of me. Well, I have been thinking of you, too, these past three years. And now we shall put these thoughts into action.*

Ganadarm crawled out of sight and crept through the forest toward Bannom. The scouts had left space between themselves and the soldiers surrounding the Drelfin fort, as though they were not party to the siege, but merely there to observe. Ganadarm crawled toward this gap.

He worked his way through the brush until he was as close as he could get without being seen. He took a deep breath and thought of Ugly Lem. Then he drew his father's sword and strode out onto the road.

The foot soldiers had their backs to him, so he was not surprised that they did not see him, but the Chumwarl Scouts allowed him to take four steps before they noticed him approaching. A man mounted next to Bannom raised an arm in Ganadarm's direction and the manhunter turned his round head.

Ganadarm halted, at his ease, fifteen paces in front of Bannom's horse. "Good afternoon, Bannom."

The Klindrel captain looked Ganadarm from moccasins to hair and condescended to reply, "Good afternoon."

"I suspect you are surprised to see me again," said Ganadarm.

"Are you the one who attacked my men at the Borderkeep?"

"I am," said Ganadarm.

"And are you also the man who was yelling at us from the rocks earlier today?"

"Yes."

"Then, no," said Bannom. "I am not surprised to see you again. Merely surprised to see you again so soon."

"You need not fear another meeting," said Ganadarm. "Our chase ends here."

"What chase?"

"Why, you have been chasing me for three years," said Ganadarm.

"Unlikely," said Bannom. "Until last fall, my company was stationed in the Saltlands."

"And I was a bandit in company with Ugly Lem."

Recognition lit Bannom's face like the sun emerging from a cloud. "Ah! That explains why you think I should know you."

"But you do know me. I am the man who gave you that scar. I am Ganadarm!"

"My apologies for not recognizing you," said Bannom.

"'Twas I who escaped you!" said Ganadarm. "'Twas I who alone went free! 'Twas I whom you have tracked in vain ever since!"

"And now here you are," said Bannom.

"Yes."

"All alone, and surrounded by my men," observed Bannom.

"I will die by their swords if I must," said Ganadarm. "But I offer you the chance for a duel."

"A duel?"

"Yes," said Ganadarm. "If you win, you can hold your head high in front of your men and tell them that you slew me in honorable combat."

"And if you win?" asked Bannom. "We are not bandits, you see. My men will not follow you just because you kill me. They will obey only the army of the Klindrel Empire."

"If I win," said Ganadarm, "your men must let the Drelfin go free."

"Ah," said Bannom with a smile. "I see. You have come out of hiding to save the Drelfin, is that it?"

"That is it," said Ganadarm.

Bannom shook his head. "I fear 'tis not so simple, Ganadarm. In the first place, my men must obey the orders of the emperor, and our orders are to help the Yellow-Eye Skirmishers burn this fortress to the ground. In the second place, our role here is supporting. Captain Harsk is in charge of the assault."

Ganadarm looked at the flaming palisade. Gaps showed where

burned poles had fallen from the gate. The foot soldiers were aware of Ganadarm now, but they did not break ranks.

"You call this an assault?" asked Ganadarm. "Smoking tiny Drelfin out of their home to be slaughtered?"

"Yes," said Bannom. "We call this an assault."

Ganadarm spat. "I call it disgraceful."

"Call it what you will, the assault will continue. There is no point to your duel."

Ganadarm's fingers tightened on his sword.

"But," said Bannom, "that does not mean your arrival is pointless."

"You will fight me, then?"

"I would fight beside you," said Bannom. "You are strong, brave, resourceful, and … well, perhaps not 'clever', but you do possess a certain cunning. Why not join us? Perhaps you were in hiding and did not hear, but the emperor offered amnesty to all bandits in the Saltlands last fall."

"Amnesty?" said Ganadarm. "But I killed one of your men the day before yesterday!"

"Well, in point of fact," said Bannom, "he was not one of my men. His commanding officer is still at the Borderkeep. So no one is in a position to argue against me, should I decide to grant you amnesty."

"Why are we talking about this?" asked Ganadarm. "Get off your horse and fight!"

"So you refuse?"

"I refuse!" said Ganadarm.

"Captain Bannom?" called the officer at the end of the ranks standing before the smoking gate. "Is there a problem?"

Bannom raised his voice to call, "We shall deal with it, Captain Harsk. But do alert your line."

Bannom raised an arm and gestured at Ganadarm. "Scouts: kill him."

The line of horses advanced.

Ganadarm crouched into a fighting stance, weight evenly balanced, sword at the ready. He grinned. This would be a good fight.

Wagon wheels rumbled inside the palisade. The scouts halted, looking with uncertainty at the burning fort. Ganadarm heard a crash and the snap of charred poles.

He turned to see a cloud of fire billowing from the flaming archway of the Drelfin fort. Within the fiery orange cloud was a rumbling wagon accelerating toward Captain Harsk's line of foot soldiers. At first, the wagon seemed propelled by a supernatural force, but looking more closely, Ganadarm saw tiny legs running along underneath it. The wagon bed was filled with potatoes.

Ganadarm grinned up at the open-mouthed Bannom. "We will meet again!" Ganadarm promised, and he dashed toward the fleeing Drelfin.

Soldiers scattered as the wagon rolled through their ranks. Smoke curled from two tattered flour sacks attached to the wagon's modified front. Little feet scurried toward the edge of the road.

The wagon left the road and they could not stop it. Two of the Drelfin dropped off in the brush, the others hung on to the axles until the wagon smashed into a tree, spilling potatoes into the forest.

Ganadarm ran toward the wreck of the wagon. He saw Tim Hill scramble out of the bushes.

"Tim!" he called.

The Drelfin seemed to not hear him. Tim jumped into the wagon bed and pawed through the potatoes. He lifted out a wiggling, snarling sack and tossed it over one shoulder. Before Ganadarm could catch up to him, Tim had jumped off the wagon and disappeared into the forest.

Other Drelfin were running, too, without any coherent sense of purpose except to get away. The foot soldiers trotted to the edge of the road, but they were too stunned to give chase.

Ganadarm would have run after Tim, but he saw that he might be useful at the wagon. One of the Drelfin was crawling away, not running. Ganadarm knelt beside him, but the crippled man refused his help. He pointed back toward the wagon and shouted something incomprehensible.

Ganadarm looked where the little man was pointing. A white-faced Drelfin lay under the wagon, his chest crushed by the wagon wheel. Ganadarm looked at the determined cripple crawling away and then back to the Drelfin lying, eyes wide with shock, under the weight of a loaded wagon. Ganadarm picked up the protesting crippled man and ran away into the forest.

And that is how Tim Hill and others escaped from the destruction of Passwatch. Before we continue, let me say a few words about these people whom Ganadarm and Tim did not know:

The man Ganadarm saved was Mo the ritesmaster. His leg had been caught between a rock and a log when the wagon went down the slope. Once everyone had regrouped, the healer, whose name was Bu, was able to remove enough pain and swelling from Mo's knee to allow him to walk unassisted.

Jamidu was the one who landed in the bushes with Tim. He took command. Leaning heavily on Ganadarm's advice, Jamidu was able to lead the group until they rejoined the rest of the Passwatch patrollers the following morning.

The stablemaster, Vahi, was the one who ensured that they were found. Vahi heard the distant whinny of a mountain stepper and convinced Jamidu that they should call out for help.

I am not certain who was the cook. Sabu said that either Kamifo or Gosher could have been in charge of the kitchen that week. Tim credited "the cook" with the idea of tying flour bags to the front of the wagon to make an impressive explosion. Both men were clever, so regardless of which one was there, I believe either could have been responsible for the idea.

The quartermaster was the one whose chest was crushed under the wagon. His body was never found. Perhaps the Klindrel buried him. His name was Gerjuvi and he had kept the Passwatch Roadhouse running for fourteen years.

CHAPTER 20
Souls

THOSE IN JAMIDU'S SQUAD were not the only ones who rejoined the main body of the Passwatch Company the next morning. A search party found a few stragglers that had fled to the other side of the ridge after the battle.

Ah, that was a mixture of smiles and tears! Everyone was so glad to see those who had been missing, but each group of new arrivals necessitated a new accounting, and a recounting of those who had been killed. The only patroller unaccounted for was, as I have said, poor Fermigo, may Knowledge have his soul.

Captain Sabu's dark face looked resigned when he finally gave the order to move out. Dusi hoped Fermigo, her classmate, would be found as they traveled toward the Highcliff Roadhouse, but she could see that no such hope was held by their beloved captain.

And he was beloved. Dusi saw how Perga and Thaki, the most senior patrollers, looked to Sabu with sympathy and gratitude for the way he accepted the responsibility of command. She saw how Sabu's calm bearing and quiet presence comforted her grieving comrades. And she felt in her heart a flutter of compassion for the man who was able to remind them of their mission while accepting their grief.

He was grieving, too. Zhaku must have meant even more to him than she meant to Dusi.

The plan, as Captain Sabu explained it, was to stay above the road and head down to the other roadhouses. They hoped to join up with other garrisons. In a day or two, they might be receiving orders from Headquarters at Roadhouse One.

Ganadarm and Captain Sabu agreed that the Klindrel Army was unlikely to send soldiers marching up the steep forested slopes above the road, so the patrollers rode at a brisk pace, sacrificing stealth for speed. With long strides, Ganadarm kept up on foot.

Because the spare horses had been left at Passwatch (there was no way to convince them to dash through the flaming gate) a few other people were on foot as well. They could not keep up as well as Ganadarm, so Captain Sabu created a small squad that would take turns riding. Tim Hill and his cat were among them. Perga was put in command.

Dusi was with the main body of patrollers. They reached the vicinity of Highcliff in less than a lithic. The odor of charred timbers told them what they would find at the Highcliff Roadhouse, but Captain Sabu decided that he, Ganadarm, and Dusi would look anyway.

As they crept through the forest toward the rim of the cliff, Sabu asked, "Are any of our people still nearby?"

Dusi opened her mind to outside resonances. The first minds she found were Ganadarm's and Captain Sabu's. Though Ganadarm's mind was jangly and Sabu's crystal clear, their thoughts were in harmony. Both minds were receptive, alert for signs of trouble. Dusi tried to focus on minds that might be ahead of her while ignoring the nearby cluster of patrollers.

That was challenging. She wondered if her mother could have taught her how to focus better.

As they drew near the edge of the cliff, Dusi thought she felt a resonance below. It felt like her people, not Children of Lith. But the Klindrel could be nearby. So she shifted her focus to the negative Elemental Realm, searching for any Thought that might have been shielded by iron.

No Klindrel was down there. And the thoughts of her own people were too faint to be detected in the negative Elemental Realm.

She pulled her focus back up into the world. Ah, there it was: several separate tangles of Thought, well beyond the edge of her normal range.

Dusi and the two men crept nearer. The smell of smoke grew stronger. Dusi realized why the distant thoughts seemed clearer than normal.

"Captain Sabu," she whispered. "No one down there is alive."

Sabu nodded. Then he grasped her full meaning. "But you can sense their souls?"

"Yes."

Ganadarm looked from Dusi to Sabu, uncomprehending.

Sabu shrugged and indicated that they should continue.

The view from the cliff was the same sad scene they had observed at Passwatch. Charred palisade poles lay scattered about the perimeter. The barracks, the stables, and the roadhouse proper were smoking shells.

Ganadarm's nostrils flared and he nodded in grim approval. "They put up a brave fight."

Dusi could see the evidence of the battle now that Ganadarm had pointed it out. The bodies of patrollers lay strewn in front of the place where the gate had been. Their brown cloaks and buckskin riding pants were covered in soot and ash. Recovering her resonance with Thought, Dusi identified several bodies that still had souls attached.

"We'll need the ritesmaster," she said.

Captain Sabu agreed.

I won't dwell on the Highcliff funeral. Dusi was sent with those who scouted the path ahead. She was grateful that Sabu had not assigned her to funeral duty. She did not want the job of handling all those bloody ash-covered bodies, confronting the souls of those who had not yet been taken to Heaven. That night, they camped far from that charnel place.

Dusi was assigned to the first watch. She lacked the energy to hold her focus for long, but she tried periodically to reach her thoughts into the negative Elemental Realm. At least, she hoped her checks were periodic. Her mind was so numb that she had difficulty keeping track of time. Finally, the sparkling lith showed itself among the treetops, and she was able to pace her efforts according to its progress through the sky. The intensity of the red light reflected by the lith indicated that the moon had risen somewhere, behind the mountain peaks.

When the lith reached its height, someone came to relieve her. She wandered back toward the center of camp, unable to see where she was going. Exhausted, she wrapped herself up in her cloak and lay down, telling herself she would find the camp in the morning.

In her dreams she returned to the fallen patrollers of Highcliff, moving among their ash-smudged cloaks and bleeding bodies. Captain Zhaku lay among them, staring up at Dusi in confusion.

"Dusi, help me," she said. "I'm falling."

"Zhaku, I'm here."

"Come, Dusi. Come."

"I'm here," she said. She grabbed Zhaku's hand, but there was no life in it. It severed itself at the wrist and the stump of the arm fell to the ground with a puff of ash.

Zhaku's body shuddered. Her lungs emitted the sigh of death.

Dusi dropped the hand and ran into the forest.

"Dusi." A whisper.

Brambles caught the skirt of her chiton. She had lost the riding pants and tunic of a Road Patroller and was now in the garment most Children of Knowledge wear.

"Dusi." Again. But where? Was the voice outside or inside?

"Dusi, help me. I'm falling." A familiar voice. Somewhere nearby.

Dusi found herself above the Highcliff Roadhouse, running to the edge of the cliff. A woman's hand clung to a rock. The wrist twisted, as though the body dangling just out of sight were swaying above an emptiness.

"Dusi," the voice gasped. The hand slipped. The knuckles flexed. The fingers clawed for purchase, nails skittering across the rough stone. Then the hand was gone.

Dusi reached the edge of the cliff and looked down at the abyss. Ash floated in the air like snowflakes. And tumbling away into the darkness was a slender woman dressed in a gray chiton.

It was her mother.

CHAPTER 21

Command Decisions

THE GLOWING RED MOON was high enough to shine on the camp when Sabu awoke. The air held the chill scent of morning in the mountains. Sabu stared up through the treetops, looking for signs of approaching dawn in the moon-tinged sky.

Someone was snuffling on the other side of the log against which he had slept. A patroller crying, doubtless in need of privacy … but then again …

He raised his head and peered over the mossy log. He saw a fellow patroller curled up on the other side, shoulders shaking. Brown woolen cloak, short haircut—all patrollers look alike from behind. But Sabu recognized Dusi.

He climbed over the log and sat down beside her. There was a little privacy here; the log and the trees hid them from the rest of the camp.

Sabu didn't ask her what was wrong. Everything was wrong. He put an arm around her and she leaned her head against his shoulder. Her face was wet and her hair smelled of earth and pitch and sweat. It was wonderful.

He held her like that, letting her cry as much as she needed. His shoulder grew warm from her cheek.

After a time—it was a short time, but to Sabu it seemed timeless—Dusi regained control of her breathing and lifted her head. He let her go, but not because he wanted to. She adjusted herself on the pine needles so that they faced each other.

"I dreamed about her," Dusi said.

"Captain Zhaku?"

"Yes …" she said. But then: "No. Not just about Captain Zhaku. Zhaku was there, at first, but the dream was about my mother."

Sabu nodded. "I see."

"It … seemed so real. Like she was really here." Dusi pressed her fist to her chest.

"Like a ghost dream?" Sabu asked.

"I don't know," said Dusi. "I've never had a ghost dream."

"But you can see spirits," Sabu said. "If it had been a ghost dream, don't you think you would know?"

"It wasn't like talking to a spirit," Dusi said. "Spirits are on the outside."

Sabu shrugged. He'd never had spirits talk to him—neither in his dreams nor while walking through the forest—so he had no idea.

"Did she say anything?" he asked.

"I … can't really remember," Dusi said. "Mostly she called my name. Oh, Sabu, it felt so good to hear my name from her again, even if it was only a dream."

He nodded. "I'm sure it did."

Dusi took out her handkerchief and dabbed at her face. "Sorry about your cloak."

Sabu looked at his damp shoulder.

"It will dry," he said. He was trying to remember things Dusi had said before Zhaku's funeral. *I can save her,* and *I can't let her go.*

"Dusi," he asked, "did you attend your mother's funeral?"

"No," Dusi said.

That explained it. Or so Sabu thought. But then Dusi added, "My mother didn't have a funeral."

Sabu was appalled. "Because she'd violated the rules of a secret society?" That seemed unjust, no matter what forbidden knowledge she had used.

"No, Captain," Dusi said. "Because she was a demon worshipper. When she died, her soul went straight to Hell."

Oh.

"So the secret society that killed your mother was …"

"The Temple of the Hunters," Dusi said.

Now the knot was untied. Dusi's mother hadn't just been misusing forbidden knowledge. She'd been serving the demon known as the Deceiver. And the Hunters had slain her to keep her from recruiting others—others such as Dusi.

"I didn't want to believe what I saw," Dusi said. "A man was visiting our apartment. Mother sent me to the reading room. They talked for a while. I read, not really listening to their voices. Then I heard my mother gasp. I came running out of the reading room to find him standing behind her. The point of his blade came out here."

Her fingers brushed her abdomen. Sabu remembered Zhaku's exit wound.

"He didn't say a word," Dusi continued. "He just cleaned his deathblade on the hem of her chiton and then pinned his mark on her."

The Mark of the Hunters, a small round badge in three colors: white on top, black on bottom, metallic wedge between. Sabu's boyhood friends had known two stories of Deceiver worshippers and the Mark of the Hunters figured prominently in the ending of each. Their parents had not discouraged such story-telling. Cautionary tales were educational.

"She didn't die immediately," Dusi said. "She just lay there, staring, like Captain Zhaku did. I held her hand. She whispered my name."

Dusi trembled. "Then her soul ... just slipped out. And I reached for it. With my mind, my eight-year-old mind. Because I didn't want to let her go. I reached, and I could see her hand reaching for me, and I thought I held it—her dead hand, her spirit hand—both of them in mine, but then ..." Dusi sighed. "Then she was just gone."

"And you know she went to Hell?" Sabu asked.

Dusi looked him in the eye. "There was no mistaking it."

"I see." Sabu studied her face. Had he harmed her by eliciting this story? He didn't think so. She looked stronger. Determined.

"Sabu, I am not my mother," she said. "My uncle took me to a ritesmaster afterward. My soul was consecrated to the Goddess of Knowledge. I am faithful to our creator. The Deceiver shall not take me."

"Dusi," he said, "your piety was never in question."

"I know it wasn't before," she said. "But now?"

"Dusi, I know how seriously you approached your studies. I've seen how eager you are to face challenges. And I've no doubt that when the time comes, you will be a good teacher. I know you to be a good servant of Knowledge."

"Thank you," she said. "Your trust means so much to me."

Sabu smiled. "You have it, Dusi."

He saw Thaki then, standing at a discreet distance, glancing his way. He nodded.

"The camp seems to be waking up," Sabu told Dusi. "Go help with the horses when you are ready."

"Thank you, Captain."

"And I thank you, Dusi."

He stood up and shook the pine needles from his cloak. The moon-red clouds now carried also the orange fire of dawn. Thaki stood aloof from the rest of the patrollers, her gaze indicating that she wanted to speak with him. He went over to the pine under which she stood, and they exchanged good mornings.

"I have the camp up," Thaki murmured. "We have no food, so we have no need to wait for breakfast. I sent them to the horses. They can be moving as soon as you give the word."

"Thank you, Thaki."

He sighed.

"Was that the word?" she asked.

"No," he said. His eyes followed Dusi as she crossed through the camp, heading to where the horses had been left overnight. "I need to think first."

Thaki followed his gaze.

"You were right," Sabu said quietly. "I am silly for her."

Thaki shook her head, curls bouncing. "You love her," she said. "But that's not silly."

"In truth it is," said Sabu. "I hardly know her."

"True," said Thaki. "But she's just the sort of woman I'd expect you to be attracted to. She's small and fawn-eyed and looks like she needs protecting."

Sabu grunted. "She wouldn't say she needs protecting."

"No," said Thaki. "She's as tough as any of us and she's only a rookie. And that's why you admire her. So, you admire her and you want to take care of her. Of such seeds do mighty redwoods grow."

"Have you been reading poetry?"

Thaki snorted. "I haven't read poetry since local school." She grinned. "But I haven't forgotten much."

"So what do I do, Thaki?"

"Do? Just take it slow. She's young, probably doesn't understand her feelings yet—"

"No, Thaki. What do I do about my impaired mental abilities? I'm trusting you to tell me that I'm being foolish."

His friend shook her head. "But you aren't being foolish, Sabu. If she gives you comfort, then you should take those moments when you need them. That won't make you foolish. That will keep you sane."

Sabu was surprised that Thaki thought he had been talking to Dusi for his own benefit. But then ... well ... perhaps she was right. Regardless, he felt no need to correct her. And he had to admit that the smell of Dusi's hair had been very ... comforting.

He studied Thaki. "You're just afraid I'll declare myself unfit for command and give the job to you."

Thaki nodded vigorously.

Sabu sighed. "Don't worry, friend. I know my duty."

"Good," said Thaki. "I don't want to hear any more foolish talk about you thinking you're foolish."

"Yes, Lieutenant."

She looked at him sharply.

Sabu gestured at the patrollers grooming and saddling their horses. "If I'm the captain, doesn't that make you my lieutenant?"

"I just thought that Perga ..."

"You're the one doing the job, Thaki. I think you volunteered."

She smiled and shook her head. "You win, Captain."

"Give the word," said Sabu. "We're riding to Deermeadow."

Sabu felt he *was* being foolish, but he wouldn't complain again. Thaki had given him permission to be in love, and he decided to trust his friend's judgment—primarily out of necessity. He had to lead these people. It was his duty, and they needed him. But he couldn't stop loving Dusi, no more than he could stifle his feelings of compassion for his company.

His focus on Dusi was a weakness, but everyone had strengths and weaknesses. Sabu's job was to be aware of people's limitations and make good use of their strengths. Now that he had admitted his own weakness, he could be more watchful of problems it might cause. And after that talk with Thaki, he thought he could count on her and Perga to watch his blind spots.

Sabu kept his company a good distance from the road as they passed Deermeadow. Dusi and Thaki reported that the Klindrel Army was camped there. To get a better view, they had climbed a tree. (Most patrollers are good tree-climbers, because the College of Forestry requires all students to pass a lumberjack test, even those studying to be librarians. Such is the power of tradition.) The palisade and all the buildings were still intact. Moreover, a work crew was trimming poles for extending the palisade. Thaki's impression was that the army planned to stay a while.

They pressed on to Redhawk Flat. Again Sabu sent Thaki and Dusi to scout ahead. He hoped to make contact with another company of patrollers, but Thaki and Dusi reported that the Klindrel were still ahead of them. Thaki had seen signs that the Redhawk Garrison had fled toward the opposite ridge. Dusi said one Klindrel company had been sent into the roadhouse, while the others continued on the march.

"They seek supplies," Tim Hill said in Knowledge's language. He had invited himself to the head of the column where Dusi and Thaki were giving Sabu their report. Tim's small, furry beast was entertaining a knot of patrollers by chasing a stick that Ganadarm dragged through the pine-needle duff.

"I wish we could have scavenged Redhawk Roadhouse ourselves," Thaki said. "People are getting hungry."

Sabu nodded.

"I hope nothing was left," Tim Hill said. "If they get food, they will not need to wait for their wagons. They will move faster."

"We need to get ahead of them," Sabu said.

"And then what?" Dusi asked.

"Merge with another company," Sabu said. *Then I wouldn't have to be captain anymore,* he thought.

Thaki squinted at him suspiciously. She knew what he was thinking.

But in truth, there was nothing wrong with that goal. A bigger force was stronger.

Yes, he told himself. *Then you'd have two companies against an army.*

A company of patrollers had fewer combat personnel than a Klindrel infantry company. Even two companies would be outnumbered by one of the enemy's. Searching for another company was really just an excuse to avoid doing what needed to be done—to avoid making the decision that sent people to their deaths. To avoid being captain.

"I wonder what Zhaku would do," Sabu said.

"Zhaku would tell us to make another attack," Thaki replied.

"But that is why she died," Tim said. "And the army did not slow down."

"I didn't say that was what Sabu should do. I said that is what Zhaku would do."

Sabu said, "We need to find a way to slow them down. But you are right, Tim, disabling the wagons did not work."

"Ah, it was a good idea," Tim said, apparently regretting that his words might be construed as speaking ill of Zhaku.

"What else could we try to slow them down?" Sabu asked.

"We could get ahead of them and defend a roadhouse," said Thaki. "But I'd prefer a plan less suicidal."

"We should be able to outsmart them," said Dusi.

"Well, our ambush *did* outsmart them," Thaki said. "But we lost our roadhouse and our captain."

"Maybe we could feint an ambush," Sabu said. "If they thought every bend in the road was a potential trap, they would move more cautiously."

"We'd have to do the real thing sometimes," said Thaki. "Otherwise, they would learn to ignore us."

"Hm," said Dusi.

"Yes?" asked Sabu.

Dusi said, "I think I know a way to convince them to advance more cautiously." She looked at Tim. "And it will make them think twice before they try to take food from an abandoned roadhouse."

CHAPTER 22
The Neargap Roadhouse

THE KLINDREL ARMY advanced as fast as they could march. The roadhouses could not slow them down. After burning Passwatch and Highcliff, the Klindrel found Deermeadow abandoned.

Some companies were left behind to outfit Deermeadow as a supply base. The rest continued on the march. No one opposed them. The gates to the roadhouses were open.

At Redhawk Flat, the Klindrel discovered twenty sacks of grain and two sacks of moldy potatoes. At Roadhouse Six, the vanguard found enough fodder to fill two wagons, as well as a nicely aged elk, which they were forced to surrender to the cohort commander when he arrived later that evening. The Klindrel left garrisons at all the intact roadhouses, ensuring their control of the road behind them.

The vanguard reached the Neargap Roadhouse on the morning of the fourteenth of Redmonth. The gate was open and they could see the roadhouse had been abandoned, so they proceeded ahead to Tuma's Bend, leaving a search of the roadhouse to a single company.

That company was the First Teekibur Reserve—a hundred farmers led by old army officers who had come out of retirement at the emperor's bidding. It would be misleading to say that none of them had ever seen combat—Klindrel children grow up fighting—but it is true that only the officers had been trained to fight as part of a unit.

The officers did not abandon all caution as they entered their enemy's stronghold. They sent lookouts to the ramparts so they could keep watch on the courtyard. Instead of allowing the men to wander among the buildings, the officers maintained discipline and dispatched small groups to search the roadhouse, the barracks, and the stables.

Dusi was hiding in the stables, and she could sense the Klindrel minds approaching. They were not listening for danger. Each seemed to have his own private thoughts, and these thoughts did not harmonize with each other.

At Roadhouse Six, they had intentionally left ox fodder in the stable to encourage searching. But here, at Neargap, the garrison had scattered the stable's grain and hay over the wooden floor to deny the fodder to the Klindrel and to camouflage the hidden patrollers.

The Klindrel soldiers entered with soft rustling footsteps. Everyone could hear them entering, but Dusi alone could tell how many were still outside the stable doors. None of the patrollers so much as breathed. They waited for Dusi's signal.

A soldier opened the gate to the stall beside her. Sabu was in there, hidden under the hay. He had to know the Klindrel soldier was in the stall with him. Dusi assumed he would give the order to attack then, but he did not.

He would not, Dusi realized. He would stay silent until she gave the signal, because those were the orders he had given. Everyone's lives depended on her. Sabu had put his faith in her competence.

Some soldiers loitered outside the doorway. Dusi was supposed to wait until all the soldiers were inside, but some were already poking through the stalls. They were sure to find the hidden patrollers.

Dusi focused on the Klindrel in Sabu's stall. She watched the thoughts falling from his mind, waiting until she saw his concentration fall.

Dusi leapt onto the divider between the two stalls and shouted, "Now!"

The Klindrel's spear was pointed down into the hay he was searching. He tried to raise it, but the stall was too small. Dusi stabbed him in the eye. Sabu yanked his battleblade through the Klindrel's hamstring, but the Klindrel was already dead.

As fighting broke out throughout the stable, Dusi thought of the Klindrel that were still outside. Whoever controlled the exits could choose when the battle would be over.

"The doors!" Dusi shouted. "Secure the doors!"

Sabu dashed out of the stall. Dusi jumped down and followed him toward the doors.

A hamstrung Klindrel fell in their path. Sabu leapt over him. Dusi sliced the enemy's throat so he would not rise.

Two Klindrel were blocking the path to the nearest doorway, battling with patrollers that had hidden in the hay loft. Sabu sidestepped a spear thrust and stabbed an enemy in the thigh.

The other Klindrel drove his spear all the way through a patroller's body, pinning him to the floor. The patroller flopped and writhed like a gaffed fish. His mouth opened, but he made only a gasping sound. Dusi recognized him as Jamidu, but she did not have the courage to end his suffering. Someone got the Klindrel from behind and he fell screaming on top of Jamidu's dying body. Dusi ran outside.

No soldiers were left standing outside the stables. Across the courtyard, three Klindrel were fleeing the barracks with the entire Neargap Company in pursuit. In front of the roadhouse, two dozen Klindrel had formed a rectangle with their spears pointing out. Ganadarm was leading Company Six out of the roadhouse, trying to organize them into a line.

A Klindrel officer standing off to one side shouted, "To the gate! Fall back to the gate!" He took to his heels when patrollers began advancing on him. They let him go.

The rest of Passwatch Company emerged from the stables.

A handful of Klindrel remained in the center of the courtyard, facing Company Six at the roadhouse and cut off from the gate by the patrollers from Neargap and Passwatch.

Passwatch Company formed a battle line. Perhaps spontaneously. I don't remember the order.

I just remember the order to charge. How good it felt to rush upon that thicket of red legs and slice it down, to hear the hated killers scream, to see their blood.

I should have been scared, but I wasn't. I felt only hatred and joy—the joy of delivering vengeance for Zhaku and for the ghosts of Highcliff.

Outside the gate, booted feet were running, but the next Klindrel company arrived too late to stop the slaughter. We had prepared for our escape by chopping holes in the rear wall of the palisade. As the Klindrel ran in, we ran out, leaving behind the dead, dying, and wounded. In the final tally, we lost five patrollers at Neargap and destroyed an entire company.

Racing away through the forest, Dusi shared a grin with Ganadarm. She felt giddy with victory.

Those stupid Klindrel—how easy it had been to lure them in! Dusi had made them pay dearly for Zhaku's death. And she would make them pay again. She would trick them at every turn!

Dusi did not stop laughing until she realized that she could hear her mother laughing with her.

CHAPTER 23

Captains

AFTER THE BATTLE OF NEARGAP, Sabu led the patrollers away from the road and down into a narrow valley. To give the healers a chance to tend to the wounded, he called a halt when they reached the redwoods.

If you have lived in Hicho all your life and never seen a redwood forest, then shame on you. But for the benefit of those who live in the colonies, I shall attempt a description:

First, imagine walking through a wood or a forest you know. Don't imagine an apple orchard—think of conifers so tall you cannot see their tops. Some of the trunks have diameters bigger than your armspan. Have you been in a forest like that?

Now imagine you are a chipmunk in a forest like that. Think of how much bigger those trees would look and how much smaller you would feel. That is what being among the redwoods is like.

Sabu didn't mind feeling small. Small creatures are good at hiding, and after the Battle of Neargap, Sabu was trying to keep his people from being discovered. A Child of Knowledge can easily hide among the ferns, but Sabu was trying to hide a cohort of three companies—about nine dozen people and the same number of horses. If he spread his patrollers out, they left a trail that was easy to find. If he kept them single file, they left a trail that was easy to follow. Sabu posted lookouts, but he hoped the Klindrel would consider his cohort to be too small to be worth hunting down.

The reader may be wondering how Sabu got the position of cohort commander. Sabu wondered the same thing. The answer is that Captain Josho of Neargap and Captain Dabermoshe of Roadhouse Six had decided to defer to the judgment of one who had already survived one battle. Sabu would have felt more comfortable following, but logic dictated that he lead.

He had led Dabermoshe to his death. Ganadarm had rallied Dabermoshe's company after the garrison captain had been stabbed in the ribs.

In all, five patrollers had died at Neargap. Sabu took responsibility for every one of them. The sad thing was that Neargap had been a victory: They had annihilated a hundred Klindrel soldiers and lost fewer patrollers than Sabu had expected. That was the difference between war and bandit hunting. In war, a captain had to sacrifice lives to achieve victory.

Sabu hoped the ambush had achieved more than that. He hoped it would make the Klindrel slow down to investigate each roadhouse more carefully. Sabu doubted the other roadhouses were preparing ambushes, but even the threat of ambush could buy the Redwood Valley a few more days. Sabu had not yet received orders from Roadhouse One, but he hoped the people of the valley were organizing an army.

Ambushes would be difficult in the farmlands along the Redwood River. The Klindrel would travel through fields, meadows, and open woodlands. They would have time to form disciplined lines, and the Road Patrol's combat techniques, which relied on isolating enemies and slipping behind them, would no longer work.

But Sabu tried not to let these worries show on his face as he walked among his people. Despite the horrors of the morning, many of the patrollers were smiling. The cooks were laughing as they handed out raw potatoes. Thaki was joking with one of the patrollers from Neargap. The husband-and-wife patrollers from Roadhouse Six were sharing a kiss.

Sabu wondered how Dusi was doing. She had looked frightened after the battle, even as she reported that she sensed no enemies in pursuit. Sabu was not certain where she was now.

The three garrisons were congregated around three trees. (Yes, an entire roadhouse garrison could sleep under the same tree. Redwoods are big, remember?) Sabu couldn't see Dusi over by the Passwatch tree, but he went in that direction, hoping to find her on the other side.

He was intercepted by Tim Hill, whose skin was currently as dark as Sabu's own.

"Captain Sabu!"

"Tim," said Sabu. "How is your cat?"

A horse had stepped on the animal's tail the day before, and Tim had been concerned that the tail might be broken. Sabu thought perhaps a tail was not such a good thing to have if it could get stepped on so easily.

"He's tired from the ride and sleeping on my cloak," said Tim. "But his tail is fine. Thank you for asking."

"I am glad to hear that," Sabu said.

"Captain, I was wondering—"

"Captain Sabu!" This salutation came in Sabu's native language.

"—if I could have a word with you."

"Of course, Tim."

"Could I have a word with you?" asked Captain Josho. The captain of Neargap Company strode up at a brisk walk, his bushy black eyebrows lowered into the frown he wore when considering serious matters. Sabu had realized that Josho did not mean the frown personally.

Behind Josho came Lieutenant Fesu. Fesu had served under the late Captain Dabermoshe of Roadhouse Six for twelve years. Fesu wore a grim expression on his flat face. Other patrollers of Roadhouse Six were celebrating their own survival, but Fesu could only mourn Dabermoshe.

"It's about military logistics," Tim said.

"We need to discuss our strategy," said Josho.

Tim switched languages even as his skin paled to match Josho's and Fesu's. "I also discuss about strategy," Tim said.

"We can all discuss it together," Sabu offered, grateful for an excuse to use his own language instead of Tim's.

Josho's bushy eyebrows lowered, but he said, "Very well. Sabu, we need to take the goldmine road back to Roadhouse One."

"Yes," said Fesu. "But not until our patrollers are well rested."

"The Klindrel are not resting!" Josho said. "They can reach Roadhouse One the day after tomorrow."

Sabu hoped they would not. He hoped the morning's ambush would make them more cautious.

"Our patrollers need time to mourn," Fesu said.

"We don't have that luxury," Josho said.

"What would we do once we reached Roadhouse One?" Sabu asked.

"Defend it, I suppose," said Josho.

"Are our roadhouses defensible?" Sabu asked.

"Our headquarters should be," Josho said. "If we have the entire Road Patrol there to defend it."

"But is that the most effective use of our patrollers?" Sabu asked. "We are trained to move on horseback and fight on foot among the trees. We know little about defending walls. We close the gate and hope the enemy goes away. That did not work at Highcliff."

"Ah," said Josho. "But if we had slings, we could drive the enemy away."

"The enemy has slings as well," Sabu said. "Bigger slings, with bigger rocks. And they have shields to protect themselves from our slingstones."

"We can make shields, too," said Josho.

"Be logical," said Fesu. "If we don't have time to get to Roadhouse One, we don't have time to make shields."

"But we do have time," said Josho, "if we leave tomorrow at the first lithic and move at a rapid walk."

"What if a horse should go lame?" asked Fesu. "We have few spare horses."

Most of the spare mountain steppers from Roadhouse Six had been given to Sabu's company. Sabu had allowed Tim to go through the horses in turn until he found one that did not mind being ridden by a cat. Then Tim had given the horse a name: "Doefoot". Such is his people's custom.

Sabu looked to Tim to see if he had anything to contribute to the discussion, but the merchant simply stood there blinking.

"Let me give you something else to think about," Sabu suggested.

Josho nodded.

"Our horses are effective at moving us rapidly through the forest, but they aren't much help inside a palisade."

"True," Josho said.

"Our battleblade tactics are effective when we can isolate an enemy and surround him, but not when he comes toward us in a disciplined line."

"We may be able to discover new tactics for such a situation," Josho said.

"Perhaps," said Sabu. "But I'm worried that maybe the only way to defeat a line of spearmen is to have longer spears or a bigger line."

"If we are on the ramparts, the length of their spears won't matter," said Josho.

"True," said Sabu.

"It will become a battle of slingstones, and we should win because our height will give us greater range," said Josho.

"Won't their size give them greater range?" asked Fesu. "Or at least bigger stones?"

"I don't know how to use a sling," said Sabu. "Do you?"

"I've used a hunting spear with a throwing strap," said Josho. "The principle is the same."

"The principle may be the same," said Sabu, "but are the weapons similar enough?"

"So you don't think we should defend Roadhouse One?" Fesu asked.

"I think I'll leave that for Headquarters to decide," Sabu said. "They know their roadhouse better than we do. They'll know how best to defend it. I think we should focus on what *we* do best."

"You think we should set more ambushes," Fesu said. His flat, pale face did not look pleased by the idea.

"Ambushes, sneak attacks, and reconnaissance missions," Sabu said. "We should fight as much as we can while we still have them in terrain where we can fight them well. Once they get past Roadhouse One, we have to fight them in more open country. Then Terkisho's *Theory of War* tells us that the more numerous, better disciplined side will win. I fear that will not be our side."

"But if our army can't win on the lowlands, why do we sacrifice good patrollers fighting them in the mountains?" Fesu asked. "If we are certain to lose, shouldn't we focus on minimizing our losses?"

"You would surrender?" Josho asked.

"Yes," said Fesu. "If forced to choose between early surrender and late surrender, it is only logical that we would surrender earlier instead of losing more lives in a futile cause."

Sabu could see the logic in that, but he said, "We are the Road Patrol. We chose this job because we wanted to keep the road safe for merchants like Tim, here. The Klindrel have taken Tim's draft animals. They have burned our roadhouses. Even if we cannot stop them, it is our duty to fight them. That is our job."

"I agree with you," Josho said. "But let us fight them at Roadhouse One."

Sabu looked to the Child of Wealth. "Tim? What do you think?"

"I think you speak too fast," Tim said.

In Tim's language, Sabu said, "I think we should fight in the forest. Josho thinks we should fight in the fort. What do you think?"

"I think we should attack their wagons and leave their soldiers alive," Tim said.

"That is interesting," said Sabu. "Why?"

"Well, I've done some calculations, and it looks like—"

"Captain Saboon!"

Sabu turned and saw Ganadarm approaching, grinning his wide grin.

"Good day, Ganadarm."

"Captain, I would like to take out a hunting party," Ganadarm said.

"Hunting what?" Sabu asked.

"Meat," said Ganadarm. "Any place as lush and green as this should have deer, elk, moose, bear, ... or at least rabbits. What would be our best direction to go looking for game?"

"Down," said Sabu. "Klindrel are up—on other side of mountain."

"How fares your cat?" Ganadarm asked.

"He seems to be fine," Tim said.

"Glad to hear it," said Ganadarm.

"Anyway," Tim said to Sabu, "given the distance that the Klindrel ox wagons have to travel, I believe we can slow the army down significantly by—"

"Saboon," said Ganadarm. "What do you and your comrades have planned for tomorrow?"

"We plan now," said Sabu. "What do you think? Josho thinks we defend fort. I think maybe look for new attack."

"What fort?" Ganadarm asked.

"We have a big fort at the bottom of the road," Sabu said. "Maybe we go there tomorrow."

"Well, if you are asking me what I think," Ganadarm said, "I think you should stay away from forts. The Klindrel like to trap people inside and burn them."

Sabu looked at Josho.

Josho shrugged dismissively.

Sabu looked to Fesu. "What do you think? Is it wiser to fight in the forest or from a roadhouse?"

"If our choice is between dying at Roadhouse One and living as bandits in the forest," said Fesu, "then I think Roadhouse Six would prefer to live as bandits."

"Thank you," said Sabu.

"But I would like you to consider this:" Fesu added. "I know a commander must sacrifice soldiers to win a war. But if you know we will lose the war, then those sacrifices are pointless, aren't they?"

"I don't think so," said Sabu.

"But you cannot give any argument for them," Fesu said.

"It is our job," Sabu said.

"But if the Klindrel own the road, doesn't that mean we are now unemployed?"

"Lieutenant Sabu!"

Sabu turned to see a small patroller leading a horse with a white blaze. Sabu recognized the horse as one of the two that had wintered in the Passwatch stables. The forest mist had plastered the patroller's hair to his forehead, but after a moment Sabu recognized the thick, dark curls as belonging to Guvo, the messenger that Captain Zhaku had sent to Roadhouse One when they had first received Tim's news.

"Guvo!" said Sabu. "How did you find us?"

"I followed your trail of trampled bracken," he said.

Sabu grinned wryly. "It's good to see you."

"I can't say I'm sorry to have missed the battles," Guvo said.

"There may yet be more," Sabu said.

Guvo nodded. "Perga told me you are in command now?"

"We have given him command of the entire cohort," Josho said. "And he has done a fine job. But that hasn't stopped us from arguing with him."

("What are they saying?" Ganadarm asked Tim.)

"I have orders from Headquarters," said Guvo.

"Very well," said Sabu. "What are they?"

"Headquarters wants all patrollers to rendezvous at Roadhouse One."

Sabu looked at Josho. "It seems the decision has been made without us."

Josho lowered his eyebrows. "A pity. You were beginning to convince me."

CHAPTER 24
Dusi's Mother

THE THREE COMPANIES moved out as soon as their leaders could get them moving. Ganadarm did not get his chance to hunt for meat. They camped that night on a stream a short distance from the Burnt Stake Mine Road. Thaki organized the watches. Those not on watch lay down underneath the redwoods.

Fighting, riding, standing watch—a soldier's work is exhausting and the day is long. Most of the patrollers fell immediately to sleep. But some could not. Combat leaves mental wounds as well as physical, and some patrollers imagined the possibility of a Klindrel counterattack. One might say they were too scared to sleep, but that interpretation lacks precision. In truth, they were too alert to sleep, too aware of danger, unwilling to surrender their consciousness when they believed their survival depended on it.

And then there was Dusi. She *was* afraid to sleep. But she did not fear the Klindrel. She feared the voice she had heard in her mind.

Dusi had barely fallen asleep when she was awoken for the watch on the eighth lithic. There had been no time to dream. She was grateful.

Dusi stood her watch as best she could. Her brain buzzed like a bumblebee, and she lacked the concentration to use her affinity for elemental Thought. She finished her watch in a sleepless stupor. When she lay back on the ground for the ninth lithic, she could stay awake no longer.

The mist is so thick in the Redwood Forest that a cold knife drawn through it will collect drops of water. Head-high ferns spread themselves thickly above the moss-covered ground, and the redwoods push the heavens away so that the sun, the moon, and the lith are never seen. Daylight is silver and comes from everywhere. Even when one is awake, the forest seems to be the setting of a dream.

Dusi followed Sabu through the ferns, watching his slender form weave in and out of sight. Though she walked so fast her feet scarcely touched the mossy ground, Sabu stayed out of reach, his strong legs gliding forward effortlessly.

Dusi longed to catch him, longed to touch him, longed to be held by him. And then she was there, rocking in his arms. She tilted her head up to him and parted her lips.

Her mother's face smiled down at her.

"There you are, my baby girl. I have caught you at last."

"It *is* you," Dusi gasped, her heart stretched between horror and wonder. She reached up with her small, chubby baby-hand to touch her mother's face.

Her mother laughed and set her down on the floor of their third-story apartment. A patch of fresh, red blood stained the bloused waistline of her mother's chiton.

"What are you doing here?" Dusi asked.

"You summoned me. With your thoughts."

"I was dreaming of—" Dusi stopped. She did not want to say whom she had been dreaming of.

"You were dreaming of that dark-skinned man in tight trousers."

"Yes."

Her mother frowned. "And now you admit it to me."

"Yes, but—" But how could she hide it? Was not her mother inside her thoughts?

"Then learn to hide your thoughts," her mother said. "I spent eight years of my life teaching you. Did you learn nothing?"

"I learned, Mother. I learned."

Her mother scowled in disgust. "You learned to be passive. You use only the weakest aspect of your power, and you use it for *him.*"

"He is my commanding officer," Dusi said, but she was no longer in the uniform of the Road Patrol. She was wearing the green-embroidered chiton she had worn when she was eight. Dusi's mother grabbed her by the bodice and yanked her close. Their faces were only a handsbreadth apart. Dusi could feel her mother's breath on her cheek.

"And why do you let him command you?"

"Mother, I—"

"Never let that man master you, do you hear me? In all things, at all times, you must be the master of him."

Dusi pushed her mother away.

The woman staggered backward. The weapon handle protruding from her back struck the wall with a clunk. The point of the blade emerged from the red stain on her chiton. She sank to the floor.

"So this is the way you treat your mother," she said.

"Mother ..."

"I've been trying to reach you for nineteen years, and when I finally do ..." She gestured to indicate the blood dripping from the point of the knife.

No. Dusi knew she hadn't done that. That had been the assassin. Her mother was just playing for sympathy. Dusi should not let herself be misled. A true servant of Knowledge would think logically.

"You claim you've been trying to reach me," Dusi said. "But earlier you claimed *I* summoned *you*. Which is it?"

Her mother reached inside her bloody chiton and withdrew the deathblade she always carried there. She tapped the flat of the blade against her palm. "You always were a sharp one."

Her mother rose to her feet and stood with her back to the trunk of a massive redwood. Her body was naked and whole, except for a thumb-width slit where the assassin's blade had exited her abdomen. The illusion of fresh blood was gone.

"You aren't really here, are you?" asked Dusi. "You're still in Hell."

"Yes," said her mother. "I am still in Hell with the All-Knowing Master. But I am also 'here', inside your soul. The two are linked."

"My soul is bound to Heaven," Dusi said.

Her mother shook her head. "That is an illusion."

"It is no illusion," Dusi said. "After you died, Uncle Kershavi took me to a ritesmaster. My soul has been consecrated to the Goddess."

"Your goddess is mighty," her mother acknowledged, "but when she encounters the All-Knowing Master, she is easily deceived."

"That is just one of the Deceiver's lies," Dusi said.

Her mother smiled. "Oh no, my daughter. No, that is one of his truths. His truths are much more terrible than his lies."

She placed her hand over her exit wound, and with two fingers she spread the lips of the puncture so Dusi could gaze inside. "This is another truth, daughter—the hole in my body that took me to Hell. But you have this same hole in your soul."

Dusi felt it then, a sharp sudden pain stabbing through the muscles of her back to emerge from her belly. She gasped.

Her mother smiled. Kindly. "That is the hole through which I speak to you. That is the hole that will lead you to Hell, as surely as mine led me."

Dusi put her hand on her back. She could feel no break in her skin, yet the pain pulsed through her.

"You cannot do this," Dusi said. "I will not let you. The Goddess will protect me."

Her mother shook her head. "Foolish child. The Goddess does not rule here. The Master does. Your uncle may have consecrated your soul when you were eight, but I damned your soul on the day you were born."

"That cannot be done," Dusi said. "My soul belongs to the Goddess unless I give it willingly to another."

"And you believe you have not yet given your soul to the Deceiver?"

"I have not."

"What of those men you killed?"

"They were attacking Children of Knowledge!"

"Were they? It seems to me they were investigating an abandoned stable. You attacked *them*."

"They are invaders," said Dusi. "We are outnumbered. Our tactics are justified."

"Anything can be justified. The question is, were your actions *good*?"

"Their actions are worse."

"So they were evil, and you are less evil. But still evil."

"I didn't say anyone was evil."

"Ah, so they were good," her mother said. "And then you killed them."

"I did what I had to do."

Her mother nodded. "Yes, you did, Dusi. You did. And I approve. Your goddess would have tried to reason with them. But your demon—your *master*—knows that the smartest course of action was pure, base treachery."

Dusi realized her mother was right. Dusi had not even considered reasoning with the Klindrel. Not once. At the first battle, when Sabu had asked her to tell him when to initiate the ambush, she had been proud. At Neargap, she had tricked the Klindrel and reveled as she killed them. Perhaps her actions *had* served the Deceiver.

But Dusi could not believe that Knowledge wanted her people ruled by the ignorant Klindrel. Knowledge wanted her people free to think for themselves. Knowledge expected her people to use their skills wisely. Dusi had been trained to fight giants—and she had proven herself competent!

"You serve the Deceiver," Dusi told her mother. "You delight in deceit. You twist truths until they become lies. I will not believe you."

"Belief does not matter," her mother said. "Regardless of what you believe, you will follow me."

"I will defy you!"

"Your foot is already on the path."

"I choose my own path!" Dusi shouted. And she woke up.

Captain Sabu was looking down at her, concern in his eyes.

"Dusi, are you all right?"

Dusi blinked in the misty morning light. She lay on a bed of moss looking up through a wreath of ferns, but she knew she had left the dream. A stick pressed into her back.

"It was just another dream, Sabu."

"About your mother again?"

She nodded.

Sabu put a hand on her shoulder. "Would you like to tell me about it?"

Tell him? Tell him—Captain Sabu, this man she loved, this man who trusted her—tell him that, since birth, her soul had been consecrated to the Deceiver?

Dusi shook her head.

"Very well," Sabu said with a gentle smile. "Go get some breakfast, then. We have a long road ahead of us."

CHAPTER 25
The Redwood Forest

THE DEITIES designed us to have the power of choice. They did so not because it amused them to see whether we would choose Heaven, Nature, or Hell, but because free choice was a condition imposed by the Laws of Nature. So Knowledge's children are born bound to her, but the choices we make determine how well that bond is maintained.

We easily forget this. People take their bonds for granted. People assume that, as long as they do not commit their souls elsewhere, Knowledge will find them when they die. For the most part, they are correct, but it would not harm them to be a little more cognizant of their duty to the Goddess.

The other thing people forget, in a society dominated by servants of Knowledge, is that some people have pledged their souls elsewhere. Students at the Hicho Seminary are encouraged to study each of the nine deities and pledge their souls to the one they can serve best. Our first ancestors—according to *The Book of the Eighty-One*—communicated with nature spirits, and these communications led to the earliest forms of nature worship. No doubt the study of demons, which began in the third generation, led some to explore the possibilities offered by pledging their souls to Hell.

I have heard some people—wise scholars, who should have known better—make the argument that demon worshippers do not exist. They claim that no one can benefit from a demon, that we are logical people, and therefore none of us would ever choose to serve a demon. But it is not so.

We are logical people, but we do not always use that logic to find the truth. Sometimes, in moments of weakness, we use logic to justify actions that are wrong. We use logic to support the falsehoods we want to believe in. We take pride in our intelligence, and the demons take advantage of that pride by making their path appear clever.

If you ever find yourself facing the Deceiver, remember that logic is not enough to defeat him. In fact, he will feed on your logic. What you need is the ability to tell right from wrong.

Dusi had that ability. She knew her comrades were justified in opposing the invaders. She did not think Sabu's decision to set the Neargap ambush had been morally wrong. But she was troubled by her mother's logic.

Killing people was not good. Dusi knew that, and she had chosen to kill the Klindrel anyway. The good thing to do would have been to attempt reason. If the Klindrel had killed her, the sin would have been theirs, not hers.

But there was no way she would ever bow her head to an aggressor and passively accept her fate. There was no way she would stand by and allow the Klindrel to kill her friends and invade the valley that had been her home since leaving Hicho eighteen years before. She would fight them every step of the way.

So what did that make her?

"Dusi, if something is troubling you ..."

Dusi snapped out of her reverie. Why couldn't she concentrate today? Sabu was depending on her to watch for the enemy.

It was Sabu who had spoken. He rode beside her on a road lined with leafy ferns. The moon and sun, both unseen, flooded the misty forest with rosy light. Three companies of patrollers stretched out behind them. They were riding among the redwoods on a hidden back road to Roadhouse One.

"My apologies, Captain," she said. "I fear I did not get as much sleep as I should have. I will not let it affect my concentration."

"Dusi," he said gently, "that was not a rebuke. These battles have been hard on you. You are doing well, under the circumstances. I just want you to know that if you need to talk about it—"

"I don't."

Sabu studied her face. He nodded.

Dusi tried to relax her mind and abandon her negative thoughts. She closed her eyes. She let the reins go slack, signaling to her mount that she was trusting it to keep up with Sabu's horse and follow the road through the forest.

As thoughts fell from her mind, she became aware of the riders behind her. Ganadarm was striding among them, but she could not distinguish him amidst the noise of the dying thoughts. Only Sabu's mind was close enough to be distinct. His thoughts seemed half-formed. They tumbled and spun as they fell away, like broken brown oak leaves buffeted by the unseen wind of his emotions. They were worries.

Poor Sabu. He wanted to help her with her troubles, but who would help him?

Dusi let this idea fade from her mind and focused on resonating with the destructive half of the Elemental Realms. It was the only way to get around the Klindrel Army's iron helmets. How she wished she had discovered the technique in college. Then she could have had time to perfect it. Why hadn't the Goddess seen fit to give her the idea sooner?

But perhaps the idea had not come from the Goddess. The destructive half of the Elemental Realms was far from Heaven's domain. Perhaps the idea had come from elsewhere.

Dusi opened her eyes. The rosy fog limited her view of the road ahead. The trunks of the redwoods were big enough that a giant could hide behind them even if he were mounted on a horse. The ground was so soft that even the hoofsteps of Dusi's own company sounded distant and muffled. If the Klindrel were lying in wait somewhere along this mining road—not likely because the main road and the roadhouses were all on the other side of the ridge—but if the Klindrel were to set an ambush ahead, Dusi's supernatural senses would be the only means to detect them.

Was the Deceiver pleased by that idea? Did Dusi's contact with the destructive side of Thought give the Deceiver an avenue into her mind? And if so, did she not have an obligation to listen to her destructive aspects anyway? Perhaps it was risking her soul, but she had to make herself strong enough to handle the risk. Otherwise, she would be failing the man who rode beside her. And failing all those minds behind, which she could no longer sense because thoughts of the Deceiver were distracting her again.

Get out of my head! she thought. But she hoped no one else was there to hear the words.

Someone had heard, though. He answered her in a voice as patient as the roots of the redwoods, which wait for droplets of fog to collect on the leaves of the ferns and slide down into the mossy earth. The voice said, *My mind is not inside yours; it is yours that is inside mine.*

The voice came from outside, resonating in Dusi's head. She glanced sidelong at Sabu. He had not heard it.

What are you? she asked. *You seem like a nature spirit, but you can't be.*

She had confused it. The reply came slowly: *But I am a nature spirit.*

You are speaking in language, Dusi said. *Nature spirits communicate with pure thought.*

Some do, said the voice. *But my thoughts are too big to share with you. I will use language. For people, thoughts and language are the same.*

This is not strictly true, but Dusi chose not to correct the speaker. He seemed bigger than the usual sort of spirit, and she did not wish to offend him.

What do you want from me? Dusi asked.

Again the voice was confused. *From you? What could you give me?*

I don't know, Dusi admitted. *Nothing, I suppose. So why did you speak to me?*

You were shouting, the nature spirit said. *I wanted you to think in a more reasonable tone of voice.* He chuckled.

Dusi shivered. How could she hear him chuckle? Her affinity was for Thought, not Emotion.

You should see the look on your face, the spirit said.

Dusi grew suspicious. *That is an idiom,* she said.

And?

Nature spirits don't use idioms.

Dusi, may I suggest that you are ignorant?

So you know my name. That doesn't frighten me.

I apologize, said the nature spirit. *I did not mean to intimidate you.*

You didn't.

You know I did. Otherwise you would not have denied it.

The mind knew her name. It seemed to be all around her. It used her language and spoke in a way that only she could hear. What was it?

I am the spirit of this forest, it said. *I know the names of all who travel through me, for I can see their thoughts, if I choose. And I have been speaking your language far longer than you have, for I learned it from the first timber cutters who came up the river to diminish me.*

I have never met a spirit that learned language, Dusi said.

The spirit thought a shrug into Dusi's mind. *People interest me,* it said.

Dusi was still suspicious.

Tell me this, the spirit said. *Why do you doubt that this voice is mine, and why do you believe that the voice you heard last night was your mother's?*

You were in my dream?

No, said the nature spirit. *You slipped from my domain and went to consort with Evil. But since your return, your thoughts have told me most of what happened.*

I didn't go anywhere, Dusi said. *It was just a dream.*

Why should I believe that lie? asked the nature spirit. *You do not.*

I want to, Dusi thought.

The spirit chuckled again.

I have problems enough in the outside world, Dusi said. *I don't need you mocking me inside my head.*

Your head is inside me, the spirit reminded her. *I can't go away; I am defined by this place.*

By which place?

By the forest of redwoods.

The whole forest? It is very big.

I am very big. But if you ride far enough, you can leave me behind.

Dusi wondered how she could leave the voice of her mother behind.

You can't leave behind the things you carry with you, said the Redwood Forest. *Oh, and if you want to keep a thought to yourself, you will have to do a better job of shielding it from me.*

Dusi scowled. "I shall practice," she said.

"Practice what?" Sabu asked.

"Ah, forgive me. I was—" She was letting her personal problems interfere with her duty to safeguard three companies of patrollers. Again.

Sabu looked at her. "You were …?"

"I was talking to a nature spirit."

"Ah." Sabu nodded and pretended not to be disturbed by the idea.

The nature spirit chuckled.

I have a job to do, Dusi said. *If I promise not to think so loudly, will you leave me alone?*

Gladly. Your evil makes you stink. But I have thought of one thing I would like from you before you get back to work.

What? she asked warily.

Can you explain what you are doing? My little neighbors among the mountain pines whisper that people have been freeing each others' souls from their bodies. Usually, people try to stay in their bodies for as long as they can.

Do you know what a war is? Dusi asked.

War is the struggle between the deities and the demons.

Yes, well, this is a war between Children of Knowledge and Children of Lith.

Hm. Perhaps that word has acquired a new meaning recently. Why do you war with each other?

We are fighting each other because they are trying to take our territory.

Ah! Like ants. Yes, I understand now.

Dusi did not know anything about ants, but the spirit ignored her confusion.

Thank you for answering my question, it said. *I will not distract you from killing those riders.*

What? What riders?

Dusi received no reply.

She closed her eyes and tried to force thoughts from her head, striving to resonate with the destructive region of the Elemental Realms. It didn't work, of course. Thoughts cannot be forced away; they must be let go.

"Captain, wait," she said.

"What is it?" Sabu asked.

She had to keep her people out of the Klindrel trap. She had to be calm. Dusi took a deep breath. As she exhaled, she found her focus, she connected with the negative Elemental Realm, and she found the riders.

"Klindrel," she said. "On the slope above us."

CHAPTER 26
The Maziban Lancers

PERHAPS YOU ARE SUPPOSING that the riders on the slope above are the Chumwarl Scouts, the men in brown-and-gray uniforms who play a central role in Ganadarm's history. However, I would like to point out that the invading Klindrel Army also had a full company of cavalry.

The Maziban Lancers were a unit of one hundred men led by Prince Welzenkam, the son of the king of Mazibo Province. The Maziban Lancers normally served as the personal guard of the king, but during the invasion, they were on loan to the new emperor, whom the king sought to impress in the hope of renegotiating Mazibo's annual tribute. Or so Boshi tells us in *Analysis of Invasion*.

What Boshi does not mention is that the Lancers got their name from a spear long enough to spit two mountain steppers lengthwise. Should this spear be lost or broken, they also had, within easy reach, a sword as long as their giant arms and an axe specially designed for splitting skulls.

Their armor was intended to intimidate. The breastplates—both those of the horses and those of the riders—gleamed a brilliant black, for they were coated in a paint made from obsidian, a glassy black rock common in Mazibo. Their iron helmets—round at the top and flared at the bottom, like a Shozumi-made school bell—were gilt-etched with stylized patterns representing fur, feathers, or scales, identifying the wearer with a fierce animal. Most intimidating from our perspective, however, were the black leather riding boots reinforced with an iron strip that ran from shin to knee.

But I do not mention this because one hundred Maziban Lancers were on the slope above Sabu's patrollers, ready to descend upon them and slay them all. No, the riders on the slope above were the Chumwarl Scouts, as you supposed. The Maziban Lancers were *behind* the patrollers, following them on the mine road.

Of course, as Sabu gave the order to halt, none of the patrollers knew this. And Ganadarm did not even know an order had been given.

Ganadarm jogged along beside Tim and his tiny horse. Tim's gray striped cat rode behind the saddle and watched Ganadarm with lazy yellow eyes. The other Drelfin reined to a halt, but Tim kept riding toward the head of the column where Captain Saboon conferred with Pergan and the two Drelfin women, Thaki and Dusi. They had all dismounted.

Ganadarm looked around at the Drelfin he and Tim were passing and asked, "Why did they stop?"

"Because the captain gave the order to stop," Tim replied.

"Why did he do that?" Ganadarm asked.

"That is what we are going to find out," Tim said. He reined his horse to a halt at the head of the company, a short distance from the four conferring Drelfin. They seemed to be arguing—or at least, Thaki and Captain Saboon seemed to be arguing. Pergan and Dusi mostly watched.

"What is the trouble?" Ganadarm asked.

"They think Klindrel are nearby," said Tim. His face showed he was not pleased by the idea.

Ganadarm, however, was quite pleased. After the rout yesterday, of course the Klindrel would come looking for another fight. Perhaps they had even hoped to set an ambush of their own! But Ganadarm could tell by the way the tiny Drelfin rode their tiny horses that they were the masters of this foggy forest. The Klindrel could not win a battle here among the rosy mist, the thick ferns, and the giant trees.

"They should keep marching and send the rear company to sweep up and ahead to ambush the ambush," Ganadarm said. "Why are they arguing?"

"Well, they aren't certain it *is* an ambush," Tim said. "Apparently, Dusi wants to follow the Klindrel and report back once she knows where they are going."

"That sounds like a good idea," said Ganadarm.

Dusi was a light-footed little creature, and on this mossy ground, Ganadarm had no doubt she could follow the Klindrel without being overheard. Maybe Saboon would let him go with her. It sounded like fun.

"But the captain says it is too dangerous," Tim said.

"Hm," said Ganadarm. "So what is Thaki saying?"

"She's, ahem, suggesting that the potential benefits justify the risk."

She was suggesting it quite emphatically. Saboon's shoulders slumped and he nodded.

Ganadarm asked, "He gave in, didn't he?"

"Aye," said Tim.

"Will he lose face now?" Ganadarm asked. "Will Pergan challenge his right to command?"

Tim glanced at Ganadarm sidelong. "I don't think so."

"Will giving in to Thaki make it harder for him to add a second wife?" Ganadarm asked.

"What?"

"Saboon wants to take Dusi for his second wife, but Thaki won't let him," Ganadarm explained. He was pleased that he had understood something about the brown Drelfin that Tim had not.

"You think the captain and Thaki are married?"

"Aren't they?"

"I don't think so."

"Then how can she keep him from marrying Dusi?"

"You think he wants to marry Dusi?"

"Dusi is a woman-Drelfin. Did you know?"

"Yes," said Tim. "Yes, I knew that."

"Well, so does Captain Saboon. He is always watching her backside like a stallion investigating a mare."

"I'm not sure Brownfolk ... watch each other. In that way."

Ganadarm chuckled. "I know what you mean, Mister Hill. Geldings are lustier than these little men. But that is why Saboon stands out."

Tim studied Saboon, who had put a hand on Dusi's shoulder. "Could be you're right," Tim said.

"I am," said Ganadarm. "She has knocked him dizzy."

Dusi left her horse with Saboon and walked toward Ganadarm.

"What does she want?" Ganadarm muttered.

"I don't know," Tim replied. "You were talking so much I couldn't hear."

"Ganadarm, I and you are to be scouting this hill," Dusi said, waving at the slope above them. "Captain says you do my orders. Understand?"

Ganadarm looked to Saboon then back at Dusi. He was a free man of the Saltlands. He would do as he pleased. But he liked Saboon and wanted to help him. As long as the Drelfin woman did not want to do anything stupid, what harm was there in letting her think she was in charge?

"I understand," he said.

Dusi nodded. "We go up walking on the feet," she said. "You be behind me, be as small as me, and very quiet. Klindrel are up there."

Ganadarm smiled and patted the hilt of his sword. "Good," he said.

Dusi sighed. "Come," she said.

Ganadarm gave Tim a shrug and a smile.

"May Yolim bless you," Tim said. "Or Kashram, I suppose."

Tim looked worried. Poor, gentle fellow. Well, Ganadarm would find out what these Klindrel were up to and keep them from harming his merchant friend.

Ganadarm followed Dusi's little backside up the slope. She had hips—slender, but still female. The differences between men and women were slight among the Drelfin. They all had flat chests and none of them had beards to shave. The men did women's work and the women did men's work. If it weren't for the hips, a man would have to wait until they pissed to tell them apart.

Maybe it didn't matter. Saboon never seemed to mind when Thaki questioned his judgment. And Tim said that Dusi had been the one who suggested the ambush at the fort. That had been fun! Worth leaving his shack for, that was certain.

So maybe it didn't matter that Dusi was a woman. Because she wasn't, really. She was a Drelfin—three feet high, with pale brown skin and magical sight.

"How many Klindrel do you see?" Ganadarm asked.

"Perhaps twenty," Dusi said.

"Ten for each of us? Captain Saboon has faith in our skill."

"He has faith in our see them and they do not see us," said Dusi. "Or hear us. Please be quiet."

"Of course," said Ganadarm, with a chuckle. "You are in charge."

Dusi followed a well-worn deer trail, which made it easier for Ganadarm to move without rustling the bracken. He was not too concerned about noise. Sound did not travel well in this misty, damp forest.

The trail wound between trees tall enough to span rivers with trunks so wide that the wall of a house could be built from a single board. Yet something of this place reminded Ganadarm of the dusty scrubland he had been raised in: That *something* was the slope of the hill. The climb was gentle. It was a foothill. They were no longer in the mountains.

Ganadarm and Dusi were quite close to the Klindrel before Ganadarm heard the horses' hooves. It was more than one horse, he could tell, but because of the mossy ground, he could not be certain it was as many as twenty.

Because the riders were so close, their noise grew louder rapidly. Dusi sat down between the roots of a tree and closed her eyes. She was not relaxing. Ganadarm knew that was how she used her magic.

He slipped in beside her, lay down in the screen of roots, and curled around her.

Her face and his were at the same level, little more than a foot apart. She frowned at him.

Ganadarm shrugged. He was hidden. What did she expect? Ugly Lem had always said that if you want to keep all your men, hide them all in the same place. Every extra hiding place is another place they can be found.

Riders passed on the other side of the huge tree. A horse snorted, possibly at Dusi, who smelled a bit like the mare she rode. Then another horse snorted, and the steady march of hoofsteps changed into the fluttering thumps of horses coming to a halt.

Ganadarm looked at Dusi. She had closed her eyes again, but the frown was concentration, not worry. Ganadarm could hear someone striding through the bracken. One of the horses on the other side of the tree took a few dancing steps, but quieted when its rider murmured, "Easy."

The person afoot stopped a short distance away. He spoke in a low voice: "Captain. We found no stretch of narrow canyon on the road ahead."

Aha! So they *had* been planning an ambush.

Another voice said, "Very well."

That was Bannom!

"In that case," Bannom continued, "we shall make our assault on their flank. How is the tree cover along the road?"

"Good," said the man afoot. "Excellent even. We could hide the entire company behind one of these trees."

"I am right glad to hear it," said Bannom. "We'll descend here. I want you on foot at least fifty yards downslope. Warn us if the enemy is close enough to hear or see."

I'm close enough to spit on you, thought Ganadarm. (He was exaggerating, but only a little.) He tensed to stand up before he even realized he had decided to do so.

Dusi put a mist-chilled hand on his cheek and shook her head.

Ganadarm clenched his jaw. Bannom, the man who had killed Ugly Lem and ordered all Ganadarm's friends executed, was mounted no more than ten strides away. Ganadarm could cut his horse out from under him before he even realized he was in a fight. If Ganadarm struck quickly, he could end the fight before the rest of the Chumwarl Scouts joined it.

Dusi locked eyes with him.

Ganadarm was not intimidated. His impulse was to stand up and toss her aside. She would fly through the air like a doll.

And then what?

Then the Klindrel would spit her like a hare and that would be the end of the cute little Drelfin whose backside Saboon liked so much. Ganadarm was willing to die slaying Bannom, but he wasn't the sort of man who endangered helpless Drelfin. Well, in point of fact, having seen Dusi cutting up the Klindrel yesterday, Ganadarm had to admit that she was not helpless. But she was still no match for ten Chumwarl Scouts. Ganadarm would have to wait until Dusi went back to warn Saboon.

The man afoot strode away through the bracken. Ganadarm actually caught a glimpse of his back as he faded into the mist. Bannom gave the rest of his men some silent signal, and they began riding down along a line that would intersect the road.

The rearmost riders were still passing by when shouts and screams penetrated the mist. The shouts sounded like men. The screams sounded like Drelfin horses, and perhaps Drelfin themselves. It did not sound like a battle to Ganadarm, for he did not hear metal ringing on metal. No, it sounded like a massacre.

Bannom's men halted to hear better. At the front of the column, Bannom turned his horse and called back, "It seems the Maziban Lancers have caught up to the enemy already. Let us ride to join them."

The Chumwarl Scouts descended at a trot.

CHAPTER 27

Chaos in the Mist

FIGHTING FROM HORSEBACK is more practical for giants. They are stronger than we are, and they have a longer reach. Our mountain stepper is used for advances, retreats, and patrols. But in hand-to-hand combat, patrollers are taught to dismount and fight on foot.

When Captain Sabu sent Ganadarm and Dusi into the forest, no one knew that there would soon be a fight. Tim Hill especially was not planning to fight. But he did dismount, because he reckoned it would be a long wait.

Mister Whiskers dismounted as well and began prowling through the ferns for something to eat. Doefoot was of the opinion that patient horses who carry heavy merchants on their backs should also get something to eat, so Tim tied Doefoot to a salmonberry bush and the little horse began to nip at it.

Tim saw that Sabu had ridden back to confer with Lieutenant Fesu and Captain Josho. No doubt they were discussing the reason for the halt. Josho's curt nod said that he didn't much like the idea, but he had to agree with it. Fesu's nervousness at being so near the Klindrel was translated to the shifting steps of his horse. And it would probably carry over to his soldiers.

This was only Tim's fifth day of military life, but already he understood a few things. Lieutenant Fesu was the most timid, so his company was put in the middle, where the need for snap decisions was least likely. Although his company's captain was dead, Fesu was still called "Lieutenant", which indicated that he was not trusted to make strategic decisions. Captain Sabu's company had taken the vanguard because Sabu was the leader of the cohort and because they had Dusi, who could sense the Klindrel even when the mist and trees hid them. This left Captain Josho's company as the rearguard, which was the best place for him: He was the most eager to get to Roadhouse One, so he would be certain to keep up.

Captain Sabu knew what he was doing. The only problem was that the Passwatch Company was sharing food that the Neargap and Roadhouse Six Companies had intended for themselves.

Among Clanfolk, this would have led to resentment unless a fair exchange was negotiated. The Brownfolk tended to act as though they were all in the same clan, but Tim suspected that even Brownfolk would get angry if the food ran out.

Fortunately, Roadhouse One was only four or five meals away. As long as the soldiers rationed their food for six meals, they would not run out. If things went well.

But Tim had already reckoned out how long it would take the Klindrel to reach Roadhouse One, and as far as he could tell, it mostly depended on how they reacted to the previous day's ambush. If the ambush had slowed them down, then the Klindrel might spend another day or two on the road. But if the ambush sped them up for some reason, the Klindrel would be at Roadhouse One before Sabu's companies could get there. Tim was not pessimistic by nature, but merchants don't achieve success by trusting that things will always work out for the best. Tim was the sort of person who makes contingency plans. He wondered if Sabu had one.

Tim need not have worried about Sabu's contingency plan. The ambush *had* slowed the Klindrel legion down. But it had also made them angry—angry enough to send the Chumwarl Scouts and the Maziban Lancers out to get revenge.

After some discussion, Captain Sabu's conference broke up. Captain Josho nodded to his partners and rode back to tell his lieutenant why they were stopped. Lieutenant Fesu scanned the upslope trees warily, but it was clear that he was done conversing as well. Captain Sabu remained beside him, giving Company Six a more reassuring presence. They had lost their captain, and Sabu knew they needed a confident leader they could follow.

Well, if Sabu was not returning to the fore, Tim would go back to him. He left Doefoot and Mister Whiskers beside the fern-covered road and went to speak with Sabu.

"Good day, Captain Sabu."

"Good day, Tim."

"May I have a word with you?"

"Certainly."

"Have you ever heard the phrase 'contingency plan'?" Tim didn't know the word in the Brownfolk tongue.

"I am not sure, Tim. What is—"

They heard murmurings among the rear guard.

Someone called, "Horses!"

Sabu cocked his head, and Fesu looked to the rear in alarm.

Tim could hear only the tapping and shuffling of the little horses in Neargap Company.

"They're behind us," Fesu said.

From somewhere in the mist, Captain Josho yelled, "Dismount and form a line!"

The rearmost rank of Sabu's company was looking back to Sabu for orders.

"Jathigo: ride back and find out what's happening," Sabu said.

The Brownman nodded and wheeled his horse toward the rear.

"Should we dismount?" another Brownman asked.

"Not yet," said Sabu. "Wait for my—"

"Charge!" roared a Redman's voice from the rear. Heavy hooves thundered through the fog. These were not small horses.

Afoot, Tim could barely see half the middle company. He had no idea what was happening to Josho in the rear.

Tiny horses and big horses whinnied challenges. The Redmen shouted exclamations that seemed to be in no language at all.

Some of Fesu's soldiers had dismounted at Josho's command. Others had remained mounted and were now looking to Fesu and Sabu for orders. In the misty distance, Brownfolk and their horses began screaming.

"Scatter!" Sabu shouted. "Scatter and hide! Regroup at the river!"

He rode toward the thunder of the onrushing enemy shouting, "Regroup at the river!"

Some of Fesu's soldiers who were still mounted turned their horses and began racing through the trees upslope—the wrong direction, but they didn't know that Dusi had sensed Klindrel somewhere up there. Thaki knew. She exhorted Passwatch Company to force their horses through the osiers and across the creek.

Tim turned and ran for Doefoot, who was dancing around the salmonberry bush with her ears back. As Tim puffed along the fern-covered road, heavy hooves galloped behind him, getting closer, closer.

Well, Tim could see no percentage in staying on the road. He ducked into a thimbleberry patch and made himself small. Ten or so full-sized horses passed by, their hooves spreading the tang of exposed soil into the air.

Tim poked his head up to see where he should run. A small knot of mounted, armored Redmen was trying to follow the Brownfolk through the osiers. Tim could hear other riders upslope. Doefoot had pulled free of the salmonberry bush and was disappearing upslope into the trees, dragging her lead rope behind her.

Tim didn't want to be alone and afoot. He ran after his horse. Maybe the rope would tangle on something and he could catch her.

As Tim crashed through the ferns and scrambled over fallen branches, he knew he risked running into the Redmen that Ganadarm and Dusi had been sent to investigate. He did not have time to make a plan for this specific contingency. So he fell back on his universal plan for any contingency: He prayed to Yolim. But despite his prayers (or perhaps because of them—how can we ever truly know?) Doefoot soon outdistanced him, and he found himself alone among the redwoods listening to the cries and screams drifting through the mist.

Tim reckoned he was pretty safe, though. At least, he was as safe as he could be on a battlefield. He heard hoofbeats, big and little, coming from all directions, so there wasn't much percentage in trying to find some place safer. Once the battle was over, he might find his horse. Or somebody's horse. Doefoot was probably not the only one with no rider by now.

He heard a two-footed lope rising above the distant noises of battle. The tread was not exactly heavy, but Tim recognized the gait of a Redman. He peered around a tree, hoping to see the Redman he knew.

"Ganadarm!" he called to the giant running through the mist.

The figure stopped and looked his way. The fog gave the face an alien appearance. Tim feared he had misidentified the runner. Then Ganadarm opened his mouth in a wide smile.

Ganadarm trotted over. "Tim! How goes the battle?"

"Can't say as I know," Tim replied. "I've been trying to stay away from it."

"And I am right glad you have succeeded," said Ganadarm. "But tell me, have you seen Captain Bannom?"

"I don't think so," Tim said. "Of course, I haven't been looking at faces, but the Klindrel I've seen have been armored."

Ganadarm spat. "Bannom will need a hundred armored reinforcements if he wants to kill Ganadarm. But wait: Perhaps this is Bannom now."

A full-sized horse was approaching at a trot. Tim ducked down and burrowed his way into a thick patch of bracken.

"Ganadarm," he whispered. "Hide."

"I'm through hiding," Ganadarm said, and he remained standing in the open with his polished sword drawn.

"Ho there!" cried a voice. And the heavy hooves approached, striking so close to Tim's hiding place that he could feel the earth shake.

Ganadarm stood his ground.

The rider addressed Ganadarm in a tone that sounded somewhat haughty: "Prince Welzenkam has ordered everyone to regroup on the road below."

Oh, thought Tim. *That's right. Ganadarm is a Redman.*

After a moment's pause, Ganadarm said, "That interests me. Will Captain Bannom be there?"

"Your captain is already there," the rider said. "Where is your horse ... or? ... Say ..."

What did the Maziban Lancer want Ganadarm to say? We will never know, for Tim, understanding that the rider's confusion would soon lead to enlightenment, leapt from the bracken and yelled "Blyeah!" right under the horse's nose.

This produced exactly the effect Tim desired. The horse reared, the rider toppled off, and by the time the horse's hooves struck the ground, Tim had moved into position to grab a saddle strap and wedge his boot inside the saddle girth.

In an instant, the lancer was on his feet, drawing his sword, but in that same instant, Tim had clambered up onto the saddle and seized the reins.

Tim cried, "Mount up, Ganadarm!"

Ganadarm vaulted into the saddle behind him. The horse started, and Tim gave it free rein to race through the trees. The black-armored soldier's curses rang out behind them.

Ganadarm's laugh rumbled against Tim's back. "Oh, Tim," he said. "I could have slain him, but what you did was much, much funnier."

CHAPTER 28
Leaves in the Wind

TO STAND AND FIGHT, or to run and hide? This is the question that confronts every soldier in every battle. Standing firm is not always a mark of arrogant foolishness. Running away is not always a mark of selfish cowardice.

The company that runs may save themselves but lose the battle. The general that stands firm may win the battle but lose the war. And even winning the war may be unwise if that victory leads to folly.

In other words, I cannot tell you whether Josho was wise to order his company to form a line and fight, nor whether Sabu was correct to order the cohort to scatter and flee. They did what they thought was best. If you must judge them, remember that the mist was thick. Neither captain knew they faced a hundred mounted lancers.

Dusi, being some distance upslope, was likewise too far away to discern the nature and number of the foe. All she knew with certainty was that Ganadarm had run off and she had twenty mounted scouts between her and the road. She heard Sabu's call to regroup at the river, and she heard Thaki exhorting Passwatch Company to cross the creek below the road. She also heard Children of Knowledge and their horses crying out in pain.

The Chumwarl Scouts crashed through the brush and bracken as they descended toward the road, while crashes in the distance suggested that other riders were coming uphill. The chaos of the battle was noisy, but it did not seem loud. Sounds were muffled by moss and fog, and Dusi felt alone in the mist, removed from her comrades' desperation on the road below.

She was calm. She was scared, but she was calm. She could deal with this. If she kept her wits about her, she could survive. Now what could she do to help her people?

Minds moved about on the road. No one was very close. It sounded like the attack had come from the rear. That would push her people ahead. Dusi reasoned that the best use of her talent would be to scout ahead and ascertain whether they were fleeing toward safety or into a third enemy force.

She ran through the trees, choosing paths where she made little noise, but not worrying about silence. The Klindrel had so many targets below that they were unlikely to pursue her.

Dusi ran, but it was not the flight of panic. She kept her mind open for resonances with other minds, and she listened to what her ears were telling her of the battle below.

Screams and shouts diminished as she left the battle behind. Dusi slowed to a walk and concentrated more on her elemental resonance. No one seemed to be lurking ahead.

She could still hear horses screaming in the distance—giant horses and mountain steppers both. She was at the road, now. She stayed off to the side and looked for a tree with sheltering roots. If she had a good hiding place, she could wait for riders to come by. If they were her people, she could join them. If the riders were the Klindrel, she could get a count and then give a report to Captain Sabu—if she could find him again.

The sudden thought came to her that he might be among the wounded. If he were dead, there was nothing she could do for him, but if he were lying beside the road, bleeding among the ferns while his comrades raced to safety ...

Dusi had to go back. Could she find him? Would she recognize his mind? If he were unconscious, would he have any thoughts at all?

No. No, the thing to do was to follow orders, go to the river, and hope that Sabu had survived the battle unscathed. He would certainly have been clever enough to escape and wise enough to follow Thaki across the creek ...

But he was also brave enough to stand and fight so that his people could flee. Dusi turned back toward the battlefield.

She was being illogical. She was no healer. If Sabu were too wounded to escape, then she would be unable to help him. But Dusi knew that if she went on to the river and Sabu did not appear, she would never forgive herself. She was not an imbecile, but she *was* in love. Perhaps I contradict myself.

Dusi glided from tree to tree, staying close to the road so that she would be able to sense people who might be across the creek. She thought of Sabu and kept her mind open for him. If he were conscious, she would find him. She was using her usual resonance techniques, not the backdoor through the negative Elemental

Realm that would have allowed her to detect Children of Lith.

When she heard the hooves, she was in the open, between trees. They were giant horses, coming down the road at an easy trot. Hoping their steps would mask hers, Dusi continued her advance, reaching the base of the next redwood just before the riders arrived.

Five black-armored mounted men passed by. The fresh blood on their long spears only strengthened Dusi's resolve to find Sabu. As soon as they had faded into the mist, she moved toward the next tree.

Something snapped a branch upslope. Dusi crouched in the ferns, closed her eyes, and focused her concentration on the noise. She found a mind, at the edge of her range, descending toward the road. It was not a Child of Lith. She ran to intercept.

As Dusi drew nearer, she became more certain that the mind was Sabu. He was moving swiftly, still mounted.

"Captain!" she called.

Sabu's little horse snorted and the dainty hooves scuttled to a stop.

"Dusi!"

She hurried to meet him.

"Five Klindrel on the road," she reported.

"Take my horse and head upslope," Sabu said, dismounting.

Dusi shook her head. Now that she had found him, she would not leave him.

"That is my order," Sabu said.

"We should stay together," Dusi said.

"We will debate my decision at another time," Sabu said. "Ride high and rejoin me later."

"Yes, Captain, but—"

Heavy hoofbeats sounded on the road, and in the forest.

Dusi thought fast. She slapped the mountain stepper on the rump, sending it running away through the redwoods. She ducked and hid herself among the ferns. Sabu crouched down beside her, his eyes glaring hot fire.

Dusi shrugged. It was a good plan. She could defend her actions later.

"Ho!" cried a voice from the road.

"Tanmarv, come back!"

"But I saw one!"

"But you won't catch it. Not unless you ride hard. And we're a long way from our remounts."

Tanmarv replied with a grudging, "Aye." His horse crashed back toward the road, and the riders continued their return to the scene of the battle.

"Those were the five I saw," Dusi whispered.

"I heard one more in the forest," Sabu said.

Dusi nodded and listened. As her ears followed the hoofsteps of the lancers diminishing in the distance, she caught a resonance with Sabu, who was listening to the same. This amplified her resonance with a third mind, also listening. She did not think it was a Klindrel, for she could sense it sharply and clearly. But then, in the same vicinity, she found another mind, obscured by the haze that Lith gave to his Children. So one Klindrel and one Child of Knowledge—a patroller had been taken prisoner. They were nearby.

Dusi looked at Sabu and signed, *One horse; two riders.*

Sabu raised his eyebrows.

Dusi signed, *One friend; one enemy.*

Sabu thought a moment, then nodded.

Dusi pointed the direction.

Sabu moved up onto the balls of his feet and motioned that Dusi should follow him. They left their cover.

They heard the horse clomping through the ferns at a walk. Sabu quickened the pace. Reaching the base of a redwood, Sabu drew his battleblade. Dusi did likewise.

The enemy horse clomped around their tree.

"That was close," Tim said.

"Very," agreed Ganadarm amicably.

"Could be yet another bunch ahead," Tim said.

"Perhaps," said Ganadarm. The idea did not seem to trouble him.

Sabu sheathed his blade and eased his way out into the open.

The horse snorted.

"Easy!" cried Tim.

"Saboon!" bellowed Ganadarm. "What are you doing here?"

"I look for my scouts," Sabu said wryly.

Dusi blushed and sheathed her blade. She stepped out beside Sabu.

"And Dusi!" said Ganadarm. "Well, it seems you have found us, Captain. Would you like to ride?"

"Yes, I would," said Sabu. He looked at Dusi. "I lost my horse."

"Sorry," she mumbled. But at least her plan had worked.

"I'm not sure this horse can carry all of us," Tim said.

"That will be no problem," Sabu said.

Ganadarm looked from Sabu to Dusi and he began to chuckle.

"What am I missing?" Tim asked.

Ganadarm leapt from the horse's back and clasped his hands into a step to help Sabu up onto the saddle. "I think Captain Saboon's scouts will be walking."

CHAPTER 29

Rendezvous

THAKI SAVED PASSWATCH COMPANY by shepherding them into the osiers and across the creek. Sabu and his squad rejoined them shortly after noon. They proceeded to the Redwood River.

Company Six had scattered in all directions. About half of them caught up to Passwatch Company along the way, and survivors continued to trickle into camp over the course of the evening. Lieutenant Fesu was presumed dead, but he was not. He eventually made his way to the river and spent the summer in a frontier village, hosted by a family that owned a nice herd of dairy sheep. He later married one of their daughters and became a lumberjack.

Captain Josho, however, was never seen again. Only half of Neargap Company survived the initial charge, and only eleven of them reached Sabu's rendezvous point on the river that evening. Four of those who missed the rendezvous survived in the mountains for a week. They eventually teamed up with a mining gang to form a small resistance unit.

Spirits were high among the Passwatch patrollers once they had Captain Sabu back, but Sabu himself was stricken by the heavy losses to the other companies.

Dusi wanted to comfort him, but she didn't know what to say. She had guilt of her own—guilt she did not want to talk about. She kept it inside. This was not wise.

Dusi fell asleep early that evening. She had not actually forgotten about her nightmares, but she was too exhausted to care. And when her mother demanded to speak to her, she was too exhausted to resist.

"You killed them, you know," her mother said.

Dusi sat up on her cot. It had been her father's, before she was born. It was still too big for her, even though she was eight years old.

"Killed whom, Mother?"

"Neargap Company, Company Six. Watching for the Klindrel was your job."

"No," said Dusi. "I was in front. The attack was from behind."
How did her mother know about that? Wasn't she dead?

"What did you do when you heard the fighting, Dusi?"

"There was nothing I could do."

"Wasn't there? Don't you have a blade?"

Dusi drew her blade, but not from a scabbard on her hip. She reached into her chiton and withdrew it from a secret sheath that lay snug along her belly. She held it up to the candlelight. Smooth, sharp edges, no serration. It was not a battleblade, but a deathblade. Tiny drops of blood dripped from its point.

"Their blood is on your blade," her mother said. "You could have run to fight beside them. Instead ..."

"It was too late," Dusi said. "Captain Sabu had already given the order to retreat."

"Ah, yes. 'Captain' Sabu. He tells his people to retreat, and then he comes to find you."

"He cares for me."

"Of course he does." Dusi's mother smiled. "You can use that, you know."

"I don't want to use it," Dusi said.

"You don't?"

"No."

"Are you certain? Because if you wanted, you could use his feelings to distract him from his duty, couldn't you? You could lead him off into the forest when his people need him most."

"I didn't do that."

"Why was he with you, instead of leading his company?"

"Because— That wasn't my decision."

Dusi's mother shrugged. "You led him to abandon his people."

"No."

"No? But he *did* abandon them for you. If you wanted him to do so, then you deceived him."

"I didn't deceive him. I didn't want him to come for me."

"No? Well, then, that means you have corrupted him, broken him, without even trying. After a defeat like that, no one will want him for a captain."

"That's not true!" Dusi shouted. She drew back her deathblade to strike.

Her mother laughed and turned her back. "Go ahead," she said over her shoulder. "I won't be the last person you murder."

Someone was shaking her awake. Dusi opened her eyes, fearing she would have to explain herself to Sabu. But no. It was Tim.

"You shouted," he said in Dusi's language.

"I'm sorry," Dusi said. "It was just a nightmare."

Tim nodded. "I know. Yesterday was a bad day. But now it is time for a new one."

Dark shapes of patrollers were rousing themselves in the gray river fog. The red moon was not up, but there would soon be enough sunlight to see by. What about her turn at watch? Had Thaki let her skip watch?

Tim handed her a raw potato. "This is your breakfast ration."

Dusi nodded and wiped it off on her leather tunic. Leather tunic, not linen chiton. She patted the hilt of her battleblade. Good. She still had it. With a crunch, she bit into her breakfast ration.

Looking around the camp, she thought she saw a few patrollers that had rejoined them overnight. Bu, the healer, was checking people's wounds. Dusi went to look for the stablemaster, to see if she could be assigned a horse.

Captain Sabu gave the order to move out after breakfast. So many horses had been lost in the previous day's confusion that Sabu ended up leaving six patrollers at the rendezvous spot to wait for stragglers. He left Bu with them in case anyone arrived wounded. (This group did find a few stragglers, but they never caught up to the Road Patrol. They spent the summer in a village downstream.)

The rest of the patrollers rode for Roadhouse One. Tim also had a mountain stepper, although Doefoot had been lost. No one had seen Mister Whiskers, either.

Ganadarm proudly rode the horse that had previously served the Maziban Lancers. To anyone who would listen, he told the story of how Tim had courageously confiscated the mount.

Dusi and Thaki rode in front, with Thaki watching for ambush and Dusi using her senses, trying not to think about her nightmare. After a time, Ganadarm rode up to join them.

"I will help you watch for enemies," he said.

"This is fog," said Thaki.

"Yes," said Ganadarm. "I know."

"We not watch," said Thaki. "We listen."

"Ah, yes," said Ganadarm. "Captain Saboon says you have very good ears."

"Not so good when your horse does his big feet," said Thaki. "Clomp, clomp, clomp."

"Oh," said Ganadarm. "Well, good thing I'm here to help you listen, then."

"Yes," said Thaki, rolling her eyes. "Good thing."

Dusi wondered if Ganadarm knew Thaki was making jokes at his expense. Perhaps his people didn't make jokes.

"You know," said Ganadarm, "this is a very strong horse. I'm right glad that Tim captured it. Little Tim!"

"Yes, yes," said Thaki. "You say. But Dusi and I are talk now."

"We are?" Dusi wasn't sure she wanted to talk.

"Yes, we are," said Thaki, slipping into the language that Ganadarm couldn't understand.

"Oh, well, don't mind me," said Ganadarm. "I'll just ride here and help you listen."

Dusi looked up at him. His eyes twinkled. Perhaps he did know a few things about jokes.

She did not have time to puzzle over Ganadarm. Thaki was serious when she said she wanted to talk.

"Sabu is worried about you," Thaki said.

"Oh?"

"He says you've been having nightmares."

Dusi shrugged. "Everyone has nightmares."

"Including you?"

Dusi shrugged. Then nodded.

"Do you—"

"No," said Dusi. "I don't want to talk about it."

"Why not?"

Because I don't want Sabu to know that my soul is bound to a demon, Dusi thought. But she said nothing.

"So he was right," Thaki said. "It *is* the nightmares that are troubling you."

Dusi shook her head. "Don't you think *everyone* is troubled by this war?"

That was a clever redirection. It implied that she was having nightmares about the battles, not about her mother. It was the sort of deception that would make her mother proud.

Thaki nodded slowly. "Yes. Yes, I do. But has it occurred to you that you might be special?"

"In what way?"

"In the way Sabu thinks of you."

"What? … Oh."

"If you have problems, then he has problems. And I'm his lieutenant right now. I can't let him have problems."

Thaki was right. Dusi was a problem.

"Thaki, I'm sorry."

Thaki shook her head. "You don't need to apologize. But if there is anything you need, anything you want to talk about, you must let me know."

"No," said Dusi. "I can handle it."

"But you don't have to handle it alone," said Thaki.

"But I will," said Dusi.

Thaki shook her head sadly. "Have it your way, rookie."

Dusi looked up to see what Ganadarm thought of all this. He was smiling at the redwoods.

"Oh," Thaki added, "and I'm taking you off night watch so you can get more sleep. People's lives may depend on your mental health."

So Thaki was qualified to judge mental health? *Dusi* was the one with affinity for Thought. She was master of her mind.

Dusi put her mind to the task of thinking things through. And the more she thought about it, the more she thought that Thaki was right. Dusi and Sabu distracted each other. If Sabu felt the same tingle she felt whenever he touched her arm, if he felt the same flood of joy she felt whenever she saw his smile … well then she was causing problems.

Lives were at stake. The Road Patrol needed Sabu to make good decisions with a clear head. He could not do that if he was silly over some rookie.

Then, too, there were facts Thaki did not know. Dusi's soul was tainted by the Deceiver. She could not be certain that all her choices were truly her own. *She* had not intended to lead Sabu astray, but she no longer had full control of her mind. And what would happen if her mother got hold of kind and noble Sabu? Dusi had evil inside her, and that was a danger to the man she loved.

Dusi *would* defeat that evil. The Deceiver would *not* win. But she had to keep Sabu out of her internal battle—for his sake and for the sake of those he led.

Dusi reached a conclusion. It did not please her, but she was strong enough, and it was the only right thing to do: Until she had control of her soul, she would not let Sabu grow close to her.

CHAPTER 30

Hierarchy

ROADHOUSE ONE sits near the Redwood River in the heart of the Redwood Forest. It has the usual barracks, stables, and roadhouse proper, but most of its buildings are outside the palisade. The training barracks, winter stables, storage cellars, wagon sheds, smithies, and headquarters building take up more space than would be practical to enclose. Sitting among the fields and villages of civilization, far from the Klindrel Pass, Roadhouse One has never been threatened by bandits. (By thieves from the villages, occasionally, but never by bandits.) In fact, one could say that the roadhouses fall along a spectrum: Passwatch perches high among the cold pines, defending the road against bandits from across the border; Roadhouse One sprawls along the foggy banks of the Redwood River, supplying the other roadhouses and organizing the maintenance crews.

By the time the Passwatch Garrison arrived at Roadhouse One, most of the road crews, wagon drivers, and stable hands were already on the road, withdrawing downriver. Sabu's people were given cots to sleep on for the night, but the quartermaster warned them not to get too comfortable.

The next morning, a gong rang to announce the start of the day. Sabu was summoned to the headquarters building while he was still putting on his moccasins.

Sabu had wintered at Roadhouse One as a rookie, but this was his first visit to the headquarters building. It was smaller than the roadhouse proper, because it did not need to accommodate giants.

A clerk met Sabu at the door and gave him directions to Patrol Commander Shiboko's study.

Sabu was confused. "I was told to see Army Liaison Visho."

"Ah, yes," said the clerk. "I misspoke. The room is his, now."

"Ah," said Sabu. "Very well."

The room in question, whoever it was, had a large sunward window. A little later in the day it would, perhaps, have provided some light, but on this dark and misty morning, the window was shuttered and the room was lit by three oil lamps. Only a few books remained on the shelves. The embroidered floor cushions lay in a heap in a corner, as though discarded. The hardwood table also sat off to one side, covered in curled-up messages and reports. In the center of the room, Army Liaison Visho had set up a writing board and a portable camp stool.

Visho was a flabby man with a face like raw bread dough. His fine woolen chiton was pinned with a gaudy brass badge at each shoulder. His blue eyes sparkled with good humor as though he were enjoying a private joke. He extended an ink-stained hand inviting Sabu to enter the room.

Sabu entered and reached for the sliding door. Visho shook his head, so Sabu left the door open.

"Sabu of Passwatch reporting."

Visho smiled. "Yes, Lieutenant, I know who you are."

He stepped over to the square table. From the myriad of scrolled papers, he selected one. "And I've read the account you wrote for me last night. You've had an interesting week."

"Yes," said Sabu.

"You may call me 'Commander'. I have taken over the Road Patrol."

He had? Could he do that?

"Yes, Commander Visho."

"And I trust I may call you 'Lieutenant'?"

Sabu hesitated only an instant. "Yes, of course."

"I know you assumed command of three incomplete companies," said Visho. "However, the Road Patrol account book—" he gestured at one of the few books left on the shelves, "—still lists your rank as lieutenant."

"Yes, of course," said Sabu.

"Good," said Visho. His eyes searched Sabu's face. "I'm glad we understand each other." Perhaps the sparkle in his eyes was not good humor. Perhaps it was the gleam of hard steel.

Visho returned Sabu's report to its place on the table. "You are in the army now, Lieutenant Sabu—under command of Army Headquarters in Hicho."

In truth? From what Sabu knew, the "army" was just an atrophied branch of the Hicho police force and "Army Headquarters" was a small handful of people charged with providing liaison officers between the Hicho Guard and the Road Patrol.

"You will find," said Visho, planting himself in the center of the Patrol Commander's study, "that we in the army are a little more particular about rank."

Sabu said, "I see."

Visho shook his head. "I am not certain you do, Lieutenant. When you lead a small garrison of soldiers, perhaps you can allow yourself to be … informal. But we are now at war. Discipline must be tight. Hierarchies must be maintained."

"Of course."

"So in the future, when someone in your command is exploring the possibility of reassignment, she should not bring the matter to me. She should bring the matter to you. And you, if you agree, should bring the matter to my adjutant. Is that clear?"

"Please pardon me, Commander Visho, but now I am confused."

Visho raised his eyebrows.

"Did someone in my command ask to be reassigned?" Sabu asked.

Visho shook his head sadly. "You see, Lieutenant? That is what I mean about discipline. She should have come to you first, don't you agree?"

"Of course," said Sabu.

"I am glad we understand each other."

"But who asked to be reassigned?"

"Your mind finder spoke to me yesterday evening."

"Dusi? Why did she—? What did she say?"

"She offered to join any scout unit I might be putting together."

"Ah," said Sabu. That was— Well, it was disturbing because she hadn't spoken to him about it. But it was also logical. "And will she be reassigned?"

Visho made a disgusted face and shook his head. "We have no scout units to assign her to. We are withdrawing. We don't need to scout our own territory."

"Of course not, Commander."

"We don't need scouts. We need defenders! The quality of our troops is abysmal."

Sabu didn't like the sound of that.

Visho raised a placating hand. "Oh, I'm not blaming you, Lieutenant. You followed your captain's orders. You did your job.

No, the trouble started here, in this office." Visho gestured to include the barren bookshelves, the shuttered window, the seating cushions discarded in the corner.

"Shiboko should have been able to hold the Klindrel off for weeks," Visho said. "The Road Patrol held nine fortified positions along a narrow road. The eighth was overrun last night, and the enemy is poised to take the ninth this morning—without a fight! I considered making a defense here, at the gateway to the Redwood Valley, but our fortifications are ludicrously inadequate, and we have the river at our back."

Visho shook his head. "No, this is no place to make a stand. I'll not sacrifice more of your comrades for Shiboko's folly."

Looked at in that light, Sabu thought perhaps he should be glad Visho had taken over. Except that the Road Patrol had a duty to defend the road.

Visho said, "I want your company ready to march in half a lithic."

So I'm not captain, but it's still my company?

"Understood," Sabu said.

"We'll march toward Hicho until we meet up with the main body of the army. Along the way, my adjutant and I will be doing some reorganizing. Some of the Road Patrol will be assigned to new companies where they can learn the combat techniques necessary to fight a war."

"And others?" Sabu asked.

Visho fixed Sabu with a measuring eye. "I was not entirely displeased with your report, Lieutenant. In fact, I was impressed."

"Thank you, Commander," Sabu said, to be polite.

"Your mind finder, however undisciplined she may be, had a good idea. Oh, not scouts. We shan't need scouts. But we might need skirmishers. I think your company's skills will be exactly what we need."

"Thank you, Commander. We will give you our best."

Visho smiled. "I am certain you will, Lieutenant."

Lieutenant. Sabu didn't want to ask, but he had to know: "Will we be assigned a new garrison captain?"

Visho shook his head. "You no longer have a fortress, so you are no longer a garrison. Your skirmishers will be a stand-alone company commanded by a lieutenant."

"I see," Sabu said. *Why do I feel so grateful?* "Forgive me for being unfamiliar with the structure of the army," he added.

"We are improvising a little," Visho admitted. "I expect most of our army will be drawn from the farmers on the plain—people with no training whatsoever. Some cohorts and companies will be formed ad hoc. But the important thing is: We will have hierarchy. We will have discipline."

"Of course," said Sabu. He was saying that a lot to this army liaison officer. But then, whatever had happened between Visho and Shiboko, it was not Sabu's business to interfere. Visho was right: Sabu *was* just a lieutenant.

"Is there anything else?" Sabu asked.

"Actually," said Visho, "I do have one more important detail. I have decided to allow the Child of Wealth and the Child of Lith to remain attached to your company."

"Thank you," said Sabu, because Visho seemed to think he had done Sabu a great favor.

Visho dismissed him, and he left gratefully. He went to the roadhouse dining hall to tell his people they would be moving out immediately. They took the news well. Sabu felt sorry to be abandoning their last roadhouse, but he could not blame his people for embracing the idea of putting off the next battle. Or perhaps they were just in a good mood because there were raisins in the porridge.

Thaki appeared at his side with a steaming hot bowl of the stuff and handed it to him. "We'll get ready," she said. "You eat."

Sabu laughed.

"Something amuses you?"

Sabu shook his head. "Remind me to give you Commander Visho's views on hierarchy," he said.

Thaki nodded. "Certainly. *After* you've eaten your porridge."

Sabu looked about the room. "Where did Dusi go?" he asked.

"She was the first one out the door," Thaki said. "You can talk to her on the road."

Sabu shrugged and sat down cross legged at the nearest table.

"Captain Sabu!" It was Tim, speaking in his own language.

"I am lieutenant, now, Tim. But what can I do for you?"

"Did I understand you to say that we will be retreating all the way to the plain?"

"Until we meet the Hicho Guard," said Sabu. "But the plain is halfway."

"But Captain—Lieutenant—your people have a lot of villages between here and the plain."

"Yes," said Sabu.

"Cap—" Tim took a breath to calm himself. He put a hand on Sabu's shoulder. "Sabu, it isn't right. And you know it. The Klindrel will raid every one of those villages. They will take your people's food. They will kill and butcher your people's livestock."

"I know all this, Tim. But they have an army. Our army will be forming on the plain."

"But you could make a stand. The Klindrel have only two months of food. And we know they are using your forts as supply depots. A few well-timed raids in the mountains could stop this army before they reach your cropland."

"That might work," Sabu admitted.

"I know it would," Tim said. "The Klindrel are cutting it too close."

"What are they cutting close?"

"I mean that their strategy depends on stealing food from you if they want to keep their soldiers fed. If they can't get to your cropland, they can't win."

Sabu saw the logic in that. "Tim, you are thinking good. But we have not the army here. The army has decided where it will be. And where I will be."

"But you Brownfolk aren't mindless Klindrel soldiers," Tim said. "You talk to each other. If you have a good idea, they will listen to you."

"Tim, you have a good idea," Sabu said. "But I am not a leader now. I am just a lieutenant. I will take your idea to the people who lead here, but I think they have already decided."

Sabu was right, of course. Roadhouse One was abandoned before the morning's second lithic.

CHAPTER 31

The River Road

THE ROAD PATROL abandoned Roadhouse One and set off at ox-wagon pace. This was hard on the morale of men and women who were accustomed to riding mountain steppers all summer long, and it was hard on the morale of the mountain steppers, who found the slow pace and flat terrain physically uncomfortable. The stablemasters pleaded with former Patrol Commander Shiboko to intercede on the horses' behalf, but Shiboko would only say that the Road Patrol was at war and had to defer to Commander Visho.

Sabu got along with Commander Visho by staying out of his way. Visho seemed pleased with Passwatch Company, for he put them in the vanguard and allowed them to ride ahead at a more comfortable pace.

The canyon of the upper Redwood River is only sparsely populated, but compared with the wilds of Passwatch, it seems like civilization. Wherever the canyon widens enough to leave some space between the river and the mountains, one can find a village. Sturdy wooden houses line the road. High fences protect vegetable gardens from the deer. Fields of flax, potatoes, and cabbage are crammed into the flat land between the houses and the apple orchards on the slopes.

As the survivors of the Road Patrol rode through these villages, people turned out along the road to watch them. Small children smiled at the procession of dainty horses, but their parents wore grim faces.

Part of Sabu's job as leader of the vanguard was to find a place for the Road Patrol to camp. Tim Hill proved to be a valuable asset in these situations. He seemed to know someone at every village. Tim did need a portion of the Road Patrol's treasury to grease the wheels of negotiation, but twice the Road Patrol was given a campsite for free, and once the villagers even turned out to dig the latrine pits.

Sabu's company often reached the evening's campsite before midday. This could have left them with idle time, but Visho had made it clear that he wanted all patrollers to be training. Sabu asked Perga to train Passwatch Company in battle line tactics every afternoon. Perga spent every evening studying relevant chapters from Terkisho's *Theory of War*.

Sabu spent his evenings talking to his people. He would have liked some time to talk with Dusi alone, but her zeal made that impossible.

On the first day, Dusi volunteered to ride back and inform the rest of the Road Patrol where they would be camping. On the second day, Dusi volunteered to help the cooks. On the third day, Dusi asked if she could practice the Klindrel language with Ganadarm and Tim. On the fourth day, Dusi joined another company's evening drills.

Sabu almost told her "no" that time. He was certain that Visho would think it highly irregular for a patroller from one company to drill with another. But Dusi said she wanted to get better, and Sabu could find no logical reason to forbid it.

On the fifth day, the Road Patrol crossed the Farbridge. The creaking wooden bridge seemed springier than Sabu remembered it, but this was the first time he had ever crossed with a company of patrollers and horses.

The Redwood River narrows at the Farbridge, then drops over a three-story cataract. It is not the gentlest stretch of river on which to build a bridge, but a bridge there is necessary: Above the Farbridge, the arable land is on the left side of the river; below the bridge, it is on the right.

Farbridge is also the name of the town they arrived in after crossing. Tim's contact was Fishurba, a tall, keen-witted woman with arms like knotty juniper. Being a blacksmith, she lived in town, but her brother, a farmer, had a sheep meadow that he didn't need to graze again until Greenmonth. Tim compensated Fishurba's brother for potential loss of forage (due to oxen, mountain steppers, and moccasin traffic) and the Road Patrol once again had a place to camp.

Sabu hadn't seen Dusi all morning because she had experienced some trouble with her saddle which caused her to fall to the back of the company. At the sheep meadow outside Farbridge, Dusi volunteered to dig the latrine pits. Then they had drills. Dusi joined the cooking squad, too, but Thaki sent her away from the cook fire as soon as it was Passwatch Company's turn to eat.

"Sit down, eat, and rest a while," Thaki told her, casting a significant glance at Sabu.

Sabu stood there staring at Dusi, holding his baked potato in his handkerchief, hoping she would sit some place where they could have a little privacy. But Dusi only gave him a nervous glance before going over to sit with Ganadarm, Tim, and Hikafa.

Sabu had seen quiet Hikafa in the company of Ganadarm frequently. It was a good combination. The giant liked to talk, and Hikafa liked to listen. And after losing Jamidu at Neargap, Hikafa needed a friend.

Sabu joined them and sat down beside Dusi. It wasn't private time, but he would take what he could get.

"I don't think I'll ever see him again," Tim said.

Ganadarm patted Tim on the back. "Fear not. Mister Whiskers is a survivor."

"But we crossed the river," Tim said.

Hikafa nodded.

Ganadarm shrugged. "He can use the bridge."

"I reckon the bridge would scare him," Tim said. "It's high, and the water runs fast underneath. He's just a little animal."

Dusi patted Tim on the shoulder.

Sabu patted Dusi on her shoulder.

She stiffened.

Ganadarm asked, "Saboon, is that bridge the only way across the river?"

What was wrong? Why didn't Dusi want a friendly pat?

Sabu realized Ganadarm had asked him a question.

Tim answered for him. "Aye, it is." He made a wry face. "I've paid enough tolls here that it would have been cheaper to buy the bridge."

Ganadarm said, "Then you should make your stand here, Saboon. You should defend this crossing."

"Commander Visho discusses that with the town people tonight," said Sabu.

"Good," said Ganadarm. "Tell him I will be in the first rank."

Tim asked, "You reckon he'll force a battle here?"

Hikafa looked up from his potato. Clearly, Sabu's answer interested him.

Sabu shook his head. "I think no battle. Visho wants no fighting until we meet our army."

"I see," said Tim. "The townsfolk aren't willing to defend the bridge, either. At least, that's what Fishurba said."

"But you cannot afford to miss this chance," said Ganadarm. "On the open field, the Klindrel can surround us, but on a bridge we shall be strong!"

Sabu shrugged. "When Visho tells me, I tell you. But I think he will say no fighting."

Ganadarm shook his head. "Ah, that is a shame. Wouldn't you agree, Tim?"

"Well, I don't much care for fighting."

"But your heart is fierce!" Ganadarm said.

"It is?"

Ganadarm began to enumerate Tim's exploits. Sabu would have been interested to learn why Ganadarm thought Tim was fierce, but his mind was not really on the two foreigners nor their conversation. Sensing that Ganadarm was expounding, Sabu thought he had an opportunity to talk to Dusi.

He shifted closer to her and murmured, under cover of Ganadarm's monologue, "Dusi, I would like to speak with you alone for a moment, if I may."

Her dark eyes showed fear, and Sabu realized that it was not his imagination. He made her uncomfortable.

"About what?" she asked.

About everything, Sabu thought. *Now I see it all. It has been no accident that I haven't had a chance to talk with you. You have been avoiding me. But why?*

"About, ah ..." Sabu groped for words.

You're afraid of me. Have I done something wrong? And if I have, do I still have time to fix it?

"Why do you keep volunteering for so much work?" Sabu asked.

"I just want to do my part," Dusi said. "I want to be useful."

What are you hiding?

"Yes," said Sabu. "Of course."

"... crashed through the gate in a cloud of flame!" Ganadarm said to Hikafa, "rescuing everyone single-handedly ..."

"Is that all you wanted to talk about?" Dusi asked.

No.

"Because Perga is done eating," Dusi said, "and I asked him to give me lessons in the two-blade technique."

"Ah," said Sabu. "Of course. Don't let me keep you."

Dusi left, still holding half her potato.

Ganadarm began describing how Tim had unhorsed a Maziban Lancer.

Perhaps I am letting my emotions confuse me, Sabu thought. *Let's look at this logically. Dusi wants to be useful. For the last five days, we haven't really needed her special talent. So it is logical that she would seek to improve herself in other ways, to make herself more versatile.*

That's what I've been doing wrong. I haven't been paying enough attention to her. When I took her out on training runs, it made her feel special, and now she looks for more training. Perhaps she is not trying to get away from me at all. Perhaps if I just reached out to her …

But that was not what her eyes had told him. Her lips had said she just wanted to be useful, but her eyes had been afraid, her back had been tense.

Sabu was a lieutenant. Understanding his subordinates was his job. And he was good at it. True, his feelings for Dusi sometimes clouded his judgment, but now he saw it clearly: Dusi wanted to avoid him.

CHAPTER 32
Spirits

SLEEP IS NOT UNCONSCIOUSNESS. Sleep is a time of relaxation, during which one's spirit is allowed to spill outside its waking shape. The souls of the dreamers writhe and twist above their bodies, like steam from a cup of hot tea dancing in the windowlight. If these souls touch, they can influence each other—that is why you will sometimes have the same dreams as the people you sleep beside—but dreams are mostly influenced by flows of Thought and Emotion through the Elemental Realms.

The flow through the Elemental Realms is turbulent. Eddies of Thought spin through our world as they tumble from Creation to Destruction. These elemental thoughts push against our sleeping minds, but our minds also push back. When we allow our souls to touch the Elemental Realms, the Thought that flows through us is shaped by our beliefs, our experiences, and our desires.

Dusi dreamed of Sabu swimming beside her as she bathed in the river. In the real world, the river under the Farbridge was much too fast to be safe for bathing, but in Dusi's dream, the water flowed slowly and gently. The place was more like the bathing shallows of Flaxfield Ford, the riverside village where Dusi had grown up after leaving Hicho. Sunlight shone through the needles of the redwoods towering overhead. The eddies of the river spoke to each other in liquid murmurs.

Sabu rolled over on his back and floated downstream. Looking lazily up at the sky, he asked Dusi why he had never seen her naked. Dusi looked down at herself and discovered she wore her trousers and tunic, even though she was bathing. She didn't want Sabu to see *her*. She wanted him to see her clothes.

"People will see what they believe to be true," Dusi's mother told her. "Give them reason to believe the best, and they will never suspect the worst."

"Thank you, Mother. That is good advice." These words came from another Dusi—a chiton-wearing eight-year-old sitting on the bank.

"It's not good advice," said Dusi—the real Dusi. "If one

always strives to do good, then one need not worry about what others believe."

Her mother shook her head sadly. "I'm afraid, my daughter, that striving is not sufficient. I wanted to be good. You know I did."

They stood once more in their third-floor apartment. The warm glow of the hanging oil lamp revealed the sheen of fresh blood on her mother's chiton.

"But when my time came," her mother said, "I was judged by the result of my actions, not by the good I had been striving for."

"It was not your time," Dusi said. "If you had lived longer, perhaps you would have forsaken the Deceiver. You still had a chance to be good. But the assassin took that chance from you."

"That is so," said Dusi's mother. "But do you know, Dusi? I do not regret it."

"No?"

"No. For you see, my connection to the All-Knowing Master gave me a connection to you. I died, Dusi, but I did not leave you. I have watched your progress every day. And, Dusi, do you know? I am proud of you."

The words took Dusi by surprise. The idea that her mother had watched over her filled her with gladness.

"Why didn't you say anything?" Dusi asked. "I felt so alone in school."

"Dusi, I couldn't say anything. You were not yet ready to let me into your heart."

"Mother, I have always loved you."

"You loved me as your mother. But you did not know *me*."

That was true. As a child, with no basis for comparison, Dusi had thought it was normal that her mother could read her mind and manipulate her thoughts. She had expected to learn such skills herself someday. When her mother left the apartment after dark to visit with secret friends, Dusi had complained, but she had not known these visits were unusual. And she had not known who those friends were.

Even after her uncle had explained that her mother had been serving the Deceiver, that some of the exercises she had asked Dusi to practice were forbidden knowledge, that she had murdered Dusi's father—even after Dusi understood that her mother had not been normal at all, she still had not understood why. Why had her mother done those things?

"But now you know," her mother said, in the dream that was not truly a dream but actually a contact between Dusi's soul and the Netherworld. "Now you understand that deception was my nature—a part of me I could not change, a trait I was born with. You know the pleasure of springing a trap well-laid. You know the necessity of using truth to distract from that which you must keep hidden. You know that 'lie' is too clumsy a word for the many paths one can take through the forest of truth. And to understand why I chose my path, all you need to know is that all the paths lead to the same place. Dusi, you will join me when you die. But until then, you have many, many choices before you. Don't make stupid choices. Be the smart girl I can be proud of."

Dusi went walking through the forest then. Some paths would lead to her mother. Some paths would lead to Sabu by the river. Some paths just wound deeper into the forest. Which was the smart path? Did they truly all lead to the same place?

Where do you want your path to lead? asked a voiceless thought. It was not in her dream. It was a thought from outside—a thought pushing her out of her dream and toward wakefulness.

"I thought you lived on the mining road," Dusi said, still half in her dream.

I am the entire forest, the spirit said. *You sleep in the shadow of my domain.*

"Why haven't I seen you since?" Dusi asked.

Because you were not looking? I was all around you.

"Have you no form like mine?" Dusi asked. She had seen spirits take the shape of people or animals before. Not all of them did, but some could.

I am not a single animal or tree, said the spirit of the Redwood Forest. *I exist wherever my trees cast their shade.*

"But I haven't sensed you when I was looking for other minds."

I had nothing to say to you.

"But you do now?"

I need your help.

"In truth?" Dusi was intrigued. "I could help you?"

You can, said the spirit. *I am glad you wish to.*

"I do," said Dusi. "What do you need?"

I need you to go here. The impression of a place flashed into her mind: the sound of a small stream crashing over rocks, the smell of osiers and streamside willows, moss-covered rocks pressing against her knees.

"I'm sorry," said Dusi. "I don't know where—"

Actually, though, she remembered kneeling on those rocks and drinking from that stream. She asked, "Is that the brook where we stopped for water yesterday afternoon?"

It is.

"I didn't recognize it in the dark," she said.

It is gloom, said the nature spirit. *Early morning gloom. For it is morning there, just as it is in the meadow where you sleep.*

"And you need me to go to that brook?"

Yes.

Dusi thought about it. It was on the other side of the bridge.

"And once I get there? Then what?"

Do you trust me? the spirit asked.

"Yes," said Dusi.

Then just go, the spirit said. *It is important.*

"I will need permission," Dusi said, waking up.

She went to look for Lieutenant Sabu.

Sabu was standing in the morning gloom, listening to Vahi, the Passwatch stablemaster, give an assessment of the horses. Sabu spotted Dusi at once, focusing on her with such intensity that Vahi broke off in mid-sentence.

"Pardon me for interrupting," Dusi said as she approached.

"What is it?" asked Sabu, his eyes searching her face.

"Lieutenant, I would like to request a … diplomatic assignment." Dusi was not quite certain how else to justify it.

"I was not aware any such assignments were available," Sabu said.

"Well," said Dusi, "I may have found one. Or rather, it found me. You see, I was contacted by a nature spirit while I slept. And it asked me to return to the place where we stopped for water yesterday."

"On the other side of the bridge?"

"Yes."

The stablemaster looked from one to the other, worried.

"Our last report was that the Klindrel hold Roadhouse One and could arrive in Farbridge today," Sabu said.

"Yes," said Dusi.

"Did this spirit say why it wished you to go back there?"

"No," said Dusi. "It just asked me to do so."

"I wish it had spoken to me," Sabu said.

"Lieutenant, when I spoke with the spirit the last time, it warned me of the approaching cavalry. If it is asking for a favor now ... well, on the one hand, I may have incurred some kind of debt, and on the other hand, it may be attempting to help us again."

"Can they help us? I thought nature spirits were neutral."

"Can Knowledge help us?" Dusi asked. "We're fighting against another deity's people. Yet we pray for her help every day."

"True," said Sabu. "Ganadarm even asks *Lith* to help us." He thought a moment. "You are right, Dusi. We need any help we can get. Go find out what the nature spirit wants."

Dusi smiled. "Thank you, Lieutenant."

Sabu nodded, but his eyes were sad and his lips were tight.

Dusi rode back across the creaking bridge before anyone could make a fuss. If Commander Visho were to decide she also needed *his* permission, she wanted to be well gone before he knew she had left. Once among the trees, Dusi took her mountain stepper off the road, so she would be hidden from any Klindrel scouts.

She rode at quick-step along the deer trails above the farming villages of the upper Redwood River. It occurred to her that she could keep going, keep riding all the way back to Roadhouse One and even up the Klindrel Road to the charred ruins of Passwatch, if she wished. Sabu would never know she had deserted.

Was that where she wanted her path to lead? The spirit's question came back to her.

No, it wasn't. She had studied nine years to be a patroller, and she was good at it. Someone needed to fight the Klindrel, and she had proven she had the skill. She was strong enough to overcome her fear and do her duty.

Was that what her mother had meant by the "smart path"? Dusi didn't think so. In the dream, following her mother's path had seemed important, but awake, Dusi could reason it out: If her mother believed that all Dusi's paths led to the Deceiver, then

Dusi needed to find a path her mother could not see. That would be the true smart path.

The place the spirit had shown Dusi in her waking dream was a half lithic's ride from Farbridge. Dusi reined back as she approached the stream and guided her horse in a soft-step descent toward the road. When they reached the place where Dusi had knelt the day before, she dismounted and allowed her horse to drink.

"Mer?"

The question came from the boughs of an alder.

"Mister Whiskers! What are you—? Wait. You! Forest spirit. Are you here?"

Call me Redwood. The voice was all around her, but she could hear it only inside her head.

"Is this the reason you asked me to come back? To find the cat?"

He misses the man who pets him.

"Tim misses him too, but— Ah. I see. You chose not to explain because you knew I wouldn't think the cat was important."

Yes, said the forest. *But the cat is important to me. I care about all the creatures that live here.*

"Even the people?"

Yes. At first, I was angry with you for taking my trees and diminishing me, but the more I listened to your thoughts, the more fascinated I became.

The cat climbed down the tree. Dusi knelt to pet it.

"The people need your help," Dusi said. "We are at war."

It is your war, said Redwood. *Not mine. I do not choose sides among the ants. I simply watch and learn.*

"You like learning? So do we, you know."

Her mind echoed with a chuckle that sounded like leaves shaking in the wind. *You worship learning.* The chuckle ceased. *That is, your people do.*

"I serve Knowledge, too," Dusi said.

You do, but you don't, said Redwood. *You are closer to Destruction than to Creation.*

"The Deceiver will not claim me," said Dusi. "I will defeat him."

How? By lying?

"I don't lie."

You have not told Sabu the truth.

"About what?"

About yourself. About why you want to avoid him.

"But if Sabu knew ..."

The cat began making its strange throaty buzzing sound. Dusi ran her hand along its soft coat of fur.

Yes? If he knew ... ?

Perhaps, being aligned with neither the demons nor the deities, the nature spirit could not understand.

"It's like this," Dusi said. "If people discovered that my soul is consecrated to a demon, they would have to do something to me. Perhaps something fatal. And then— then I would never get free."

How long do you plan to live with your soul split?

"As long as I have to. Until the Deceiver gives up."

Can demons give up? Redwood asked. *And if they did, what would happen to the balance of our world?*

"I ... don't know." These cosmological questions had not been addressed at the College of Forestry.

You hope to defeat this demon with strength, Redwood said. *But you are rotting inside. Every deception weakens your resistance to the Deceiver.*

"Everyone lies sometimes," Dusi said. "Knowledge understands that some lies are necessary."

This is not about whether Knowledge is willing to accept you. This is about whether the Deceiver has the power to steal you. Other servants of Knowledge can sway in the storms and never fall, but because of the rot inside you, you are vulnerable. You must stand straight and tall. If you waver, you will crash to Hell.

"But you believe I do have a chance to go to Heaven?"

As you are? No. You must either change the way you are growing, or you must eradicate the rot within.

"You're saying I have to stop lying to people."

Not only that. You would have to stop hiding things from people.

"But some things I must keep hidden."

Yes, said Redwood. *It is your nature.*

"My mother said the same thing—in my dream."

That was not a good dream, Redwood said. *That is why I woke you.*

"But you're saying she was right, that all my paths lead through deception to the Deceiver."

Perhaps she was right, said Redwood. *If that is true, then you need to think about leaving the paths.*

"What do you mean?"

You want to walk the path to your goddess, but your mother has twisted it, so that it leads to her demon. You can free your soul by leaving the path and giving up on both.

"Ah, I see. You want me to become a nature worshipper."

Redwood chuckled. *No. I just want you to free yourself of the demon. I can help you do this, but my help would also cut you off from Knowledge.*

"Once I was free, could I be consecrated to Knowledge again?"

Perhaps. But then you would be susceptible to the Deceiver again. The two grow intertwined, and Knowledge is weak against his pull. If you wished to serve the deities, the God of Justice would be a better choice. Against the Deceiver, Justice is mighty.

"But I wish to serve Knowledge. That is what my people were created for."

Not all of your kind serve Knowledge.

"No. But I will. If deceit is leading me down the wrong path, then I will choose a path without deceit."

Can you?

"I will."

How?

"I will start by telling the truth to Sabu."

That would be a good start, said Redwood. *I am sorry you will not accept my help, but perhaps you will accept his.*

"I should be able to do this without help," Dusi said. "But thank you anyway, Redwood. I will think about what you have said."

She scooped up the cat in her arms, mounted her horse, and rode carefully back to Farbridge.

CHAPTER 33

Looking Back

THE ROAD PATROL WITHDREW from Farbridge, and Passwatch Company was again in the lead, scouting for the next campsite. Whenever they passed through a village, men and women stopped working, children stopped studying, and people gathered in the road to ask questions.

As commanding officer of the advance guard, it was Sabu's job to tell them the Road Patrol was just passing through. *We didn't defend Farbridge, and we won't be defending your village, either,* he thought. His actual speech was more diplomatic, but that was the truth of it.

When he explained that the Road Patrol was trying to rendez-vous with the Hicho Guard to form an army, some villagers even volunteered to join. Sabu put these under Perga's command with orders to march swiftly enough to stay ahead of the supply wagons. On foot, they could not keep up with Sabu's people, but he might be able to assign them to some other company when the Road Patrol camped that evening.

The squad of volunteers trailing behind gave Sabu an excuse to keep looking over his shoulder. But from the careful expression on Thaki's face, he could tell she wasn't fooled. She knew he was really looking for Dusi.

When Passwatch Company camped at midday, Dusi was still absent. Thaki assigned a squad to dig the latrines. Sabu watched the road, waiting for Perga and his volunteers to be passed by a lone rider.

Sabu hoped the Klindrel had not found her. Perhaps she was riding with another company. Dusi wouldn't desert the Road Patrol. Sabu was almost certain of it. But he was also certain she wanted to get away from him.

Had he done something wrong? Had he said something that made her dislike him? She seemed … fearful. Perhaps the horrors of the battles on the road had caught up to her.

Sabu tried not to think about the past—especially not about the ambush at the Neargap Roadhouse. Everyone had been so wild. He wasn't certain his blade had killed any of those men, but he had certainly given the order. Red-skinned giants writhing in the blood-soaked mud …

Sabu did not think about the past. The Goddess had granted him a logical mind, and he would not allow his emotions to undermine his reason.

Except perhaps where Dusi was concerned.

Maybe that was the problem. Maybe he wasn't looking at this logically.

Dusi was avoiding him. Why?

Something about him frightened her. What?

Sabu wondered if she had confided anything to Thaki. The two of them were friendly, though perhaps not quite "friends". It was hard for Thaki to be friends with a rookie. She didn't think they were on the same level.

What had Thaki said? Something about many paths and perfect babies. She had said rookies thought life was dramatic, and Sabu had disagreed. But Thaki hadn't been talking about rookie-Sabu. She'd been talking about rookie-Dusi.

Thaki had warned him to take it slow. She had warned him that Dusi would be unsure of her feelings.

Sabu knew how to deal with his feelings: He gave them to the Goddess and received sanity in return. But maybe Dusi couldn't do that yet. She was overwhelmed.

She carried herself with such confidence that Sabu sometimes forgot she had just graduated from college. And now she was stabbing giants, falling in love, and living every day in fear that the Klindrel would overtake her company. Sometimes even Sabu felt overwhelmed.

He couldn't keep her out of the fighting. That was a burden everyone had to bear. But if his feelings for her were making that burden heavier, then he had to let her go.

He should have realized that back at Roadhouse One.

Perga and the volunteers were nearly at camp. They had marched briskly. Sabu found Tim and asked him to be certain they all got water when they came in.

Sabu went to check on Thaki and the latrine-digging crew. Thaki had chosen mostly second-years. They had once been a big class, but now they were down to six. When he joined them, the second-years were engaged in their favorite pastime—running the Road Patrol.

"We should never have left Farbridge," said Sijo, the only female in the second year. "That bridge was the only defensible position between Passwatch and Hicho."

A couple of the second-years nodded. A couple of them looked sick at the idea of fighting again.

Zerdegi, who was becoming something of a leader among them, said, "We left Roadhouse One to the Klindrel. We left Farbridge to the Klindrel. I think Visho means to abandon the whole Redwood Valley."

"Commander Visho is leading us to join with the Hicho Guard," said Sabu.

Zerdegi jumped. He hadn't known Sabu was there.

Hikafa nodded a greeting. The quiet third-year often spent time in the company of the second-years. He was probably the only latrine-digger who had volunteered.

"Sijo is correct," Sabu said. "That bridge was defensible. For an army. Are we trained to fight like an army?"

Sijo bit her lip and looked guilty.

Sabu turned to Zerdegi. "We've abandoned some positions, yes, but how would you have held them? How would you have held Highcliff?"

The questions were rhetorical, but Zerdegi found the courage to answer them anyway. "By ambush," he said. "The way we won at Passwatch and Neargap."

Sabu met the second-year's eyes. Zerdegi's classmate Jamidu had died at Neargap.

"You think those were victories?" Sabu asked.

Zerdegi didn't answer.

Sabu sighed. "Perhaps you are right. Perhaps we should have remained in the mountains and fought the Klindrel among the trees. You are good at it. You have all proven your skill." He looked at Mishu and Therva, two of the more timid ones, to let them know he had faith in their skill, too. "But what you aren't seeing, Zerdegi, is that it doesn't matter what we do *best*. What matters is what most needs to be *done*. Commander Visho has decided that our top priority is putting an army together. That's logical, isn't it? It would be difficult to defeat the Klindrel without an army."

Some of them nodded.

"So we'll go downriver," Sabu said. "We'll get more volunteers. And in a week or two, if all goes well, we will meet up with the Hicho Guard."

Zerdegi said, "Visho must not think very much of us if he's not willing to let us fight until we join the Hicho Guard."

Sijo asked, "Who gave him the authority to take over the Road Patrol, anyway? Why didn't he leave Patrol Commander Shiboko in charge?"

"A fair question," Sabu said. "Do you remember Terkisho's chapter on 'Chain of Command'?"

They nodded. They were only eighteen months out of school. Of course they remembered Terkisho's *Theory of War*.

"Well, you may have noticed that in the Road Patrol, chain of command is not as strict as Terkisho describes it. Commander Visho thinks this will lead to trouble in a war. We don't have time to debate everything. We have to make decisions and act on them."

Hikafa nodded. The third-year was intelligent enough to see where Sabu was going.

"Now when Commander Visho told Patrol Commander Shiboko to step down, Shiboko had a choice. He could either decide to stay in command of the Road Patrol, or he could accept the chain of command. The fact that he stepped down means that he thinks we have a better chance to win the war if Visho commands the Road Patrol. And that means doing things Visho's way."

Sijo looked skeptical. Zerdegi looked confused, which meant that he might be getting the message.

"So whose orders should I follow?" Sabu asked. "Should I do what Commander Visho wants, or should I do what I think Patrol Commander Shiboko would want? Well, Shiboko has stepped down. I know what he wants: He decided I should take orders from Visho. And that is why we will keep riding downriver until we find the Hicho Guard."

Even Sijo was thinking now.

"Thank you, Lieutenant," Hikafa said.

"You're welcome," Sabu said.

"Lieutenant?"

Sabu turned to see Perga standing nearby. Sabu smiled. Perga usually called him "Sabu", but that would have undermined the lesson.

"What can I do for you, Perga?"

"I'd like to discuss the new recruits, Lieutenant."

"Certainly," Sabu said.

He and Perga walked through the meadow until they were standing well away from the rest of the company.

"So how did your charges fare?" Sabu asked.

"They did well enough," Perga said.

"You certainly kept them moving."

"Rookie zeal," Perga said.

Sabu chuckled.

"Sabu, did you mean what you said over there?" He nodded back toward the second-years. "Do you really agree with all of Visho's decisions?"

Of course not. But he wouldn't undermine the Road Patrol's commanding officer.

"I understand the reasons behind them," Sabu said.

"Was he right to abandon Farbridge today?" Perga asked.

"Was I right to hold Zhaku's funeral when you needed me to rejoin you? Was I right to enrage the Klindrel at Neargap?"

"You think you were wrong?" Perga asked.

"I don't know," Sabu said. "Perhaps I should have done things differently. But those were the decisions I made, and I have to live with the consequences."

"I was wrong to wait for you, wasn't I?" Perga said. "I should have gone to evacuate the roadhouse."

"Perhaps," Sabu said. "But they managed on their own."

"When I have blades in my hand," Perga said, "I know just what to do. I never have to think. When you put me in command of people, sometimes I feel paralyzed. Anything I do seems wrong."

"I can understand that," Sabu said.

Perga shook his head. "No, Sabu, don't you see? You know exactly what to do. Maybe you don't always guess right, but you always *lead*. Half the second-years are wetting themselves thinking about another battle, and the other half think they should be leading the Road Patrol. You just told them all exactly what they needed to hear. The next time they have to fight for you, they'll all fight better. Because of what you told them just now."

"Ah. Thank you, Perga."

Perga put a calloused hand on Sabu's shoulder. "Zhaku picked you for a reason. She trusted your judgment, and we do, too. Captain, Lieutenant—it doesn't matter what Visho wants us to call you. You are our leader."

"Thank you."

"But Sabu …"

"Yes?"

"When you pass one of his orders on to us, make sure it's an order you believe in. Because we are trusting you to tell us when it is time to give up our lives. Don't let anyone else make that decision."

Sabu didn't know how to reply. He stood staring at his friend, at the man whose skill he so admired. Sabu had been so relieved to let Visho take the burden of command. Perga had just called him a shirker, while giving him the finest compliment he had ever received.

Perga nodded toward the camp. "Dusi's back."

Sabu looked. Dusi drew his eye like a torch. Her pale face shone brightly in the noonday sun. She was standing off to the side with Tim and Vahi the stablemaster. Vahi had taken Dusi's horse. Tim was petting his cat.

Dusi glanced at Sabu. Even at a distance, Sabu could see her fear. Poor thing. He should have realized how much her feelings frightened her.

Dusi's shoulders heaved as though she were drawing a deep breath. She began walking toward him.

Perga said, "I need to … talk to Thaki."

"Thank you," Sabu said.

He met Dusi halfway.

"Good day, Lieutenant." Dusi gave Sabu her lopsided grin. It looked weak, perhaps because she hadn't smiled in days.

Sabu smiled, hoping it would give her strength. "Good day, Dusi. I am glad … you have returned."

She gave a tight-lipped nod.

He was glad to have her back, but he wouldn't be keeping her much longer.

"You found Tim's cat?" he asked.

"Yes." Her shoulders relaxed a little. "I'm sorry, Lieutenant.

The nature spirit did not want to help us. Against the Klindrel, I mean. It just wanted to return Tim's cat."

That was almost funny.

"Well, it's a good thing it didn't tell you," Sabu said. "I wouldn't have let you go back for a pet."

Dusi nodded. "I think perhaps it knew that."

Sabu wished they could just keep talking. This was more than she had said to him in days. He asked, "Is the spirit intelligent, then?"

Dusi's eyes widened. "I'd say so. It understands theology better than we do. It watches every living thing within the forest. It knows our thoughts. It—"

"You make it sound like a deity!"

"Well, it is not as powerful as the deities," said Dusi, "but it is closer. A nearby bonfire seems hotter than the distant sun."

Sabu laughed. "Well said!"

Dusi smiled. He loved that smile.

Just keep talking to me, he thought.

"So it spoke with you?" he asked.

"Yes, it—" Her smile was washed away by uncertainty. "Yes."

And now he'd somehow pushed things too far. Somehow, he had reminded her that his interest was about more than his duty to the Road Patrol.

"Sabu, I have something I need to tell you." Her voice was heavy now.

"Dusi, you don't need to say it."

"But I—"

"No, Dusi." Sabu shook his head. "I know you've been trying to avoid me. And I understand why."

"You do?" She looked mortified.

"Dusi, it's nothing to be ashamed of. It happens to patrollers all the time. If it weren't for this war—"

No. He shouldn't speculate about how things might have been.

"Anyway," he said, "I understand why it's too intense. And why ... you need to leave my company."

Now she was frowning at him as though he were a puzzle. "Sabu, what are you saying?"

"I'm saying that I will request a transfer for you."

"A transfer?"

"Yes," said Sabu. "To another company. Or ... or perhaps Visho needs a messenger."

That was something Dusi would be good at, and it would make it easier for Sabu to take her back into Passwatch Company if she changed her mind.

"So you want me to leave?" she asked.

No. No, he wanted to stand this close to her forever. To smell her hair. To look into her deep brown eyes.

"Let's just say I understand why you need to leave," he said.

Dusi slowly shook her head. "No, Sabu. I don't think you do."

"But—"

Aren't you in love with me? he didn't ask.

"Listen," she said. "Redwood—the nature spirit—said I have to tell you something."

Tell me what? "Very well," he said. "I'm listening."

Dusi took a deep breath. "Do you remember what I told you about my mother?"

Sabu nodded. Her mother had been murdered by the Temple of the Hunters because she was a demon worshipper. It was not something Sabu was likely to forget.

Dusi swallowed. "Well, there's more."

Sabu waited, scarcely breathing.

"The nightmares I have ... are not truly dreams. My mother speaks to me. She wants me to serve the Deceiver, too."

"But you won't," Sabu said.

Dusi shook her head. "I won't," she said. "But it's ..."

And then she was in his arms, and he couldn't say whether he had reached for her or she had reached for him. All he knew was that she was crying and he was petting her hair.

"It's so hard," she said. "She's my mother. And I still love her. She twists the truth to break my will, but I still love her. I still miss her. I still want her back."

"Oh, Dusi." It felt so good to hold her.

She pushed away and looked up at him with tears in her deep, dark eyes. "But she damned me, Sabu. When I was an infant, she gave my soul to the Deceiver."

Sabu opened his mouth to speak, but Dusi's words had knocked the wind out of him. Giving an infant to a demon? How was that even possible?

"But you said—" Sabu coughed some life into his voice. "You said your uncle took you to be consecrated to Knowledge."

"He did," Dusi said. "And I was consecrated. But we didn't know what Mother had done to me."

"But the ritesmaster would have known. Wouldn't he?"

Dusi shook her head. "Redwood says that Knowledge is weak against the Deceiver. The demon must have deceived even the ritesmaster."

"But … can't you feel the Goddess in your soul?"

"Sometimes," Dusi said. "I think. The nature spirits say I belong to both—that Knowledge and the Deceiver are fighting a war over me."

"So you can still decide?" Sabu asked. "You can still choose to serve the Goddess?"

Dusi's words were steel: "I made my decision long ago. I fight my mother's legacy every day."

"And you win?"

She nodded. "Every day."

"Oh, Dusi."

"I'm sorry, Sabu. I should have told you."

Sabu was feeling stunned. "I can see why you didn't."

"So that's why I wanted to leave," she said.

"Oh." Sabu had forgotten that they were making arrangements for Dusi to leave. "I had thought …"

"You thought I wanted to leave because I'm in love with you," she said.

Sabu nodded. It seemed silly now. But really, his feelings were trivial compared with—

"Sabu, I *am* in love with you."

"You are?"

"Yes. You knew that."

"Then stay," he said. "Because I'm in love with you, too."

"Even though the Deceiver has a claim on my soul?"

"It doesn't matter," Sabu said. "It's just one more battle that we'll have to fight together."

CHAPTER 34

Marching and Camping

THE KLINDREL ARMY MARCHED into Farbridge at noon the next day, while the Road Patrol continued to withdraw. That evening, word reached camp that the Klindrel had taken Farbridge without a fight. Commander Visho told his subordinates that orders would soon be arriving from Hicho, but Tim Hill took out his pocket ledger and showed Sabu that this estimate was based on hope, not arithmetic.

Visho had them all on the road before the sun rose the next morning, and this was, you recall, late Redmonth, so the sun was rising quite early. The wagon drivers kept the oxen moving at a hard pace all morning long, until word came from the rearguard observers that the Klindrel had not yet broken camp at Farbridge.

Indeed, the Klindrel were to stay at Farbridge for several more days, waiting for supplies until their first pulse of horse wagons caught up to them. Meanwhile, the Road Patrol crept slowly toward the plain.

Passwatch Company continued to have camp chores and training exercises scheduled throughout the days and evenings, but now Sabu and Dusi were able to find time for private moments together. Dusi was no longer looking for ways to avoid Sabu, and Thaki helped by insisting that Sabu take himself off duty now and again.

People in love are intensely interesting to each other, but dreadfully boring to everyone else. I shall spare you the details. They spent their time as lovers do—exchanging childhood memories, sharing their views of classic philosophical conundrums, and kissing. In other words, they did nothing of interest to the reader, although I will say that the kissing was quite good. If you are a young person considering whether to fall in love, don't worry about the kissing. It is actually very pleasant, and once you are in love, it won't seem silly at all.

Sabu felt guilty for enjoying these happy moments while the clouds of war overshadowed the peaceful Redwood Valley, but he had to admit that Thaki was correct: Being with Dusi relaxed him, and being relaxed helped him to be a more rational leader.

And yet, the time he spent with Dusi was not entirely without worries. Sabu feared for Dusi's soul.

The way Dusi described it, her soul belonged to two powerful supernatural entities, Knowledge and the Deceiver. Against another demon, Dusi's decision to serve Knowledge would have had more power. But because the Deceiver dwells in Knowledge's blind spot, the Deceiver could pull Dusi toward himself every time she engaged in deception. Whenever Sabu had asked Dusi to spy on the Klindrel or spring an ambush, he had been pushing her soul one step closer to Hell.

After a week of thinking about it, Sabu finally convinced himself that Dusi had only one solution.

"You have to consecrate your soul to Justice," he told her as they lay concealed in the tall grass, with his head on her chest. "If Knowledge cannot free you, you must go to the deity who can."

"I will free myself," Dusi said. "I have driven my mother from my dreams."

"How?"

"By controlling my thoughts ... using techniques she taught me when I was small."

"But you aren't cured," Sabu said.

"I don't have the nightmares," Dusi said. "That's good enough for me."

"But the link to the Deceiver is still within your soul," Sabu said. "What if something awakens it again?"

"I just won't let that happen."

"Dusi—" he rolled onto his belly so he could look down into her deep, dark eyes, "—you can't fight a demon by yourself. You need divine help."

"The ritesmaster consecrated my soul to Knowledge when I was nine. If that wasn't good enough, I don't see what a servant of Justice can do for me."

"I thought the Redwood spirit explained that."

"He didn't, really," Dusi said. "He just said that Knowledge is weak against the Deceiver, and Justice is strong."

"So?" he asked.

"So?" she echoed.

"So shouldn't you give some thought to serving the God of Justice?"

Dusi shook her head. "I don't want to serve Justice. I want to serve Knowledge. Besides, if I went to Justice's Heaven, then I wouldn't see you anymore."

Sabu grinned. "Maybe Knowledge would let me visit."

"I don't think it works like that."

Sabu wasn't really sure how it worked, but he suspected Dusi was right. He wanted to tell her they were a long way from worrying about death, but they weren't: Word had reached camp that the Klindrel were moving again.

The Road Patrol kept moving, too. And as they marched down the Redwood Valley, they drew more and more volunteers. Most of these people came in ones and twos, but the College of Forestry supplied an entire company of lumberjacks, who spent their evenings practicing vicious axe techniques. To Sabu, the idea of chopping into a leg seemed barbaric compared with the precise tendon surgery he had taught his people, but he could find no logic behind his opinion. Looked at logically, it was all barbaric ... and evil.

Sabu could not deny the evil in what he had done. He had ordered his people to kill the people of another deity. That was wrong. Absolutely.

It was justified, of course. He had given those orders in an attempt to protect the road and defend the people of the Redwood Valley. That evil was a necessary part of his duty. But no matter how necessary it was, his part in the Klindrel deaths diminished his soul.

He had come to accept that. He believed that Knowledge understood his rationale and that she would take his circumstances into account when she judged him. The same would have been true for Dusi, had her mother not served Evil.

On the last day of Redmonth, the Road Patrol and the Redwood Valley Volunteers met the messenger who had been sent to Hicho three weeks earlier. He gave Commander Visho the message from Army Headquarters: The Hicho Guard is mustered and ready to march; fall back toward Hicho; we will meet you on the road.

Sabu noted that the second-years were grumbling less about Visho's decision to withdraw. They were impressed by how much the cohort had grown, and they were warming to the idea of joining with an even larger force from Hicho. The talk changed from "We should have defended Farbridge" to "Wait till the Klindrel see how big our army is."

Overall, spirits were rising until the rearguard reported that the Klindrel Army had finally caught up.

On the second day of Orangemonth, the Road Patrol camped near the village of Tomivo. The Klindrel Army camped in the village of Uppermost Pikomi—almost within galloping distance.

That night, Commander Visho called his subordinates together and announced that it was time to stop running. They now had no choice but to stand and fight. Sabu agreed.

At first light the next morning, everyone in Tomivo was awake and watching the Klindrel. But in Uppermost Pikomi, the Klindrel seemed to be settling in. Our people waited all day for an attack that didn't come.

Which is not to say that the Klindrel were living peacefully in the village they occupied. The Maziban Lancers left Uppermost Pikomi at midmorning and came back that afternoon with sacks of wheat and bleeding carcasses of mutton. And that evening, we heard word from the villages that had been raided:

Only the village of Jakubi had offered any resistance. At the other villages, the Maziban Lancers had presented disemboweled corpses from Jakubi and received food without a fight.

Our people were angered by these raids, but they saw no way to prevent them. Spreading our troops out to defend every village would have opened the way for the Klindrel to march past and raid downriver.

Now the grumbling started again—especially among the volunteers, who had joined expecting to fight. Sabu tried to keep his own company calm, but in truth, he hated the idea of standing by and watching the Klindrel ride out on their raids—not just because of the massacre at Jakubi, but also because of the timing. It was still early Orangemonth, and the villagers' only food was the last of their winterstock and the early potatoes. Many people would be going hungry—unless they ate their draft and dairy animals.

On the second day of camping and watching, the Klindrel Army was visited by horse wagons. Tim Hill and Ganadarm found a good vantage point and watched them intently as they rolled into Uppermost Pikomi. Sabu and Dusi went to see what they had learned.

"I reckon that was every horse wagon left in the legion," Tim said, consulting his pocket ledger. "Not quite as many as they started with."

"Thanks to our bravery in the mountains!" said Ganadarm.

Tim checked his figures. "Aye. And I reckon some horses must have gone lame. The emperor had to push them hard to get them here so fast."

Dusi said, "He could not be pushing them too hard, I think, if men on foot must wait two days for them to catch up."

Tim said, "Well, they aren't just traveling along with the army like our ox wagons." He opened up his ledger and showed Sabu and Dusi his figures. "I reckon they made a trip from Farbridge to Roadhouse One and back, while the army was marching from Farbridge. You see, they don't have enough horse wagons to move all their supplies in one trip."

"How much supplies have they?" Sabu asked.

"Oh, quite a bit, I reckon. But not much of it here, yet. You see, a lot of their wagon space is taken up by forage for the horses and for the oxen crossing the mountains."

"That is why the soldiers waited in Farbridge?" asked Sabu.

"Aye," said Tim. "They had to wait for their supply chain to catch up."

"And now it is catched up," Sabu said.

"Well, now," Tim said, "that's an interesting question. I'm not sure how far they can march on what the wagons brought today. I reckon that's why they've been raiding your villages." He nodded in the direction of the forest lining the valley. Sabu saw the sparkle of sunlight on distant armor. The Maziban Lancers were returning from another raid.

"Why don't you attack?" Ganadarm asked.

"We wait for more soldiers from Hicho soon," Sabu replied.

"I wonder what *they* are waiting for," Ganadarm said. "They outnumber you. You have no armor. And even if you had shields for everyone, no one knows how to use one."

"Could be that this is as far as they want to extend their supply line right now," Tim said. "I reckon their ox wagons won't get here for another—" he flipped some pages in his ledger, "—twenty days."

"But they can use horse wagons," Sabu said.

"Oh, aye," Tim agreed. "On this end. But they don't have enough horse wagons for the entire supply chain. Most of it has to be moved with oxen."

"So they will wait here long," Sabu said.

Dusi frowned. "And while they are waiting, they eat our sheep, our baby potatoes, and what we have left in our cellars."

"Aye," Tim said.

"If they are short on food, you should try to steal their horses," Ganadarm said. "The raiding parties wouldn't be able to range as far."

"We do not steal," said Sabu. "We catch stealers."

"Well," said Ganadarm, "I respect your virtue. But this *is* a war."

"No, that is not what I mean," said Sabu. "I mean we do not know how to steal."

"Oh," said Ganadarm. "Well, Ugly Lem taught me all about horse thieving. I think the four of us can steal most of those horses all by ourselves ... or at least turn them loose."

"The four of whom?" asked Tim.

"You, me, Saboon, and Dusi," said Ganadarm.

"Me?" said Tim.

"Yes," said Ganadarm. "I think you would make a right good horse thief."

"I'm not a thief," said Tim.

"But you could be a good one," said Ganadarm. "I would show you how."

"But Tim is not a soldier," Dusi said.

"No," said Ganadarm. "But he *is* a fighter. He escaped from a Klindrel prison with a little help from me. He escaped from a hundred Klindrel soldiers all on his own. And he stole the horse that I rode here on. Bandit, soldier, thief—whatever you want to call him, Tim is a good man to have with you."

Dusi tilted her head to one side and looked at Tim. "And if we take Tim, he can get a better count of the supplies."

"And he's good with horses," said Ganadarm.

"Are you serious?" Sabu asked. "Or do you jest?"

Ganadarm shook his head. "I do not jest, Saboon. I think we can do it."

Dusi looked from the giant to Sabu. "Would Visho let us go?" she asked.

Sabu thought a moment. If Tim were right, if the Klindrel did have supply problems, then cutting down the range of their raids would be a clever thing to do.

"I think I can make Visho see wisdom here," said Sabu.

But the question was whom to take. Ganadarm was certainly the right person to consult for horse-stealing strategies. Dusi's mind-spotting talent would give them an advantage on a moonless night. Sabu wanted Perga along—Perga always made him feel safe in a fight. And Vahi the stablemaster would show courage where horses were involved—even giant horses.

As for Tim ... well, Dusi and Ganadarm were right: Tim was good with horses and he was good at counting supplies. Of course, that good head would be useless if Tim panicked inside the enemy camp.

"What think you, Tim?" Sabu asked. "Do you come with us?"

"Yolim help me," Tim said. "I don't know, Lieutenant Sabu. Could I have a bit of time to think about it?"

CHAPTER 35

Raiding the Raiders

IF YOU VISIT UPPERMOST PIKOMI today, you would never guess that it once hosted the Klindrel Army. Apple trees line the country lanes along which the villagers fled when the Klindrel arrived. Cheerful-faced families now live in the houses that, during the invasion, stood empty and looted along the cobbled streets, gaping at the invaders with broken-doored entrances and smashed-shuttered windows. Fluffy lambs graze the meadows where the Klindrel pastured their giant-sized cavalry horses. Barley grows where the camp followers pitched their tents. In Uppermost Pikomi, the Klindrel Invasion has been forgotten.

And so it is throughout the Redwood Valley. The days of my youth are taught to today's youth as history. The elders remember, but most of them were children at the time. In order to live their lives, they had to learn to forget.

But brave deeds should not be forgotten. Our culture does not revere heroes (as evidenced by the fact that we must borrow the word "hero" from the Klindrel) but we should at least admire heroism. Tim Hill was just an honest merchant, no more praiseworthy than anyone else who fought in the war, yet his deeds and the courage it took to perform those deeds—these things are worth describing for future generations. When the time comes to finally fight the demons, I hope all our people can be as brave as this one Child of Wealth.

Tim did not see himself as brave as he lay on the cold soft earth of the field, hidden from view by the darkness and the waist-high flax. Tim felt shivery and vulnerable. He was not a soldier, and he had no idea why he had let Ganadarm talk him into joining the mission to sneak into the Klindrel camp. "Flattery does not come cheap," was the saying in the Hill Enclave, and Tim reckoned he should not have bought Ganadarm's fanciful embellishments. But he had bought them, and now he was wondering what the price would be.

He asked Yolim for help, but in a vague and general way. He reckoned Yolim wasn't the kind of god who helped folks sneak around and steal horses. But Yolim was all Tim had, so he prayed to Yolim.

Tim wondered if he should pray for forgiveness. But no. That would be insincere. He hadn't actually done the stealing yet.

Of course, Tim wasn't really stealing. The Redfolk would lose their horses, the Brownfolk would gain the horses, but *Tim* wouldn't get anything—except killed, maybe.

That was no excuse, though. Helping thieves was as bad as stealing. If Yolim made an exception for war, Tim had never heard about it.

But Tim had decided to come along anyway. He reckoned that the Klindrel were the worse thieves, the worse sinners. They were using those horses to steal potatoes and grains that could have been used for seed stocks. They were occupying the Brownfolk's land. They broke into houses and killed people who got in their way. Tim couldn't stop them, not by himself, but he could help the Brownfolk take the horses that allowed the Klindrel to range so far. If they covered less ground, they would steal less food and ransack fewer towns. Looked at that way, Tim was actually *preventing* theft.

He wondered if Yolim would look at it that way.

Ahead of Tim, Sabu began crawling forward. Tim followed him.

They passed under a fence and crawled down into a roadside ditch. It was wet country, and the Brownfolk built high roads to shed the rain. The ditch itself, of course, was soggy.

In the mostly cloudy, moonless night, Tim could barely make out the shapes of his companions. Dark-skinned Sabu was beside him, and Dusi was on Sabu's other side. The stablemaster was there somewhere, but his outline was disguised by Ganadarm's huge silhouette. On the other side of Ganadarm was Sabu's friend Perga, who fought with two blades.

Tim had made his skin darker than Sabu's so that he would blend into the night. The Klindrel had sentries somewhere on the other side of the road, and unless Tim had misinterpreted Sabu's body language, Tim and his five companions were about to climb out of the ditch and cross that road, relying purely on the darkness to hide them.

Sabu waved an arm, confirming that Tim's assessment had been spot on.

They scuttled over the gravel-topped road like snake-hunting badgers—low to the ground and ready for a fight. Tim didn't feel low enough or ready enough.

Sabu did not pause in the ditch on the other side, but rather kept them moving onto the open meadow. Tim ran bent over double, mimicking the lieutenant. With his nose near his knees, he could smell the fresh grass as he crushed its leaves beneath his leather boots. The grass smelled green and healthy, but it was not high enough to hide anyone—the meadow had been well grazed that spring. Soon the greasy smell of sheep dung was added to the mix.

Tim's companions did not run silently. He could hear Sabu and the stablemaster puffing. Their feet whisked through the soft grass.

Ganadarm ran with a different cadence. Despite the giant's weight, his steps brushed the ground only lightly. His shallow breaths were quiet—an admirable feat of concentration from a man whose snores could wake the camp.

Tim tried to control his own breathing and found that the effort to breathe silently made him light-headed. When Sabu lay down on the ground, Tim joined him gratefully, not caring about the fragrant pile of sheep dung into which he put his right knee.

The Brownfolk's sheep were gone from the meadow now. The Redfolk had commandeered the pasture for their horses. The nearest horse was a dark shape fifty paces away.

As Tim got his breath back, he realized that Sabu would not have lain down in the middle of the open meadow simply to rest. Dusi must have given him some warning signal. Perhaps a Klindrel sentry had seen them running. Perhaps she had spotted a sentry hidden among the horses. Perhaps someone from the torchlit camp in the village was walking this way.

They lay on the meadow grass a good long while. Tim listened for Klindrel footsteps, but none came.

Sabu crawled through Tim's field of vision and arrived at the massive form of Ganadarm. Sabu whispered something. Ganadarm whispered back and pointed. Sabu nodded.

Ganadarm rose to a crouch. Perga did likewise, as did the stablemaster after Ganadarm tapped him on the shoulder. The three men moved off and were soon lost to sight in the darkness.

Sabu looked to Dusi. She shook her head. Apparently this head shake meant, "No one has spotted us," for Sabu immediately signaled an advance. At a more reasonable pace this time, Sabu, Dusi, and Tim crept toward the nearest horse.

The horses were picketed in the meadow by ropes running from their halters to wooden stakes driven into the turf. Each horse was powerful enough to pull up the stake or snap its halter, but their training held them in place. The picket was simply a reminder of where they were expected to stay.

The first order of business was to separate the horses from their pickets. Ganadarm's trio was assigned the cavalry horses in a different part of the meadow. Tim, Dusi, and Sabu were responsible for the wagon horses.

Tim drew his blade from its sheath. It was a long, nasty serrated knife that the Brownfolk called a "battleblade". Well, fair enough. This was a lot closer to battle than Tim had ever wanted to come.

Sabu had found the blade for him … somewhere. Tim wondered if the blade was new or previously owned. If the latter, then it had not done its poor owner much good. Tim was glad he only had to use it for sawing through rope.

He found the nearest stake. The horse stood close beside it, head hanging, eyes drooping, dreaming some horsey dream.

Tim slipped his blade under the rope, close to the stake, and put his foot on the slack to give himself something to pull against. He had practiced this in camp.

Tim knew that cutting the rope would not be silent. In fact, it would probably wake the horse.

"Easy, big fellow," he murmured in his deepest voice. "Easy now."

The horse's ears twitched.

"Eeeeeasyyyyyy."

With a quiet *riiiiip!* Tim sliced through the rope.

The horse opened one eye and looked at Tim suspiciously. But the horse didn't shy.

As the three of them passed from stake to stake, cutting the ropes, some of the more nervous horses began shuffling their feet. Tim left the cutting to the Brownfolk and tried to keep the horses calm. They wanted the horses to run away, but not before it was time.

The little ripping noises of the knives blended into the background of the shuffling hooves and snuffling noses. If he were a foreigner camping out in a strange land—which, in fact, he was—Tim might mistake the knives for the call of some night bird. But only a person ignorant of horses would fail to notice that the animals were reacting to something passing through the herd.

Fortunately, the Klindrel infantry were, in general, ignorant of horses.

After Sabu cut through the last rope, he straightened up and looked at Dusi. Dusi gave a nod. Brownfolk could be so expressive with their heads! This nod, like the head shake earlier, meant that no Klindrel were on the way.

Then they waited. Ganadarm was supposed to boost Perga and the stablemaster onto two of the cavalry horses and then come over by himself to lead the wagon horses away.

Sabu seemed to grow nervous as the wait dragged on. Tim wanted to put a hand on his shoulder and say, "Eeeeasyyyy!"

He didn't. But he did realize that he was calm now. In soothing the animals, he had soothed himself.

A challenge rang out through the night. "Who goes there?"

Ganadarm answered in his Saltlander accent, " 'Tis I, Ganadarm!"

Tim's blood felt suddenly chilly.

"One of the wagon horses is loose," Ganadarm called to the sentry. "I think it slipped its picket."

"Oh," said the sentry.

A short while later, Ganadarm arrived, leading one of the wagon horses back to the herd. He looked down at them. All Tim could see of his face was his broad, white smile.

Ganadarm said, "You let this one wander too far, Saboon. You were supposed to keep them together until I arrived."

"Yes, yes," whispered Sabu. "But now hurry."

Ganadarm's smile broadened. He vaulted astride the wagon horse. The gelding widened its eyes, unsure how to react to this development.

Whether the horse had been ridden before or not, it decided to accept Ganadarm's assertion that it would be ridden now. It carried Ganadarm at a walk around the herd, stirring the other animals.

The horses began drifting from the pickets, following a certain mare that had established herself as their leader. Ganadarm trotted through the herd, trying to catch up to the mare.

The horses beside him went to a trot. To stay ahead, the mare went to a trot.

"Hey!" called a sentry. "What are you doing?"

"Captain Bannom ordered me to move the pickets," Ganadarm called.

"Who?"

"Captain Bannom!"

The horses didn't like the shouting. They were moving faster now.

A tug on Tim's tunic reminded him that he was not supposed to be watching. He followed Dusi and Sabu across the meadow. The Brownfolk moved with swift strides, keeping low. Tim alternated between trying to match their posture and trying to match their pace.

"Horses loose!" called a sentry who was less easily confused.

"Horses loose, horses loose ..." the cry was passed down the line.

Figures began moving among the torchlit camp on the edge of the village. Men began shouting. Sabu and Dusi continued toward the village—now at a run. Tim struggled to keep up, no longer worrying about his footsteps or his breathing. He could hear two horse herds galloping. It was unlikely anyone in the Klindrel camp could hear him running.

Backlit shadows emerged from the camp. Sabu and Dusi changed course to avoid them, but more men came running from another direction. Sabu and Dusi stopped.

As Tim caught up to them, the two Brownfolk dropped to the ground. Dusi lay at an angle across Sabu's legs, as Ganadarm had told them to do if they needed to hide in the open. The trick worked—at least to Tim's eyes. They appeared to be some sort of formless lump, looking more like mole diggings or a rock than like two people. Tim sprawled over Dusi's legs and hoped the Klindrel would be fooled.

With his body pressed to the ground, he could feel the Klindrel feet pounding toward him, out of rhythm with his own thudding heartbeat. He could hear their loose scabbards clacking against their legs as they ran. Face down, he would never see it coming if a soldier decided to put a sword into him.

Then they were so close he could hear their breath. One of them broke stride to veer around the pile of bodies. A booted toe stepped on Tim's hand and pressed it into the ground.

Then the running giants were past, their footsteps receding into the distant gallop of the horses.

Tim lay there, sweat-soaked and shivering. Dusi crawled out from underneath his legs and stood up, but Tim did not move.

"Tim," Sabu murmured, very quietly in Tim's ear. "Tim, we must go into their camp now."

"You go," Tim whispered.

"You cannot stay here," Sabu said.

I can't move my legs, Tim thought.

"Tim?"

Dusi knelt down by Tim's other ear. "Tim," she said gently. "Are you hurt?"

"They— they stepped on my hand," Tim said.

"Tim, look at me," she said.

Tim lay motionless.

"Tim," said Dusi. "You talk to grass. We do not hear what it is that you say."

Tim turned his head. "I shouldn't be here," he said.

Dusi nodded. "Yes, you should. You are Tim Hill, strong soldier of Clanfolk. Only soldier of Clanfolk. You must fight because you are the unique item."

Tim sat up and stared at her. Was she crazy?

"I'm the stupid item!" he said. "I should have stayed home with my wife!"

"But you did not stay home with your wife," Dusi said. "So you must be here the hero now. So get up."

Tim looked at her.

"Get up," she said.

Tim thought about explaining how he couldn't move his legs, but he had already sat up.

"If I die, I shall be sorely mad at you," he said.

"Yes, yes," said Dusi. "Up, up."

Tim got up. After all, he couldn't lie in the meadow until morning.

They moved cautiously now. The sounds of alarm were behind them. Ahead, the camp lay quiet and alert.

About sixty paces from camp, the Brownfolk stopped so that Dusi could whisper something into Sabu's ear. Sabu nodded and altered course, aiming for a larger tent that loomed blackly on the edge of camp. When they reached it, they crouched in the darkness underneath one of the ropes tethering a tent pole. A giant snored on the other side of the canvas.

They waited next to the tent while Dusi used her Brownfolk magic. Tim could hear two men somewhere inside the camp conferring about something. Among the camp followers, a baby was crying.

Tim thought of his own babies, grown big now, but not yet grown up. There had been times when he had envied the Klindrel Army's custom of bringing women and children along. But not right now. Now he was glad that his family was safe on the other side of the mountains, far, far away, and he wished he were with them.

Dusi waved a pale arm, indicating that no one nearby was awake. They scuttled through a gap of dim orange torchlight and stopped in the shadow of the next tent.

They played this game of hop-toad-hop for a while, working their way around the perimeter of the camp. Dusi's magic was good enough that no one saw them. That was why Sabu had wanted her along. Sabu had wanted Tim along because he needed an accurate supply count.

When they reached the corner where the rows of tents met the houses of the village, they began scuttling from house to house. They found the empty supply wagons lined up along the main street. The supply tent was pitched in the center of the village.

Two men stood guard at the entrance. All the sides and corners were well lit by torches around the village plaza.

They skirted the plaza, keeping in the shadows when they might be in view of the guards. When they reached the back of the tent, Dusi strode boldly out into the torch light.

Tim froze, but Sabu pushed him, and Tim had no choice but to scurry across the plaza as quickly as he could.

Dusi dropped to the cobbles and casually slithered under the canvas wall. Tim did likewise. Then Sabu joined them in the supply tent.

It was different from the way it had been when Tim had seen it last. Of course, that had been in Kanabur in the daylight, but those were not the differences that came immediately to mind. It was smaller. And it was emptier.

Tim moved across the cobbles, bare where he had expected sacks of wheat, barley, and potatoes. The supply tent held only a few spare weapons and the iron, wood, leather, and canvas that would be needed for equipment maintenance. Had all the food been distributed through the camp already?

Tim looked for the tally poles—and nearly jumped from his boots when he saw the supply master sleeping on a bedroll in the splash of torchlight at the tent's entrance. Why hadn't Dusi told him?

Well, Tim should have been scared, but right then, he *had* to read the tallies and no sleeping giant would stop him. He found the supply master's stool and set it up by the wheat tally pole.

He climbed up. Running his fingers along the smooth pole, he could feel the splintered lines scored into the wood. The supply master continued to breathe deeply and evenly.

The front of the wheat tally pole showed how much had been taken into the supply tent since leaving the Borderkeep. When Tim returned to the Brownfolk camp, he could compare that with the Kanabur tally and figure out how much wheat was still coming on the ox wagons.

On the back of the wheat tally pole, he found the count of wheat handed out—which was tallied from the top down—and wheat spoiled and discarded—tallied from the bottom up. A score mark separated the two tallies and showed that ninety-five percent of the wheat had been handed out and five percent had spoiled. Tim gave it a quick double-check against the "wheat carried" side. Yes, the totals matched. The supply master had no more wheat.

Tim checked the other poles. The barley and potato tallies likewise showed that everything that had not spoiled had been distributed to the camp. The army had nothing except what the raiders brought in and what the followers had hoarded in their tents.

Tim looked down at the supply master and wondered how the man could sleep.

CHAPTER 36

The First Battle

SABU'S RAIDING PARTY got very little sleep that night. Ganadarm, Perga, and Vahi the stablemaster rode into camp at about the ninth lithic, having scattered the bulk of the Klindrel horse herd across the farmlands of the valley and through the forested hillsides. Sabu, Dusi, and Tim did not return until half a lithic later, and then they were required to give a report of what they had learned. (Dusi actually fell asleep during the report and had to be awakened and ordered to her sleeping place.)

The mission had been accomplished, but as the sun rose on a new day, our officers did not yet understand the consequences of that success. Maburbi, however, with the advantage that comes from writing twelve years after the battle, provides an excellent account of that morning in his book *Defense of the Redwoods*.

According to Maburbi, who actually interviewed Klindrel officers after the war, the first consequence was a duel between Prince Welzenkam and Commander Felk. Welzenkam, captain of the Maziban Lancers, accused the infantry of incompetence for not guarding his horses. Felk said he had warned Welzenkam against spreading the horses out because it thinned the sentry perimeter. In fact, that was why he had asked Welzenkam to assign his Lancers to watches along the road. Welzenkam replied, as he had when the request was made, that elite cavalry companies do not stand watches. To which Felk replied—and perhaps these words were the main reason for the duel—that the Maziban Lancers were infantry now.

The duel was fought at first light. Welzenkam was so vexed by the loss of his horses that he had not slept, and observers of the duel reported that Commander Felk slew the Prince of Mazibo easily.

At the duel's conclusion—I would say "bloody conclusion", but such is the conclusion of every duel among Children of Lith—the Klindrel Emperor gave the order to prepare for battle. This had the desired effect of preventing further duels and forcing the disparate units under his command to unite toward the common goal. And also, perhaps, he hoped to capture our supplies. Within a quarter-lithic, the Klindrel were advancing on our camp in Tomivo.

So the theft of the Klindrel horses caused the First Battle in three ways: It created a strategic problem that the emperor hoped to resolve by seizing more land, it created a political wildfire that the emperor hoped to put out by exhorting his men to fight together, and it created a humiliation that the emperor hoped to erase with a glorious victory.

Before proceeding to an account of the First Battle, I should acknowledge that I have already given that name to Zhaku's ambush on the Klindrel Road. At the other end of the spectrum, Thamikaber's *War History* describes the battle of Tomivo as a minor frontier skirmish, inconsequential compared with the battles that were fought when the Hicho Guard finally arrived to join in the defense of the Redwood Valley.

But we shall call the battle of Tomivo "the First Battle". For one thing, it was the first battle in which an army of ours clashed with a foreign army on a major scale. For another thing, all citizens of the Redwood Valley refer to it as "the First Battle" to this day, and only the most thick-headed of Thamikaber's students insist on referring to it as "the Tomivo Skirmish".

Thamikaber has no account of the battle except to mention that it occurred, so if you want to learn more about it, I suggest you read Maburbi. Maburbi's account will give you an abstract overview of the events, such as you might expect to find in Terkisho's *Theory of War*, had Terkisho not been already long dead at the time of the Klindrel Invasion.

For example, Maburbi will tell you that the Klindrel Army arrayed itself with six cohorts on the line and four held in reserve. In each of the five gaps between cohorts stood an orange-cloaked Vakadool, a master of elemental Earth and Motion, whose task was to counter any "Drelfin magic". (We knew no magical combat techniques, but the Klindrel feared otherwise.) The company of Maziban Lancers—now afoot, with their lances merely long, unwieldy spears—had the flank on the enemy's right, while "a band of skirmishers" formed a thin line in front.

Of course, Maburbi leaves out details that will be of interest to anyone who has been following the story I tell here. For example, Maburbi does not mention that these skirmishers were in fact Captain Harsk's Yellow-Eye Skirmishers, the ones who had burned down the Passwatch Roadhouse and massacred the garrison at Highcliff. It is also of interest to note that Captain Bannom and the Chumwarl Scouts, who had assisted the skirmishers at Passwatch, were no longer in the vicinity, having been given the assignment of searching for the lost horses.

So some of the enemies familiar to us were present at the battle, and some were not. I hope you aren't expecting revenge in this chapter. If so, you will be disappointed.

Ganadarm was only a little disappointed that he did not see the uniform of the Chumwarl Scouts among those arrayed for battle on the field before him. Mostly, Ganadarm was excited. He thanked Kashram for the chance to fight, and he thanked Kashram for the raid the night before—for giving him one last laugh at the Klindrel before he died.

This looked like the sort of battle Ganadarm had always wanted to die in—fighting against the Klindrel and greatly outnumbered. In fact, our numerical disadvantage was even worse from Ganadarm's perspective, astride the horse he and Tim had stolen from the Maziban Lancer two weeks before. We were outnumbered five to one, but because we were each individually half the enemy's size, it looked like ten to one.

The high horse gave Ganadarm a perspective better than most of ours. In fact, the only people who saw the battle as Maburbi describes it were those who read Maburbi's account afterwards. The actual battle looked more like Ganadarm described it in the stories he told later. I should probably give you one of those stories, but I am trying to stay closer to the truth than Ganadarm did. Let me compromise and show you the battle as I think Ganadarm actually saw it.

The Drelfin formed lines in imitation of the Klindrel cohorts they could see in the wheat fields. The lines were too close to camp to allow time for an orderly retreat, but Ganadarm didn't mind. He didn't plan to retreat.

The Drelfin carried makeshift spears—farming and gardening tools that had been given a pointy end. The spears were short, but deadly enough if the wielder could somehow get by the enemy's armor. The Drelfin themselves had no armor. Most of them did carry crude shields made hastily of wood. Their little arms were too weak to take the full force of a blow, but perhaps some of them would get lucky and deflect an attack or two before they were slain. Ganadarm had seen them in training. He did not have much confidence in their will to hold a line.

Somewhere behind the Klindrel's wall of spears, helmets, and shields, a man with a hammer struck the iron bar the Klindrel use for signaling—three strikes in slow succession. The thin line of skirmishers advanced. The black eyes painted on their yellow shields scowled across the green field of spring wheat. Drelfin shifted from foot to foot, but their officers gave no commands.

The Klindrel skirmishers advanced about halfway, then halted in the middle of the battlefield. Yes, they had slings.

The Drelfin had no weapons that could come close to the range of a Klindrel's sling, but they did have a plan. Their horse squads filed through gaps between the infantry companies. Ganadarm, astride his stolen horse, rode beside Lieutenant Saboon.

The first stones began raining down on the Drelfin while the horsemen—that is, the horsemen and horsewomen—were still forming their line. Like the Drelfin, Ganadarm held up his shield to protect his head. The wood was stout, but Ganadarm mistrusted the straps of Drelfin sheep leather.

Please let me live to cross blades with these Klindrel, Ganadarm prayed. *I do not fear to die, but please, not by sling.*

A Drelfin spoke the word that Ganadarm understood to mean "charge". Ganadarm urged his horse toward the line of scowling eyes. Tiny Drelfin horses and riders charged beside him.

The Drelfin thought that anyone with a sling would feel compelled to draw a different weapon when confronted by a line of charging horses, but Ganadarm was not surprised that the Klindrel stood their ground.

They lobbed volley after volley over the heads of the riders and into the assembled ranks of infantry. Ganadarm thought a few men were also targeting him. He separated himself from the rest of his company, so that stray shots would not strike his companions.

As he drew near enough to see the skirmishers' faces, Ganadarm grinned. They did not look like men ready to die. They looked like men who had been sent to fight Drelfin in the service of a weak emperor. The Drelfin could win this battle. The Klindrel knew that Kashram was not on their side.

Not until the last instant did the Klindrel skirmishers drop their slings and draw their swords. Saboon's soldiers leapt from their saddles and drew their longknives. Now these Klindrel would learn the lesson their comrades had already learned on the road: Never let a Drelfin get behind you.

Ganadarm remained mounted and charged directly into a knot of Klindrel. His horse surprised him by rearing and striking with its hooves. The technique was effective. These Maziban beasts were true battle horses!

Ganadarm used his shield to guard his left leg while striking down at soldiers on his right side. He crumpled one man with a helmet-denting blow. He stabbed another in the nose. Someone stepped inside his guard and tried to throw him off the horse, but his horse pivoted to push the assailant over.

Ah, the skill of his horse was nearly unfair! It *danced* on its hind legs, allowing Ganadarm to clear out a circle around himself. The Klindrel dared challenge him no longer.

The timid Drelfin ponies, abandoned by their riders, trotted daintily away from the fighting. The Drelfin had orders to fight afoot, and they were doing a good job of it. Hamstrung Klindrel lay everywhere, writhing in agony.

Ganadarm looked for a place he could attack without trampling Drelfin and found a group of Klindrel bunched in a circle to protect their backs. With a shout, Ganadarm charged.

Drelfin parted to let him attack. The Klindrel raised their blades to meet his charge. His horse veered from the fence of blades. One of the enemy must have struck the beast in the hind leg, for its rump dropped, tumbling Ganadarm onto the ground.

He rolled to his feet, sword and shield at the ready. Beside him, the horse tried to rise, screamed, and sat down again. Ganadarm used the bulk of the struggling animal to defend his back as he turned to face the soldiers.

Ah, they were glad to fight a man their own size. Ganadarm could see it on their faces. Five, perhaps ten, closed around him, each eager to deal the killing blow. He backed one youth away with a feint at his face, but then all he could do was parry. Swordtips tore his tunic, ripped his trousers, found his unprotected skin. Cuts opened on his arms and legs—even his cheek—

but he could feel none of them, so hard was he concentrating on circling his blade and twisting his shield.

A moment's more courage and they would have him. Thus would fall Ganadarm, gloriously avenging the deaths of his father and Ugly Lem!

But it was not so. Klindrel started dropping, cut or stabbed from behind by three swift-striking blades. Two of these were wielded by Pergan, whose arms moved as fast as the wings of a sparrow taking flight. The third blade was little Dusi's, darting here and there like the beak of a woodpecker pecking ants off a tree. Ganadarm found an opening to stab a man in the throat, but the foe was already collapsing from a thrust up his armored apron.

Dusi met Ganadarm's eyes and shouted, "Behind you!" It was in her language, not Ganadarm's, but Kashram was with him and he read the flick of her eyes in the universal language of battle. Ganadarm turned and thrust at a man leaping over the fallen horse. The thrust slid off the soldier's breastplate, but the force of the blow was enough to deflect his leap. The foe's swinging blade missed Ganadarm's skull. Instead, it just barely nicked his eyebrow.

The Klindrel landed with one foot on the wounded horse. The screaming beast kicked and thrashed with its good legs, knocking the Klindrel's feet out from under him. Ganadarm would have taken advantage, but more Klindrel came rushing at him from the direction of the head and the tail.

As the fallen man tried to rise, Ganadarm stepped on his shoulder and leapt over the horse, leaving the rushing foes on the other side. For an instant, he congratulated himself on his cleverness, but then he realized he had left Pergan and Dusi behind. The Klindrel were not pursuing Ganadarm. They were joining the fray that Pergan and Dusi were somewhere in the middle of.

A Drelfin grabbed the hem of his tunic and tugged it hard. Ganadarm looked down into the little face of Thaki, the other woman.

"Do you no hear the sound?" she asked. "Diggle, diggle, diggle, diggle. That means run away!"

Ganadarm blinked at her. She slipped behind him and started pushing.

Ah, yes. He could hear it now. The Drelfin signalman was whipping his baton around the inside of an iron triangle, making the noise that Thaki had imitated. Lieutenant Saboon had told him that would be the signal to retreat.

Beyond his screaming horse and the knot of skirmishers, Ganadarm could see the lines of the Klindrel advancing, hundreds and hundreds of gleaming spearpoints coming to claim the battlefield.

Thaki was pushing him back toward the Drelfin lines. The rest of Saboon's people were already obeying the signal.

Ganadarm ran to join Saboon.

CHAPTER 37
Sacrifice

FROM SABU'S PERSPECTIVE, of course, things appeared different.

The Klindrel skirmishers looked like a forest of legs. Sabu did not look into their eyes. He did not watch the swing of their shoulders. He saw the set of their legs and inferred where the openings would be.

The soldier in front of him stood with right hip cocked, sword pointing at Sabu's face. Sabu sidestepped, and the Klindrel's sword thrust into the space where Sabu had been.

Sabu countered with a thrust of his own, but the Klindrel, savvy in close-quarter combat, met the attack by driving the edge of his yellow shield into Sabu's face. Sabu fell on his back among the green leaves of wheat.

His opponent's legs shifted in, rising up on the balls of the feet. The sword was poised to skewer Sabu where he lay. Sabu raised his wooden shield.

Steel flashed into the Klindrel's boot. A scream sounded from high above. Sabu rolled to his feet to see one of his patrollers emerge from behind the wounded leg. It was Bovushimo, the sixth-year with a scar on his lower lip from a riding accident. He was an awkward rider, but graceful when he had both feet on the ground.

Gosher the cook jabbed a blade up inside the Klindrel's armored apron and the soldier collapsed in pain.

"Are you hurt?" Gosher asked, as Bovushimo ended the Klindrel's life with a deep thrust through the eye.

"I'm fine," Sabu said.

Sabu nodded to Bovushimo, who came to stand on the other side of him.

"Where next?" Gosher asked.

Sabu made a quick assessment. They had stopped the hail of slingstones—which was their goal—but they had no easy way to disengage. Their mounts had run from the skirmish and were now trotting along the line of volunteer infantry, trying to leave the battlefield. The fighting in front of Sabu had broken up into several clusters, and his people appeared to be outnumbered in all of them. Sabu knew this was an illusion—his people were in there somewhere among the legs, using the Klindrel's cohesion against them—but this knowledge did not make it easier to tell where he and his two companions would be needed most.

Then the signaler began clanging the retreat. Now Sabu had to pull his people out of the battle without exposing their backs to the enemy.

"To me, to me!" he cried to the knots of combatants. "To me and form a line!"

Gosher looked at him uncertainly. They had practiced line techniques, but they were not very good at them.

Patrollers came to Sabu's call. In twos and threes they broke away from the Klindrel and ran to join the line. Zerdegi, the second-year who showed the most leadership potential, turned his back to the enemy. A Klindrel sword came crashing down on his head, breaking open his skull.

Vahi the stablemaster was trying to help Mishu to his feet. Mishu had fallen off his horse at the start of the battle, and he had remained kneeling in the wheat while his comrades fought. Sabu prayed that Knowledge would bring Mishu to his senses before Vahi was engaged by the Klindrel skirmishers.

But the skirmishers were not engaging. They were letting the patrollers regroup. In fact, the skirmishers were falling back, leaving bodies giant and small lying on the field.

Why were they falling back? Ah, yes. Now Sabu saw it. The ranks of spearmen were advancing. Small gaps opened in the line of spears and shields to allow the skirmishers to pass through to the rear, but this did not slow the advance. The spearmen marched over top of the bodies of the wounded. As they approached Ganadarm's screaming horse, one of them broke ranks and ran ahead to slit the horse's throat so that it would not kick while his company climbed over it.

Ganadarm himself was in position on the end of Sabu's line. Sabu hoped Dusi was somewhere in the line, too.

"Company, backstep!" Sabu called. "One, two, three, four, five, six! One, two, three, four, five, six!"

The line grew ragged as they withdrew. Some were backstepping faster than others.

"Stay in the line!" Sabu called. "Guide to me."

He knew why they did not, however. Sabu's backstep was not as fast as the advance of the spearmen.

Sabu wondered about those spears. Would the Klindrel throw them once they got in range, or would they keep them for stabbing? He hoped the spears would be thrown. The volunteer infantry would not have the courage to stand against a wall of spears. Even his disciplined, veteran patrollers were wavering.

The signaler whipped his baton around the triangle again. Sabu was not certain what that meant. Was there another cohort on the field somewhere that was also being ordered to disengage, or was Commander Visho trying to tell Sabu to get his people out of the way faster?

Sabu guessed the latter.

"On six, turn and run!" he yelled. "On six, turn and run! One. Two. Three. Four—"

That was enough for the weaker-willed. Sabu's line began to disintegrate.

"Five."

Now only the patrollers between him and Ganadarm were still in line.

"Six!" he shouted.

Sabu turned, glad to see most of his patrollers already well ahead of him. He wanted them all in front, so he could keep an eye on them. And if the Klindrel started throwing their spears, he would have been ashamed if someone else's back had been a closer target than his own.

Sabu sheathed his battleblade and ran after his people. The patrollers were well rested after two days without travel. They were strong runners, and Sabu had to work hard to keep up with them. No iron tip punctured his gasping lungs. No wooden shaft shot through his pounding heart. The Klindrel had decided to hold their spears.

Sabu was now close enough to the battle line that he could see the faces of the Redwood Valley Volunteers. They looked scared.

"Hold the line!" an officer shouted as Sabu's people ran past his. But with the Klindrel coming next, the order must have seemed illogical. The central company turned and ran away behind the retreating Road Patrol.

Maburbi will tell you what happened next. Companies on

either side also crumbled away and our center collapsed before the Klindrel had even reached throwing range. Some companies on the flanks held, but only long enough to get smashed by "the steel-capped wave of Klindrel infantry", as Maburbi puts it in *Defense of the Redwoods*. He claims that only the Shady Creek Spear Company, a unit of professional trappers and hunters, slew a significant number of the enemy. But anyone I've talked to says that the Shady Creek Spear Company distinguished themselves mostly by their willingness to lie shamelessly about their accomplishments.

We abandoned the field of battle to the Klindrel, and we abandoned Tomivo as well. The Klindrel did not pause long to savor their victory. They pursued us down the river, raiding villages on the way, so that our officers were obliged to keep our people marching until the Klindrel were willing to stop and make camp.

But do not think for a moment that I am belittling those who fled that day. No, that would be hypocritical. The thing to remember about the men and women who were routed from that field is that they fled together. They did not run for home and leave their comrades behind to die in their places. No, they fled with their comrades beside them. Of those who survived the First Battle, I know of only one who was not with her company by the time Commander Visho called a halt to the retreat that evening. In fact, the army was actually bigger than it had been at Tomivo, for many new volunteers joined as the army passed through their villages.

In camp that evening, Sabu saw Thaki pacing among the patrollers, fingers twitching as she surreptitiously counted Passwatch Company. He walked over and took her by the hand.

"They're gone, Thaki."

Thaki nodded her curly head. "I know," she said. "I just want to know how many are gone."

"You've counted three times," Sabu said.

"I've forgotten someone."

"Vahi is helping the other stablemasters sort out the remaining horses."

"Ah." Thaki nodded. "Of course."

Sabu looked into her eyes. He didn't want to let go of her hand.

"I thought he was invincible, Sabu. I thought no one could lay a blade on him."

Sabu nodded. Ganadarm had told him that Perga and Dusi had been overwhelmed by Klindrel soldiers. Sabu hoped they had escaped somehow and were even now making their way back to camp, but that was just a story he was telling himself to get through the rest of the day. He didn't believe it.

"Perga was good with his blades," Sabu said. "But not even Perga could escape so many giants."

"Yes he could have," Thaki said. "He just didn't."

"You think he couldn't run because he was trying to protect Dusi."

Thaki nodded and let go of his hand. "I'm sorry."

Sabu wasn't angry. "I suspect you are right," he said. "Staying to protect an injured comrade is something Perga would do."

"What was the rookie thinking, diving into a mob of giants?"

"I suspect she just got excited. Perhaps she was trying to save Ganadarm."

"I'm sorry," Thaki said. "Oh, Sabu. I'm so sorry."

He held her while her shoulders shook. It was good for her. He could not cry himself. His duty was to give his emotions to the Goddess and accept cold, rational judgment in return. Because he was the commanding officer. He had to be the strong one. He had to take care of Thaki. Because it was too late to do anything for Perga and Dusi.

Mister Hill was standing nearby, trying to watch Sabu without looking at him. The cat twined itself around Tim's trouser legs. Sabu looked over at the campfire near the ox wagons, where Commander Visho stood. The other officers were beginning to gather.

"Thaki, would you take care of Tim's cat, please? I don't want it to disrupt the council meeting."

Thaki nodded.

Sabu led her over to Tim and explained the situation. Tim agreed.

"That wasn't really about the cat, was it?" Tim murmured as they walked through camp.

"No," said Sabu. "It wasn't."

"Is there anything I can do for *you*?" Tim asked.

No. There isn't. "I'm fine, Tim."

"... Of course."

"I hope you're prepared for the meeting," Sabu said.

Tim shrugged. "Well, I have my ledger."

Visho had called the council meeting to discuss strategy with his officers. Sabu had asked that Tim be included because Tim's accounting skill had proven so valuable. Visho had agreed. He had been impressed by Tim's part in the previous night's raid.

Also in attendance was Elder Shoto, who led the meetings of the General Council of the Vozohicho Academy. For the benefit of those raised in places where mainland geography is not taught in every school—here, I am thinking of the colony islands, but I fear the same could be said of those districts of Hicho where Hicho is assumed to be the only city in the world—for those people, let me say that Vozohicho is the largest city in the Redwood Valley and it was as intellectually influential then as it is now. The Vozohicho Academy was, even then, independent of the Hicho Academy—officially independent for two generations and practically independent for much longer. In short, if our people had considered themselves as citizens of states, and if the Redwood Valley had been one such state, then Elder Shoto would have been the head of that state. Be certain that when he spoke, he spoke for more people than himself.

Even though Sabu had grown up far from Vozohicho, he recognized the elder's name when introductions were made. For a while, he was awed to be part of a discussion that included this wise and honored elder. But as the discussion went on, he saw that Elder Shoto was quiet. And Sabu realized that Elder Shoto knew little of war and that he was wise enough to listen to those who did.

But how much did they know? The day's defeat had shown Sabu how inadequate his people were for fighting army-against-army. And as Commander Visho outlined various strategic options, Sabu realized that Visho had no idea what to do.

In fact, Visho even concluded his outline of the situation with, "Such are our options as I believe them to be, but which of them is the wisest course of action, I do not know."

Perhaps the others present were having the same thoughts as Sabu, for none of them ventured to help Visho choose.

Finally, it was Tim who dared to speak. "You lost today," he said. "But you are close to the win."

"How so?" asked Commander Visho.

"The Klindrel have little food," Tim said. "Sabu and I saw this with our eyes. They will be hungry soon."

"Perhaps," said Commander Visho. "But you also said they would be getting supplies soon."

"Not soon," said Tim. "Not soon enough. They will be hungry for days before the ox wagons will come. And today they move themselves one day farther from food."

"I fear they will be feeding themselves from the stores of the villages they conquer," said Elder Shoto.

Jerfashi, the captain of the lumberjack company, nodded. "Yes. I suspect that is why they attacked us today—to take the food in Tomivo."

"Well, we just have to make a stand, then," said Captain Poshovi of the Shady Creek Spear Company. "Stop them from getting any more."

"They still outnumber us," Commander Visho said. "I don't see how we can make a stand until we join with the Hicho Guard."

Elder Shoto smiled at Sabu. "You are quiet," he said. "What do you think?"

Until this moment, Sabu had thought he was there to receive orders. But if Elder Shoto wanted him to form an opinion …

"It seems like Tim and I have been fighting this army a long time now," Sabu said. "We've tried a few things, and some of them have worked. But win or lose, we always have to run away."

He thought it over a moment. "I apologize. That was incoherent."

Elder Shoto shook his head. "No, it made sense to me. You are saying we don't have the military capability to stop them. We can only attack them indirectly."

"That is what I say, too!" Tim said. "Carry food away from the villages. Leave them nothing."

"They still have the ox wagons coming down from the mountains," Visho said.

"Burn the ox wagons!" Tim said.

"How?" asked Visho, amused.

"You— you—" And then Tim's face filled with such warmth that Sabu suspected he had been ignited by the flame of Knowledge. "You burn the bridge!" he said. "At Farbridge. It is the only way to cross. Burn the bridge, and the ox wagons will never arrive."

"But the enemy legion is between us and the bridge," said Commander Visho.

Tim waved his hands dismissively. "Sabu is tricksome. He will find a way."

"In truth," Sabu admitted, "that *is* the sort of thing my people could do."

"But the Klindrel can still get food by raiding the countryside," Commander Visho said.

Tim shook his head. "No. When they move you out, you must take all food with you. Leave them nothing to steal. Can you not see?"

"Perhaps I see," said Elder Shoto. He put his palms together and pressed his fingers to his lips. Everyone remained quiet, giving him a chance to complete his thought.

He looked them in the eye, each one in turn. Sabu thought he saw a gentle smile—gentle and sad.

"We need to remove all the food from their path," said Elder Shoto. "Slaughter all the animals and eat what we can. Defend as much grain as we can and destroy the rest."

Tim's eyes widened in horror. "No, not destroy. I did not mean that."

Elder Shoto smiled. "I know you did not. You are a faithful servant of Wealth. But we lack the means to carry *everything* away. Some food and some animals must be destroyed. This is a thing we can do, if the need is great enough. Our deity will understand."

"It is too much," Tim said. "Too much waste."

"People will soon go hungry," Sabu said.

"Yes," Elder Shoto said. "It will be like the Time of Dragons."

"Will people do it?" asked Captain Jerfashi.

Elder Shoto nodded. "They will once Visho and I explain it to them. Within a week, this valley will have no food left to steal."

"I did not mean that," said Tim. "I did not *mean* that."

CHAPTER 38
The Survivor

I SAID I KNEW of only one survivor who did not rejoin her company after the First Battle. That was Dusi, of course. I wish that Perga were also among the survivors, but he was not. This is what happened:

Dusi and Perga were attempting to extricate Ganadarm from an unwinnable fray when the Klindrel signaler gave the command for the lines to advance. As the heavy clangs of the Klindrel hammer sounded through the battlefield, our own signaler began whipping around the triangle to tell Sabu it was time to retreat. The Klindrel skirmishers were also retreating to clear the way for their advancing infantry. The Klindrel disengaging from Thaki's squad turned to find Ganadarm's fallen horse between them and their lines.

Dusi had just collapsed a Klindrel skirmisher, so she had a good view of these soldiers coming up behind Ganadarm.

"Behind you!" she cried.

But she could do no more, for she was surrounded by the enemy.

Dusi thrust at the nearest knee. The knee jumped back. Dusi sidestepped a sword and shifted inside the enemy's guard. She poked a hole in his trousers and dodged past him.

She glimpsed Perga confronting a pair of legs. Dusi dodged behind those legs, using the Klindrel's body to shield her from the others. She thrust her battleblade behind the enemy's knee and ripped the serrated edge through the tendon. One less for Perga to worry about.

As the stricken soldier fell, the sky opened around Dusi and she saw that the Klindrel were retreating from the fray. Perga stared at her openmouthed, with blood spurting from a gash in his neck. His eyes rolled up in the back of his head, and he fell to the ground.

Then the skirmishers who had come from behind Ganadarm's horse were rushing down upon her. She turned to face the leader and raised her shield to block his sword. The blow struck her shield squarely, knocking her to the ground. A boot heel smashed her ankle into the soil of the wheat field as the retreating skirmishers passed over. Then they were gone, leaving Dusi lying among the dead and wounded Klindrel, near the screaming horse.

Her shield arm rang with numbness from the shock of the blow. When she rose to her feet, pain shot through her ankle. Dusi clenched her teeth and convinced herself to remain standing.

She measured the distance to her line. How *fast* could she walk on that ankle?

Dusi sheathed her battleblade and began limping away from the advancing Klindrel infantry. She was strong. She was tough. She would push through the pain, because she was a survivor.

But she was not the only one who could endure pain. A hamstrung Klindrel pushed himself up on one good leg as she passed. His jaw clenched. With a mighty heave, he lunged toward her, swinging his sword down at her unprotected head. Dusi flung her numb shield arm in an arc across her body, catching the Klindrel's blade on her shield and slapping it aside.

The Klindrel fell in front of her and rolled to right himself. She drew her battleblade, pushed off with her good foot and fell on the Klindrel, stabbing at his face. The point of her blade scraped against his eye socket and slid into his brain.

Dusi pulled her battleblade out and rolled off the Klindrel's spasming body, landing on her aching shield arm. She caught a glimpse of the Klindrel skirmishers retreating through gaps in the infantry line. The line was closer now. Her own line was still far away.

The Klindrel whose brains were on her blade was twice her size. Dusi discarded her shield and crawled inside the dying man's stinking embrace. Before he even stopped twitching, she covered herself with his torso, tucking her arms and legs in close to her body so that she would not be seen. She lay curled up under the corpse and waited to see if she would be found.

Presently, she heard the sound of the Klindrel's segmented armor, a multitude of thin metallic scrapes as segment slid against segment, like a field full of crickets with well-oiled scissors for legs. The impact of their boots on the soft earth was so quiet that they seemed almost ghostly as they advanced, green wheat rustling about their ankles.

Then they were upon her and she could hear their breath as they huffed under weight of sword, spear, shield, helmet, and armor. An entire company of panting men passed over her, cursing when they stumbled over their fallen comrade's body.

Then they were gone and Dusi could breathe again under the weight of the heavy corpse. She listened until she was certain the susurration of armor and the clack of loose scabbards was distant. Then she risked a peek from her hiding place.

The horse was finally dead, but several of Perga's victims were still writhing in pain nearby. In the direction of Uppermost Pikomi, Dusi could see four Klindrel cohorts held in reserve. She was caught between them and their front line. If she tried to flee, she would be seen, but if she stayed, she would be found when the Klindrel came to collect their dead.

The spirits of the dead were all around her, but she forced them from her mind using the same techniques that had kept her recent dreams safe from her mother's hauntings. Dusi was master of her mind and she would focus it on the task at hand.

She decided to crawl away on her belly. The field was flat, but it was not flat like a table. It was above the annual floodplain, with gentle rolls of higher ground and faint creases of drainages. Dusi crawled into such a crease and followed it upward toward a grove of flex-fir.

She left her shield behind but kept her battleblade. She believed she might need it.

By the time she reached the grove, the numbness in her shield arm had relaxed to a dull ache. Her ankle had swollen and the tight cuff of her trouser leg bit into her skin.

Dusi used the tip of her battleblade to slit the cuff of her trousers, picking out stitches in the seam one by one. As she worked, she tried to decide what to do next. She knew the Klindrel had overrun her comrades' position. She was now behind enemy lines.

Her calculation had two unknowns: How far away would her army go before they encamped again, and how fast would they move? Dusi feared she could not catch up on her swelling ankle. She needed a day or two to rest it, preferably in a place where she could keep it in cold water. Tomivo was the nearest village, but the Klindrel probably occupied it now. Dusi did not know this part of the Redwood Valley well, but weren't there always lumber villages near the edge of the forest? A place like that might be far enough off the main road that the Klindrel would not bother with it.

Dusi left the grove shortly after the fifth lithic, aiming for the line of redwoods in the distance. She walked upright, hoping that she could cover the ground faster on two legs than she could on all fours, and hoping that her ankle injury was the sort that heals faster with exercise. She had to stop and rest more often than she would have liked.

Before the lith set, she found a road to follow. Walking was less painful on a firmer surface. You see, her forearm and her ankle were not her only problems, now. Her hip was sore from carrying her injured ankle, and the knee of her good leg was aching from the stress of her awkward gait. She was asking her body to do what she would never have asked from a lame horse. If she did not take some care, she would be lame in two legs, and two were all she had.

She was following a curve of the road between two apple orchards when she heard hoofbeats behind her. She slid off the road into the ditch.

Careless, she thought as she crawled out of the ditch and into the orchard. *No one should be able to sneak up on you, Dusi.*

The orchard grass was tall, nearly waist high. She knelt at the base of a tree and tried to open her mind.

From the sound of the hooves, she knew the riders were on giant-sized horses. Dusi reached for the destructive side of the Elemental Realms and detected the decay of stray thoughts popping from the world like bubbles of foam from a river eddy.

"Captain Bannom," said a voice.

Horses reined to a halt. Dusi guessed about a dozen of them.

"In the grass there," said the voice. "Something crossed through the ditch and went into the orchard."

"Interesting," another voice replied. "Vilmon, call out. See if it's a Drelfin."

A voice spoke up in Dusi's language. The accent was as choppy as a one-armed woodcutter. "Hello. We see you. Come out now."

Dusi held still. The Klindrel thought they could trick *her?*

The first voice decided, "It's probably just a deer."

"Well, deer or Drelfin," said the one that gave the orders, "it's not a horse. And we're supposed to be finding horses. We ride on."

"Aye, sir."

One man dismounted, and the horses clomped away down the road.

The sounds of bees and birdsong returned to the orchard. After a time, the soldier who had been silently assigned the task of staying behind to watch for her gave up his vigil. He jogged off after the others.

Dusi smiled. She had out-bluffed them and out-waited them.

Traveling on the road was now too risky. Dusi stayed in the orchard until nightfall.

After sunset, she followed an empty irrigation ditch up toward the hills. When she came to the headgate where her empty irrigation ditch met a flowing creek, she took a drink and soaked her ankle. Her bruised arm was feeling better. She could grasp her moccasin in her hand without fear of dropping it.

It was still night when Dusi reached the redwoods at the edge of the Redwood Valley. Choosing a bed among the ferns well away from any paths, she settled down to sleep. She hoped the new day would bring her some food.

When she awoke, she was back in the apple orchard, watching the Klindrel Army march by.

"You can hide from them," her mother said. "But you cannot hide from me."

Dusi controlled her surprise. It was the first time she had seen her mother since confessing the true nature of her dreams to Sabu. A part of her wished she had not been too exhausted to ward her mind before going to sleep. A part of her was glad to see her mother again.

"Hello, Mother," she said calmly.

"Nor can you hide your thoughts from me," her mother said. "I am in here with you. You have no other place to hide them."

Dusi shrugged. "Then you know how much I want you gone."

"Yes," her mother said, smiling down into her face. "And I know how much you want me to stay. You are almost ready to serve the All-Knowing Master. You did good work today."

That was true. She had found a way to hide in the middle of a battlefield, and then she had eluded the enemy's patrols.

"I did what I had to do to save my life."

"Of course," her mother said. "And the Master approves of how you used his gifts. He wants you to live."

"I wasn't using any gifts."

"All your lies, tricks, and deceptions belong to him," her mother said. "Haven't you learned that yet?"

That wasn't true. Dusi was clever, and that cleverness was her own.

"No," said her mother. "You got your cleverness from me. And every time you use it, you serve my master."

"I serve the Children of Knowledge."

"You fight the Children of Lith."

"They are invading our lands."

"And you must use deception to defend our people," her mother said. "I understand. As I said, the Master approves."

She was lying. Either that or she was telling only the part of the truth that served her purpose. Dusi would not let herself be manipulated.

Her mother shook her head sadly. "You still don't understand, do you? Every deception brings you closer to me. Every single one. The fact that you are condemning your soul in service to our people just makes your damnation sweeter."

Dusi awoke then to the sound of a chattering squirrel. She was lying among the ferns in which she had fallen asleep. Mist hid the tops of the redwoods from view, and dew dripped from the fronds onto her face. Dusi sat up. The squirrel on the tree in front of her added his final words, then scurried around to the other side.

Ah, good, said Redwood. *I see you are awake.*

Dusi blinked a moment. She tried to listen to the thoughts inside her own head. She could no longer find her mother in there. Her resonance with Redwood was too strong.

"Did you send that squirrel to wake me up?" she asked.

Yes. Your dream seemed to be disturbing you … at least the part of you that was still a part of me.

Dusi thought about this. "Thank you," she decided.

She tried to rise to her feet, and pain flamed in her ankle. She sat down with a mossy thump. The ache in her arm had diffused up into her shoulder overnight. The ache in the knee of her good leg had not gone away, and she now had the usual back stiffness that she got from sleeping on the ground.

"Redwood," she said, "I need to return to my people."

Your villages are not far away.

"Not those people. The army."

She forced herself to her feet.

"Redwood," she asked, "if you have power over this entire forest, does that mean you have the power to help everything in this forest?"

The forest is my body, Redwood said. *Of course I use my powers to help it.*

"What about me?" Dusi asked. "Can you help me?"

I do help you, said Redwood. *But you are asking me to heal you.*

"Yes," said Dusi. "That is the help I need."

I am not so certain, Redwood said. *Your body will heal by itself long before next spring arrives.*

"But I need to walk now."

Then walk.

"You will not help me?"

You are not mine, Redwood said. *You are part of me while you are here, but you are not mine. Your soul is divided between Heaven and Hell.*

Dusi sighed. "Thanks for reminding me."

But I did help you, Redwood said. *By waking you up.*

"Well, thank you for that, at least."

You should not trust those dreams.

"I know," Dusi said. "Redwood, did you see me escape from the Children of Lith yesterday?"

No. But you told most of the story in your thoughts before you went to sleep.

"Did I do anything wrong?"

Right and wrong are for the deities to judge. Nature spirits are more concerned with balance.

"Oh."

Your balance has tipped only a little since I last spoke with you.

"Tipped? Which way?"

Toward evil, of course. I told you that Knowledge is weak against the Deceiver.

"So my mother was telling the truth?"

About what?

"She said that every deception serves the Deceiver."

Not every deception. Just your deceptions. Because your soul is rotting.

"She said that by serving my people I am damning my soul."

Perhaps, said Redwood. *You can fight the Children of Lith with deception, but not the Deceiver. Deception is the essence of his nature.*

"If that's true, then why did my mother warn me?"

I don't know, said Redwood. *I assume the warning served the Deceiver's purpose.*

"Then I can't let her manipulate me," Dusi said. "I have to do my duty, no matter the cost to me."

I doubt the answer is so simple.

"Simple or not, I'm going back to Sabu."

I thought you wanted to go back to your army.

"I do."

But your Sabu is not with the army.

"He's not? What happened to him?"

Do not fear. He is well. He and the Child of Lith and the Child of Wealth all passed through my forest last night.

"Only three of them?"

Yes. Only three of them. No cat.

Sabu, Ganadarm, and Tim behind enemy lines? It sounded like another special mission.

Dusi moved her foot in a circle, trying to loosen the pain in her swollen ankle. She said, "I need to go with them. I know you can't help with my injuries, but can you at least help me find them?"

Yes, but that is not the help you need from me.

"You are offering to separate me from the Deceiver."

Yes.

"But that will also separate me from the Goddess."

And from your mother.

"There must be a better way," Dusi said.

Perhaps. But I do not know it.

"Please, just help me find Sabu."

CHAPTER 39
Threewells

THIS IS HOW SABU, Ganadarm, and Tim came to be sneaking through the redwoods:

Lieutenant Sabu was ordered to explain the Starvation Strategy to the villages behind enemy lines. He had been second-in-command of the ambush on the Klindrel Road. He had led the ambush at Neargap. He had led three garrisons through the mountains to Roadhouse One. And he had led the reconnaissance mission that confirmed the Klindrel were low on food. According to Commander Visho, Sabu was the patroller most qualified to lead this mission.

Visho added that Sabu's company would be well cared for. He was reorganizing the Road Patrol into a cohort of Roadhouse Skirmishers. Passwatch Company would be combined with Deermeadow Company and a few volunteers to round the numbers up to six dozen.

Visho also suggested—perhaps insisted—that Sabu take Ganadarm along. This was wise. If Ganadarm had stayed with the army, he would have been subordinate to a stranger, and that could have led to unpleasantness.

Of course, Ganadarm was glad to have such an assignment. He looked forward to sneaking around behind Klindrel lines and sabotaging their battle plans. It was the sort of thing Ugly Lem would have done. Also, Ganadarm had noted the absence of the Chumwarl Scouts on the battlefield, and he hoped to find them and Captain Bannom somewhere in the Drelfin countryside.

And as for Tim Hill ...

Tim stood a respectful distance from Sabu and Thaki as they discussed the merger with Deermeadow Company. Sabu kept calm, with a face like granite, while Thaki grew increasingly more animated in her gestures and increasingly louder in her expressions of incredulity. Tim had been in enough arguments during his married life to tell that Sabu was winning.

They argued until Thaki's objections shortened to single-sentence mutters. Sabu replied to her with monosyllabic murmurs. Finally, Thaki's shoulders slumped and she trudged off to assume temporary command of the company. Sabu heaved a sigh. Tim sighed in sympathy. When a man argues with a woman, he loses even when he wins.

Although Tim had sympathy for Sabu, he chose not to pass up this opportunity. It might be his only chance to speak with the Brownman before he left on his mission, and the fact that Sabu was tired of arguing gave Tim a powerful bargaining position.

"Lieutenant Sabu?" he called as he approached. "May I speak with you?"

To Sabu's credit, he did not sigh heavily at these words. Nor did he cut to "What is it?" Instead he presented a calm face and said quietly, "Of course, Tim. What can I do for you?"

"You can choose me as one of the people for your mission," Tim said.

Sabu opened his mouth to reply.

Tim asked, "Before you say no, would you please listen to my reasoning?"

Sabu nodded.

Tim kept his face as calm as Sabu's, but he smiled inwardly. Tim had chosen to speak in his own language so that Sabu would have more difficulty articulating objections.

"First," said Tim, "I am capable. I proved that during our midnight mission in the Klindrel camp."

Sabu nodded.

"Second," said Tim, "I have skills you need. I know the roads, and I know how the trade flows through this valley."

"Third?" asked Sabu.

"And third," said Tim, "I am not one of your soldiers, so taking me away will not weaken those whom you must leave behind."

Tim smiled openly now. He had spoken in his language, but he had made Brownfolk arguments. To say no, Sabu would have to provide counterarguments, and Tim thought he was too tired to do so.

Sabu remained silent for a long while, studying Tim's face. Finally he said, "Tell me your real reason."

"Beg pardon?"

"Tell me why, Tim. You say why *I* want you to come. But why do *you* want to come?"

"Oh, well ..." Tim hadn't prepared for this. "Does it matter?"

Sabu nodded. It did matter.

"I don't want to come," Tim admitted. "I'm scared. But I have to come anyway."

"Because ...?"

"Because I'm the one who gave your leaders the idea that they should destroy their wealth."

"You feel guilt?"

"Aye," Tim admitted. "Or at any rate, I feel responsible. If your people give up so much and then the Klindrel get supplied anyway ... Well, I just have to stop those wagons, Sabu. I have to. Or at least, when I face Yolim, I have to be able to say I did all I could."

Sabu nodded. "Go to sleep then," he said. "I will wake you in half a lithic."

... and that was how Tim was selected as the third member of Sabu's squad.

Three days later, as Tim stood outside a spacious two-story house in the village of Threewells, he wondered if maybe they shouldn't have taken along an additional person. You see, Tim had been given the assignment of standing watch while Sabu conferred with the village council. This was a job Ganadarm could not do. A red-skinned giant lounging around in the village square would have been conspicuous. So Ganadarm had been hidden in a nearby apple orchard.

Tim would have preferred to be hiding with Ganadarm. He wished they had a Brownman along who could "play lookout" as Ganadarm called it. Instead, the Brownfolk had shaved Tim's head and given him a chiton to wear.

The bald head was conspicuous, but not as conspicuous as Tim's own fuzzy pate would have been. Without Clanfolk hair to give him away, his brown skin would make him look like a Brown-man—at least to the Redmen. Tim did not feel like a Brownman, and even the Brownfolk admitted that he could be mistaken for them only at a distance. Still, "at a distance" was where they hoped to keep the Klindrel. And so they would, if Tim did his job as lookout.

But it was not his exposed *head* that bothered Tim. No, what bothered him was the chiton.

It was a dress. Pure and simple, that's what it was. Thaki had explained that, no, it was a long, seamless tunic, but if so, then where were the trousers? Even the slightest breeze found places that Tim did not want caressed by the wind.

It was a dress, and it was not even a *modest* dress. His arms were completely *bare*. And seamless? Was it ever! The right side of the garment was held closed by only four pins. Tim walked with his arm covering the gaping holes until Sabu and Thaki chastised him for not looking natural. In Tim's opinion, the chiton was a bit *too* natural. Civilized people should not expose so much skin.

So Tim stood in front of the house in the village square and tried to look natural—at least from a distance—while all the people who went to the well paused to stare at his bare arms and bald head. The scabbarded blade issued to him was hardly concealed beneath his flimsy garment. Little children gathered in small clusters to discuss and point at the stranger in their village. Tim hoped no Klindrel came, for even the least observant of them would surely notice the entire village was staring at Mister Tim Hill.

A boy with long, dark hair came striding down one of the roads Tim was in charge of watching. He spotted Tim, and his pace quickened. The boy crossed the square purposefully and stopped in front of Tim, staring up at him with solemn green eyes.

"Good day," said Tim, in the boy's language.

"Good day," the boy replied. "Are you the Child of Wealth?"

"Why do you ask?"

"My parents told me to warn the short-haired man who travels with the bald Child of Wealth."

Tim took in the boy's drab gray chiton and the stray bits of grass that clung to its skirt. "You cut hay today," Tim said. "We passed you as we came in."

"Yes," said the boy. "My father gave you directions. Is the short-haired man here?"

"He is inside," said Tim.

The boy bit his lip. Apparently, his parents hadn't mentioned anything about interrupting a council meeting.

"You can tell me this message," Tim offered. "I will tell him."

The boy thought a moment, then nodded. "Tell the short-haired man that Children of Lith are riding down the road."

"Which road?" asked Tim in alarm.

"That one," said the boy, pointing. "The one I came in on."

Tim knocked on the door. "Sabu," he called. "Riders coming."

He looked down at the boy, who continued to stare with solemn eyes. "Ah, thank you," Tim said. He fished around in his coin pouch and found a sixth-thozi. "For you," he said, handing the coin to the boy.

The boy studied it. He looked up at Tim quizzically. Tim remembered then that it was not the custom in the Redwood Valley to pay children for small favors, but it was too late to take it back, and he didn't have time to explain. Sabu came out with a hunted look.

"Which road are they coming on?" Sabu asked.

"Our road," Tim said, pointing.

Sabu nodded. "Come with me."

They left the solemn-eyed boy and the staring people in the village square.

Sabu led Tim to a smaller house at the edge of the village and rapped on the yellow-painted door. No one answered. Not surprising. It was an Orangemonth day, beautifully warm. Most people were outside.

Sabu pushed on the door. It was not locked. Apparently, the village of Threewells was far enough off the main roads that the people did not fear burglars.

"Follow me," said Sabu.

"What are you doing?" Tim asked.

Sabu shook his head and passed through the house to a back window. The reed mats had gone unchanged too long and the shutters had been left open to freshen up the dank smell. Sabu peered out, then indicated that Tim should take a turn.

The Klindrel were on the road as the boy had said, but they were no longer advancing. Instead they were waiting while some of their number trotted through the orchard where Tim and Sabu had left Ganadarm.

"Now what?" Tim asked.

"We go on a different road," said Sabu.

"But what about Ganadarm?"

Sabu shrugged. "We are no help for him now."

Tim knew that wasn't right. Ganadarm had freed him from prison. He couldn't just let Ganadarm be captured.

"What if we distracted them?" Tim asked.

"How?"

"I don't know," Tim said. "We could call out to them. Make them chase *us* instead."

Sabu looked Tim up and down. "They have horses," he said. "How fast do you run?"

Tim had no answer for that.

"I also do not want him captured," Sabu said. "But if they capture us, too, then who will burn the bridge? We must go."

Tim thought of all the Brownfolk who would go hungry— even the solemn-eyed messenger boy, assuming that Sabu had convinced the Threewells council to destroy their food supplies. He had to admit that Sabu was right. Tim's personal debt to Ganadarm would have to be satisfied after he had ensured that the sacrifice of wealth was not in vain. That was a debt he owed to Yolim.

"All right," Tim said.

Sabu nodded and led Tim out the door.

"We walk normal," Sabu said. "Down that road." He pointed. "Behave like walkers, like normal people. Not soldiers."

"Aye," said Tim.

They set off on a road leading moonward that would put several fields between them and the orchard the Klindrel were searching.

"More slow," Sabu warned. "We have no hurry. We are traveling philosophers."

"Aye," Tim agreed, and he tried to slow his pace.

A voice spoke up from behind a garden fence: "Tim."

"Eep," Tim gasped, stopping in his tracks.

"Ganadarm?" Sabu asked.

"Saboon," the giant replied.

Tim still could not see him. The poles of the fence were as tight as a roadhouse palisade.

"We thought you were in the orchard," Sabu said.

"I was," Ganadarm replied. "But when Bannom's men came riding up, I thought I had best come warn you."

"How did you escape?" Tim asked.

"Ah, 'twas not easy, my friend," Ganadarm said. "Fortunately, I espied them approaching from my perch in an apple tree. If not for that, I would never have had enough warning to enact my plan. But I did see them, and I realized that the tracks we had left in the grass would give me away. So my first task was to make more tracks to convince them I could be hiding somewhere in the orchard. Once that was done—"

"Excuse me," said Sabu. "We should go to the forest while they seek in the orchard."

"Oh," said Ganadarm. "Yes. Quite right."

"But Ganadarm cannot pretend to be a wandering philosopher," Tim said.

"Fear not," said Ganadarm, vaulting over the fence to stand above them. "I shall hide myself in the road ditch." He smiled his broad grin. His terra-cotta face was no less cheerful than it had ever been, despite the scabbed-over cuts on his cheek and eyebrow.

Sabu thought a moment, then nodded. "Let us go."

And so the three of them left Threewells, Tim pretending to be talking to Sabu and trying to act as though he did not see Ganadarm skulking along beside the road.

The road ditch in which Ganadarm walked turned out to be an irrigation canal, with running water knee-deep on Ganadarm's trousers. But the giant did not complain. He merely chuckled at the thought of the Klindrel searching among the apple trees while Tim and Sabu walked casually along a different road in plain sight.

"Are they *still* in the orchard?" he asked.

"Yes," said Sabu.

Ganadarm chuckled.

"Ah," said Sabu. It was not a good sort of "ah".

Tim looked. It was difficult to tell at this distance, but some of the Klindrel seemed to have noticed them. One of them pointed. With no other warning, ten Klindrel were shortcutting through the barley fields, riding toward the road that Sabu had chosen.

"What is it?" Ganadarm asked, from the ditch.

"They've seen us," Tim said.

"Have no fear," Ganadarm said. "They have not seen me, and you look like civilians."

"They come," said Sabu.

"They won't come," Ganadarm said. "They wouldn't go so far out of their way."

"Ganadarm," Tim said, "they are coming now."

"What? All of them?"

"Half of them," Tim said. "Riding through the fields to cut us off."

Ganadarm's jolly demeanor disappeared. "Bannom knows something," he said. "Perhaps someone we visited yesterday tipped them off."

"I do not know," Sabu said. "But they ride to us."

"Here," said Ganadarm, holding up his hands. "Let me lift you across the water."

Sabu nodded and scrambled down the side of the road. Ganadarm caught Sabu by the waist and carried him over the irrigation canal to set him on a headgate. Tim was next. The two men climbed down into the dry canal blocked by the headgate. The giant climbed over and joined them.

They ran through this canal between fields until they reached the next headgate. Water seeped from the bottom and fed a lumpy colony of moss.

"Now what?" Tim asked.

"We open it and cover our tracks," Ganadarm said. He lifted Tim and Sabu out and opened the headgate.

"If they saw us on road," Sabu said, "they know where we go."

"Perhaps," Ganadarm acknowledged as water flowed under the gate and around his ankles. "But when the ditch overflows onto the field, it will start to get muddy for their horses."

"So we go downstream?" Sabu asked.

"Upstream," said Ganadarm. "They will go downstream be-cause it looks like we are trying to make that way more difficult for them."

Ganadarm climbed over the headgate and waded into the canal. The water here was knee-deep on the giant and flowing swiftly because the gate to the cross-canal was now open.

Ganadarm turned his back to them. "Each of you grab one shoulder."

Tim grabbed Ganadarm's shoulder and hung on with both hands. Sabu did likewise on the other shoulder. Ganadarm hooked his arms behind and grabbed their legs to give them extra support.

Tim and Sabu rode upstream on the giant's back. Ganadarm kept his head hunched below the level of the orchard grass lining the canal so that they would not be seen. By the time they reached the next side-canal, Ganadarm was gasping for breath. He collapsed on the bank, and Tim and Sabu clambered off. The three of them slithered through the grass and into a vineyard.

"We hide here?" Tim asked, thinking perhaps Ganadarm could use a rest.

Sabu shook his head. "We must go more," he said. "They will see we are not down and will then look up. They will find smashed grass where we climb out."

"Bannom is a fair tracker," Ganadarm agreed.

"But the grape trees will hide us long enough," Sabu said. "Be small, Ganadarm. We will reach the forest soon."

CHAPTER 40

The Safety of the Forest

AS SABU, TIM, AND GANADARM CREPT through fields on their way to the forest, another person was creeping away from the forest on her way toward Threewells. She had no chance of being mistaken for a member of the civilian population. Her battle-blade's sheath was visible on her hip. Her tunic-and-trousers marked her as a member of the Road Patrol even from a distance. Up close, the drops of blood on her uniform would reveal her as a combatant.

Dusi had been shadowing her friends for three days, limping along deer trails and soaking her ankle in cool streams. The soaking had helped. She limped less, now, and she believed the knee would stop aching soon.

She knew she was gaining on them. A wind spirit had carried word of their passage to Redwood, and he had pointed Dusi in this direction. She would catch them by evening. And her ankle had healed enough that she would not have to worry about slowing them down.

So Dusi crept away from the safety of the forest. She slithered through fields. She crouched and ran through dry irrigation canals. She skulked through vineyards and lurked in orchards. And she kept her senses open because she was in enemy territory. Klindrel could appear anywhere.

She was crawling through a flax field when she first caught the faint buzz of stray thoughts at the edge of her senses. She sensed the thoughts, but she could not be certain they were Klindrel. After all, she was nearing a village.

Dusi abandoned her resonance with the destructive side of the Elemental Realms and focused on thoughts present in the world. Yes, she could still detect those minds. They must be Children of Knowledge.

She could not discern individual minds. From this distance, the village was a noisy blur. She would not be able to tell if Sabu were there without going closer.

Dusi took a direct line to the village, scuttling swiftly through the flax. The less time she spent in the fields, the less chance

Klindrel patrols would have to catch her in the open. Soon she reached a shallow ditch at the edge of freshly scythed hay meadow just above Threewells.

This was not the time to be careless. Before poking her head up, Dusi opened her senses to resonate with anyone looking for something. It was a specific state of mind that would be more likely to match a Klindrel patrol than a worried citizen of Threewells.

She sensed no resonance with that thought. Now it was time to use her eyes.

But as she was letting the resonance go, something brushed her mind. Someone was behind her. Someone searching? No. The mind behind her had *found* something. That was why the resonance had been imperfect.

Dusi looked over her shoulder. A Klindrel was afoot, running alongside the trail she had made through the flax field. Behind him four riders—one of them leading the running man's horse—kept pace at an easy trot. They wore the uniform of the Chumwarl Scouts. Three days ago, they had been interested only in finding stray horses. Apparently, this was no longer the case.

Dusi's tracks led straight to her. She had no time to double back and create false trails. But perhaps the scouts would assume she had continued across the hay meadow and into the village.

Dusi took an oblique angle away. She hoped the Klindrel would be so focused on her trail that they would not notice her motion among the flax. If they spent even a little time in the village, Dusi could go back the way the Klindrel rode in. She just needed a some luck.

A horse snorted.

"Over there!" shouted a soldier.

The riders turned toward her.

Peering through the flax, she saw three riders approaching. The man afoot was somewhere else. The one holding the spare horse remained behind.

So, then, only three to defeat. Could she do it? Not likely. Perga had once told her that a three-on-one fight was unwinnable unless he could turn it into a two-on-one before crossing blades. Dusi drew her battleblade anyway. Perga's hypothesis deserved a fair test.

The riders reined to a halt well out of range of her tiny blade. "Do you speak Klindrel?" one of them asked.

Dusi's instinct was to pretend she did not. After all, why give away information to the enemy? But her next thought was, *And if they think they cannot talk to me, how long will I live? I have a better chance of winning an argument than winning a fight.*

Dusi sheathed her battleblade. "Yes," she said. "I speak Klindrel."

"Good," said the leader. "My captain wants to speak with you. Take off your belt and leave your weapons here."

Dusi slipped her meatknife and battleblade off her belt and laid them on the earth. But she kept the belt and put it back on: It held her trousers up.

She looked up at the leader. "Let us speak with captains, then."

"Tie him up," the leader said. "I don't trust him."

"I am a her," Dusi said as the two subordinates dismounted.

The men paused and looked up at the leader.

He shrugged. "Tie *her* up, then," he said. "Damn Drelfin all look like little boys anyway."

As Dusi rode to meet the captain, she wondered if she ought to have done things differently. She could not have outrun them. They were five and they had horses. She could have fought them, but probably not for long. No, she decided, this was probably the best of all possible outcomes.

Which was discouraging, since she was riding wrapped in rope with her belly across the leader's lap. He kept her in place by jabbing his elbow into the small of her back. With his other arm, he held his helmet over her head.

The helmet, apparently, was an impromptu technique for inhibiting "Drelfin magic". Dusi wondered how they knew she had extraordinary elemental senses, but later she would learn that the Klindrel assumed *all* the brown Drelfin had dangerous magical powers.

The iron helmet didn't really bother Dusi, since her trick for evading iron's interference would still work, if she needed it to. She would have liked to grumble to herself about being smothered by a stinky helmet, but the truth was, it had only the usual smells of iron, sweat, and leather. And the smell of the Klindrel's hair reminded her a little of Sabu's.

No, all she had to complain about was the indignity, really. Perhaps some torture would come later, but the Klindrel soldiers seemed to be a practical sort of people who would execute prisoners rather than torture them. There is a difference between ruthless and cruel.

Dusi also felt embarrassed at letting herself be tracked. She would have felt better if she had known that the Klindrel had been looking for Sabu, Ganadarm, and Tim and that they had abandoned their pursuit of her friends when they discovered her just outside Threewells. I cannot with any certainty say that Dusi's capture aided Sabu's escape, but it would be nice to think so.

As soon as Dusi had come to terms with being packed like a sack of flour, the ride stopped. Her tightly bound body was passed down and set on sweet-smelling, drying grass—a hay meadow.

There followed a murmured discussion in which it was decided that forcing the Drelfin to wear the helmet while answering questions was too ridiculous. So the helmet was removed and Dusi found herself in the midst of five swordsmen, each holding his sword ready to plunge into her neck. Yes, that would certainly make a person reluctant to attempt any magical attacks. In fact, Dusi felt reluctant to breathe.

A soldier knelt in front of her. "Good day," he said. "I am Captain Bannom."

Dusi looked up into the face of Ganadarm's hated enemy. After listening to Ganadarm's tales of how Bannom had surrounded Ugly Lem's Band, imprisoned the survivors, and led them to their execution, she had imagined a cruel man with cold eyes, a nose like a vulture's beak, and thin lips twisted into a sneer. In fact, his lips were full and expressionless, his nose was in proportion to his placid, round face, and his eyes ... well, his eyes had the color and hardness of steel, but they were not cold—they were questing, searching her face for answers.

She knew this was Ganadarm's Bannom because he bore a white scar through his left eyebrow. I suppose a Child of Beauty would have found this scar sinister, but Dusi knew he had been clipped by Ganadarm's sword three years before, and the scar was simply a logical consequence.

"Do you understand me?" Captain Bannom asked.

Dusi nodded.

"Good. Lieutenant Marl says you are a girl in boy's clothing. Is that true?"

"No," said Dusi. "I am a woman. And this is *my* clothing."

The captain considered that, flitting his eyes over her body.

"You have a girl's chest," he said.

"I said I am a woman," Dusi replied. "Not a mother."

"Very well," Bannom said. "You are a woman. Did you know that among our people, men and women do not fight each other?"

Our men and women don't fight each other, either, Dusi thought. But she knew what he meant.

"Yes," she said.

"If you help me," Bannom said, "I will give you a dress. You can walk away, go back to your mother, and my men won't harm you."

"My mother is dead," Dusi said.

"Oh." He blinked. "I'm sorry."

She stared hard into his steel eyes.

He met her gaze calmly, studying her.

He said, "I need to know about the men you were traveling with."

"I am alone," Dusi said.

Bannom nodded. "Perhaps," he said. "But perhaps you travel with two Drelfin men dressed as civilians, one bald and one with hair as short as yours."

Dusi shook her head. "I am alone."

"But you have seen them."

"I have seen many men," Dusi said. "With many sorts of hair."

"Have you seen a man like me?" Bannom asked. "A man who looks like a Klindrel but wears his hair in a long black queue?"

"I have seen many Klindrel," Dusi said. "Too many."

"This one has no helmet and no armor," Bannom said. "And his clothes are filthy."

"I cannot help you," Dusi said.

"I think you can," said Captain Bannom. "I think you know where these men are. I think you can help me find them."

Dusi shrugged. "I will not betray my people for a dress."

Bannom smiled pleasantly. "I see."

And now what would he do with her? Dusi didn't want to be imprisoned. To tell the truth, she also hoped to avoid torture and execution. But most important was to make certain Sabu got away. She could do that only if she gave Captain Bannom a reason to take her along.

"But the Saltlander I could betray," Dusi said.

Bannom's shoulders relaxed a little, as though he, too, had been worried about what to do with her.

"You know where he is?" Bannom asked.

"No," she said. "But I can find him. I am a magic tracker."

"A tracker?"

Dusi nodded. "Magic tracker. I could find him … if you promise the other two can go."

"Oh? That is a high price to pay for one man," Bannom said.

"But it is he whom you wish to catch," Dusi said.

"I would prefer to catch all three."

"You want him most," said Dusi. "He is the bandit who gave you the mark above your eye."

"So he has reminded me," said Bannom. He did not sound angry. Perhaps he was even amused.

"He is the reason you hunt these men," Dusi said. "I will bring him to you, but you must let the other two go."

Bannom shook his head. "I fear you are mistaken. This Galadarn—"

"Ganadarm."

"Thank you. This Ganadarm is no longer a threat to the Saltlands. And I do not carry grudges over fights that I won. But if I *did* have something against him personally, I would not let it interfere with my duty to the Klindrel Army. Is that clear?"

"Then why do you want him?"

"I must find all three," Bannom said. "They have been visiting villages and trying to organize people against us."

Dusi shrugged. "So why should I help you?" *Give me a reason. Any excuse to travel with you and keep you from finding Sabu.*

"You care about the two Drelfin?" Bannom asked.

Dusi nodded.

"If you help me find them, I will give them a chance to surrender. We'll take them prisoner instead of killing them."

One of his men looked dubious.

"We will find a way," Bannom insisted. "We'll find a cozy cellar and keep all three of you there until the end of the war. It should be over by Yellowmonth."

Dusi pretended to think about it, but she knew it was her best chance to help Sabu.

"Very well," she said. "I will help you find them."

Her mother's laughter echoed in the back of her mind.

CHAPTER 41

Betrayal

I HAVE OFTEN WONDERED who told the Klindrel that Sabu, Ganadarm, and Tim were organizing resistance. It must have been someone from a village they visited before Threewells.

Of course the trio would draw attention. Sabu was a stranger in the vicinity. Ganadarm, though he did not enter the villages, would appear to be a giant even at a distance. And Tim, no matter how good his disguise, would still be foreign to them.

But this was not merely a case of someone asking the authorities to deal with three suspicious strangers. No, the informant revealed that the three men were convincing villages to destroy food rather than hand it over to the Klindrel.

What induces someone to turn against his or her own people? Was the informant hoping for special treatment? Did the informant get a new "dress"?

One might like to think the informant was coerced. One might like to think Captain Bannom threatened to put everyone to the sword unless the villagers told him who had advocated destroying food. But I doubt it was that way. This little betrayal was not an isolated incident.

In *Analysis of Invasion*, Boshi names entire village councils that decided to cooperate with the invaders. She tells of ferries that accepted looted money in exchange for transporting Klindrel units across the Redwood River. People had seen their defenders retreat, and when they were left to the mercy of the invaders, they chose to cooperate. This may have been logical, but it was not good.

Dusi cooperated, too, in a way. She rode behind Captain Bannom with her cheek against his brown-and-gray uniform, using her elemental talent to look for her friends in places where they might be hiding. Her mother would laugh and say, *Soon, soon,* but Dusi kept looking, because she believed she could help Sabu if she found him before one of Bannom's men did. She was acting like a good patroller, looking for a chance to help with Sabu's mission, but mostly she was concerned about Sabu. She wanted him to escape the Chumwarl Scouts. If necessary, she *would* sacrifice Ganadarm and even Tim. There were rational reasons for giving Sabu's life priority over his subordinates' lives, but Dusi knew those rational reasons were not hers. She did not try to justify her feelings. She loved Sabu. He simply meant more to her. And when the time came to make a quick decision that could save his life, she needed to be prepared to make that decision without hesitation—regardless of the consequences.

Captain Bannom visited several villages that day, trying to discover whether Sabu, Ganadarm, and Tim had been there. The villagers eyed Dusi uncomfortably as they answered his questions. Clearly, they inferred that they could also be trussed up and taken for a ride if they did not cooperate.

"I think they spoke the truth to you," Dusi said up to him as they rode out of Wheatfallow. "The men you seek have not been here."

"I know," Bannom said over his shoulder.

"You know?"

"Those villagers were honest men," Bannom said. "I can tell an honest man by looking in his eyes."

Dusi did not ask him what he saw in her eyes.

They camped that night in a wheat field and destroyed a dozen bushels with their careless trampling. Armies do not respect fields.

Dusi could not keep her mother from her dreams that night. Her mother mocked her and laughed at her, but Dusi remained silent. She would not reveal her plan.

They rode out the next morning, looking for a village where Sabu had been. At the height of the third lithic, they found one. The village square was lit by a bonfire. It sizzled under the scattered drips of rain that fell from the gray clouds. The smell of burning grain and roasting meat filled the air.

"Ho!" cried Bannom as he reined his horse to a halt before the assembled villagers.

The villagers turned to face him and his scouts. Their expressions were grim, but they were not surprised.

A young elder, one just beginning to grow his beard, stepped forward. "You find nothing here," he said. "We burn all foods."

Bannom studied the assembled villagers. "Yes, well, we are not here for your food."

Bannom's scouts exchanged uneasy glances. Perhaps they were

not seeking food, but they had counted on a little enforced hospitality to round out the provisions they carried with them.

"We are looking for one Klindrel and two Drelfin," Bannom said.

The villagers remained silent, standing in the heat of the crackling flames.

"From your fire, I know they have been here," Bannom said. "Which way did they leave?"

"We say nothing," said the young elder. He looked about for support. "We say nothing even if you kill us."

"Kill you?" said Bannom. "Why should we bother? You will soon starve to death."

He led his scouts out of the village at a slow walk.

"Are all your people such fanatics?" Bannom asked as they rode toward the next village.

"What is fanatics?" asked Dusi.

"A fanatic is someone who would die for an idea."

"A good word," said Dusi. "What do you call someone who would kill for an idea?"

Bannom chuckled. "A soldier."

Dusi's mother laughed inside her head. *Ah, we are all soldiers, then, aren't we, Dusi dear?*

Dusi ignored her.

"Why did you come?" Dusi asked. "Why are you in our lands?"

Bannom shrugged. "The emperor wants the glory of conquest. And the barons are giving him a chance to show how well he can do."

"So how well so far?" Dusi asked.

"Oh, that depends on whom you ask," Bannom said. "The commanders are happy because we have taken plenty of territory. But the common soldiers hate fighting you."

"Why?"

"Because you look like children to us," Bannom said. "Who can brag about killing children? And also because you fight nasty. For every man you kill, you cripple twenty, leaving us to kill them ourselves."

"You kill your own wounded?"

"If we have to. A man who cannot fight is better off dead."

"Have you no healers?"

"You mean men who can make a hamstrung man whole again? No. Magic is rare among us. Kashram expects a man to take care of himself. If a man cannot march ... well, better to die swiftly by a comrade's sword than to be abandoned and torn apart by wild beasts. That is no way to enter Kashram's Heaven."

In *Consequences of the Klindrel War*, Chohu corroborates the fact that the Klindrel slew their own wounded, but Chohu presents this as an example of Klindrel barbarism. To Captain Bannom, it was simply necessity—grim, yet pious. The Klindrel soldiers were not monsters, despite how our historians choose to depict them. True, the invasion was horrific, so I understand why Chohu expresses horror. But those of us who drew our battleblades and committed horrors of our own—we cannot be so quick to condemn the common Klindrel soldier.

Ideas spread like fire, as the saying goes, and for the Starvation Strategy, the simile was literal. In village after village across the Redwood Valley, plumes of smoke marked the acceptance of the new plan for fighting the Klindrel. At noon the next day, Captain Bannom found a hill from which he could survey the countryside.

"That's the one we passed through half a lithic ago," he said, pointing out a nearby village to his lieutenant. "There's a village by the river that has just gotten wind of the idea." He pointed to a distant plume of smoke. "You can see word moving from the forest toward the river."

Indeed they could. Small puffs marked bonfires that were just starting. Gray clouds of smoke marked villages where the bonfires were underway. Villages that had destroyed their food reserves were marked by faint wisps of black ash rising from the cooling embers. The curve of the idea was charted across the face of the valley.

"So which village are they in, Captain?"

Bannom surveyed the terrain. "None of them," he said. "They are letting the civilians carry the idea themselves. Our quarry went into the forest there." He pointed. "They'll cross those foothills sometime this afternoon and start again the next morning on the other side."

"So you think they'll keep moving up the river valley?"

Bannom nodded. "That's what I would do." He turned to Dusi. "Don't you agree?"

There was no sense lying to him—not if she wanted his trust. "Yes," she said.

"So we'll cross the creek there," Bannom said. "And aim for that gap. Unlike them, we can travel in the open. We'll reach their next target before they do."

"You could let them go," Dusi said. She waved her arm at the columns of smoke marking the villages of the valley. "The fires will burn without them. You need not chase them now."

"Spreading insurrection is treason," said Lieutenant Marl.

"'Tis," agreed Bannom. "Although technically, until the Drelfin surrender the province to the emperor, they can't commit treason against him."

"So let the men go," Dusi said.

Bannom shook his head. "I can't. I have my orders. And the emperor will need someone to blame for this."

"You mean someone to execute," said Dusi.

"Aye," agreed Bannom. "And if I don't find them quickly, he might execute me."

"Forgive me," said Dusi. "But that troubles me little."

"I know," said Bannom. "But consider this: The sooner we capture them, the better I'll look. I might be able to ask for favors. I might even be able to save one or two of them from execution."

"But not all three?"

"No, I fear someone must take the blame. But if we capture this Ganadarm fellow, we can make him take most of it."

So Bannom might be able to save Sabu.

Dusi's mother giggled softly in the back of Dusi's mind.

"What if the emperor will not listen?" Dusi asked.

"The sooner we bring Ganadarm in, the better chance I have of being heard," Bannom said. "Help me find him, Dusi. Today or the next. We may not have much time."

Dusi ignored her mother's laughter. "Very well. Let us cross that ridge and see what we see."

Later in the day, as the clouds in the sunward sky began to turn gold against the blue, they topped a ridge surveying the Mill River Valley, a peaceful green dale blanketed by polygonal fields and bisected by a vigorous tributary of the Redwood River. Bannom made observations as they descended along a vineyard road, and Dusi leaned off center to look around him at where he was pointing.

"They'll camp somewhere there," he said. "They'll aim for that village at the top of the valley. It's closest to the forest, and the firewood grove will give Ganadarm good cover. The question is, where are we most likely to find all three together?"

"In the grove," Dusi said. "Unless Ganadarm stays in the forest."

"You had best hope Ganadarm comes out. Otherwise, we shall capture only the Drelfin."

"We should hide in the grove," said Dusi. "Then we will capture him if he comes to the grove, and if he stays in the forest, we can find him by watching how the other two come out."

"Aye," agreed Bannom. "Good thinking."

" 'Tis not so easy to hide twenty horses," observed Lieutenant Marl. "Even in a thick grove."

"You would leave the horses in the apple trees there," said Dusi. "Away from the firewood grove."

"Aye," said Bannom. "The slope of the apple orchard would screen the horses from view." He grinned. "When this war is over, Dusi, maybe you should join the Chumwarl Scouts."

"I like my scouts," Dusi said.

"I'm sure you do," said Bannom gently. "Well, let us make camp among those rocks there. We shall need an early sleep so we can get started earlier than they do."

It took Dusi a long time to get to sleep that night. The orange moon climbed high into the sky and shone on her face. Every time she dozed off, her mother's laughter awakened her. Finally, she found a dreamless sleep, only to be shaken awake by Captain Bannom.

A faint orange glow above the moonward mountains was all that remained of the moon for the night. The sky held no sunlight yet, but the stars peeking through the clouds were beginning to fade.

Fog blanketed the valley below. Captain Bannom discussed the terrain with his lieutenant, perhaps to refresh the lieutenant's memory of what they had seen the previous evening, perhaps to show his men that he still knew where they were going.

They descended into the mist.

Before the men could grow nervous, Captain Bannom found a road, which they followed with fog-muffled hoofsteps. The road seemed to come into existence only ten paces ahead. Behind them, it vanished. The Chumwarl Scouts could see each other only as dark shadows, but they trusted their captain's memory and sense of direction. They trusted the orders he gave. They trusted his judgment in taking along the androgynous Drelfin who claimed to be willing to help them. If one admires the way Sabu led his patrollers, one must also admire how Bannom led his scouts. The two men were not so different.

Deeper in the valley, the fog was thicker and the moon was hidden by the mountains. The Chumwarl Scouts picketed their horses among the apple trees. Bannom removed the rope from Dusi's ankles so she could walk with him to the firewood grove.

The grove proved to be a dense wood of whiteoaks with thick trunks and head-high crowns of tangled branches. The giants had to crawl on hands and knees. Bannom tied Dusi's ankles together again and made her crawl ahead of him.

Dusi led Bannom to the far edge of the grove while the others spread themselves out among the whiteoaks. Dusi had claimed that she needed to be on the edge closest to the forest because the minds of the scouts would interfere with her resonance, but in truth, she just wanted to get Bannom alone.

They found a place where the branches were high enough to allow Bannom to stand up, and there they waited in the gloom.

When the sun rose, bringing foggy gray light to the gnarled trees, Dusi saw they had concealed themselves well. They would not be visible from the forest or the road. But most importantly, she and Bannom were not within eyesight of the other scouts.

The warm sun diminished the fog to a fine golden mist. The Chumwarl Scouts were so quiet and still that the grove's squirrels scampered through the branches heedless of the men below. Robins busied themselves gathering food for their babies, while chickadees made occasional comments on the weather.

The sun was heading for mid-morning before Dusi felt a mind that was not hiding in the grove. It was Sabu. His mind was divided—half wary for danger, half quiet and contemplative.

Bannom looked at her sharply and she knew she had given Sabu away. Dusi held up her palms to forestall his question. She closed her eyes and expanded her awareness until she could sense Tim.

Tim's mind jittered. Dusi could not sense Tim's emotions, but she could see the way his worries jiggled his thoughts.

Dusi leaned toward Bannom and put her bound hands on his hip to steady herself. "They are on the road now," she murmured. "Coming this way."

She could feel his back tense. Bannom gave the whistle of the tufted titmouse. The grove became silent and alert.

As Sabu and Tim drew closer, Dusi opened herself to the destructive side of the Elemental Realms. Yes, Ganadarm was with them, coming toward the grove. That was good. She didn't want to hunt him in the forest.

The three men stopped. They exchanged words—Dusi could see the conversation falling from their minds.

Ganadarm left the other two. He moved toward the grove, wary. Sabu and Tim continued on the road.

"That way," Dusi whispered, pointing with the index fingers of her bound hands.

This was the tricky part of the plan. Bannom wanted Ganadarm to come deep inside the grove before the scouts ambushed him. Dusi had told him she would adjust their position as Ganadarm approached so that Ganadarm would not stumble over them on his way in. Bannom would give the signal to spring the trap when he had a square view of Ganadarm's back.

Bannom went where Dusi indicated, closer to the edge of the grove, farther from the rest of his men. He moved in a crouch, keeping his head below the gnarled mass of limbs above. He moved quietly. And most remarkably, he did this while carrying Dusi on his hip, for she could not sneak very quietly with her hands and feet bound.

He set Dusi down and looked a question at her.

She pointed to indicate Ganadarm's position.

Bannom adjusted himself so he could peer between two oaks at the path Ganadarm was most likely to use.

Dusi leaned against his muscular back and pressed her cheek against his fog-dampened cloak. He smelled of days in the saddle—honest smells of sweat, leather, and horses. She put her hands on his belt, as though to steady herself.

Bannom looked down at her quizzically, not realizing she had just taken his knife from its sheath.

Do it, her mother said. *Betray this man and join me.*

I lose my soul either way, Dusi replied. *And I won't betray Sabu.*

She pushed away from Bannom gently. Then, with both hands, she stabbed the knife into his kidney. Bannom gasped in pain.

Dusi's connection to Heaven snapped, and her soul fell toward the Deceiver with a stomach-sickening lurch.

... I wonder sometimes if Captain Bannom had a wife. Did he have small children who lived among the camp followers? Did someone find his parents and tell them that he died, or were they left to wonder? It has been fifty-seven years since the war, and I still weep for him.

CHAPTER 42

The Heroic Duel

UP UNTIL THIS POINT, Ganadarm had been enjoying his adventures with Saboon and Tim. True, Saboon was a harder man now that his little sweetheart was dead. And Tim was nervous about posing as a brown Drelfin, despite being able to make himself as brown as he wanted. But the mission reminded Ganadarm of the best days of his life. He was sneaking across countryside patrolled by Captain Bannom and the Chumwarl Scouts. He was hiding in orchards and ditches and thickets. Burning down the bridge would be more impressive than anything Ugly Lem had ever done, even during the Saltlands Uprising. And Ganadarm enjoyed watching Tim lose the soft mannerisms of a merchant and acquire the wary, stealthy habits of a bandit. Tim still thought of himself as hunted, but Ganadarm and Saboon would show him he could also be the hunter. Ever since Tim had escaped from the Drelfin fort, Ganadarm had known the little man had great courage.

And so on the eleventh of Orangemonth, Ganadarm approached the oak grove with a light heart. He would hide. Saboon and Tim would visit the village. Ganadarm would watch for signs of trouble. Then they would reunite and continue on their way toward the bridge they planned to burn down.

In short, Ganadarm's morning was going well until he heard a sudden, sharp intake of breath just as he entered the oak grove. Ganadarm froze.

A man staggered into his line of sight, drawing a sword. It was Bannom!

The Klindrel captain held one hand against a bleeding wound on his back. His incredulous gaze was not on Ganadarm, but on the trees from which he had come.

"She stabbed me!" he croaked—addressing the trees, or perhaps the heavens.

Bannom's knees buckled. He dug the point of his sword into the ground to keep himself upright.

Bannom looked at Ganadarm and his head lolled weakly. "To me," he gasped. "And to the road," he added. "Stop them," he murmured.

Bannom's face was pale and sweaty. His breathing was quick and shallow. He collapsed to one knee, then fell forward.

Swords slid from scabbards throughout the grove, but Ganadarm didn't care who else might be there. Beating away the tangled oak branches, he crossed to the dying man. With a toe, he rolled Bannom over to face the sky. Bannom's eyelids twitched.

Ganadarm drew his sword and pressed the point to Bannom's chest. "This is what we have been struggling toward?" he asked. "This is our great duel?"

Bannom shivered.

Ganadarm thrust his blade through Bannom's heart. His enemy convulsed and died.

Ganadarm slid his sword free of Bannom's body. He contemplated the dead man's face.

Not a word. In death, as in life, Bannom did not find Ganadarm worthy of his attention.

Movement in the trees caught Ganadarm's eye. Dusi stood there with a bloody knife clenched in her teeth. She sawed at ropes that bound her wrists. Severed ropes lay at her feet.

Ganadarm felt too empty to be confused.

"Hello," he said. "We thought you were dead."

Dusi freed her wrists and spat the knife into her shaking hand. She was even paler than Ganadarm remembered.

Dusi screamed something in her language. Ganadarm understood only that she was yelling something to Saboon. The little Drelfin woman grabbed his wrist and tugged it.

"We must go," she said.

She was right. Ganadarm caught a glimpse of scouts moving among the trees. Always, always he ran from them. He never stood to fight.

A face appeared on his flank and Ganadarm thrust his sword into it savagely. The scout fell onto his backside. Ganadarm followed Dusi out of the grove and into the surrounding sheep meadow.

"This way," she said, tugging him away from the road.

"But Saboon and Tim are on the road," Ganadarm explained.

Two scouts burst from the trees. With a roar, Ganadarm charged them. He slashed the nearer opponent's blade offline and slammed into him, leading with a forearm to the jaw.

The scout flew backward and crashed into a tree trunk. The second scout turned to watch his comrade's flight and Ganadarm stabbed him in the side.

Ganadarm sprang away from them. Neither man looked inclined to attack him now.

"This way," Dusi begged. "Please. This way."

Ganadarm sighed. She was right. He must escort her to safety. Saboon and Tim were men. They would take care of themselves.

Ganadarm broke into a lope, matching Dusi's pace easily.

Dusi's breath came in heaving gasps. Tears made streaks on her dirty face. She stumbled to a halt in the open meadow.

Five scouts emerged from the grove and ran toward them. One called, "Surrender or die!"

Ganadarm sheathed his sword and bent to pick Dusi up. She raised a hand to forestall him.

The scouts closed the distance.

Dusi wiped her sleeve across her wet face and closed her eyes.

Ganadarm considered drawing his sword again, but dying beside a grubby Drelfin woman in the middle of a sheep meadow did not seem very heroic. He put one arm on her back and bent to scoop her up at the knees.

But apparently, she had only been taking a moment to draw the Klindrel away from the road. Before Ganadarm could lift her, her eyes flashed open and she shouted, "You can catch us never!"

Then she bolted, with the Klindrel scouts just three steps away.

Ganadarm followed. This time Dusi was difficult to catch. Her tiny legs blurred and her little elbows pumped as she sprinted toward the forest.

Ganadarm shot a glance at the five Klindrel behind him. They were running shoulder-to-shoulder, which meant they could run only as fast as the slowest man. Ganadarm could outrun the slowest man. Even the short-legged Drelfin woman could. The scouts gave up before Ganadarm and Dusi reached the trees.

After that, there was nothing heroic to be done. Dusi started limping a little, so Ganadarm picked her up and carried her deeper into the forest. The scouts went for their horses and rode along the edge of the trees for a while, but they were afraid to split into small groups and afraid to go in too far. Evading a herd of timid scouts was not a challenge for a man who had been raised by bandits in the Saltlands. If Bannom had been with them, Ganadarm could have taunted them to make the game interesting, but without Bannom, there was no joy in eluding these men.

When it became clear that the scouts would not follow deep into the forest, Dusi said they should circle back to the road and look for Saboon and Tim. Ganadarm acquiesced.

He wondered if Saboon and Tim had found any excitement. Unlikely. Bannom was dead, and the world was empty of all joy.

CHAPTER 43

Twisted Tangles

HAVING COME SO FAR with Dusi and the Chumwarl Scouts, perhaps we should remind ourselves that Sabu knew nothing of Dusi's capture. To Sabu, Dusi had been dead for a week. He was no longer numbed by shock. He had given up hope of seeing her again.

So when he heard a stranger's voice croak, "She stabbed me!" he did not realize that meant Dusi was in the oak grove.

Tim froze in the middle of the road. Sabu reached inside his chiton and withdrew his battleblade.

"To me," the stranger called weakly. "And to the road."

Something fell to the ground. Then Sabu heard the slick sound of swords being drawn. The grove was full of soldiers.

Sabu had nowhere to hide. The meadow on the other side of the road had been grazed so close that no grass was left above ankle height. The forest was too far away, at the very edge of sprinting distance.

Ganadarm's voice came from the grove, disappointed and incredulous: "This is what we have been struggling toward? This is our great duel?"

Soldiers were rustling between the trees now.

Ganadarm said faintly, "Oh, hello. We thought you were dead."

He was talking, not fighting. Who was in there? Friend or foe?

Sabu opened his mouth to call to Ganadarm when the air was split with a loud cry in his own language: "Sabu! It's an ambush!"

Dusi! That was her; that *had* to be her! She was alive!

Four giants in brown-and-gray quartered tunics emerged from the trees, swords drawn. No visible armor and no shields.

If Perga had been at Sabu's side, they might have had a chance against four giants. But Perga was not there. It was only Tim, who had not even remembered to draw his blade yet.

Had Sabu not heard Dusi's voice in the grove, he might have tried to run away, and the giants might have caught him—or at least Tim. But Sabu knew the woman he loved was in there somewhere, so he grabbed Tim by the chiton and dragged him into the grove. The soldiers followed.

Now everyone was crashing about. A cry of pain from Ganadarm's direction suggested that things were not going well for somebody, but Sabu did not think it had been Ganadarm's cry.

Sabu ran between the trees, taking Tim in deeper. He stopped in a concealing cluster of trunks and tried to figure out where the Klindrel were.

Ganadarm emitted an incomprehensible snarl. One giant grunted. Another gasped.

"This way," Dusi begged. "Please. This way."

She was speaking quietly—to Ganadarm, not to Sabu.

Sabu wanted to run toward her, but he kept his wits about him. Dusi was the only person who could see everyone in the grove. If Sabu tried to run after her, he might meet a horde of Klindrel. If he stayed put, Dusi would be able to find him.

Tim grabbed his shoulder and pointed up into the treetops.

Sabu looked up. All he could see were green leaves and tangles of slender branches. He looked a question at Tim.

Tim jumped and caught a branch. With grunts and wiggles, he wove his body upward into the canopy.

Ah, Sabu thought. *Good idea, Tim.*

He sheathed his blade and climbed up, too, until he was high above the ground.

In the distance, a voice cried, "Surrender or die!"

Sabu doubted Dusi and Ganadarm would surrender. He hoped the giant could protect her.

"You can catch us never!" Dusi replied in mangled Klindrel.

So she was running away. Good.

But Ganadarm must have told her that Sabu and Tim were nearby.

Ah. Sabu understood it now. Dusi knew exactly where he was. She was trying to draw the Klindrel out. Sabu held his position and hoped that Dusi's tactic would work—but not so well that the Klindrel actually caught her.

Leaves rustled. Sabu and Tim held still. The rustling grew louder as the soldier came closer. The branches were woven into a thick canopy just above head height, and this was only waist height on a Klindrel. The enemy could move through the grove only with difficulty.

The giant came into view below Sabu's feet. He was crawling. His back was to the sky.

Sabu contemplated the point on the uniform where the four rectangles met. It was a nice target.

But Sabu did not strike. The success of his mission did not depend on killing this Klindrel. It depended on escaping the entire company.

"Seen anything?" a voice below asked.

A silent reply.

"Nor have I," said the voice. "Let's stay together. Watch my back?"

Again the leaves rustled, but this time the sound diminished.

A short while later, a man called, "To the horses! To the horses! The vixen killed Captain Bannom. We can't let her escape!" After that, all the rustling died away and the grove was silent for some time.

Sabu did not descend until the birds had started chirping again. No one jumped out to stab him when he hit the ground, so he motioned for Tim to come down as well. The two men crept to the edge of the grove and Sabu poked his head out to look around.

The mist was lessening as the sun climbed higher. The meadow was green and growing. The lith was sparkling high above the mountains.

They ran to the forest as fast as Sabu could make Tim go. If they were spotted, Sabu wanted as much of a head start as he could get. But no one pursued them.

"What now?" Tim asked, when they had reached the safety of the redwoods.

Good question, Sabu thought. *Not back to this morning's camp. Someone might be tracking us from there. But not too far away, either, because we don't know where Dusi went.*

"We wait here," Sabu decided. "Dusi will find us."

Tim got a funny look on his face. "Are you sure that was her?"

Sabu nodded. "Yes, I am. I hear that voice in dreams every night since the battle."

If Tim had further doubts, he kept them to himself. They waited in silence until they heard their friends approaching.

"Saboon!" called Ganadarm. "Look who I found!"

It was indeed Dusi, his dear Dusi, somehow alive after Tomivo, somehow returned to him after he had given up hope.

Sabu wept as he embraced her. I trust the reader will not judge him too harshly for this. Sabu was always a pious, rational man, yet in this moment, he found he could not rein in his emotions. He was overcome by his joy at seeing Dusi again, and perhaps he was also grieving for the loss of Perga.

Dusi wept, too, and she let Sabu think it was for the same reasons.

CHAPTER 44
Farbridge

SOME PEOPLE ARE AWARE of their souls and some are not. Why do I say this? And what is the difference between a person and a person's soul?

Simply put, the soul is that part of you that will continue to exist after your body dies. When you walk to the market, when you hand over your coins, when you lift the plum to your mouth, bite through its skin, and suck in its juices, then you are a person, a union of body and soul. You may think it is your body that does the walking, the buying, the eating, but no, your soul participates, too. The union is so perfect that you sense no separation.

On the other hand, when you pray for the Goddess's blessing, when you sit and contemplate a geometric puzzle, when you dream, then you know it is your soul that does these things. Your body is present, of course. You may be aware of your breathing or your heartbeat. But such actions concern only your soul.

If you ever change the way your soul is aligned, you will be different on a fundamental, metaphysical level. The connection you have with the Elemental Realms will shift to a different place, and even if you have lived your entire life unable to sense the Elemental Realms, you will sense that shift.

So when I say that Dusi's soul now belonged to the Deceiver, I am not stating a hypothesis. I am not telling you what Dusi feared. I am relating an observable fact.

And yet, this fact was observable only to Dusi. The others did not know she had lost all connection to the Goddess of Knowledge. And if they noticed any difference in her behavior or demeanor, well, any oddity could easily be attributed to her time in captivity. Her friends expected her to be somewhat affected by the ordeal.

Dusi took advantage of this. When Sabu assumed she had been mistreated, she did not correct him. When Tim expressed sympathy, she did not point out how much safer she had felt as a prisoner rather than as a combatant.

Ganadarm was the only one who fully realized that she had gained Bannom's trust and then stabbed him in the back, but he was not familiar with Dusi's link to the Deceiver, and he was so mournful over the loss of his enemy that he did not discuss Bannom's death with Tim and Sabu.

So Dusi fooled her friends into thinking she was still good. And this deception was easy because she was still on their side.

She had allowed the Deceiver to trap her, to put her in a situation where she had to betray either her friends or Bannom. But even though the Deceiver had won, she could win, too. Her desire to help her friends had been used for evil, but now she could use that evil to help her friends.

Deception and trickery, which had always been easy for her, were even easier now that she was no longer trying to be honest. She no longer had to deny her impulses. She no longer had to question her destructive intuition.

And so, as she lay in concealment at the edge of a high cliff overlooking the town of Farbridge, she felt confident in saying, "We aren't going to be able to burn that bridge down. We'll have to knock it down instead."

"Knock it down?" asked Sabu. "It looks quite stout."

"But remember how it bounced when we rode across?" Dusi asked. "One of the piles is loose."

"If the force of that water hasn't knocked it down," said Sabu, "I don't see what we can do."

Tim, too, was skeptical. "Burn it down, knock it down—how do we get past those guards?"

Indeed the Farbridge did have guards at each end. They were difficult to count at this distance, but they looked like two squads of ten.

"We can sneak around them in the dark," Sabu said.

"Or we can create a diversion," said Dusi. "Something that will pull them away."

"Such as?" Tim asked.

Dusi said, "Perhaps your friend Fishurba will have some ideas."

"Well, she said she would be here soon," said Tim.

Fishurba, the Farbridge blacksmith, did indeed arrive a short while later. She brought three chitons—one for Dusi, who was still in her Road Patrol uniform, and clean chitons for Sabu and Tim.

"Now you won't stand out like gray sheep in a white flock," Fishurba said.

Fishurba was the one who had suggested this lookout point. She was keenly interested in any action that would impede the Klindrel. However, the sentiment was not universal.

"When your army rode away," Fishurba said, "the people felt abandoned. Many are saying that the Redwood Valley would not be starving if you had stayed to defend the bridge. Our town has become a Klindrel supply base. The market has reopened, and we're trading with the Klindrel. The local lumber company has negotiated a contract with the Klindrel garrison captain, so the lumberjacks have work again. I fear we'll be in the Klindrel Empire before Hicho even acknowledges we are at war."

"So your people will not help?" Tim asked.

"There are some people who will not help," Fishurba said. "But *my* people will help. What do you need?"

"We need to destroy the bridge," Sabu said. "Burn it down or knock it down."

"That wood won't burn," Fishurba said. "Not after the rains we've had this spring. It would take a month of drought to dry it out."

"Is one of the piles loose?" Sabu asked.

Fishurba nodded. "Upstream pile, second one on this side. But it is just loose at the base. It hasn't rotted through."

"Is there any way we could push the pile over?" Sabu asked.

"It's solid redwood," Fishurba said. "If the river hasn't pushed it over, I don't see what we can do."

But Dusi saw. She suddenly saw it very clearly. "We can pull it," she said. "The river is pushing it against a rock, keeping it in place. If we pull it toward shore, the bottom will slip loose and bring the bridge down."

Sabu looked to Fishurba.

"It might work," the blacksmith conceded. "But we can't be certain."

"I'm certain," Dusi said. *But please don't ask me how I know.*

"Ho! The first wagon has arrived!" This cry came from Ganadarm, who was the only one still at the lookout point.

They rushed to join him. Tim pulled out his pocket ledger and murmured to himself.

A small squad of soldiers and one ox wagon were visible on the opposite bank of the river. As they crossed the bridge, Dusi fixed her eyes on the point where the road emerged from the trees. But no more wagons came.

"Only one wagon?" Sabu asked.

"It's loaded only lightly," Tim said. "I reckon it's just tents and camp equipment."

"So this squad will be setting up tents," Sabu said.

And digging latrines, Dusi thought.

"We still have time?" Sabu asked.

"Not much," Tim said. "We surely can't wait for darkness."

Sabu thought a moment.

"Fishurba," he asked, "how many people do you have?"

"Enough to cause trouble," she said. "But not enough for a direct confrontation on the bridge."

Dusi's hand moved to the hilt of her battleblade—or rather, to the hilt of the battleblade that Tim had quite willingly handed over to her. It felt good to be wearing one again.

In the town below, an officer of some sort came out to greet the new arrivals. Sabu expressed hope that some guards might be pulled from the bridge to help with setting up the new supply tent, but the guards only rotated.

Dusi's companions discussed whether a tactical advantage could be gained by attacking during the next changing of the guard. Dusi's newly sharpened instinct for treachery told her the answer was no. She kept her thoughts to herself, however. The others were arriving at the same conclusion.

Once the wagon was in place at the chosen campsite, the oxen were unhitched and led back to the bridge. A grassy area below the high water mark provided an impromptu meadow.

In a breathy voice, Tim said, "They've decided to graze the oxen right below the bridge!"

"Is that good?" Ganadarm asked.

"It's a sign from Yolim!"

Sabu and Fishurba looked at Tim quizzically.

"First Dusi gets this idea that we should pull the bridge down. Then the Klindrel put oxen right where we need them. The gods are helping our side!"

Dusi knew her knowledge had not come from the Goddess,

but it was best to let Tim think otherwise.

"I pray that Kashram aids us as well," said Ganadarm.

"Me too," said Tim. "Or I would, if I prayed to Kashram. Anyway, we need some rope, Fishurba."

"And a diversion," said Sabu.

"And an assassin," said Fishurba.

"What?" asked Dusi.

"See those two Klindrel saddling horses? They're messengers. If you can't stop them, then an attack on the bridge is pointless."

CHAPTER 45
Ganadarm Rides Again

NOW SOME READERS may have immediately grasped the importance of stopping the two Klindrel messengers, whereas others would prefer a more detailed explanation of Fishurba's reasoning. To the latter, I promise an explanation will be given, but not immediately, for you see, the less you understand Fishurba, the more you understand Ganadarm, who couldn't understand Fishurba at all.

The Drelfin murmured to each other and put on their new dresses. Tim explained only that Ganadarm was to go with Dusi and Saboon, while Tim went to town.

Then they were off, with Saboon leading Ganadarm and Dusi on a run through the forest.

Ganadarm stayed behind Dusi so he would not have to look over his shoulder to be sure she was keeping up. In a dress, she looked much more like a woman. Of course, so did Saboon.

Ganadarm had not asked her why she had stabbed Bannom in the back. She was a woman, not strong enough to face a man like Bannom in direct confrontation.

And Ganadarm? Had he been strong enough? Or had he run away like a coward every time?

He was running now, dashing between the trees. The air felt good in his lungs. He had to admit that running always felt good, whether he ran away from a battle or toward it.

They ran until they reached the edge of the forest, where Saboon paused to survey the countryside. Saboon did not see whatever it was that he feared, and they resumed their run, leaving the forest to cross a sheep pasture. They found a path and followed it between fields until they drew near a meadow where Drelfin were putting up stacks of hay.

Saboon slowed to a walk as they approached the hay meadow. The Drelfin in the meadow looked up in surprise.

Saboon conferred with the field workers. Dusi cast nervous glances in the direction of the town. Saboon spoke with quiet urgency. The Drelfin workers frowned, casting worried glances at Ganadarm. Eventually, Saboon convinced the Drelfin to go work in a distant corner of the meadow. They left behind two hay forks.

Dusi looked up at Ganadarm and said, "Ganadarm, we need you to sit here by the road."

"I will," said Ganadarm. "But even sitting down, I will be seen."

Dusi shook her head. "No. Because we cover you with hay."

These Drelfin are clever, Ganadarm thought, as Saboon and Dusi built a haystack around him. *They would make good bandits. Maybe they would like to come back with me to the Saltlands someday.*

Soon he was concealed in hot, green darkness.

He waited, and as he waited he realized that some of the old joy had returned to him. They were about to spring another clever trap.

Ganadarm had not been waiting long when he heard two horses approaching at an easy walk. The clacking of scabbards and the slicing of scaled armor told him the riders were soldiers. If those clues were not sufficient, one of the Klindrel confirmed his assessment by shouting, "Out of the way, Drelfin. We are messengers on imperial business."

"My apologize," said Saboon. "Should you like to drink of water?"

The other Klindrel said, "I could use a drink, Yibbo. The sun's getting warm."

The horses halted, right beside Ganadarm's hay stack.

"All right," said the one called Yibbo. "Where's your water?"

Saboon grunted something in Drelfin. The Klindrel shouted. The horses squealed.

Ganadarm assumed this was the signal. He burst from the hay.

Saboon had caught his opponent's trouser leg with the hay fork and was dragging him off the horse. For a moment, it seemed that the other leg would remain mounted. Then the soldier's booted heel slipped over the saddle and the soldier tumbled to the ground.

Saboon whipped the fork free of the soldier's trousers and slammed the butt end into the side of the soldier's helmet. Ganadarm drew his sword and leapt to impale the Klindrel.

"No stab! No stab!" Saboon yelled.

Ganadarm halted, the point of his sword poised above his enemy's throat.

"Why not?" asked Dusi.

The question was moot in her case. Her longknife was hilt-deep in the other Klindrel's eye. She braced her foot against the chest of the supine corpse and pulled her blade free. Ganadarm could see why Saboon loved her.

The Klindrel whom Saboon had saved rolled away from Ganadarm and drew his own sword.

"No stab!" Saboon yelled. "We need his clothings."

"We do?" Dusi asked.

The Klindrel eyed the three of them nervously.

Ganadarm charged the messenger and locked swords. Stepping inside the man's guard, he drove his left fist up into the man's unprotected jaw. The Klindrel's head snapped back.

Dusi slipped behind the enemy and Ganadarm gave him a push so that he fell over Dusi's body. Saboon drove the butt of the pitchfork down into the man's gut.

Saboon cried, "Horse!"

Without knowing why, Ganadarm snatched a rein as a horse went by.

The rein went taut. Ganadarm tugged, holding the beast to a circle. Its frenzied kicks punched the air. Just when Ganadarm thought it might slow down, it stepped on the surviving Klindrel. The man gasped, and the spooked horse made four more circles. Finally, it played itself out and Ganadarm was able to convince it to stand still.

There. Ganadarm had the horse. But why did Saboon need it?

Saboon said something to Dusi. She looked puzzled a moment, then nodded in comprehension. The Drelfin began removing clothing from the soldier Saboon had asked them not to stab. The soldier, for his part, stared at the sky with glazed eyes while gasping for breath.

"What are you doing?" Ganadarm asked.

"We get you a uniform," said Dusi. "Clean uniform. No blood." She held up the trousers and inspected the hole Saboon's pitchfork had made. "Well, little blood."

"Why do I need a uniform?" Ganadarm asked.

"You must carry a message," said Saboon. "Tell all Klindrel soldiers that the bridge is gone. They will get no food."

Ah, they wanted him to play Klindrel.

"And if you can't destroy the bridge?" Ganadarm asked.

Saboon shrugged. "We must."

"The bridge is not important," said Dusi. "The idea is important."

Dusi gestured at the man she had killed. "If we drop bridge and he says bridge is fine, then plan fails. Army stays strong because they say, 'Oh, food is coming.' But if *you* say food is not coming …"

"You want me to pretend to be a Klindrel soldier."

"Yes," said Saboon.

"You want me to run away from your fight." He always ran. Every time. "Like a coward."

Dusi put her tiny, grubby hand in his. "No," she said. "Not like a coward. Like a bandit."

"But I want to be like my father. He wasn't a bandit, Dusi. He was a warrior."

"Ganadarm," she said. "We do not always get to be what we want."

Ganadarm thought about it: riding through Klindrel territory, pretending to be a messenger, spreading tales of a terrible Drelfin uprising that destroyed all the supply wagons. Dusi was right. It seemed daring, not cowardly.

Every time Ganadarm had tried to confront Bannom, he had found a reason to run away instead. Ganadarm had feared this was due to innate cowardice. But his fear of cowardice was his only fear. He ran not because he was afraid, but because he liked running.

He liked escaping. He liked getting away with something.

And now he had a chance to ride off and fool the entire Klindrel Army.

Ganadarm started changing clothes.

CHAPTER 46
The Farbridge Uprising

AFTER SENDING GANADARM OFF, Sabu and Dusi hastened to
Farbridge, leaving the shocked farmers to deal with the naked
soldier and the dead one. In retrospect, this seems irresponsible.
But at the time, it was war.

Meanwhile, Tim sat in Fishurba's house at the center of the
Farbridge Uprising. You see, Fishurba was the local leader of the
Nightrunners, a secret society devoted to spreading information in
Klindrel-controlled territory.

In one sense, the Nightrunners came into being when Sabu set
out on his mission. Sabu's three-person squad could never have
visited all the villages in the Redwood Valley, but the Nightrunners took the Starvation Strategy to the places that Sabu,
Ganadarm, and Tim could not go. So in one sense, this secret
society formed spontaneously.

In another sense, the Nightrunners were built on a foundation
that had been laid long before.

Consider, for a moment, the Order of the Lock. This secret
society is charged with the confiscation and suppression of forbidden artifacts. Given that all land-based foreign trade must pass
through Farbridge, it seems very likely that they would want to
station a member there.

This is just a guess, of course. Fishurba certainly never revealed
anything to me. But let us suppose for a moment that my guess is
correct and that Fishurba was an agent for the Order of the Lock.
That still would not account for all the other Nightrunners.

I imagine the Order of the Lock requires very few members in
the Redwood Valley because artifact-making skills are rare. The
Order of Joined Minds, on the other hand, probably covers the
valley like a blanket. Mind-reading confidence artists are common
among our people. There must be some system in place that keeps
such miscreants from working village after village.

So the Nightrunners were probably using communication
protocols that had been established for several other secret
societies. But of course, I don't know, and anyone who did know
never told me. The societies are secret, after all.

All Tim knew was that Fishurba surely had a lot of people organized. From time to time, someone would knock on the door to give Fishurba a breathless update on how things were progressing. Her husband would pretend to need to check on something in the backyard. Tim would brazenly listen in.

As near as Tim could tell, things were going bad. Fuelwood was easy to find, but a cart was not. Fishurba solved that problem by handing over a pouch with enough money to buy a cart at double price.

As the cart was being purchased, word reached Fishurba that the Klindrel had finished setting up tents on her brother's sheep meadow.

"Are the soldiers staying there or coming back toward town?" Fishurba asked.

"I don't know," the runner said.

"Find out."

The runner left to find out.

Digo came back into the house with a mint leaf for Tim's tea.

"Why is it you leave whenever anyone comes to the door?" Tim asked.

Digo looked at Fishurba. "I don't want to know what she's up to," he said.

Fishurba chuckled.

"Why not?" Tim asked.

"It would make me nervous," Digo said.

"You are nervous anyway," Tim said.

Digo shrugged. "If I knew, I would be more nervous."

Someone knocked on the door.

"Excuse me," Digo said. "I must go check on the ducks' water."

Tim couldn't understand it. If *his* wife had been organizing an uprising in the Hill Enclave, he'd want to *know*.

Actually, that was crazy. Besi would never organize an uprising. He wondered what she *was* doing. He had left home nearly two months ago, and it seemed like he'd been away two months too long.

News kept coming in. Two Klindrel soldiers had stopped the empty cart and asked a lot of questions before they let the driver go. The newly arrived soldiers were guarding their empty tents.

The lookout across the river had signaled that the main body of ox wagons was approaching.

This last bit of news meant that the wagons would arrive in half a lithic. Tim had told them where to post the lookout to get the timing right.

Tim began to wonder what he would do if his friends did not come back in time. Fishurba and Sabu had assumed that Sabu would be in Farbridge before the wagons. But if he was not … well, Tim didn't think he could do his part without their help.

Another knock on the door. When Fishurba opened it, she let in Dusi and Sabu. Tim breathed a sigh of relief. Dusi flashed him a smile.

Sabu gave a brief accounting, mostly to let Tim know that Ganadarm would not be joining them.

"Is your squad ready?" Sabu asked.

"We are," Fishurba said.

"The whole town is buzzing," Sabu said. "The Klindrel, the market-goers, the townspeople. I've never seen so many people look so wary."

"Shall I give the signal?" Fishurba asked.

Sabu asked, "Are you ready, Tim?"

"Yes," said Tim.

He spoke the word in someone else's language, but it felt like he was speaking with someone else's tongue. He had bargained for trouble when he had left his townhouse to go spy on the Klindrel Army, and he had surely gotten it. He had been in and out of prison, he had pushed a wagon through a burning gate, he had stolen horses, and he had read tally marks by touch in the presence of a sleeping giant. If Besi knew … Well, he was glad Besi didn't know all the things he had done. Anyway, he had now agreed to pull a bridge out from under twenty Klindrel soldiers, and it scared him to realize that this might not be the most dangerous thing he had done this year.

"Good," said Sabu. "Let's get in place. Fishurba, give the signal."

Smoke rose above Fishurba's smithy. Tim followed Sabu and Dusi through the streets of Farbridge, trying to look like just another Brownman. A short while later, they reached the street where Fishurba had told them to wait.

A lumberjack walked by with an axe over one shoulder and coils of stout rope over the other. He hung the rope on a gate and continued around the corner.

Tim took the rope, and they continued toward the river. One block from the bridge, they turned into a narrow, mossy alley. Sabu knocked on a red door.

The girl who opened the door couldn't have been much more than twelve or thirteen. She gestured toward a front room and latched the red door behind them.

The front room was dark. The window was shuttered. Sabu peered out through a crack.

Only one of them needed to watch. They all knew what was happening.

Fishurba's people had pushed a cart of burning fuelwood into a haystack beside the corral that the Klindrel had built for their messengers' horses. The soldiers would be forced to organize a bucket chain.

They were in the house with the red door because it had a good view of the guards at the bridge.

"There's an officer approaching," Sabu reported. "Get ready to move, Tim. Dusi ... do your best. Go when the time is right. I trust your judgment."

He clasped her hand, then released it, the entire gesture so brief that it almost might not have been.

Sabu peered out the window again. "They're distracted. We go now, Tim."

They stepped out the front door into the bright light of day.

"Match my pace," Sabu said.

Tim did so. He wanted to sprint, but this would be a bad time to draw the soldiers' attention. He was a bald man carrying a rope to the rapids below the Farbridge while a corral was catching fire. His Brownfolk dress would not be sufficient to convince an onlooking Klindrel that he was on legitimate business.

Don't look, don't look, don't look, he told himself, keeping his eyes on Sabu's heels.

And then Sabu's sandals were stepping over the edge of the bank and Tim was following him down into the tall grass where he could smell the earthy scent of oxen.

"Did we make it?" he asked.

"So far," said Sabu.

Tim studied the oxen. They did not seem concerned by Tim and Sabu's sudden appearance. And of course they should not be. These were the fine, gentle beasts bred by Clan Hill.

If these two oxen had been, in fact, the very two oxen that Tim had planned to use on his trade run that summer, it would have been so great a coincidence that it could have been explained only by divine intervention. But in fact, the two oxen belonged to one of his cousins. Even so, Tim believed they had been placed there by the hand of Yolim.

The yoke for the oxen had been placed in a nearby willow thicket by one of Fishurba's people. Tim dragged it into place while the oxen watched him sadly.

"I know, I know," Tim murmured. "But this will just be a short pull."

And he spoke to them in this way as he secured the yoke, keeping the oxen calm and calming himself as well. With snuffly sighs, the great beasts accepted their fate.

Tim fastened his end of the rope to the yoke.

"Ready when Dusi is," he said.

Sabu gave no reply.

Tim looked up from his work.

Sabu, with the other end of the rope, was already running toward the bridge.

CHAPTER 47

The End of the Rope

DUSI WATCHED the guards through the crack in the shutter. The house felt deserted. Dusi didn't know where the girl who had let them in had gone. She wondered if the girl had a mother.

Dusi's muscles felt loose and relaxed. She had already run cross country and killed a man today. Her body felt ready for action.

She had become used to this. The possibility of combat didn't bother her. Killing didn't bother her. Because she was now evil.

Her evil nature would let her recognize the proper time to strike. All she had to do was trust in the Deceiver's instinct for weakness.

Seven guards left with the officer to go fight the fire. One set off across the Farbridge, doubtless to convey orders to the guards on the other side. That left only two.

Dusi couldn't win against two, but she knew how to even the odds.

Dusi opened the door and ran from the house shouting, "My baby! My baby!"

Both guards looked her way and reached for their swords, but their hands relaxed when they saw her awkward stride, her flailing arms, her flapping chiton. They didn't notice the bulge of her barely concealed battleblade. They didn't notice she was wearing tree-climbing boots.

"My baby!" she cried in the Klindrel tongue. "She is trapped!"

Dusi waved at the clouds of smoke rising from the haystack fire across town. "My house is all fire!"

She tugged on the nearest soldier's sword arm, but he refused to move. Perhaps he was suspicious, perhaps he was bewildered. Dusi didn't know. She was too close to see his face. She reached inside her chiton, drew her battleblade from its scabbard, and drove it up into the soldier's groin.

The soldier gasped and his body tightened on Dusi's blade. She released it and in its stead took his sword from his scabbard as he collapsed.

The sword was long and heavy, but Dusi knew how to use its weight. She swung it two handed at the other guard's legs. A bone snapped.

Dusi dropped the sword, reached inside her first victim's armored apron, and yanked her serrated battleblade free.

The one with the broken leg called for help, but he could not rise to fight her. Dusi turned her back on them. Blood flying from her blade, she ran onto the bridge.

The guards at the other end were looking her way, but they had already lost the race to the undermined pile. Dusi sheathed her blade, slipped over the edge of the bridge, and lowered herself onto a crossbeam.

Sabu was on the bank below the bridge, swinging a rope weighted with a logging hook. He let it fly toward Dusi.

Dusi dropped flat on the crossbeam, reached down, and caught the logging hook at its apex. She looked at Sabu to let him know she had it.

Sabu held her gaze an instant, then he turned and ran downstream toward the oxen and Tim.

Dusi looped the rope over one shoulder. She wiggled her toes to be certain they were snug in the tree-climbing boots she had borrowed from Fishurba. The soft-soled boots had a spiked leather pad at the toe. The spikes bit into the wood, and Dusi's toes hung onto the pad. The College of Forestry had taught her to use such boots. Now she would find out if she still remembered how.

The pile was a single log, shaved of bark, with a girth that Dusi's arms could almost encompass. Dusi dug her spikes into the log and lowered her weight onto the toe of one boot.

The boot held.

Dusi pressed the other toe into the log. Step by step, she descended toward the base of the pile and the rushing water of the Redwood River. Crossbeams creaked as the turbulent water bounced the pile against the underwater rocks.

Something plummeted past Dusi's head. She looked up to see a Klindrel soldier leaning over the edge of the bridge. His boots were useless for climbing so he was dropping them on Dusi. The second boot glanced off her upraised arm, but Dusi held fast.

Dusi uncoiled the rope from her shoulder, wrapped it about the pile, and secured it with a logger's hitch.

The giant swung over the edge and landed with his bare feet on the crossbeam above Dusi's head. He drew his sword, but he was still too high to reach her.

Dusi looked downstream. She could swim, but could she swim hard enough to reach the bank before the current carried her into the rapids?

It didn't matter. She couldn't abandon the rope. She couldn't give the Klindrel a chance to cut it.

Dusi climbed up to engage the enemy. Through the pile, she could feel Tim putting tension on the rope; she could feel the Klindrel soldier maneuvering on the crossbeam. Dusi reached inside her chiton and drew her battleblade.

The Klindrel crouched and jabbed at her. She was still out of reach, but his reach was longer than hers. Unless she got her feet under her, she couldn't dodge, counterattack, or block. She needed to get up on that crossbeam.

Dusi maneuvered carefully around the pile, putting it between herself and her opponent. He countered effortlessly, grabbing the pile and swinging to the beam on the other side.

There was her opening! Dusi spiraled upward and, with her free hand, grasped the beam he had just left. She hooked her weapon hand over for extra support. With her feet she pushed away from the pile to gather momentum.

The Klindrel glided into a low stance and drew his sword in an arc around the pile.

Hanging from the beam, Dusi twisted her swinging legs, hoping to deflect the blow by kicking him in the arm. But she was too slow. His sword hacked through her wrist and bit into the wood.

Dusi lost her grip and fell toward the water. In front of her eyes, just out of reach, her severed hand fell with her, still clutching the battleblade.

CHAPTER 48

Dear Sabu

FROM THE TALL GRASS DOWNSTREAM, Sabu saw Dusi fall. As she passed the rope, her hand shot out and caught it, sending vibrations all the way to the yoked oxen.

An object splashed into the water. Sabu thought it was Dusi's battleblade, but something about it hadn't looked quite right.

He did not have time to puzzle it out. A half dozen Klindrel soldiers were running across the bridge, shouting down at Tim.

Two soldiers remained above Dusi, leaning over the edge of the bridge to watch their comrade, who secured himself in a sitting position on his beam. Below, Dusi still clung to the rope. Her body dangled limply, but one hand held fast.

"Let go," Sabu said. "Why doesn't she just let go?"

The Klindrel on the crossbeam hooked his knees and dangled over backward. Sabu saw what he was about. With his long body, long arms, and long sword, the Klindrel could reach the rope.

He would cut it. And the sacrifices of the Redwood Valley would be in vain.

Sabu swallowed the sickness rising in his throat.

"Start the oxen, Tim."

"What? Dusi's still on the rope!"

Neither man bothered with the other's language.

"We must pull the bridge down *now.*" Sabu spoke with heat, but icy dread gripped his heart.

"The bridge will fall on top of her," Tim protested

"I know."

Tim shook his head. "I don't want to be responsible for her death."

Tim didn't want to be responsible? *Tim* didn't want to sacrifice Dusi?

Sabu grabbed Tim's chiton so hard that a shoulder pin snapped open. "You aren't responsible," Sabu said. "I am. I'm the one killing her."

"Sabu, I can't do it!"

"Think of all the families going hungry today," Sabu said. "Think of all the babies starving. All because we promised we would stop those supply wagons. We *promised*, Tim! Now drop that bridge."

CHAPTER 49
Revenge

WITH HIS FEEBLE LITTLE WILLOW SWITCH, Tim whipped and whipped his cousin's oxen.

"Hey! Hey!" he cried. "Ho! Ho! Hey! Hey!"

The oxen strained. The rope vibrated with tension.

"Ho! Ho! Hey! Hey!"

The oxen took one step forward.

"Hyah, hyah!"

A grinding vibration traveled along the rope. The oxen pulled.

"Hyah, hyah!"

Something in the bridge snapped. The oxen were moving now.

"Hyah, hyah!"

Tim drove them up the bank.

"Hyah, hyah!"

He drove them through the willow thicket.

"Hyah, hyah!"

He drove them and whipped them, dragging the pile from the collapsing bridge until it caught on rocks at the water's edge. Tim whipped and whipped, and when he saw that the oxen would go no farther, he swapped his stroke and whipped his own back:

Hyah, Tim! Spy on the army!

Hyah, Tim! Warn the Brownfolk!

Hyah, Tim! Kill the quartermaster!

Hyah, Tim! Starve the babies!

Hyah, Tim! Drop the bridge!

Hyah, Tim! Drown Dusi!

All that matters is your revenge. All that matters is your revenge.

CHAPTER 50

Letting Go

I DON'T THINK TIM ever forgave himself.

Sabu would never talk about it. Oh, he could explain it. He could explain that he saw a choice between what he wanted to do and what had to be done. He could explain that a moment's more delay and the Klindrel soldier would have cut the rope.

But he never really talked about it. He never said how it made him feel.

I think I know how it made him feel. Whenever anyone mentioned the town of Farbridge, I could sense his thoughts sliding back to that day, and I could see the pain of memory in his eyes.

And as for me? I didn't blame them. I didn't blame either one of them. I admired them for their courage. I still do.

I didn't intend for this to be a memoir. I wanted to tell you what happened during the Klindrel Invasion. I thought that if I talked about Dusi as though she were someone else, then my account would be more objective. Or at least, since everything has to come from some perspective, I hoped to give you several to choose from. So you could see the war as Tim saw it, as Gana-darm saw it, as Sabu saw it. And as Dusi saw it.

Dusi didn't know about the argument between Sabu and Tim. She was hanging above a river, bleeding from a severed limb, wondering when the soldier above would climb down and kill her.

The pain in her arm was turning her vision dark with shock, but painful and dark was how she had expected death to be. That was how her mother had died.

She regretted losing her soul to the Deceiver. She was a Child of Knowledge, and she felt she belonged in Knowledge's Heaven. Because she was smart. And because she didn't want to be evil.

She had thought she could win. She had thought she would be able to trick the Deceiver. She had thought that once the war was over, she would be able to get free of the demon somehow. She had thought she was strong enough to climb to Heaven with her bare hands, but now that one hand was missing, she didn't feel so strong.

And yet she did not ask Knowledge for mercy. She had no connection to the Goddess. Another thing severed. No deity, no mother, no hand. Just a tiny woman dangling from a rope above a roaring river in the shadow of the redwoods.

She remembered, then, the last time she had been in Farbridge. The spirit of the Redwood Forest had awakened her from a dream. And she wondered if the spirit had power here, underneath the Farbridge.

I have some, Redwood admitted. The thought came easily into her mind. Dusi realized he had been aware of her the entire time, just waiting for her to open her thoughts to him.

"How much?" she asked.

How much do you need?

Dusi thought about it. Did she need enough power to regrow an arm, fly into the sky, and kill the man above her? Not really. She just needed a place to be after she died. A place that wasn't Hell.

Then I have enough, Redwood said.

"What do I have to do?" she asked.

You have to let go.

Let go? Was she still holding on to the rope?

"Be gone!" said Dusi's mother. "Let us share this moment in peace, you wooden-hearted being who pretends to be a person. Dusi is mine! I brought her into this world, and the time has come for me to show her the way out."

Redwood gave no reply, and Dusi saw that the darkness had closed in around her. She was dreaming, drifting, falling, dying. She was conscious, but not inside her physical body. She held her mother's hand with her weapon hand no longer severed, somehow made whole by the death-dream.

"Finally," said her mother. "Finally I can take care of you as I should have while you were growing up. Finally I can do more than feed you. I can show you how to be a woman. I can help you find your way. The paths of death are just as tangled as those of life, dear Dusi, and you will need my guidance. Finally, I will be there for you."

Dusi was weak, alone, and frightened. And these words were exactly what she wanted to hear.

"I wish I could believe you," Dusi said. "But you have not been sent to guide me in death. You are here to take me to Hell."

Her mother said, "Dusi, you do not know the true nature of the realm created by the All-Knowing Master. In truth, it is not a life of torment and misery. His domain has joy, peace, and even love."

"Love?" asked Dusi. "How can one trust love from the Deceiver?"

Her mother looked into her eyes. "Trust in my love, Dusi."

Dusi's skepticism wavered. "Can there truly be love in Hell?"

" 'Hell' is not the right word, Dusi. I fear our people have been horribly misled. And those few of us who learn the truth … well, true knowledge of the afterlife is forbidden. Yes, Dusi, that is why I was slain. Because I had learned the truth."

The old pain came back, and Dusi hated that assassin for taking her mother. How foolish! How spiteful and petty to kill a woman just for knowing that Hell was actually as good as Heaven.

Except it couldn't be. If Hell and Heaven were equally good, then good and evil had no meaning.

"Why are you here?" Dusi asked.

"To be with you at your death, Dusi. As you were there for me."

"I couldn't save you," said Dusi.

"I did not need to be saved. Nor do you. Come with me."

She still held Dusi by the hand.

"What if I refuse?" Dusi asked.

"You cannot refuse, daughter. You are dead."

"If I cannot refuse, then why hasn't the Deceiver claimed me already?"

"Don't you think it is gentler this way?"

"I think the demon is evil. I think he does not care for gentleness."

"I am proof that he is not evil. He loves us so much that he has allowed me to come back to you."

"I will not go."

Her mother smiled. "Then what will you do?"

"I'll … join Redwood. He offered to protect me from Hell."

"You would give your soul to a tree?"

"Yes," said Dusi, "if that is the only way to sever my connection with the Deceiver."

"Dusi," said her mother, "this is the only way to sever your connection." She let go of Dusi's hand, stepped back, reached inside her chiton, and withdrew a deathblade.

"The tree wants you to kill me. That's all you have to do to become one of his kind. Just kill your mother." She offered the blade. "Go on. Take it. If that is truly what you wish."

"Redwood?" Dusi called. "Is that true?"

No reply.

Her mother's smile softened. The blade vanished. "Oh, Dusi, I knew you wouldn't. You're my little girl."

Her mother reached out a hand. "Now, come."

Dusi took the hand once more. It felt warm, soft, and fleshy. It was real.

She had her mother's hand, and nothing pulled them apart now. Her mother wasn't falling away to Hell. She and Dusi were in the same place.

Dusi gave the hand a squeeze and looked into her mother's eyes. She said, "Goodbye, Mother."

And then she let go.

CHAPTER 51

The Redwood River

I REALIZE NOW WHY it has been so easy to write about Dusi as though she were another person. She was.

When I let go of my mother's hand, I let go of many things. I let go of the arrogant presumption that I was strong enough to defeat the Deceiver on my own. I let go of my conviction that I had to solve my problems without help. I let go of my hope of reaching Knowledge's Heaven. I let go of my life.

Sabu and Tim had thought Dusi would die, and part of her *did* die that day. I was born.

I let go of the rope and trusted Redwood to take care of the rest. He was the only one who could help me. Once I accepted that help, everything became easier.

I hit the water with a splash. Then I was under, and everything had changed. The world's sounds were liquid. The light was green and thin, shining above me. I floated on the darkness below.

Thank you, Redwood, I thought. *This is peaceful.*

I apologize, he said. *It is about to become painful.*

Tim and Sabu found me on a rock downstream. My severed arm was still bleeding. My unsevered arm was broken in two places. I had bruises on my head and abrasions all over my body. But Redwood's friend the river spirit had washed me to a place within their reach.

Tim and Sabu ran away with me and found a family that would take me in. Tim got Fishurba to hire me a healer. She was a *good* healer, but she couldn't convince my hand to regrow. She said my body no longer believed that it needed a weapon hand to be whole.

One night, I asked Sabu why he wasn't with the Road Patrol. He said the war was over. He said we had won.

This was not strictly true. The Klindrel were deserting, their army was disintegrating, but people were still fighting, and the garrison at Farbridge was still trying to repair the bridge. But the war was over for Sabu.

CHAPTER 52
The End of the War

IF YOU WANT A SCHOLARLY ACCOUNT of how we won the war, you can read Boshi's *Analysis of Invasion*. I disagree with some of her analysis, but she has most of the facts correct. However, since so many people read only Thamikaber's *War History*, I feel that I should make a few things clear:

Although our army retreated from the fields of Tomivo, the first blows to weaken the Klindrel had already been struck. Earlier, I explained how releasing the Klindrel horses started a quarrel between the infantry and the Maziban Lancers. The Starvation Strategy also tested the bonds of camaraderie. As food grew scarce, fights broke out over the distribution of tiny spring potatoes and scavenged pots of grain.

And then the messenger came.

He said, "I ride with news for the supply master."

And the sentry on duty asked, "What news is this?"

The messenger's terra-cotta face took on grim lines. "News from Farbridge, and even that is more than I should say."

"Have the ox wagons been delayed?"

"That is for the officers to tell you or to keep to themselves, as they decide. Now kindly tell me where the supply master can be found."

Legitimate messengers followed, of course, but among the common soldiers, their messages mixed with Ganadarm's in a swirling muddle of rumor:

The bridge is gone. But they'll have it rebuilt in two days. No, the food will come across by ferry. Farbridge is rioting and the garrison has been destroyed. The ox wagons have turned back and no food will ever come.

So when Thamikaber writes that the war was won when a secret society assassinated the Klindrel emperor, he is ignoring the circumstances. Had the Klindrel been strong, the assassination would not have stopped the army.

The Klindrel had many soldiers ready to lead the army in the emperor's stead. And General Felk actually did so. He was a cunning general, savvy not only in military strategies but also in political tactics. He could have used the emperor's death to inspire his soldiers to seek revenge. Felk could have led those men all the way to Hicho. He could have—if the army had been strong.

But the army was weak, thanks to Ganadarm's heroic ride. Before Felk could consolidate support, many companies had already left for Farbridge. After all, if there were food in this Kashram-cursed valley, it would be there. And if the Farbridge garrison couldn't figure out how to get it across the river, well, perhaps they just needed extra help.

That is why dropping the bridge was so important. If the bridge had remained standing, truth would have defeated the rumors, food would have replaced fear, and the soldiers' spirits would have been rising at the very moment General Felk took command.

I admit that the impact of the assassins was dramatic. I concede they did us all a great service. But it was not the assassins who saved us. It was Sabu, Ganadarm, and brave Tim Hill.

And especially we were saved by the courage of the people of the Redwood Valley. Let us never forget that they sacrificed all their food, trusting that their neighbors would do the same, believing that Sabu would complete his mission.

General Felk's first order as commander-in-chief was the order to withdraw. He did not retreat from our army. He simply decided that the wisest course of action was to withdraw from the valley. General Felk held his remaining companies together, and on the long march home to Kanabur he lost only nine men.

Those who chose to flee without the benefit of Felk's leadership did not fare as well. Our people had given up their food, but they had not given up their meatknives, their cleavers, their scythes, their pruning poles. Men retreating in twos and threes were hacked to pieces by mobs. Men retreating by the dozen were hunted down by ad hoc combat units led by game finders and lumberjacks. Those who retreated as full companies learned to keep their sentries close to camp rather than let unseen Drelfin slay them in the dark.

By the time the war was truly over and the last Klindrel was on his own side of the mountains, our people had a reputation for savage ferocity that would astonish anyone who has spent time among the cheerful, prosperous people of the Redwood Valley.

I should also like to say a few words about the conspiracy theory. It seems that someone discovered links between the Deceiver and certain Klindrel who were close to the emperor in the year before the Klindrel Invasion. The conclusion I was expected to draw from these rumors was that the Deceiver himself was trying to destroy us and that we had been saved only through the intervention of assassins from the Temple of the Hunters.

Well, perhaps. But the Deceiver guards his secrets closely. Whether the conspiracy story is true or not, we would not have learned the story unless the Deceiver wanted us to hear it.

CHAPTER 53

The Rest of the Story

THE KLINDREL INVASION made me who I am. I have led a wonderful life since then. Sabu was a kind and loving husband. Our children have grown up to be responsible and intelligent. I have no regrets.

Ganadarm spent the rest of the summer hunting down disorganized companies of retreating Klindrel. He spent the autumn under Sabu's command, helping rebuild the Passwatch Roadhouse. He left Passwatch the following spring. He told us he was returning to the Saltlands, but Tim said that Ganadarm ended up in the province of Falkadwen, where he made a name for himself during the Falkadwen Uprising. I assume he enjoyed it.

Tim Hill never received the recognition he deserved for his courageous efforts, neither from our people nor his own. However, he did convince the Enclave Council to seek the return of Clan Hill's livestock, and an agreement was negotiated with General Felk. So Tim got his cattle back, in the end, and the Empire did not ask for the return of the coins he had scattered in the muddy street.

At the rebuilt Passwatch, Tim's cat was adopted as a mascot. I learned to wield a battleblade with my remaining hand, but I can't say my heart was in it. I had changed in other ways, too—Sabu said my smile had become symmetrical—but I was still a mind finder and that skill proved useful from time to time.

While Sabu and I served at Passwatch, Tim visited us every year. He never asked anyone to pay him for the cat.

Later, when we lived in the Redwood Valley, Tim and his son continued to favor us with infrequent visits, even though we lived off the main road. And for many years after Tim was too old to travel, his son kindly carried on the tradition alone.

Sabu went to Knowledge's Heaven nine days after his eighty-first birthday. We were asleep, but the Goddess let him kiss me goodbye in my dreams. A rare privilege.

Four times over the course of our marriage, we expressed sorrow that we would not be together after death. But we never expressed regret. Our ultimate separation is a fact we both accepted.

I wanted our children to be servants of Knowledge—to be like their father, to take the path I could not. I am pleased that they agreed with me.

I never pursued the possibility of Heaven for myself. That hope was one of the things I let go when I dropped into the Redwood River. Knowledge and the Deceiver are so close; if I had reached for the Goddess, I might have been unable to fight off the demon. I was no longer foolish enough to believe it was worth the risk. And as for the other deities, what would have been the point? Sabu was going to Knowledge's Heaven, not anyone else's.

As the years went by, this decision became easier to live with. Ganadarm had once told me that he knew servants of Nature who help people overcome the grip of demons. I went to the Saltlands to learn from them. Over the course of my too-long life, I have helped seven souls escape the Deceiver. Sabu said I was serving the Goddess in my own way. I think he was right.

I am sure some of the neighbors will be surprised to learn that my soul has been consecrated to Nature for fifty-seven years. And people will be shocked to learn that I once wrestled with a demon.

I have kept silent about my mother and the Deceiver all my life. My excuse was that I did not want to bring my mother's shame to my children, but I think, perhaps, I was also worried about my mother.

She was kind to me, you see. She gave me to a demon before I was old enough to talk, but she was kind to me. She taught me things. She was my mother. I suppose I still wish I could save her somehow.

But she was taken from me when I was eight years old. And I never saw her again. Oh, I thought she was speaking to me during the war, but that woman in my dreams could just as easily have been a dream-puppet of the Deceiver. She gave her soul to him. He knew all her thoughts and feelings. It would have been no effort at all for him to pretend to be her.

My children will not have to wonder. I will not haunt their dreams. I am going now into the forest to become a nature spirit.

When Redwood tells me to, I will drop my body and keep walking to the place where he wants me to be. If anyone needs to speak with me, look for me there.

Works Cited

NOTE FROM DUSI'S SON: Mother died (or "disencorporated", if you prefer) before completing this list of cited sources. I believe she simply did not know the protocol. After all, this is her only scholarly work. I am certain she intended no disrespect by the omission. (Any disrespect she intended is clear from her text.)

Boshi's *Analysis of Invasion*. A consideration of factors leading up to the Klindrel War and an analysis of factors figuring in the outcome. Available at the Academy and in all Invasion scholars' libraries.

Thamikaber's *War History*. The Klindrel War as seen from Hicho. An excellent complement to Mother's work. Widely available in Hicho.

Chohu's *Consequences of the Klindrel War*. An examination of the impacts that the Klindrel War had on our people and theirs. Available at the Academy library.

Maburbi's *Defense of the Redwoods*. An explanation of the events of the war written for the people who lived through it. Available at the Academy and the College of Forestry.

Terkisho's *Theory of War*. Still the definitive text on warfare. Available wherever the theory of war is taught.

Acknowledgments

I'D LIKE TO THANK MY WIFE, Sierra Stoneberg Holt, for reading an earlier draft of this novel and making helpful comments. Lorraine Heisler also read the novel and suggested several improvements, as did Andrea Howe of Blue Falcon Editing. The story is better for their efforts.

Rose Stoneberg, D.V.M., advised me on ways small people might ride horses. Christine Doyle, M.D., explained how people might react to various nasty wounds. Even so, this book should not be mistaken for a primer on either horseback riding or people stabbing.

Clay Cooper's MisCon lectures on tracking and ambushes had a strong influence on this book, as did Joseph Zieja's Military in Fiction advice and Jack Anderson's experiences as detailed in *Warrior: ... By Choice ... By Chance.* Thank you, gentlemen, for your writing advice and for your service to our country.

This is a fantasy novel. Although I made an effort to get certain details right, other details are wrong. The inaccuracies and exaggerations that improve the story are intentional and those that detract from the story are mistakes. I'll let the reader decide which is which. That said, the reader should be advised that three-foot-tall people really can seize a combat advantage against a six-foot-tall foe if they are willing to gang up on him, rush in close, and attack his legs. I would like to thank my children, Zora and Linden, for their demonstrations of this effective technique.

About the Author

JASON A. HOLT has a Ph.D. in mathematics. He is fluent in Czech, and he lives on a remote Montana cattle ranch. In other words, he is well qualified to write fantasy novels.

To learn more about Jason, visit `JasonAHolt.com`.

To learn more about the world of Edgewhen®, visit `edgewhen.com`.

CHRONOLOGY OF EDGEWHEN® ADVENTURES

1002: The Dragonslayer of Edgewhen
1311: The Artificer of Dupho
1500: The Klindrel Invasion

and coming soon:

1577: The Bladesman of Darcliff
1670: The Burglar of Sliceharbor